Thy Will Be Done

Marcus Power

To Aisling, for her unwavering support and patience.

Chapter 1

Although I was just a young child at the time, I have never forgotten the chaos and excitement that consumed the parish as we eagerly awaited the appointment of our new priest. In the weeks leading up to the announcement, the exuberant spirit of the close-knit parish committee had reached a feverish level that seemed to infect everyone who came into contact with them. As always, there were a few overly zealous committee members who seemed completely fixated on the matter and spoke of nothing else from morning till night. It was rumoured at the time that several members of the parish committee had completely lost the run of themselves and should have been certified due to their unconventional behaviour. However, their fellow committee members had speculated that their uncharacteristic attitudes and antics were undoubtedly a side effect of the intense anticipation and excitement that surrounded the impending appointment and were therefore overlooked.

The parishioners appeared to be anticipating a momentous occasion, an event comparable to a divine revelation or even the Second Coming. Their excitement was palpable and had spread throughout the entire parish. It was hard to believe that they were merely awaiting the appointment of a humble parish priest, rather than the arrival of the Messiah himself, descending from heaven on a majestic white horse and wielding a shining, double-edged sword.

Although many years have passed since then, I can still vividly recall an incident that occurred just days before our new priest was appointed. The incident, which became known as, 'The Splinter Group,' remained the topic of gossip for many years afterwards. The incident itself involved a handful of committee members who had secretly gathered in the church, where they were stumbled upon, fervently reciting decades of the Rosary, as they anxiously awaited the appointment of the new priest. When my mother, who was the chair of the parish committee at the time, was informed of the covert prayer service, she publicly referred to the participants as a 'Splinter Group,' thus giving it its name, and threatened to expel them from the committee. Back then, my mother was a formidable force within the higher echelons of the parish committee, and nothing ever happened without her knowledge or consent.

Although my mother was hurt and felt belittled by the incident, she refused to be outdone by her fellow committee members. Instead, she channelled her anger and frustration into her unwavering faith and devotion to our Lord. Our sitting room had been transformed into a sacred sanctuary. My mother knelt for hours on her arthritic knees, lost in prayer before the Sacred Heart of Jesus that hung on the wall. Her lips moved in a gentle whisper as she sought solace from our Heavenly Father. With her head bowed low and her eyes closed in deep reverence, the evil bitch almost appeared angelic as she prayed. The flickering flame from a solitary candle illuminated the image of our Saviour, with his arms outstretched in a gesture of love and forgiveness. The crown of blood-soaked thorns on his head enhanced the surreal atmosphere that I found myself trapped in.

After a couple of days had passed without any news of a new priest being appointed, my mother became disheartened. She could not understand why it was taking so long for such a simple appointment to be made. After all, it was just the selection of a new parish priest, not the next Pope. Despite this, she resolved to deepen her level of devotion and embarked on a strict fast, abstaining from all solid foods, in the hope that her sacrifice would speed up the selection process. Our small and cluttered sitting room, no longer provided the peaceful sanctuary that she required for her devotional practices. My mother decided that she needed to worship in God's house instead of her own, with all its distractions and temptations, and as an eight-year-old child, without having a say in the matter, I was dragged along to the church.

Inside the church, the sweet and earthy scent of incense filled the air, which caused me to sneeze incessantly, much to the annoyances of my mother, as she fully immersed herself in the Stations of the

Cross. She followed the exact path that Jesus had walked on that dark Friday as he dragged his cross up to the summit of Mount Calvary. At each Station, she bowed her head in reverence, her aged fingers traced the well-worn Rosary beads that had been passed down from her late mother (another religious nut), as she reflected on the immense suffering that Jesus had endured to save our lost souls.

For two full days and nights, she had survived on only water and black tea. On the third day of her fast, the diocese finally announced the appointment of a new priest, Fr. O'Connell, who was rumoured to be a highly experienced and respected member, of the clergy. My mother responded to the announcement as if she had just witnessed puffs of white smoke billowing from the chimney of the Sistine Chapel, signalling the beginning of a new papacy, rather than just the naming of a new parish priest. After my mother had quelled her excitement, she emerged from her fast looking exhausted and famished, as if she had just spent forty days and nights in the desert without food or water. She complained endlessly of debilitating headaches and crippling hunger pains, as she savagely devoured a full Irish breakfast. While under her breath, she vehemently cursed those who had secretly gathered in the church behind her back.

In the days that followed, the committee members were consumed with unbridled enthusiasm as they eagerly compiled to-do lists in preparation for the imminent arrival of the new priest. However, behind closed doors, the chosen few of the committee's inner circle had gathered and whispered amongst themselves, causing envy and resentment among the other members. While the majority of the dedicated parishioners had welcomed the appointment of the new priest, the announcement had also unleashed a wave of mixed emotions that not only engulfed, but also divided, the committee members as it washed over them.

'An injection of fresh blood, just what the parish needs,' had been whispered in some dark corner. However, there were a few senior members of the parish committee who, despite having faithfully served under their outgoing spiritual leader for over two decades, remained silent and sceptical. They were concerned that their highly sought-after positions within the committee's inner circle, which they so proudly held, could be compromised or threatened.

The outgoing parish priest, or ousted, as some of the parishioners had described his sudden departure, was veiled in secrecy. Lost his marbles was one of the rumours that circulated, fathered a child was another. Neither rumour was ever confirmed nor denied, leaving his devoted flock with nothing but unanswered questions, as they sought solace amidst the rumours and gossip. Within days of the old clergyman's departure, his once-familiar residence of over twenty years had been stripped back to its bare walls and completely renovated, transforming it into a pristine new home for his successor. Not a single trace of the old priest remained; it was as if he had never existed.

Upon his arrival, Fr. O'Connell was warmly welcomed by the parish committee. Each member had gone above and beyond to impress their new shepherd. The members had set aside their petty differences and joined as one for the welcoming ceremony, exuding a strong sense of unity and devotion for the benefit of their new priest.

The old, neglected Parish Hall, which stood next to the church, was not immune to the frenzied excitement of the committee members, as they poured their hearts and souls into transforming the old, rundown space for the big day. Over the course of several weeks, the committee members had painstakingly removed years of accumulated dirt and grime. They had relied heavily on good old-fashioned elbow grease as they vigorously scrubbed and buffed the entire hall to within an inch of its life. After the hall had been thoroughly cleaned, they applied a fresh coat of gleaming white paint to the ceiling and walls. The committee's unwavering commitment and diligence had completely transformed the once dull and dreary Parish Hall.

The stale, musty odour that lingered in the old hall had been replaced by the overpowering fresh smell of lemon-scented bleach, which stung the senses and brought tears to your eyes as you inhaled the air. The old, worn tables, which used to wobble with even the slightest movement, were hidden beneath brightly coloured tablecloths and adorned with platters of mouth-watering sandwiches and freshly baked cakes. Upon entering the newly decorated Parish Hall, many of the parishioners experienced a sensory overload as the pungent tang of lemon-scented bleached clashed with the enticing aromas of freshly baked cakes, as they mingled and vied for dominance.

The school choir, which I had been reluctantly forced into as a child, had rehearsed for weeks prior to the arrival of Fr. O'Connell. Sadly, when our big moment arrived and the spotlight shone down on us, we struggled courageously, but failed miserably, to hit the right notes. Parents cringed in their seats as their precious offspring belted out incoherent hymns with unwavering enthusiasm. A collective sigh of relief swept through the audience as the final note faded into the air. Some parents were overheard whispering amongst themselves, 'Thank Christ, it's over,' and 'Jesus, I thought it was never going to end.' The cramped and overcrowded hall, filled with proud parents, and doting grandparents, then erupted into a thunderous round of applause and cheers, much to the delight of the children in the choir, myself included. We all beamed with pride as we looked down from the makeshift stage, completely oblivious to our less-than-stellar performance.

The female members of the parish, including my mother, had gone to great lengths to look their best for the occasion. Each woman proudly displayed her own unique style as they strutted around the Parish Hall, like a flock of colourful peacocks, craving attention. All the women had donned their finest Sunday dresses and had their faces plastered in makeup. I couldn't help but notice that some of the women, actually looked better without the heavily applied cosmetics. It appeared as though the various coloured powders and blushers had been hastily applied without the assistance of a mirror. And many of the women in attendance were sporting new hairstyles; they all seemed to be vying for the coveted title of best-dressed woman. I couldn't understand what all the fuss and excitement was about; it was as if the Holy Father himself had graced us with his presence.

I was eight years old when Fr. O'Connell entered my life. My twisted religious nut, of a mother had invited him over for tea.

'We would be delighted to have you over for tea, Father. A nice cup of tea and a slice of lemon-drizzle cake.' I overheard her say into the phone, in a voice that was unrecognisable to me. I couldn't believe that the woman I heard speaking on the phone and my mother were indeed the same person. Before Fr. O'Connell arrived, I found myself exiled to the sitting room with a bar of chocolate and a bottle of fizzy orange, which was a rare treat in itself.

I knew she was embarrassed of me. She never bothered to hide her disdain or resentment towards me, and I reciprocated those feelings, although I kept them to myself. After my mother and the priest had finished their tea, they joined me in the sitting room. As they entered the room, I turned to face them and was immediately overcome with fear upon meeting the priest's penetrating stare. He stood, blocking the doorway, his intense gaze never wavered as he pulled out a pack of cigarettes from his coat pocket. He tapped one out and lit it; the smoke curled around his head like a sinister halo as he exhaled. His dark, looming shadow engulfed me as he stepped into the room. He towered over me with his imposing frame and intimidating presence. The combination of my overwhelming fear and the thick, acrid smoke from his cigarette made the air in the room feel heavy and suffocating.

His pale complexion was almost translucent, making the veins in his neck stand out like tiny blue rivers. The top of his head was completely bald, save for a few stray hairs that resembled blades of grass on a barren field. Delicate wisps of silver hair clung to the back and sides of his head as if frantically trying to hide his baldness. Deep, weathered lines etched his ageing face; each crease told its own tale of battles fought, and lessons learned. His expression remained stoic, revealing no emotion, as he held his gaze on me.

In a moment of sheer terror, I quickly turned my head back towards the television, convinced that I had locked eyes with the devil himself. My mother's hand grabbed me by the shoulder and roughly dragged me up off the sofa. Resistance was futile, as she pulled me across the sitting room floor. When I opened my eyes, I found myself standing before the imposing figure of the priest, his stern gaze fixed on me. The old biblical tale of Isaac bound on the altar, as his father Abraham stood over him with his hand raised, ready to deliver the fatal blow, flashed through my mind. Was I being offered up, her only son, the perfect Eucharistic offering.

'Well, child, don't just stand there staring at the floor like a simpleton,' she snapped, as she grabbed me by my hair and forced me to look up. My gaze quickly shifted from the floor to the yellowed, nicotine-stained ceiling above.

As our eyes met for the second time, another wave of paralysing fear washed over me. My mother's hand slapped against the back of my bare arm, urging me to speak. Reluctantly, I raised my trembling hand to meet his. He stepped forward, his hand outstretched. As he approached me, his broad shoulders cast a dark, menacing shadow that slowly crept along the wall, intensifying his already intimidating presence. His pale, wrinkled hand, with thick blue veins running through it, completely swallowed mine as he squeezed tightly.

'Hello, John, I'm Fr. O'Connell. It's nice to meet you,' he said in a deep, controlled voice that commanded respect. His firm grip and intense gaze only heightened the fear that had already consumed me. My mother's hand clamped down on my shoulder, her fingernails dug into my flesh, like the sharp talons of a hawk swooping in for its prey. She shook me violently, her words laced with venom, as her uncontrollable anger erupted like molten lava, scorching everything in its path. She had returned; her pretence had finally shattered, unable to be contained once the façade had crumbled.

Unfortunately, as the years passed, my initial impression of Fr. O'Connell was confirmed. He was not a good or holy man; he was a sick, twisted paedophile. My daily existence had become a terrifying and inescapable nightmare, as that evil bastard repeatedly defiled me. My mother had practically handed me to him on a silver platter; she must have known what that evil bastard was doing to me. I was just an innocent child; I had no way of avoiding or stopping the abuse that he so easily inflicted upon me. Even if I had spoken out back then, my allegations would have been rejected without even being considered. The reason being, Fr. O'Connell was highly revered and respected by his devoted parishioners and fellow clergy. Any accusations of such a depraved nature made against him, would have been deemed blasphemous.

Throughout my childhood and early teenage years, I felt completely numb and disconnected from the world around me. Each passing day only added to the pain and shame that I carried around with me in silence. My mind and body felt like two separate entities, lost and adrift in a vast, unforgiving void, unable to find a way out. Fr. O'Connell was a deceitful, malicious predator, who preyed on the vulnerable, and had successfully hid in plain sight, behind the protection of his white collar and the safety of the church. He had exploited his position of authority and trust within the community and had continued to do so undetected for so many years without any opposition or consequences. As a result, his unchallenged actions left me broken and scarred.

Chapter 2

My mother and 'O'Connell,' as I called him (though never to his face), had developed a very close relationship, which I'm sure was the talk of the town at the time. Most days after school, my mother would send me over to O'Connell's house.

'Now, John, run along over to Fr. O'Connell's house and help him with any chores that need to be done,' she'd command. His house was only a short distance from ours, about a fifteen-minute walk at most, even at a snail's pace. I always tried to prolong that short journey for as long as humanly possible, hoping that I would be kidnapped or killed by a speeding car along the way. Anything would have been better than reaching my dreaded destination.

Every time I approached his house, my entire body tensed, as if preparing itself for the brutality that awaited behind his dark mahogany door. At the entrance to his garden, there was an old, weathered, wrought-iron gate that always squeaked and shed flakes of peeling paint as I pressed down on the rusted latch to open it. Beyond the gate, his neglected garden was a chaotic mix of wildflowers and weeds. Reluctantly, I always closed the gate behind me, and then began the slow, terrifying death march up the winding driveway, which was practically hidden by the overgrown bushes that ran along either side of it. With each hesitant step that I took towards his front door, I fought fiercely against the raging waves of apprehension that tossed me about like a discarded piece of driftwood. I had considered running away many times, but as an eight-year-old child, I had nowhere to run to, and even if I did, the consequences would have been horrific.

The haunting memory of standing in front of O'Connell's door had seared itself deep into my mind, leaving an indelible mark that refused to fade despite the passing of time. As I stood facing his door, my heart pounded against my chest like a caged animal desperate for freedom. The sound of its rapid beats echoed in my ears, drowning out all other sounds. My body shook uncontrollably, as beads of cold sweat ran down the length of my spine. I always closed my eyes as I forced my trembling hand to press the doorbell, while at the same time, I desperately prayed that the bastard wouldn't answer. Or even better, that he had fallen down the stairs, and lay lifeless in a crumpled heap on the floor. However, just like all the other prayers that I said back then, it went unanswered. 'Ask, and you shall receive,' what a load of pure shite!

When the door opened, I would be ushered straight into the sitting room. The curtains were always drawn, regardless of the hour, and the only source of light in the room came from the television screen. On the coffee table, there was always a bowl of sweets and chocolates proudly displayed.

'It's just like being at the movies,' he would say with a smile, revealing his badly stained teeth and stale smoker's breath.

When he was finished using me for his own sexual gratification, his demeanour would suddenly change. His previously calm expression would contort into a mask of rage, his fists clenched, and his body trembled with anger as he lashed out at me. He would beat me severely for 'leading him into temptation,' as he called it. In those fits of rage that consumed him after he had defiled me, he would loom over me, shouting aggressively and calling me all the filthy names that he could think of. Then, he would order me to get dressed and get out of his sight.

After I had dressed, he would tell me to go and wait in the car, which provided a temporary reprieve from the traumatic ordeal that I had just endured. As I sat alone in the car and waited for him, the images of his depraved cruelty flooded my mind. It felt as though each horrifying image that flashed through my mind was taunting and haunting me at the same time. I couldn't understand why this was happening to me, I had done nothing wrong. Why was I being so severally punished? I desperately struggled to hold back the tears that threatened to flow, determined not to show any emotion or pain. Once his anger subsided, he would join me in the car. His old, wrinkled hand would rest on my trembling knee as he settled himself into the driver's seat, grinning with satisfaction as he handed me a bar of chocolate, which I assumed was my reward. Although the sweet, rich chocolaty taste in my mouth, helped to replace his vile taste and odour.

I always dreaded the short drive back home. The air in the car was heavy with unspoken tension, as both victim and abuser sat side by side, and the suffocating silence between us only added to the discomfort. The fear that he instilled in me during that brief journey lingered and haunted me throughout the night. As he parked the car outside my house, he would shift in his seat to face me, his penetrating gaze burning into me. My eyes stung with unshed tears as I turned to meet his gaze. His vice-like grip on my upper arm tightened with each passing second, forcing me to close my eyes as waves of excruciating pain shot down the length of my arm.

'If you ever breathe a single word about what happened between us to your mother, or anyone else for that matter, you'll end up on a missing person's list, never to be found,' he whispered into my right ear. His voice was low and chilling, and the menacing look in his eyes assured me that he would stop at nothing to guarantee my silence. I felt like a prisoner, trapped and suffocating in my own little, dark, and isolated world with no chance of escape.

Every time I returned home from Fr. O'Connell's house, I always ran straight up the stairs and into the bathroom to wash away the filth of his sin. My mother never questioned anything, and even if I had mustered up the courage and told her, my dark secret would have fallen on deaf ears. After all, my abuser was not only her lover; he was also a well-respected pillar within the community. The consequences for concocting such a heinous story would have been horrendous. I felt trapped and vulnerable, like a bird with its wings cruelly clipped. I yearned to speak out, and cry for help, but I had no one to confide in, not even my own mother. Her abusive nature and unpredictable, violent outbursts had kept me imprisoned in a never-ending cycle of fear and isolation.

Looking back, I never had a chance of living what would be deemed a normal childhood. Despite my mother's popularity within the parish committee and the wider community, she was a completely different person behind closed doors. The persona that she had adopted for her social standing within the community was in stark contrast to the person who I knew at home. Once she was within the safety of our house, and away from prying eyes, she would abandon the façade, and her cruel sadistic nature would appear.

Her most treasured possession was a whip, which she kept on the top shelf of her wardrobe, hidden beneath her clothes. The whip had a short, solid wooden handle with thin braided strands of leather tightly coiled around it. Each strip of leather was well-worn and frayed from years of use. If, in her deluded and irrational mind, she concluded that I had committed a sin, she would violently drag me up the stairs. My hair would be brutally pulled and twisted in her unrelenting grip, as her fingernails dug deep into my scalp. My young, frail body was mercilessly jerked and flung against the unforgiving steps, sending jolts of pain right through me. Each step was a brutal and painful experience as my body crashed against the hard wood, the heavy impact left me reeling, my head spun and my vision blurred. In a desperate attempt to escape her evil clutches, I writhed and thrashed in agony, like a fish on dry land, as she dragged me from step to step. However my feeble efforts were no match for her iron grip.

As we entered her bedroom, my head always collided with the doorframe, with a little guidance from my mother. The dimly lit room cast our tangled shadows along the back wall as they struggled against each other. Once inside, the beating continued as she unleashed her rage upon me. Each kick and punch landed with acute precision and brutal force, leaving me doubled over in agony. As her fists slowed and her breathing became laboured, the onslaught finally came to an end. Exhausted from her seething rage, she would collapse onto the bed in a heap, her chest heaving violently with each laboured breath. Eventually, after gathering herself together, the proceedings recommenced and I was forced to strip naked and stand exposed in front of her full-length mirror. She would then flick her lighter and take a long drag, her piercing gaze remained fixed on me as she blew smoke in my direction. I stood there, exposed and vulnerable, as she coldly stared at me with a cigarette dangling from her fingers. Although humiliated, I was grateful for the brief respite from her vicious assault.

As our eyes met in the mirror, a tremble of fear coursed through my body as she slowly rose from the bed, her movements deliberate and calculated as she stubbed out her cigarette in the ashtray. My eyes followed her in the mirror as she crossed the room, opened her wardrobe, and reached inside. My reflection's eyes widened in terror and desperation, as if silently pleading for mercy as she closed the wardrobe door and turned to face me, the whip held tightly in her right hand. I knew there was no escaping her wrath.

Then, she would hand down my sentence, ten of the most brutal lashes that left behind a trail of raw, bleeding flesh. As the whip tore through my skin, the sound of its crack reverberated throughout the room, followed by a searing pain that felt like hot knives slicing me into pieces. While, the scars on my body served as a constant reminder of her sadistic sense of justice, the emotional wounds cut even deeper, haunting me for years to come.

My mother truly believed that each brutal lash was necessary for my salvation. She justified this barbaric punishment by stating, 'If Jesus, our Saviour, endured the whip to cleanse the world of sin, then I too needed to suffer the same fate when I had sinned.' After she had administered the whipping, she would pull me up off the floor from where I lay, shaking, and curled up in the fetal position. As I knelt, bloodied, and battered, I felt completely humiliated and exposed as my pathetic reflection stared back at me. Tears streamed down my face as I watched my blood trickle down my beaten and lacerated body. My body trembled uncontrollably as the pain and fear coursed through every inch of my being.

'Watch the sin running off of you,' she spat out the words, as she held me upright by my hair with one hand, while the whip shook violently in her other clenched fist. The punishment was meant to make me reflect on the sin that I had committed, a sin of which I was completely unaware.

My father passed away when I was just three years old. Unfortunately, I have no memories of him. I often wished that I could remember something about him, anything, like the sound of his voice or the way he smiled, but alas, there was nothing. My mother never spoke of him; she never even mentioned his name. Her silence on the matter, coupled with her volatile nature, made me too afraid to ask about him. There were times when my mother was out of the house, and I would take the opportunity to rummage through the drawers and closets, hoping to find some trace of my father before she returned home. However, my frantic searches always ended in disappointment, as I never found anything, no personal belongings, not even a single photograph, and as time passed, any thoughts I had of him simply faded.

I often wondered if my deluded mother saw herself as a divine being and believed that I had been conceived by the Holy Spirit, similar to the Virgin Mary's Immaculate Conception. She always portrayed a holier-than-thou attitude, and often looked down on those who did not share her beliefs, and she never shied away when it came to expressing her moral point of view. However, behind her back, she was not as loved and admired as she thought. There were quite a few who could not tolerate or even stand the sight of her. I had once overheard her being described as 'obnoxiously pious,' by one of her fellow committee members. At the time, I didn't know what the words meant, but I still smiled to myself, knowing that it wasn't a good thing. However, my mother seemed to have her spies strategically placed throughout the committee, as even comments that were whispered in secret somehow managed to reach her burning ears. Although she remained unfazed by those who did not share her sense of self-importance and often dismissed them as 'ignorant and jealous.'

My deluded mother, and her equally disturbed lover, O'Connell, had effectively isolated me from the outside world. They had confined me within the four walls of our house, using my bedroom as a prison cell. I spent my days and nights in fearful solitude, anxiously waiting behind my bedroom door for the inevitable horror that would come. The other children who lived on the street either avoided me or were forbidden from playing with me. Although they never held back when it came to the bullying or name-calling. It was relentless. The neighbours never spoke out or questioned anything; some of them must have suspected that something sinister was happening behind our closed door. Maybe they just gossiped amongst themselves, or turned a blind eye, just like God and Jesus had. Regardless of what they thought or suspected, I was left to suffer my cruel fate alone, in silence.

Throughout my childhood and adolescent years, my mother rarely spoke to me, and when she did, it was usually in an abusive or degrading manner. However, there were times when she and O'Connell would disappear into her bedroom, and I would have to turn up the volume on the television to drown out the grunts and groans coming from above. Once they had finished, O'Connell would always retreat to the bathroom. The sound of the shower running echoed through the house as he purged himself of the sin he had just committed with my mother. After they had whispered their goodbyes in the hallway, and she had waved him off from the front door. My mother would then join me in the sitting room, her cheeks, flushed and her hair, a wild, tangled mess. Her once carefully applied makeup had turned into a smudged and streaked disaster. For a brief period of time after O'Connell's visit, she was a completely different woman. The old bastard obviously knew how to perform beneath the sheets.

On those occasions, my mother would sit next to me on the sofa, gently tousling my hair as she lit a cigarette. The naked flame always captivated me as it flickered and danced at the end of the match, before she blew it out and inhaled deeply. She would sit in silence, lost in her thoughts, her gaze fixed on the circles of smoke that she exhaled towards the ceiling.

Those brief moments of tenderness were rare and fleeting, but I cherished them nonetheless. I knew that as soon as her cigarette burnt out, that peaceful moment would come to an abrupt end.

It was during one of those peaceful, fleeting moments, that my mother told me how she hoped and prayed that I would one day become a priest, just like Fr. O' Connell. I would simply smile up at her in silence, wanting that precious moment to last as long as possible, while at the same time, I was scared shitless of upsetting her. So, when she took it upon herself and told O'Connell that I wanted to become a priest, a statement that couldn't have been any further from the truth, that sick fuck was only delighted. He assured my mother that he would take me under his wing to guide and mentor me in living a life devoted to serving God and the Church. As If, I hadn't suffered enough under that sanctimonious prick throughout the years. My choice of career was not optional; just like everything else in my life back then, my mother decided it for me.

Chapter 3

I had just turned seventeen when I first entered the seminary. It was early autumn, and the leaves on the trees had already begun to change colour. The vibrant hues of red and orange danced among the golden-brown leaves, creating a picturesque scene that adorned both the trees and the ground. I have always loved the autumnal colours and the soft crunch of the leaves beneath my feet. It was a sound that I eagerly awaited every year as my birthday approached. From a young age, I had convinced myself that the changing leaves were a special birthday gift, bestowed upon me by Mother Nature herself.

O'Connell accompanied me on my first day at the seminary. He had offered to drive me there, much to the delight of my mother. On the morning of my departure, my mother informed me that she had some urgent parish committee business to attend to, which required her utmost attention, and therefore was unable to join us. I was relieved, as her presence would have only added to my already crippling sense of dread and foreboding.

The car journey was a nightmare. Not only did O'Connell reek of sweat and stale cigarettes, but his massive bulk left little room for movement. As we drove towards the seminary, I felt confined and claustrophobic, wedged between the car door and my oppressor. The air in the car felt heavy, making it difficult to breathe as the tension between us grew with each passing mile. Each time he changed the gears, his elbow dug into my side with brute force, causing me to wince in pain. His intentional blows sent my body into survival mode, as every muscle tensed.

Throughout the journey, O'Connell's eyes remained fixed on the winding roads, his hands tightly gripped the steering wheel as if his life depended on it. His menacing aura sent shivers down my spine.

Despite my efforts, I struggled to remain calm. My trembling hands and pounding heart were clear signs of the fear that consumed me. I felt small and powerless as I sat next to him. The constant fear and threat of his physical and emotional abuse that had haunted me for years, still held a powerful grip over me. I spent most of the journey with my eyes closed, pretending to be asleep. However, my mind was a chaotic mess, filled with the worries of what awaited me once I entered the seminary.

The hour-long journey was travelled in complete silence. As soon as O'Connell parked the car, he quickly hopped out and lit a cigarette. I watched as he inhaled deeply, the silent journey had obviously taken its toll on him as well. I remained in the car, hesitant to leave the safety of the passenger seat. The seat belt was wrapped tightly around me, providing a false sense of security against the unseen dangers that I feared surrounded me. As I peered out from behind the smudged windscreen, a wave of anxiety washed over me as I took in what would become my new home for the next seven years.

The building that stood before me resembled an old Gothic castle, similar to the ones seen in those outdated black-and-white horror movies. As I took in my new surroundings from the safety of the car, a sense of foreboding settled in the pit of my stomach, confirming my initial fears, as the looming silhouette of the ancient edifice shrouded everything in sight. O'Connell threw me a look as he lit another cigarette, my cue to join him, I assumed. I unbuckled my seat belt and slowly stepped out of the car. As I approached him, he grunted and flicked his half-finished cigarette to the ground, crushing it beneath his freshly polished shoe. I ignored him, even though I could feel his penetrating stare boring into me. I shielded my eyes from the blinding rays of the early morning sun, using my hands as a visor as I tilted my head back and marvelled at the colossal building that seemed to spread in every direction, creating the illusion that it reached the distant horizon. It was hard to fathom that such an imposing structure, centuries old, had been built by mere mortals. It seemed like an impossible feat.

As I gazed up in awe at the ancient edifice sprawled out before me, my mind momentarily drifted back to the time of the Egyptians. Their magnificent pyramids and monuments have stood for thousands of years, a testament to their advanced civilization. And despite the advancements that have been made in science and technology through-out the years, renowned archaeologists from around the world remain perplexed and are unable to fully explain the incredible feats achieved by our ancestors. The secrets of the Egyptians remain buried deep within the tombs of their great pharaohs, hidden beneath the warm, golden sand. I couldn't help but wonder what secrets lay hidden within the walls of the ancient edifice that loomed before me.

As O'Connell and I approached the main entrance, we were greeted by a tall, thin priest named Fr. Conroy. He welcomed us with a firm handshake and a friendly smile. His hunched posture, possibly due to his height and thin build, gave the impression that he could snap in half at any given moment. His pale, gaunt face and sharp, hooked nose not only lacked a bit of sunlight but also gave him a slightly menacing appearance. His small, black, beady eyes resembled those of a crow, and his full head of dark, slicked-back hair only added to the image of Count Dracula that had entered my mind. A wave of dread washed over me, as if I were about to enter his lair.

Fr. Conroy had the arduous task of not only welcoming but also looking after all the new and some very enthusiastic recruits, a number of whom were already displaying a holier-than-thou attitude. One particular seminarian had boldly expressed his desire to become the first Irish Pope, and had his sights firmly set on conquering El Papa's throne in Rome. It became quite evident that O'Connell and Fr. Conroy were very well acquainted. It transpired that both men had entered the seminary at the same time many years ago, and had remained close friends ever since. I watched as their faces lit up with joy as they shook hands and embraced each other as old friends do. I tried to imagine them as two young, God-fearing men, full of enthusiasm and naivety, as they embarked on their calling to save lost souls.

My fellow seminarians and I stood at the foot of the large, weathered granite steps that led up to the main entrance. Fr. Conroy welcomed us all as he positioned himself on the third step, elevating himself to a higher plane. He seemed to relish the attention of his captivated audience, as he regaled us with one story after another about his own wonderful journey as a servant of God. I found it difficult to listen to him; it felt as though he was simply playing a role, like an actor performing for an audience in front of him. Very little of what he said resonated with me. Although the odd loose word did penetrate, such as obedience, redemption, and my personal favourite, unrequited love for our Heavenly Father, I soon zoned out after I heard that. I was convinced that both God and Jesus had abandoned me, turned a blind eye, and left me, an innocent and defenceless child, at the mercy of that twisted paedophile, O'Connell.

After Fr. Conroy, had finished reciting his well-rehearsed welcoming speech, he then shared some of his vast knowledge about the eerie building that stood behind him. He spoke at length about its history and construction, from the first sod being turned right up to its most recent renovations. With his carefully chosen words, Fr. Conroy's passion and authority were clearly evident, unveiling the deep bond he had forged with the seminary over the years. Although the manner in which he spoke, one could have easily believed that he had single-handedly built the entire structure, laying each granite stone, one by one, with his own bare hands. When he had finally finished speaking, he turned to face the building and stood in silence for a brief moment, gazing up in reverence before ascending the steps. We followed in silence, like a flock of obedient lambs being led to the slaughter.

At the top of the steps, stood two wooden doors, flanked by a beautifully carved stone archway. The doors were open, as if awaiting our arrival. Before we entered, I stole a brief moment to gaze once again at the enormity of the mysterious edifice sprawled out in front of me. I felt spellbound, completely entranced by its grandeur, as I tried to take it all in. However, my reverie was quickly interrupted when I heard my name being called, and we began to make our way inside.

Once we stepped inside the building, it was as if time had stood still within its walls, preserving the ambiance of a bygone era. We were transported back to a dark period in our history, back to a time when the Catholic Church held a dominant role in society and maintained a much firmer grip on the people, albeit through fear. While it is undeniable that the church has lost its way throughout the centuries, as it repeatedly failed to adapt and remain connected with the people in an ever-changing world, it remains trapped in its antiquated customs and rituals, chained to its dark past. Its once revered monastic vows and belief in an all-powerful living God, seem to hold little, if any, relevance in today's modern society.

Our new world is fast-paced, leaving little time for traditional religious practices such as holy orders and sacred sacraments. We are constantly bombarded by bright lights and noise, and our lives are consumed by impatience, senseless violence, and the most unimaginable suffering inflicted upon so many innocent people around the world. As a result, we have become desensitised to the inhumanity that exists among our fellow human beings. Our society is plagued by pent-up anger and madness, fuelled by our own egos. In such a world, the idea of taking a moment to kneel and pray, offering reverence to a divine being hidden above the clouds, seems ludicrous. Our new world is a cruel and damaged place, where God's faithful messengers are eagerly awaited, like a hungry wolf awaits an innocent lamb.

Once I crossed the threshold, my seven-year sentence began. My crime, I was an innocent victim of circumstance, thrown into the seminary and hidden away from the rest of society, all because my deranged mother decided that I didn't fit in. Against my will, I was forced to offer up my life to a God that I didn't believe in, promised that my sacrifice would be rewarded with eternal salvation. I was abandoned and hidden among the shadows that slowly moved throughout that dark and disturbed place of secrecy, where whispers echoed off the ancient stone walls, and secrets lurked around every corner. The seminary was shrouded in an air of mystery, and completely isolated from the outside world.

The interior of the building exuded a heavy, oppressive atmosphere, enveloped in a deafening silence and an eerie stillness that embodied the entire place. Dark-stained timber panels sheathed the walls from floor to ceiling, which seemed to enhance the sombre and foreboding ambiance that filled the air. Religious icons were strategically placed along the hallways at eye level, ensuring that they were not overlooked. Those images seemed to embed themselves into our subconscious minds, leaving a lasting impression. And despite the numerous rows of tall, arched, Gothic-style windows that were scattered throughout the building, the cold, uninviting edifice remained cloaked in darkness, with only faint rays of light penetrating its gloomy interior.

The deeper Fr. Conroy led us into the building, the more anxious I became. My imagination ran wild with dark, disturbing thoughts and images. The dimly lit hallways cast long shadows that flickered and swayed along the floor and walls as we trailed behind them. I was convinced that an unseen presence was lurking within the shadows that surrounded us, and the eerie silence only heightened my unease. It felt as though something sinister was waiting to be unleashed. Even the faint scent of incense that lingered in the air added to the ominous atmosphere. With each step, the suffocating feeling seemed to intensify. Despite my hatred of home, I found myself longing to return to that evil house.

My fellow seminarians and I listened as Fr. Conroy droned on endlessly about the history of the place. His animated gestures and over-the-top enthusiastic tone had worn thin among the group. He seemed oblivious to our boredom, or perhaps he was just so caught up in his own performance that he didn't notice. Despite this, he continued to tell us one story after another, inspiring stories, as he called them. Most of the life-sapping tales related to past pupils who had served their time within these same walls before being sent out into the world to spread the word of God.

'Not unlike all of you here today,' he said with a smile.

As we followed our enthusiastic guide throughout the building, I couldn't help but notice the amount of crucifixes that we encountered. They seemed to be everywhere, some were freestanding, while others hung on the walls. The lifelike depictions were so realistic that one could almost feel the agony etched on the face of our Lord. Regardless of which hallway we walked along or room we entered, a crucified Jesus stared intently back at us. I found it unnerving to be constantly confronted by such a horrific image. Even our modest dorms were not exempt from the eerie gaze of the crucifix, one hung on the back of the door and another above the bed. The crucifix seemed to hold a mysterious power that could not be ignored. I struggled to sleep with the crucified Jesus looming over me, so every night I removed it from the wall and placed it face down under the bed. As soon as first light entered my room the following morning, I rehung it before anyone noticed it was missing.

Chapter 4

The seminary was a poisonous place, akin to a concentration camp, and veiled in a toxic, suffocating atmosphere. We were deceived, corrupted, and completely brainwashed. Each of us endured some form of abuse, whether it was psychological, physical, or sexual; the most vulnerable among us suffered all three. Our days were extremely challenging, and the misery etched on the faces of my fellow seminarians told of their unspoken suffering. What made it even worse was the fact that they had chosen to enter the seminary, unlike me, who was forced against my will. They truly believed that God had called them to this path, and they were simply following their destiny. It was absolute madness, and I couldn't help but question their sanity for choosing such a fate.

Our daily routine started at five o'clock in the morning. We were forced to shower under the lecherous stares of the senior priests, their eyes lingering on our naked bodies with predatory hunger. It appeared they had been assigned the task of ensuring that we were cleansed of all our impurities. Ironically, it was those same priests who had entered our dorms and violated us during the dead of night, rendering us unclean. It was degrading having to shower in front of our abusers, while they leered and whispered amongst themselves as we washed their filth from our bodies, it was sickening.

After showering, we quickly dressed while still under their perverted gaze. We then made our way to the chapel for morning mass. As soon as the service ended, we headed straight to the dining hall for breakfast. Every morning, the dining hall was filled with a heavy silence, as if the weight of our shameful secrets from the previous night lingered in the air. The senior priests sat at a slightly elevated table at the top of the hall, which gave them a clear view of the entire room. They laughed and joked amongst themselves as they enjoyed their breakfast; they seemed completely oblivious to their own hypocrisy. Those same priests who preached about purity and absolution by day would fall from grace during the darkness of night, as they succumbed to their carnal desires.

Each day in the seminary seemed to drag on endlessly, it felt as though we were trapped in a never-ending cycle of prayer and study. We were bombarded with lectures on subjects that were completely alien to me, such as theology, religious history, and the scare sacraments. I often struggled to grasp the basic principles of each subject and felt overwhelmed by the amount of material that was thrown at us. As a result, I felt anxious and stressed as I tried to keep up with the heavy workload.

Although the days were difficult, they paled in comparison to the nights. The fear that consumed us as darkness descended was indescribable. Every footstep or creak of a floorboard sent a warning signal that danger lurked just beyond the door of my room. I spent my nights lying awake, terrified, praying to a God that I didn't believe in, hoping that no one would enter my room. However, my prayers were always in vain, as an unwanted guest always arrived during the dark of night. The darkness seemed to make us even more vulnerable, we were trapped like helpless animals, and left to the mercy of our captors.

Our dormitories, which should have been our sanctuaries and places of refuge, became breeding grounds of fear. There were no locks on our doors, which left us vulnerable. It was usually after midnight when the priests entered our dorms; each had their own little fucked-up fantasies and dark, twisted desires that needed to be catered for. Once spent, your unwanted guest would leave without saying a single word or even making any eye contact. There was one particularly disturbed individual who always blessed himself as he left the room.

'God bless you,' he'd whisper, while making the sign of the cross as he gently closed the door behind him.

And then, there was Fr. Conroy; he was a right sick fuck behind closed doors. When he had finished having his wicked way with you, he would retreat into the shadows of the room. He insisted that you remain naked while he watched and smoked from the dark corner. Then, just like all the others, he would leave without saying a word; although his lips always curled into a sinister smirk as he closed the door.

As soon as he'd left the room, I would open the window, although the fresh air made little difference as it collided with the remnants of his dark desires and twisted gratification. Tears streamed down my cheeks as I removed the crucifix that hung on the wall and placed it face down under the bed. As I lay on the bed and stared up at the ceiling, my body throbbed with a sharp, stabbing pain, as my blood seeped onto the sheets.

The day of my ordination was a complete fucking nightmare. My mother and O'Connell wore false, exaggerated smiles across their bitter faces. They insisted on taking numerous photos, with one standing on either side of me, like proud parents displaying their accomplished offspring. After seven long, hard-fought years of being constantly belittled and brainwashed, the seminary had finally conquered me. I had officially become an ordained priest, a man of the cloth. In their eyes, I was now ready to be sent out into the world to spread the word of God.

Little did they realise that all their years of relentless physical and emotional abuse had created a monster. For seven long, insufferable years, I lay dormant, hidden away from the prying eyes of a fickle, judgmental society. I had endured the most unimaginable suffering as a child; I had been beaten, raped, and abused in every way humanly possible. And then, just for good measure, I was thrown into the seminary, like an innocent lamb tossed in among a pack of hungry wolves, abandoned and forgotten.

I emerged from my seven-year cocoon, like a butterfly breaking free from its chrysalis, shedding the layers of fear and vulnerability that had once tightly bound me. I was no longer the prey, no longer the victim; I had evolved into a vengeful predator. My time had finally arrived to confront those who had failed me as a child. As I stood between my mother and O'Connell, a grown man consumed by an insatiable desire for revenge, the scars of my dark past were etched deep into my soul, a constant reminder of the pain and betrayal that

I had endured. Despite the forced smiles that we wore for the camera, the tension between us simmered beneath the surface. The bright flash of the camera momentarily blinded me. As I regained my sight, we posed for yet another photo. I smiled to myself as I contemplated whom I should kill first: my mother, or O'Connell.

Chapter 5

U nbeknownst to me, O'Connell had arranged with the bishop for me to begin my vocation in the parish of my childhood, under his guidance. I couldn't believe that I was being sent back to the place where I had endured years of pain and suffering. The very parish I had desperately longed to escape as a child, the same place that haunted me every night as I closed my eyes. I later discovered that O'Connell had concocted a story, telling the bishop that my ageing mother was in poor health and that having me close by would be a great source of comfort to her. The mere thought of returning to the place of my dark childhood flooded me with unwanted memories and left me devastated.

Saying mass for the first time on the same altar where I had served as an altar boy for so many years, was nerve-racking. Under the watchful eye of O'Connell, I approached the pulpit and slowly raised my head to meet the silent gaze of the congregation. Despite my best efforts to compose myself, my entire being quivered. I felt as though everyone was waiting for me to slip up, including O'Connell. Thankfully, the ordeal passed without incident. After the service, O'Connell said a few words. He spoke highly of me as he welcomed me back into the parish. The two-faced hypocrite. His kind words and warm welcome were well received among his faithful flock, as a round of applause ensued after he had finished speaking. Charlatans, the lot of them, blinded by their own ignorance.

After seven long years, I had returned to the dreaded place that still haunted my nights. While the landscape appeared unchanged, I knew that many people had likely moved on, and some may have even passed away. However, for me, the painful memories remained raw and unhealed, like an open, festering wound, that slowly continued to spread and became more contaminated with each passing day.

As the parishioners left the church, I stood outside the main entrance and offered my hand to anyone who was willing to accept it. I noticed a glimmer of recognition in the eyes of some of the parishioners; their minds seemed to be working overtime as they tried to place me from the past. I shared a false smile and exchanged pleasantries with a few elderly parishioners who had accepted my outstretched hand and welcomed me into their parish. I watched with a sense of detachment as O'Connell's faithful flock slowly made their way from the church grounds back into their own mundane lives. Some of them looked back over their shoulders, trying to catch another glimpse of their new priest, as they whispered amongst themselves.

My new position as a priest, came with a small, two-bedroom house, I finally had a place all to myself. Every time I turned the key in the lock, a wave of peace and contentment washed over me. It was my own little sanctuary, leaving the chaos of the outside world behind. My mother often stopped by after attending the morning mass. I never understood why, if ever there was an unwanted guest, she topped the list. As she walked through the house, her critical eye scanned every corner, and then her unfiltered comments and criticism followed.

'The walls could do with a fresh coat of paint, and a new carpet in the sitting room and hall would really brighten up the whole place,' she would say. Fuck off and die, often ran through my mind as she spoke. After criticising and finding one fault after another within my home, she would then make herself comfortable at the kitchen table and expected to be waited on hand and foot.

What struck me the most during those mornings, as we sat facing each other over coffee, she showed no signs of guilt or remorse. She seemed completely at ease as she babbled on about her own busy life. The past was never mentioned; had she somehow erased it from her psyche, never to be revisited or spoken of again. It was as if all the beatings that she had inflicted upon me for no apparent reason other than to satisfy her sadistic desires had been completely forgotten. How could she sit opposite me, sipping coffee and devouring cake as if nothing had ever happened between us.

One morning, after saying mass, as I sat across from her at the kitchen table, listening to her incessant chatter; not a single word that left her mouth registered with me. Her voice became nothing more than a muffled background noise. As I drained my cup, I decided that she would be the first to go. After all, everything was her fault. She had beaten and abused me since I was a young child, and she had also invited that evil bastard O'Connell into our lives. My mother was the toxic, cancerous root that had destroyed my childhood. Occasionally, I forced a weak smile as she rambled on and on, while internally, I was desperately fighting to quell the rage that was rising from deep within. If you only knew what was coming, you worthless bitch, I thought to myself, smiling as I placed my empty cup back down on the saucer.

I had settled into my new role as a priest reasonably well, considering the circumstances that had landed me there. Despite my hatred of the priesthood, I found solace in the newfound freedom it provided. The only positive aspect of becoming a priest was the house that came with the position, and with the house, came a housekeeper, it was all part and parcel of the whole deal. Ann was the housekeepers name; she was a warm, friendly woman in her late forties or maybe early fifties, it was hard to tell her exact age. Like many of the other women around her age that were involved in the parish committee, she dressed conservatively. Ann was short and slim, she seemed to be letting her dark hair fade away naturally, as it was streaked with grey and she had the most beautiful dark brown eyes. I surmised that she must have been quite attractive in her younger days. Ann arrived promptly at nine o'clock, not a minute before or a minute after, every Monday, Wednesday, and Friday morning. She did absolutely everything for me, she cooked, cleaned and even kept my laundry up to date, and the fridge and presses were always well stocked up. I never had to lift a finger in that house, Ann mollycoddled me as though I were her own son. At first, I felt very uncomfortable around Ann. I didn't want or need her to come to my home. I viewed her as an intruder, invading my private and personal space. My house was my sanctuary, a place where I could find peace and solitude away from the harshness and pain of the outside world.

Growing up under the brutal regime of my deranged mother, I had developed a profound deep-seated hatred towards women. My sadistic mother was the only female figure in my life for the first twenty-five years. As my twenty-sixth birthday approached, I still had not been intimate with a woman. The seven years I spent secluded in the seminary, hidden away from the outside world, didn't exactly help my situation either. Throughout those seven years, I had very little, contact with the opposite sex. There were occasions when a group of nuns would arrive at the seminary for what we were told was a 'special retreat,' and who were we to question our superiors. The nuns would be whisked off to a part of the building that only a select few had access to. I often wondered if the Monsignor had mixed up his words and actually meant to say 'a special treat' rather than a special retreat. The mystery surrounding the nun's retreats only added to the intrigue of our secluded life in the seminary.

During my time in the seminary, it was drilled into us that women were the root of all evil. 'Look how easily Eve seduced Adam in the Garden of Eden, and as for the mayhem that Magdalene one caused,' one of the priest had said, in a raised voice, during a lecture on religious history. As a result, I acquired a deeply disturbed and damaged view of women, through no fault of my own. It was very much a consequence of the toxic environment that had surrounded me for so many years.

A few months had passed before I began to relax around Ann. It was a slow process of breaking down the barriers and gaining the trust of an outsider. Over time, I warmed to her and allowed her into my troubled and chaotic life. Ann appeared to know exactly how to approach and handle me; she treated me as though I were a rare and delicate species that required the greatest of care. Eventually, It reached the stage where I not only enjoyed our little chats over coffee, but I also looked forward to them. The perception of women, which had been embedded in me throughout the years, began to change. There was no comparison between Ann and my deluded, sadistic mother, or even between Ann and that ancient biblical whore Magdalene.

Ann became a welcome distraction from my otherwise dull existence. I became almost childlike as I eagerly awaited her arrival each morning, consumed with a feverish excitement that I struggled to contain once she had entered my house. Her presence alone seemed to awaken a primal urge within me that I had never experienced before. As I sat opposite her, obsessed with curiosity and arousal, my imagination, fuelled by passionate thoughts and wild desires, only intensified my longing for her. I longed to touch and hold a naked woman's body against mine, to experience the intimacy and pleasure of entering a woman. Experiences I had been denied due to the way my deluded mother had raised me.

My traumatic past was buried deep within my psyche. It would often visit during the dead of night without warning, turning pleasant dreams into terrifying nightmares. I would wake up screaming, drenched in cold sweat, my heart pounding against my chest as if trying to escape my haunting past, only to find myself alone in bed with the light still on. I had to remind myself that my mother and O'Connell, could no longer hurt me. My former tormentors had grown old and weak; they had become the vulnerable ones, just like I had been all those years ago. Our roles had now reversed; I had become the predator, and they were the prey.

I had reached the point of no return; my entire being was consumed by a burning desire for revenge. My senses were heightened, like a crazed, hungry animal silently stalking its prey, lurking in the shadows, waiting patiently for the right moment to pounce. Night after night, sleep eluded me as I stared up at the cracks in the ceiling, thinking of ways to end her miserable existence upon this earth. She deserved a slow and painful departure from this world, one of unbearable suffering. As I lay there, pondering my next move, like an old grandmaster contemplating the final move required to annihilate his opponent. I couldn't help but smile as a solitary tear rolled down my cheek. My time had finally come.

Chapter 6

I pulled out from the school car park with a throbbing headache that felt like a hammer pounding against my skull. I had spent the past two hours in a classroom full of eight-year-old children, answering one ridiculous question after another about, God, Jesus, and Holy Mary. And if that hadn't been bad enough, the torture not only continued, but also intensified as a choir of high-pitched, squeaky-voiced children, stood at the top of the classroom and began singing hymns in preparation for their forthcoming First Holy Communion. The deafening noise of the children voices lingered in my ears, as I drove away from the school.

The primary school was located just around the corner from my mother's house. Despite our strained relationship, and my deep-rooted hatred for her, I found myself drawn to her house. As I drove the short distance, the toneless voices of the children echoed in my head, which undoubtedly caused a momentary lapse of reason, leading me to make the ludicrous decision to visit my mother.

As I drove around the block for the second time, a wave of doubt and uncertainty washed over me. I chain-smoked one cigarette after another, questioning my sanity, before I finally parked outside my mother's house. After parking the car, I strolled over to the corner shop and bought a lemon-drizzle cake and a pack of cigarettes. Once outside the shop, I eagerly tore open the pack of cigarettes, tapped one out and brought it to my lips, with the flick of the lighter, I inhaled the familiar smoke and let out a sigh.

'What the hell am I playing?' I quietly muttered to myself, my eyes were firmly fixed on her house, which I had aptly named 'The House of Horrors.' After a final, long, hard drag, I flicked the butt to the ground and headed across the road towards her house.

My mother's eyes widened in surprise as she opened the door and saw me staring back at her. After a brief moment, once her initial shock had settled, she stepped aside and invited me in. As I followed her into the kitchen, an uncomfortable silence hung between us. She gestured for me to take a seat at the kitchen table. My eyes scrutinised every inch of the place while she busied herself in the kitchen with her back to me. A number of years had passed since I last set foot in her house, yet it appeared just as I had left it.

Within minutes of sitting at the table, a torrent of memories engulfed me like a tidal wave, threatening to drown me in their intensity, leaving me gasping for air. The vivid images of my mother's violent outbursts, with her clenched fist pummelling down on me and her piercing voice screaming insults, played out in my mind like a chaotic and unsettling slideshow. I could feel the weight of her fist and hear the sharpness of her voice, as if it was happening all over again.

I remained silent, my back rigid as she always demanded, my eyes fixed on the back of her head. Beneath the table my hands were clenched into tight fists, my fingernails digging into my palms as I fought against the rising rage and anger that begged to be unleashed. Lost in her own world, my mother hummed a tune, completely oblivious to what was conspiring behind her.

Suddenly, I felt a strange and powerful presence surrounding me. I could feel it, even though there was nothing tangible to touch or see. It was as if my return to the house had awakened the lost and frightened soul of my horrific childhood, which had been dormant and trapped in my absence. And now that I had returned, it felt as though we needed to reunite in the fight against the evil bitch standing with her back to me, humming away absentmindedly as she gazed out the kitchen window.

The relentless barrage of horrific memories continued to assault my mind, images that were deeply ingrained in my psyche and impossible to forget, completely overwhelmed me. Closing my eyes, I hoped to escape the memories. However, the onslaught raged on, bombarding me with one disturbing image after another. Suddenly, my horrific thoughts were interrupted by her voice.

'Lemon-drizzle, my absolute favourite, how thoughtful,' she said, completely unaware that she had just winched me away from my tormented mind. As I opened eyes, I forced a smile. I watched as she poured the tea into her prized China, which was usually reserved for special guests and occasions. I couldn't help but wonder if my social status had elevated since becoming ordained. I could sense her discomfort, which both excited and unsettled me. After she had cut the cake into neat slices, she then took her seat across from me. We were sitting in the exact same spots as we used to sit all those years ago, when she was the dominant mother and I was the terrified child. But now, I was no longer the scared and helpless child I used to be.

'So John, tell me, how is Fr. O'Connell treating you these days?' she asked, as crumbs fell from the side of her mouth as she chewed on a piece of cake. Her question felt like a knife being thrust and turned deep into my side. I struggled to hold my tongue and steady myself, determined not to lose control. I reminded myself that I was no longer the helpless child that she had preyed on all those years ago. But, upon hearing her words, the memories surged back, unleashing a storm of chaos in my mind. I fought hard to remain composed as my mother looked at me with a confused expression, probably wondering why I was taking so long to respond.

'Everything is fine, couldn't be better,' I replied, struggling to contain my growing anger. 'You were so lucky to have such a fine man like Fr. O'Connell to take you under his wing at such a young age. Look at the man you have become. I'm so proud of you, John,' she said.

That was the final straw, her words were too much for me to handle.

'Fuck you and O'Connell,' I shouted, as I lunged myself across the table, and drove my clenched fist into the side of her fat, red face.

The impact sent her flying from her chair, she landed hard on the cold, tiled floor. I quickly moved around the table and pulled her up off the floor, I then threw her up against the wall. Her poisonous blood flowed from her mouth and nose, she was dazed, and confused, yet still conscious. I dragged her roughly out into the hallway, banging her head against the walls as we made our way to the stairs. It was a mammoth task to haul her heavy bulk up the narrow staircase. With each creaky step we encountered on the old, worn staircase, I cursed the evil bitch for the countless times she had brutally pulled me up the same stairs by my hair.

'How do you like it, you sadistic bitch?' I screamed at her as I kicked and violently dragged her by the hair. Handfuls of her blue-rinsed hair came away in my hands as we struggled from step to step. Finally, I managed to get her into the bedroom and threw her onto the bed. Exhausted, I collapsed onto the floor and lay on my back, my chest heaving as I gasped for air. I remained there until my breathing returned to somewhat normal. Slowly, I pulled myself back up onto my feet, a smile spread across my face as I realised the gravity of what I had just done.

I sneered at the pathetic sight of my mother, her limp body sprawled across the bed like a discarded rag doll. A wave of rage and disgust washed over me as I viciously pounded my clenched fist into her bloodied face. Breathless, I slumped onto the chair facing her vanity unit, my body trembling with exhaustion and adrenaline, as I struggled to light a cigarette. In the mirror, my eyes were fixed on our reflections. My mother's face was bruised and battered, a stark contrast to my own cold and emotionless stare. A twisted smile spread across my lips as I watched her slowly dying. Finally, I was free from her evil curse. I sat and smoked, savouring the moment I had dreamt of for so many years, as I blew circles of smoke towards her.

I was halfway through my second cigarette when my phone rang. The sound jolted me out of my thoughts and I fumbled, dropping the damn cigarette on the floor. I quickly extinguished it under my shoe while looking down at the lit-up screen. O'Connell's name stared back at me. What the fuck does he want? I thought as I answered the call.

'Hello, Tom,' I said.

'Hi, John, just a quick reminder that the parish committee meeting is at seven tonight, and not eight as previously mentioned,' he said.

'Thanks for the reminder, Tom. We'll chat later, I'm in the middle of something at the moment,' I replied, hanging up before he had a chance to reply. If he only knew that I was in the process of murdering his lover. I glanced at my watch, it was almost five o'clock, in the evening. I still had plenty of time before the meeting.

I stood up from the chair and walked over to where my dying mother lay. I placed my hand on her neck and felt a faint pulse, the bitch was still alive. Knowing that there was no chance of her making a recovery, it was only a matter of time before she passed away. I decided to leave her, suffering and clinging onto the last bit of life that was left in her, as if I was teasing her with false hope. I then made my way into the bathroom to freshen up, leaning in to the mirror, as I washed away the speckles of my mother's poisonous blood. As I lifted my face from the cold water in the sink, it suddenly dawned on me that my mother, the chairperson of the parish committee, would be expected to attend and chair the meeting. As I checked my reflection for any traces of blood, that I may have missed. I couldn't help but smile at the thought that even at death's door, my mother was still causing me problems. I needed to come up with an excuse to explain her absence from the meeting.

After giving it some thought, I decided that I would tell O'Connell and the other committee members that my mother had fallen ill with a stomach bug and would not be able to attend the meeting. Before returning to her bedroom, I took one last look in the mirror as I dried my face and hands. With no visible sign of any blood, I carelessly tossed the soiled towel onto the floor as I felt the bathroom.

As I re-entered her bedroom, a strange sense of calmness enveloped the room, as if it was shrouded in a peaceful stillness. A soft whisper, echoed in my ears, urging me towards the wardrobe. Hesitantly, I moved across the room, as if in a trance. It felt as though a mysterious presence had taken control of my actions. Once again, I heard the same soft whisper gently coaxing me as I reached up to the top shelf, where the whip lay patiently waiting to administer the punishment for the brutal act I had committed. I had broken the most sacred of the Ten Commandments: 'Thou shall not kill.' It was an unforgivable mortal sin, resulting in instant separation from God and spiritual death of the soul, with no hope of redemption.

I stood facing my dying mother, a twisted smile across my face as I began to strip. 'Look what you have created, you evil bitch,' I sneered, as I turned to face the full-length mirror. Raising the whip above my head, I brought it down with a sharp crack against my trembling flesh. I cried out in excruciating pain as the leather tore through my skin. I repeated the action nine more times, completing the required ten lashes, just like my mother used to administer. The old familiar sting had returned with a vengeance, and my body shook uncontrollably, as my blood trickled down my pale, torn skin like a crimson river. Despite the unbearable pain, I felt a sense of satisfaction as the whip trembled in my right hand.

'Watch the sin run off of you,' I whispered, as I looked in the mirror at the reflection of my dying mother lying motionless on the bed.

The pain coursed through my entire being, causing me to drop to my knees. As I caught my reflection in the mirror, my soulless eyes stared back at me. The excruciating pain mixed with the sight of blood aroused me, I became hard and excited. I relieved myself in the shower as I watched my blood disappear down the plug hole. After drying off, I struggled to dress myself as my clothes stuck to my open wounds. I then returned to her bedroom. She was still breathing, barely clinging to life. It was as if the stubborn bitch was refusing to die. Although she was still alive, I knew there wasn't much life left in her. I decided to leave her as she was and attend the meeting. I would return later to finish the job.

Chapter 7

Throughout the entire meeting, I was completely absorbed in my thoughts and oblivious to everything that was said. My mind was solely fixated on how to make my mother's death appear natural or accidental. Realistically, it was impossible to claim that she had died of natural causes, due to the fact that one whole side of her face and head were completely caved in. As my mind entertained various different scenarios of how to finish off the evil bitch and dispose of her body, I was suddenly brought back to reality by a hand landing on my shoulder. It was Helen, one of the do-gooders who had dedicated her life to the parish committee, with her big round glasses perched on the end of her nose peering down at me.

'Sorry Father, I didn't mean to startle you. Would you like another cup of tea or coffee?' she asked. I nodded silently, my mind was still consumed by thoughts of disposing of my mother's body. Helen must have taken my nod as a yes, as she proceeded to refill my cup.

O'Connell chaired the meeting, due to the absence of my mother. And, just like all the other parish committee meetings that I had attended in the past, it was a complete waste of time, as all the usual bullshit was just repeated from the previous meeting. The committee discussed, upcoming events, fundraisers, and the topic that caused the most excitement, the annual trip to Lourdes. As I looked around the room, a sense of boredom and mundanity emanated from many of the committee members. Although they appeared content with their lives, simply going through the motions, never daring to raise their heads above the parapet as they waited for the final curtain to fall.

After the meeting, O'Connell approached me and asked about my mother's well-being. He wanted to go straight over to see her, which was the last fucking thing that I needed. I reassured him that there was no need, as she had already gone to bed, and that I would be checking in on her as soon as the meeting was over.

'Okay, I'll leave it until the morning. I'll drop by after saying mass to see how she's doing,' he said. 'John, will you lock up, and don't forget to set the alarm. You know what the little bastards are like around here.' With that, he turned and left the room. I stood at the doorway of the parish hall, smoking and patiently waiting for the last few committee members to shut up, put on their coats, and fuck off home so that I could lock up the place.

On the short drive home, all I could think about was that evil bitch lying dead or almost dead on her bed, and what the fuck was I going to do with her body. As soon as I entered my house, I went straight up the stairs and into my bedroom to change my clothes. It felt somewhat inappropriate to have murdered my mother while wearing my priest's outfit. It was ironic to think that in the end, the priest she had always wanted me to become was the one who ended her earthly existence. The phrase 'be careful what you wish for' entered my mind, as I peeled my shirt away from my torn skin, the fresh wounds stung and brought tears to my eyes. It had been over seven years since I had last endured the crack of the whip, and in that moment, everything came flooding back.

After taking a handful of painkillers and washing them down with a large whiskey, I made myself a sandwich and headed to the sitting room and turned on the television. As I flicked through the channels, I had my road to Damascus moment. I jumped up from the sofa and hurried into the hall, grabbing my coat from the rack. I reached into the pocket and retrieved my cigarettes and lighter. My plan was to start a house fire, making it appear as though my mother had fallen asleep while smoking in bed. It seemed like the perfect solution, and I wouldn't have to worry about disposing of her body. Feeling pleased with myself, I returned to the sofa and my sandwich. A quick glance at my watch revealed that it was almost nine o'clock. I turned on the evening news, not because I had any interest in what was happening around the world, I just needed my daily fix of that sexy blond news reader.

At ten-fifteen, I returned my mother's house. The entire place was shrouded in darkness, I turned on the light in the hall and made my way upstairs to her bedroom. As I leaned over her motionless body to check her pulse, I couldn't fucking believe that she was still alive. The worthless bitch seemed to be clinging on tightly to whatever little bit of life remained in her. I walked over to the window, drew the curtains, and turned on the light. I sat down at her vanity unit, lit a cigarette, and inhaled the toxic nicotine as I watched her lying there, completely helpless.

As I smoked and watched her reflection in the mirror, the flashbacks returned. Horrific, violent images flooded my mind, the whippings and the beatings that she had so easily bestowed upon me. She must have known that O'Connell was having his wicked way with me, yet she just turned a blind eye as her only child suffered at the hands of that twisted pervert. As I stood up, I stubbed out my cigarette on the mirror and calmly walked towards the bed.

With one final glance at my nemesis, the evil bitch who had destroyed my life. I smiled and picked up the reading lamp from the bedside table and then repeatedly drove its base into the side of her head. Exhausted, I collapsed to my knees and wept uncontrollably, finally releasing all the pent-up emotions that had been trapped inside of me for many years. I remained on the floor for what felt like an eternity. My tears seemed endless; I couldn't tell if they were tears of sadness or joy, as I was completely overwhelmed with a sense of relief. It was as if a pressure valve inside me had been released, and all the trauma that I had been holding onto throughout my life came rushing out in one sudden burst. Struggling to stand up, I steadied myself against the bed and looked down at her.

'It's over,' I said, as tears streamed down my cheeks. 'You worthless, sadistic bitch. It's finally over.'

I flicked the lighter and held the naked flame to the duvet, and watched as the fire quickly spread across the bed. After placing the pack of cigarettes and the lighter on the bedside table, I stepped back to avoid the intense heat. With a twisted sense of satisfaction, I watched as the flames engulfed her. I quickly ran to the wardrobe and snatched the whip from the top shelf, that cruel instrument of pain had left me both physically and emotionally scarred. For some unknown reason, I couldn't bear to let it burn alongside its master. Perhaps it was the sudden awakening of some dark and unsettling memories, or maybe it was my own insatiable desires that compelled me to save it. As I took one last look at the cruel, cold-hearted bitch who had brought me into this fucked-up world, as she lay on the bed surrounded by bright orange flames.

'I hope you burn in hell for all eternity,' I said with a smile, as I left my mother for the very last time. The fire spread at a ferocious pace, I descended the stairs, two steps at a time, moving swiftly through the house and leaving by the backdoor.

Fifteen minutes later, I was back within the safety of my own four walls. My heart was pounding as beads of sweat dripped from my forehead and into my eyes, causing me to blink incessantly, and my clothes clung to my skin, drenched in a cold sweat. In the kitchen, I took a bottle of whiskey from the press, unscrewed the lid, and swallowed two large mouthfuls in quick succession.

'She's gone forever,' I whispered to the empty house as I lowered the bottle. A sense of overwhelming relief and freedom washed over me. Justice had finally been served; the defendant was guilty as hell and, in the end, she paid the ultimate price for her heinous crimes: the death penalty. From my lowly beginning as a victim, I had slowly risen through the ranks from jury to judge, before finally reaching my pinnacle role as executioner.

As I swigged from the whiskey bottle, I closed my eyes and sank into the stillness of the dark sitting room. It felt as though I was cocooned in a bubble of tranquillity shielded from the outside world. However, my calm and peaceful state was abruptly shattered as thoughts of O'Connell flooded my mind, dragging me back into reality and sending me spirally into a dark and anxious mood. I knew that disposing of that evil bastard would not be an easy task. As I drowned another mouthful from the bottle, I smiled, relieved that I would never have to lay eyes on my sadistic mother again.

Chapter 8

The half bottle of whiskey that I had consumed must have sent me into a deep sleep. I was abruptly awoken from my drunken slumber by someone repeatedly knocking on my front door. With a pounding headache and my mouth bone-dry, I dragged myself off the sofa and stumbled into the hall.

'Hello,' I said, upon opening the door. I widened my eyes and put on a shocked expression as the two police officers looked solemnly at me. Although I had been expecting them before I drifted off, I still needed to act surprised when they showed up on my doorstep.

'Hello, Fr. Doyle,' one of the officers said in a sympathetic tone.

'We apologise for disturbing you. Unfortunately, we have some bad news. May we come in?'

'Yes, of course,' I replied, struggling to maintain my composure, not knowing how much longer I could keep up the façade. As they entered the house, I stepped aside and closed the door behind them. I quickly ushered them into the kitchen, my heart racing as I tried to divert their attention away from the half-empty bottle of whiskey on the coffee table in the sitting room.

As we entered the kitchen, I turned to face the two officers and noticed that the three of us were standing in a perfectly formed triangular shape, with each of us representing a point where the angles meet. My mind drifted back to my school days as I silently recited the Theorem of Pythagoras in my head. 'The square of the hypotenuse is equal to the sum…' The uncomfortable silence and my private geometry lesson were soon interrupted by the older officer, who spoke in a solemn tone,

'I'm sorry to be the bearer of bad news, but there has been a terrible fire at your mother's house. I regret to inform you that your mother passed away in the fire.' The officer's delivery was reminiscent of a sad sonnet, his words dripping with genuine sorrow and regret. I found myself wanting him to repeat those words, but I knew such a request would be inappropriate to ask. I remained silent for a moment, pretending to process what should have been devastating news. And then, it was my turn to put on a convincing performance.

'Oh no, not my mother. She's the only family I have,' I whispered, my voice barely audible. I turned and placed my hands on the kitchen table, using it to steady myself. Slowly, I lowered myself onto the chair, my body trembling with emotion. It was a performance worthy of an Oscar. As I raised my head to meet the gazes of the two officers, I noticed their furrowed brows and tense expressions, they clearly looked more upset than I was. My eyes began to fill with tears. I was on a fucking roll.

'I'm so sorry for your loss, Father,' said the older officer with a sympathetic look on his face. To my surprise, the younger officer was struggling to hold back the tears as he asked,

'Would you like me to make you a cup of tea?'

'No, thank you. I think I'm going to need something a little stronger,' I replied, as I slowly stood up from the table and shuffled into the sitting room to retrieve what remained in the bottle of whiskey. On my return journey, I grabbed a glass from the draining board and sat back down at the kitchen table, keeping my gaze fixed on the floor. I poured myself a small one, not wanting to give off the wrong impression. I begrudgingly offered my two unwanted guests a drink, but they both quickly declined, citing some nonsense about being on duty. The younger officer then got up and went over to the sink, he filled and turned on the kettle. The cheeky little fecker, I was annoyed, as I had not offered them any tea or coffee. All I wanted was for the two of them to fuck off and leave me alone so that I could saviour the moment I had been waiting for all my life. The younger officer made two cups of coffee and then sat back down at the table across from me.

'Would you like me to call someone for you, a family member or friend?' asked the senior officer.

'No, thank you. I'll take care of that in a little while. Right now, I just need some time to process everything,' I replied.

'Of course, I understand. It's a terrible shock to receive such devastating news.' I hadn't noticed which one of the officers had spoken, as my head remained bowed towards the table. 'Yes, it's absolutely dreadful. I don't know how I'm going to cope with the loss of my mother. We were very close,' I replied, avoiding any eye contact. My gaze was firmly fixed on the glass that my hands had surrounded. In one quick scoop, I raised it and drained it, only to find myself craving a refill.

'Do you happen to know which hospital they have taken her remains to?' I asked.

'St. Vincent's Hospital. We can take you there if you'd like,' offered the older officer. I never did catch either of their names.

'No, thank you. It's very kind of you to offer, but I'm sure you both have enough to do without driving me around the city,' I replied.

'It would be no trouble at all. If we can help in any way, please just let us know,' insisted the older officer. It would be a great help if both of you just fucked off and left me alone, crossed my mind, as I stared down into the empty glass that was trapped between my hands.

'I just need some time to let everything sink in. I still can't believe she's gone. It's such a tragedy, and what an awful way to die,' I said, while trying to force out a few tear.

'I can only imagine how difficult it must be for you to come to terms with such a horrific tragedy,' said the older officer sympathetically.

'If you are sure there is nothing we can do to assist you, we'll be on our way.' He pulled out a business card from his coat pocket and placed it on the table with his name and contact number.

'Here's my number. If you need anything, please don't hesitate to call me at any time.' As they both stood up from the table and made their way out towards the front door, the older officer turned to face me. His expression was filled with pity and sympathy, as he said, 'I'm so sorry for your loss, Father. And please, if you need anything, don't hesitate to call me.' As we shook hands, I forced a sad smile. After their patrol car pulled away, I closed the door and made my way back into the kitchen. I refilled my glass and drained it in one, I was proud of my performance as the grief-stricken son.

After the police left, I downed another couple of whiskeys before I called O'Connell, my dead mother's lover. He sounded genuinely upset on the phone and offered to come over and be with me during my 'time of need.' I declined his offer, as he was the last person I wanted next or near me on what was the happiest day of my life. I told him that I needed to be alone to process and come to terms with the cruel way my mother's life had ended. As I poured another drink and embraced my celebratory mood, I told myself that this was the start of a new beginning. However, my mood soon darkened and I had to rein myself in. There were important matters to attend to, such as identifying my mother's body and arranging her funeral.

As her next of kin, it was expected of me to go to the hospital mortuary and identify my mother's body. The mere thought of it filled me with dread. I had to switch roles once again and revert back to playing the part of the grieving son. I drained another glass of whiskey before calling a taxi to take me to the hospital. I knew that I was well over the limit and unfit to drive. Twenty-five minutes later, the doorbell rang. I opened the door to find a short, plump, grey-haired man with a pleasant smile standing before me.

'Hello, did you order a taxi?' he asked in a strong Dublin accent.

'Yes, I'll be with you in two minutes,' I replied.

'No problem, take your time,' he said as he turned and made his way back down the garden path and out to his car.

I left some lights on in the house to act as a deterrent. I then set the alarm and locked the front door. As I made my way to the waiting taxi, I was not in the mood for any idle chit-chat from the driver. Over the years, I have found that hairdressers, and taxi drivers in particular, often feel the need to offer their opinions and solutions to all of the world's problems. I settled into the backseat of the taxi and gave the friendly-faced driver my destination. I closed my eyes and rested my head on the headrest, giving the impression that I needed a nap. The driver seemed to take the hint, as he remained silent throughout the entire journey, which was quite unusual for a taxi driver, as normally they never shut up.

Chapter 9

U pon entering the hospital, I approached the reception desk. Behind the desk sat a large, muscular, bald-headed Eastern European security guard. He had a tattoo emerging out from under his shirt collar and extending up behind his ear, but I couldn't make out the design of the tattoo. The man's head was bowed towards a magazine that he seemed engrossed in. I pretended to cough in order to get his attention. As he raised his head to investigate who had disturbed him, our eyes met. He wore a serious, don't fuck with me expression on his clean-shaven face, and his sheer physical size only added to his intimidating demeanour. A sign reading 'approach with caution' would not have been out of place. His stoic expression never changed as I explained to the overgrown meathead who I was and why I was there. He simply nodded at me before he picked up the phone. After a brief conversation in his native tongue, he hung up the phone and said in broken English,

'Please take a seat.' He then continued to explain in a drawn-out manner, as he struggled to find the right words, that someone would be with me shortly. As I followed his instructions and took a seat, I had a bad feeling that I was in for a very long night.

True to his word, and much to my surprise, a young foreign woman appeared from behind a set of double doors within a few minutes of me taking a seat. After briefly speaking with the security guard in their native tongue, she turned her attention towards me and introduced herself with a friendly smile, and asked me to follow her. She was slim and agile, moving lightly on her feet, I struggled to keep up as we made our way along an outdated corridor that was in need of a fresh coat of paint. Eventually, we arrived at a small waiting room, it had a television mounted on the back wall and several hard plastic chairs arranged in a semi-circle facing it.

'Please take a seat, a staff member will be with you shortly,' she said as she turned and left the room.

As the effects of the whiskey began to fade, I could feel a throbbing headache coming on. Just as I lowered the volume on the television, a nurse entered the room. She was an attractive woman, approaching middle age. As I looked at her, I couldn't help but wonder how much longer she could fight against the aging process before the inevitable lines and wrinkles appeared. She offered her condolences with the same sympathetic expression that the police officer had worn earlier. I wondered if the sympathetic look was something they were trained to do in order to help in situations like this. After a brief chat, she asked me to follow her. My patience was wearing thin as my hang-over kicked in. I felt as though I was being led on a wild goose chase, going from one room to the next. All I wanted was to get this over and done with as quickly as possible.

The nurse knocked on a door marked 'private' and entered without waiting for a response. I followed her into the room, where a very, young-looking doctor immediately stood up from behind his desk and extended his hand. He expressed his condolences for my loss and apologised for keeping me waiting. He then explained that he had been delayed in the emergency room, where he had to attend to a motorcyclist who had collided with a truck. The motorcyclist had unfortunately passed away. Christ, this young doctor was having one hell of a rough night, I thought as he continued to grip my hand tightly.

'Please, Father, have a seat,' he said, gesturing to the only other chair in the room.

He then explained that my mother had suffered severe burns and that identifying her would not be a pleasant or easy task. He asked if I was familiar with any jewellery that she may have worn regularly. I simply nodded in response, my pounding headache had taken over and I was no longer capable of thinking, let alone engaging in conver-sation. We left his office and walked a short distance to yet another room. Before he opened the door, he turned to face me and placed a hand on my shoulder, telling me to prepare myself. As we entered the room, my eyes immediately fell upon my mother's body lying on a trolley, covered by a white sheet. As we stood there, looking down at her body, he slowly and reverently lowered the sheet, revealing her charred shoulders and head.

Christ, the young, fresh-faced doctor had not exaggerated. What lay before me on the trolley looked like something out of a horror movie. I quickly turned my head away, convinced that I was going to vomit. The doctor pulled the sheet back up over her, quickly covering the sickening sight. He gently placed his hand on my shoulder as I began to force out the tears, my body shaking. It was another Oscar-worthy performance. He then lifted the sheet slightly down along her side, making sure to only expose what remained of her charred hand and arm. His earlier question, asking if I would be able to recognise any of her jewellery, now made sense.

'Do you recognise the jewellery?' he asked.

'Yes,' I replied. On her right hand, she always wore two gold rings and a gold bracelet, which, if my memory served me correctly, appeared shortly after O'Connell arrived on the scene. As he gently lowered the sheet, he asked me if I would like a little time alone with her. I simply nodded and thanked him. He smiled compassionately as he turned and left the room. Once the door had closed behind me and I knew that I was alone, I pulled the sheet back from her face. The evil bitch never looked better. As I stared at her charred remains. I felt nothing, no guilt, no remorse, no sense of loss, absolutely nothing. 'You must be as cold as fucking ice,' I gently whispered to myself, smiling as I covered her up.

The nurse led me back to the waiting room, where I found O'Connell sitting with his back to the door. As he turned to face me, he looked shaken as he raised his tear-drenched eyes to meet mine. He stood up and embraced me. I felt the urge to push him away and set him on fire, just like I had done with that charred bitch lying lifeless on a trolley in the mortuary. I struggled to control my emotions, as the intense hatred I felt towards him had reached its boiling point. With the nurse still in the room, I had little choice but to accept his embrace and condolences. I fought hard trying my best to maintain the façade of a grieving son.

Later that night, as O'Connell drove me home from the hospital, he asked if he could take care of my mother's funeral arrangements.

He struggled to hold back the tears as he spoke, telling me how much of a dear friend my mother was to him and how much she was loved and respected within the community. He continued on and on, it was pathetic listening to him blubbering as he wiped his eyes. All I could do was bite my tongue as his empty words flowed in one ear and out the other. I agreed to let him look after my mother's funeral arrangements, knowing that if it were up to me, I would have buried the evil bitch in a bog, wrapped in a black sack.

Chapter 10

In addition to handling my mother's funeral arrangements, O'Connell also took it upon himself to celebrate the requiem mass himself on the day of the funeral. It was a difficult service to sit through, not because I was grieving, or heartbroken, on the contrary, I couldn't have been happier. The toxic, manipulative bitch who had plagued me for so long was now permanently removed from my life. For me, the service was unbearable, due to all the lies and bullshit that O'Connell spewed out of him throughout the ceremony. As I sat and listened to O'Connell's words about my mother's supposed greatness and the irreplaceable void she had left in the parish, I felt sickened by the hypocrisy of his words from the pulpit. Seething with anger and frustration, I kept my head bowed towards the floor.

Occasionally, he would pause mid-sentence to compose himself, apologising to the congregation as he wiped away his tears for dramatic effect. As I sat watching and listening to O'Connell's performance from the altar, I realised just how much I wanted to end his pathetic life. After the service, my mother was cremated, which slightly amused me, as I got to watch the evil bitch go up in flames twice. From as far back as I can remember, my mother always said she wanted to be cremated. She had a terrible fear of being buried underground.

'The thought of all those rats and worms feasting on me,' she used to say. So in the end, the evil bitch got her wish.

The days following her funeral were difficult, although not in the usual way that bereaved families suffer when grieving the loss of a loved one. I was sick to death of people approaching me, shaking my hand, and expressing their condolences, and asking the same question repeatedly. 'Is there anything we can do for you, Father?' It was exasperating. Despite their good intentions, I found myself suffocated by the constant sympathy and attention. I struggled to maintain my composure and had to bite my tongue on several occasions to avoid saying something I would later regret. All I truly wanted was to escape from the well-meaning but suffocating presence of the sympathisers, well-wishers, and the do-gooders. Ideally, I just wanted everyone to fuck off and leave me alone.

Several days had passed since my mother's funeral, and the overwhelming outpouring of condolences was becoming too much for me to handle. As I approached O'Connell, I slipped back into my role as the grieving son and explained to him that I needed to take some time off to process the overwhelming grief of losing my mother. O'Connell readily agreed to my request.

The spiel I gave O'Connell was a blatant lie. I didn't need any time alone to grieve or come to terms with anything. I was just so tired of all the sympathetic nonsense that people were bestowing upon me. It infuriated and sickened me. It was exhausting to keep up the charade of mourning someone who had caused me so much pain. Those people who were offering me their hand in sympathy had no idea what that woman was truly capable of. They had never witnessed her sadistic alter ego, and even if I had told them, they wouldn't have believed me. Despite her Jackal and Hyde personality, the community only ever saw the side of her that she wanted them to see, the parish committee chairperson who did so much for the church and the people of the parish. For so long, she had hidden her true sadistic nature behind a façade of a fake smile and her rosary beads, deceiving all those around her.

I thought that taking a life for the first time, would have deeply affected me, and weighted heavily on my conscience. However, I felt nothing, no guilt or remorse. It was as if I had simply crushed a wasp under my foot. Although I couldn't have been happier with the outcome. After the fire service had completed their technical examination of the house, their report concluded that the fire was accidental, and was most likely caused by the victim falling asleep while smoking in bed. I couldn't have written the report any better myself. There was no evidence found at the scene to cause any suspicion, resulting in the case being closed and classified as a tragic accident. It was the perfect murder.

Exactly one week after my mother's funeral, I arrived into the quaint town of Kenmare, in County Kerry. I had booked a reservation at a charming family-run hotel just on the outskirts of the town. As I pulled into hotel car park, I was immediately struck by the breathtaking sight of lush emerald-green forests and gently rolling hills, creating a beautiful picturesque backdrop. Several years ago, I had stayed at the same hotel during an exchange organised by the seminary. I spent a week in Kerry, while one of the Kerry lads spent a week in Dublin. I checked in as Mr. John Doyle, not Fr. Doyle, as I didn't want anyone to know that I was a priest. If felt strange not wearing my usual black suit and white dog collar, which I had become so accustomed to.

The receptionist handed me the room key and said with what looked like a forced smile, 'Your room is number twenty-seven on the first floor.' Exhausted from the gruelling four hour drive, I collapsed into the soft welcoming embrace of the bed. Closing my eyes, I tried to retrace my footsteps of the past week. It had been a tumultuous journey, from violently taking my mother's life, to attending her funeral, to now finding myself in County Kerry, lying on a king-size bed in a hotel, staring up at the ceiling. I must have dozed off, when I woke the room was cold and dark. My watch read seven-thirty, the open window in the room explained the chill in the air.

I took a hot shower to remove the chill from my body. And although hungry, I had no desire to go down to the hotel's restaurant or bar, for the simple reason, I didn't want to mingle or have to engage with people. The thought of getting dragged into some bullshit meaningless conversation with a stranger just for the sake of being polite, which so often happens in such places, did not appeal to me at all. I decided to order room service, a steak dinner with all the trimmings and a nice bottle of French red wine to wash it all down.

The main reason for my brief break was to catch my breath, gather my thoughts, and regain my focus. It had been one hell of a rollercoaster ride since I disposed of my mother. While I was relieved she was gone, I couldn't help but feel disappointed that she had gotten away so lightly. I had wanted to inflict so much more pain and suffering on her before she passed over. The night of her death was a blur; everything happened so quickly and spontaneously. Nothing was planned; it all just unfolded before my eyes, as if I had been a spectator and not the perpetrator. Since that night, I have yearned for peace and quiet, away from the prying eyes of the parishioners and especially the parish committee, who closely observed and gossiped amongst themselves about how I was coping as I navigated my way through the grieving process.

I needed to devise a plan to eliminate O'Connell. That bastard had inflicted unrelenting pain and suffering on me throughout the years, and I wanted to replicate the same misery upon him before he drew his final breath. However, separating O'Connell from his devoted followers was going to be a problem. He was constantly surrounded by people, from early morning until late in the evening. Ideally, I would have abducted him and held him captive for several days in a secluded cabin deep in the forest. There, I would have mercilessly tortured him until he pleaded with me to end his miserable existence. He would have endured even more agonising pain as a result of his pleas. However, realistically, that was never going to happen. If O'Connell were to suddenly disappear, even for a brief period of time, the parish committee's blue rinse militia would immediately sound the alarm.

What should have been a few days of rest and reflection, had turned into three days and nights of complete turmoil. I was unable to relax or even think clearly, and sleep only came when I drank enough to pass out. My mind was racing, frantically trying to figure out how to put an end to O'Connell's time on this earth. Whatever plan I devised, needed to bulletproof. I couldn't afford any mistakes or slip-ups. Despite my desperation for revenge, I also needed to consider the consequences of my actions. Nothing rash, I had to gather myself and carefully plan every aspect, right down to the smallest detail, so when the time came, the plan would be executed with total precision. Although one thing was certain. It was only a matter of time before I ended O'Connell's miserable, fucked-up double life.

On the third and final day of my short break, I woke up early, took a quick shower, had breakfast, and then checked out of the hotel, all within an hour. I drove back to Dublin on autopilot. O'Connell now consumed my every waking hour, and even during the brief periods of sleep, that washed over me, he would appear in my dreams, as if taunting me. It felt as though I was teetering on the edge of a cliff, one wrong move away from falling into insanity.

I arrived home and pulled into the driveway. After entering the house, I unset the alarm and gathered the scattered mail from the floor. As I made my way to the kitchen, I placed the mail on the table and filled the kettle. The long drive home and the lack of sleep over the last couple of days had left me feeling completely exhausted. In an attempt to perk myself up, I made a strong cup of coffee. I then took a seat at the table and began sorting through the mail. It was the usual mix of bills and junk, along with some mass cards. These were obviously from people who knew my mother, no doubt offering me even more sympathy. However, I had no interest in reading the cards or finding out who had sent them, so I tossed them straight into the bin without even opening them.

Feeling tense and anxious, I scrolled through my phone contacts until I found O'Connell's number and called him. He answered with his usual charm, asking about my well-being and how I was coping under the circumstances. I filled him with a load of bullshit, telling him that I had spent a lot of time over the last couple of days lost in prayer and deep reflection. He believed every single word. I ended the call by telling him to take the following morning off and that I would say the morning mass. A sense of relief washed over me as I hung up the phone, a smile tugging at the corners of my lips, reassured me that my plan was coming together.

As I lay on the bed, smoking one cigarette after another, my eyes fixated on the ceiling, which was crying out for a fresh coat of paint, I began to question my sanity. 'Am I a psychopath? I nervously asked myself. How could I have a seemingly normal conversation over the phone with someone that I wanted to kill? 'Am I normal or abnormal?' Or perhaps I am broken and deranged, just like my dear old mother was. I closed my eyes tightly, afraid of what I might discover if I delved to deep. The thought of being capable of such dark, twisted urges, left me feeling unsettled. Once again, sleep eluded me, only this time I had scared myself.

Chapter 11

Despite the several plug-in heaters that were scattered around the room, the parish hall was frigid. The effects of my bad hangover and lack of sleep only intensified the chill that ran through me. I sat across from O'Connell, my former abuser, and my dead mother's old lover. I watched as one of the blue rinse militia refilled his cup. He ate with greed, devouring slice after slice of fruitcake. He reminded me of a spoiled, overweight child at a birthday party, trying to eat as much cake as possible before it was all gone.

As I sat and watched O'Connell frolicking about with his devoted flock, a seething rage consumed me. I struggled to suppress my intense hatred towards the depraved pervert sitting across from me. And to make matters worse, I was wedged between two overweight Holy Mary's, one stank of cheap perfume and the other of piss. Both were quietly whispering to themselves while clutching their Rosary beads. Occasionally, I caught them glancing up at me, as if seeking my approval. I ignored their childish glances, and gave off the impression that I was fully engaged in what was being said around the table. I always viewed the parish meetings as a complete waste of time and energy. Two hours of meaningless chatter, two hours of my life wasted, never to be regained. I knew O'Connell hated the meetings just as much as I did, but for some of the old dears in the parish, they lived for them. For some, it was all they had to look forward to. How sad, I thought, as I scrutinised the weary faces of those gathered around the table adorned with cakes and biscuits.

As the meeting dragged on, my long-simmering resentment and contempt for O'Connell had reached boiling point. I wanted to confront him and demand answers about my childhood. Why did he do so many terrible things to me when I was a child? However, I realised that what I truly needed was to regain control of my emotions and calm the fuck down before saying or doing something I would regret, especially in front of O'Connell's devoted flock. I knew that patience was my greatest ally, I just needed to bide my time until I had a plan in place. O'Connell had arranged to drop a couple of the old dears home after the meeting, so I knew he would not be hanging around. This meant there was no chance of a confrontation, which, in hindsight, was a blessing in disguise. As I watched, O'Connell leave the room with the two old dears waddling a few paces behind him, struggling to keep up, I couldn't help but wonder if he was doing both of them.

I could feel my insatiable craving for vengeance growing stronger by the minute, and I knew I couldn't suppress it for much longer. My impatience was wearing thin, and the only thing that gave me comfort was knowing that O'Connell's fate was in my hands. I would decide the hour and the day of his sudden departure from this forsaken world, and there was nothing that his God or Jesus, could do to save him cometh the hour.

The following day, I invited O'Connell over to my house for dinner. Under the pretence that is was a thank-you dinner for having taken care of my mother's funeral and for the kind words he had said about her on the day. Throughout the meal, I laid it on thick and heavy, telling him how grateful I was for all that he had done for my mother and me over the years. He was revelling in the praise and admiration I lavished upon him, until I dropped a fucking bombshell.

'Tom, now that I am a man, do you not find me attractive anymore?' I asked. The worthless bastard almost choked on the mouthful of food that he was chewing on. I watched with amusement as he struggled to compose himself. He didn't answer; he sat opposite me in a complete state of shock. He seemed incapable of any movement or speech. He was frozen, like a deer caught in the headlights of a speeding car, completely fucked, and he knew it.

'Do you not understand the question?' I asked. His response was hesitant, his voice trembling as he spoke,

'John, that was a long time ago, a very dark period in my life. It's all in the past, and I think it's best for everyone that we leave it there, let's put all that behind us, and move on.'

'Well, the thing is, Tom, no matter how hard I try, I just can't seem to put it all behind me and move on. Believe me, I have fucking tried. I was only an innocent, helpless child back then, and you, on the other hand, were a fully grown man with the protection of the church behind you. I had no one to turn to, not even my own mother, because you were fucking her as well, mother and child. You sick fuck,' I said, my tone filled with anger and hatred.

'John, please. That was a long time ago. Things are very different now, I have changed,' he said. 'It's late, and I think I have overstayed my welcome. I'll make a move and let you get some rest. John, you have suffered a terrible loss, and you need time to heal to process everything.' The quiver in his voice seemed to have spread throughout his entire body, causing him to shake uncontrollably.

'You've changed? I highly doubt that. Although, one thing I do know, is that I have changed. I am no longer the vulnerable one, the weak one hidden away without a voice. Yes, things have certainly changed. Now you sit before me, the weaker of the two, the vulnerable one. How does it feel to have the roles reversed?' I asked as I lit a cigarette.

'John, I think it's best if I leave. You've had quite a lot to drink and I understand that you are grieving the loss of your mother. Let's call it a night and forget about the whole incident,' he said, trembling like a stray dog that had been left out in the cold and rain overnight.

'Forget? Forget, how very fucking convenient that would be for you. Did you honestly think for one moment that I would forget about all the times that you stripped, touched, and buggered me? Not to mention all those other disgusting things that you did to me, forcing me to perform filthy acts on you when I was just a child. You knew that I had no one to turn to, no one to help or hear my cries. You preyed on a helpless child. You are nothing more than an evil, fucked-up pervert,' I replied.

'John, please, forgive me. That was a long time ago and I am deeply sorry. I was going through a very difficult period and was under a lot of pressure. I acknowledge that I made some terrible mistakes back then, but I assure you, I have truly changed. I am a completely different person now, I am no longer the confused man I once was,' he pleaded. I could smell the fear and desperation emanating from him.

'Bollox, you're still the same evil, twisted pervert I met all those years ago, a leopard never changes its spots. Although, I have to give you credit, you are a master at hiding your true self. You certainly know how to turn on the charm when it suits you,' I said.

'John, this is insane. It's not helping either of us. I was a heavy drinker back then, completely out of control. Sure half the time, I didn't even know what I was doing,' he said.

'Out of control, I suppose that's one way of putting it.' I replied, as I stood up abruptly from the table. My sudden movements scared him, his eyes widened with fear, as I opened another bottle of wine, smiling to myself.

'Tell me, Tom, is this the same wine that you were drinking back then? The same wine that made you lose control of yourself, the same wine that made you do all those dirty things to me when I was a child?' I asked.

'Stop, John. Please, enough, you have made your point, now please stop,' he pleaded. I looked down at him, sitting at the table, his head bowed and his hands shaking. He was not only petrified; he was a broken man. The once almighty O'Connell had fallen, and there was no way he was getting back up.

'Let's go into the sitting room, it's a lot more comfortable in there,' I whispered seductively into his ear, as I refilled the two glasses.

'No John. I've had enough, things have gone way too far. I'm going home,' he said.

'Things have gone way too far. If only I could have said that to you all those years ago.

And, if I did, would you have stopped? Well, would you? I asked, my voice raised and menacing.

'Please John, stop, enough,' he whimpered as tears rolled down his old grey face.

'Stop, please, stop. Those were the very same words I can remember sobbing to you on so many occasions. Although, the one thing that I can vividly remember is that you never did stop, not until you were completely satisfied. No matter how hard I begged or cried, you never did stop,' I said. He stood up from the table.

'That's it, I'm leaving. Things have gotten way out of hand, you've had far too much to drink,' he said.

'Fuck you O'Connell,' I snarled as I grabbed him by the throat and threw him up against the wall.

'Stop John, please, I'm begging you,' he pleaded, as I dragged him into the sitting room and threw him down onto the sofa.

'Take off your clothes. We're going to watch a movie, just like we used to all those years ago,' I said, my words dripping with venom.

'Strip,' I shouted, my impatience and anger were getting the better of me, now I was the one losing control. I walked over to the cabinet and opened the drawer, reached in and retrieved a large kitchen knife that I had placed there earlier in the day.

'John, please. We can work this out. You need to calm down,' he pleaded, his voice trembling with panic. I grabbed him by the arm and pulled him up off the sofa, and slammed him against the wall. I held the blade just below his Adam's apple, and whispered into his ear.

'Strip, or I'll slit your fucking throat.' He slowly removed his cardigan and shirt. In a fit of rage, I slapped him across the face with an open hand, just as he had done to me countless times in the past. Realising I meant business, he removed the rest of his clothes.

The almighty untouchable O'Connell, stood before me naked, scared, and vulnerable, the very same way that I had stood before him all those years ago. Our roles, were well and truly reversed. The look in his watery eyes, said it all.

'Sit down Tom, let's watch a movie together, for old times' sake,' I said. He sat down on the sofa, trembling, as tears streamed down his face. I stood in front of him and undressed. Once naked, I lowered myself down onto the sofa beside him.

'Now Tom, this reminds me of how things used to be when I was a young boy. Do you remember when we used to sit next to each other on the sofa, both of us naked, with the curtains drawn and the room dark? Does it bring back any memories?' I asked with a smile. I pressed play on the DVD player, which I had loaded with a porn movie earlier. It didn't take long for me to become fully aroused as I watched the two women on the screen pleasuring each other.

'I remember this used to happen to you when we watched a movie together,' I said, pointing to my erect penis. He didn't respond. Out of pure frustration, I slapped him several times across the face and head with my open hand. He began to cry, just like I used to as a child. I grabbed him by the hair and forced him to take me into his mouth.

'This is what you enjoyed, remember? You worthless piece of shit,' I sneered, gripping his old, grey head tightly as I emptied myself into his mouth, feeling a surge of pleasure as he gagged and struggled to breathe. During his fit of coughing and gagging he rolled off the sofa and onto the floor. I stood up and placed my bare foot on his throat, putting all my weight onto it and pressing down as hard as I could. A cruel smile spread across my face as I watched him struggle and gasp for air. Eventually, I removed my foot and made my way to the kitchen to retrieve the bottle of wine. The rush of endorphins flooded my body, making me feel invigorated as I refilled our glasses. Returning to the sitting room, I set the glasses down on the coffee table before I roughly dragged O'Connell up from the floor and threw him back onto the sofa.

'Drink,' I snarled, handing him a glass of wine; after all, he had bought the damn thing. He took a sip, his face contorting in disgust as he tried to wash away my taste.

'John, I'm deeply sorry for all the pain and hurt that I have caused you over the years. Please, John, forgive me. I am truly sorry,' he pleaded, his body shaking as he fought back the tears. I couldn't bear to listen to any more of his pathetic bullshit. With a clenched fist, I struck him on the jaw, the sound of bone cracking filling the air as he fell to the side. I drained my glass and lay back on the sofa, watching him whimper like a whipped dog. He was fucking pathetic.

The moans and groans coming from the television quickly diverted my attention away from O'Connell. It didn't take long for me to become aroused again. I stood up from the sofa and delivered a series of vicious blows to the head of my already defeated opponent. I was far from finished with him, this worthless bastard was going to suffer. I grabbed him by the hair and threw him face down onto the sofa, and entered him with as much force and violence as humanly possible. He cried out in agony, pleading for me to stop, I continued to aggressively thrust myself into him again and again. Once spent, I threw the pathetic excuse of a human being to the floor and took a swig from the bottle of wine. I felt invincible as I looked down at his old, pallid, wrinkled body curled up in the fetal position.

'It's not very nice Father, is it?' I asked. He remained silent, lying on the floor like a wounded animal. The defeated look in his eyes told me that he finally understood the gravity of his actions. I reached down and grabbed his hair, pulling him upright as I placed the knife against his throat.

'Get dressed,' I snarled, it was an order, not a request. As he dressed, I watched him, just as he had watched me all those years ago.

'We're going for a little drive. If you try anything foolish, I swear, I'll slit your fucking throat. Do you understand?' He simply nodded, unable to speak. He was scared and traumatised, unable to comprehend the situation that he found himself in.

It was all so alien to him. O'Connell had gone from predator to prey, his entire life turned upside down in the blink of an eye. I dragged him into the kitchen and got his coat from the back of the chair where he had left it earlier. I removed his phone and keys from the pocket, turned off the phone, and turned to face him.

'Let's drive to your house,' I said. As we walked towards the front door, I firmly gripped his arm and reminded him that if he tried anything stupid, I would slit his throat. In the driveway, I opened the boot of my car and removed a gym bag. The drive to his house was only a few minutes, but if felt like an eternity as he continuously begged for forgiveness. I ignored him, in my mind I was already playing out the final scene of his life. As we pulled into his driveway, I kept the knife firmly pressed against his side and warned him not to try anything heroic.

It had just gone midnight when we entered his house. The transition from the car to the house went smoothly without incident or any cause for suspicion. Even if he had wanted to run or cry for help, his body was no longer capable of any such feats. Once inside the house and the door was firmly closed behind us, I lost complete control of myself and viciously attacked him. My hands shook with rage as I lunged at him, years of pent-up anger and hatred were released, as I repeatedly kicked and punched my former abuser during the frenzied attack, while he lay helpless on the ground.

I then dragged him up the stairs; it was as if I had been transformed into a crazed killer seeking revenge. At the top of the stairs, I opened the trapdoor leading to the attic and forced him up the ladder, pushing him from behind. After a toilsome effort, we eventually made it into the cramped attic space. Despite my exhaustion, I managed to force a smile as I opened my gym bag and took out a notebook, pen, and a length of rope. O'Connell's swollen tear drenched eyes almost doubled in size when he saw the rope.

I told him to copy the note that I had already written. I needed the note to be in his handwriting. He simply stared at me in complete disbelief. A hard open right hand across his face, quickly brought him back to reality.

'Write the fucking note,' I shouted, as I delivered a few more slaps to his already badly bruised face. I then tied one end of the rope to a rafter and dangled the noose in front of him, causing him to panic. As I pulled him closer, I held the tip of the blade to the corner of his eye.

'Write the fucking note,' I commanded, pressing the blade against his skin and drawing a thin line of blood from under his left eye. The sight of his blood trickling down his face filled him with terror, causing him to cry and tremble hysterically. I had already written the suicide note, it was a full confession of his vile and twisted dark past. When he had finished copying the note word for word, I made him sign it, he had an unmistakable signature. I then forced him to sit at the edge of the attic opening, as I placed the rope around his pale neck. He sat there shivering, as tears streamed down his cheeks. I placed my hand on his shoulder and looked into his watery eyes.

'Are you truly sorry for everything you did to me in the past? I asked.

'Yes, John, please believe me, I am so sorry. I am begging you, I'll do anything you want. I have a lot of money stored away. It's all yours. Please, John, I am begging you, don't do this,' he whimpered. His voice was low and broken, no longer resembling the man he once was.

His words were nothing more than a pathetic plea from a guilty and condemned man trying to save himself. As our eyes met, I smiled sympathetically. He let out a sigh of relief, as a glimmer of hope appeared in his eyes. It was as if he thought he had been given a reprieve, a full pardon, and all was forgiven. However, just as a sad, sorrowful smile began to emerge across his badly beaten and bloodied face.

'Fuck you,' I whispered as I pushed him.

Chapter 12

O'Connell's staged suicide had the desired effect on the community that I had hoped for. One of complete shock and devastation, the parish shrouded in a dark cloud of grief and sadness. The poor old blue rinse militia, had gathered at the church for the ten o'clock mass. They were shocked and overcome with grief when Michael, the sacristan, informed them that the morning service was cancelled due to the sudden tragic death of Fr. O'Connell.

It was O'Connell's unfortunate housekeeper who stumbled upon the horrifying sight, her employer's lifeless body hanging naked from a rafter as she opened the front door. She informed the authorities, as soon as she had regained some form of composure. As the news quickly spread throughout the parish, the crying and wailing erupted. I was unfortunate enough to run into a few members of the parish committee on my way back from the shop. They were wailing like a group of feral banshees, and were only short of tearing off their clothes, putting on sackcloth, and covering themselves with ashes.

I, on the other hand, was extremely impressed with my handiwork. The police forensics team had thoroughly examined the scene and concluded that there was no evidence of forced entry to the property or any indication of foul play. They also stated that they were not seeking to question anyone else in relation to the incident. After their preliminary investigation, their report cited the cause of death as suicide. While I was pleased with the outcome of the investigation, I couldn't help but feel a little flummoxed. After all, I had given O'Connell quite a beating and as for them saying there was no sign of forced entry, they really needed to take a closer look. Despite the police shortcomings, I was on a high, having successfully committed two murders and both cases now closed. One was filed as an accidental death due to a house fire, and the other as a tragic case of suicide.

The local rag and community radio station extensively covered O'Connell's untimely demise. 'Beloved parish priest dies suddenly,' seemed to be the headline that most of them ran with. The news reports mentioned all the great work and accomplishments that O'Connell had achieved throughout his life as a servant of God. And how deeply shocked and saddened the whole parish and the greater community were, and how much he will be sorely missed.

What shocked and deeply saddened me was the fact that the word suicide was never mentioned. Every article I read, stated that O'Connell had died suddenly, but provided no more details. I couldn't understand it, the police knew, the housekeeper knew. Christ, the poor woman had found him dangling, with the letter lying on the floor beneath him. Why had they decided to hide this information from the public? The suicide note, which I had so carefully composed, revealed O'Connell's dark and twisted soul and forced him to confess his sordid past. The parishioners deserved to know the truth about the man they so greatly admired. They needed to know that O'Connell was not the person they believed him to be. His true identity as a vile paedophile needed to be exposed and brought to light. My thoughts were in disarray as I tried to figure out what had happened to the note. Who had taken it, and why was the truth about O'Connell being hidden.

The bishop personally called me to express his condolences on what he referred to as, 'shocking sad news.' Once again, I had to pretend to be a grieving man mourning the loss of a loved one. During our brief conversation, His Grace never mentioned the word 'suicide.' The reason for keeping the true cause of O'Connell's death a secret, consumed my every waking hour. Who had made the decision to keep the contents of the suicide note concealed? Surely, only His Grace would have the authority over such a sensitive matter.

O'Connell's housekeeper had been first on the scene, and she had found his lifeless body hanging from the rafters. I began to wonder if the housekeeper had destroyed the note after reading it, before anyone else had the chance to read it. And if so why? Who in their right mind would want to protect such an evil depraved pervert after reading the contents of such a note. I was incensed. I wanted the note to be out in the public domain, so that everyone knew the real O'Connell, not the one, the whole parish was mourning over. I thought my plan was perfect, completely bulletproof. The note, lying on the floor beneath his lifeless body, should have been enough to tarnish his name forever.

The only plausible explanation I considered was that the house-keeper had destroyed the note after reading it to protect O'Connell's reputation among his devoted parishioners. Or, alternatively, when the police arrived and read the note they may have contacted the bishop and, along with the housekeeper who was now sworn to secrecy, decided to withhold O'Connell's true cause of death and the note from the public. After all, the church was already dealing with enough scandals and did not need another one rearing its ugly head.

Chapter 13

O'Connell's funeral, was a grand affair, with the bishop himself presiding over the requiem mass. The church was filled to capacity, with not a single empty seat or dry eye in sight, (except for mine, of course). Several priests from neighbouring parishes also attended to pay their respects. One by one they took command of the pulpit, sharing kind words and amusing stories about their deceased friend. I knew that my own personal stories about the deceased vile predator lying in the wooden box would undoubtedly surpass them all, but I had to refrain.

Before the service, the bishop approached me and asked if I would like to say a few words during the mass. I quickly declined, once again, slipping back into my role of the grieving man, consumed by overwhelming grief as I struggled to come to terms with the loss of a loved one. I began to really turn it on, and the lies kept coming. I explained to him that the relationship between O'Connell and myself was akin to that of a father and son. As I had never known my biological father, the bond between us was particularly meaningful and had only grown stronger over time. In the back of my mind, I couldn't help but think if he only knew the truth. While I was on a roll, I decided to take it even a step further and told His Grace that I was still grieving for my late mother. By the end of our conversation, or rather, my performance, it was clear that His Grace regretted coming anywhere near me.

O'Connell was laid to rest in Glasnevin Cemetery. The scene at his graveside was pathetic. Members of the parish committee and the blue rinse militia, formed a choir of never-ending wailing and tears. Each of them threw a single red rose into the freshly dug grave, which only intensified the outpouring of emotion. It was almost comical to witness. As I peered into the grave, I saw the coffin adorned with red roses. In that single moment, I wished for that vile creature, O'Connell, to be resurrected, only to be slowly eaten by rats as he lay helpless in his wooden box.

On the third day after O'Connell's burial, I received a call from Fr. Liam, the bishop's secretary, pretty much summoning me to his residence for a meeting. I was convinced that the purpose of the meeting was to discuss O'Connell's suicide and the contents of the note. As soon as mass ended the following morning, I hurried to His Grace's residence, eager to hear about O'Connell's suicide note. I arrived a little earlier than expected, not wanting to risk being late. As I stepped out of the car, I couldn't help but reflect on the vow of poverty I had taken, despite being surrounded by such opulence.

As I approached the entrance, I was greeted by a tall, thin man who introduced himself as Fr. Liam. From his appearance, I guessed he was in his early fifties. He had a thick mane of silver-grey hair and a thin moustache of matching colour, he looked lean and sprightly. His beady grey-blue eyes, framed by gold-rimmed glasses, seemed to observe everything around him. Despite having spoken over the phone a number of times, we had never met in person before. As we shook hands, he wore a big smile across his face and came across as a very polite and friendly sort of fellow.

As he ushered me inside, he walked at a brisk pace that I struggled to keep up with. I lagged several steps behind as we approached a large, dark-brown mahogany door at the end of the corridor. He seemed a little impatient as he stood by the door, waiting for me to catch up. Once I arrived by his side, he smiled and opened the door, walking into the room ahead of me and introducing me as I followed behind him, like a school child about to be reprimanded by the headmaster. His Grace slowly rose up from behind a large antique desk and made his way around it to greet me, extending his pudgy hand. We shook hands firmly and he gestured for me to take a seat. He gave a slight nod to Fr. Liam, which must have been a sign to leave, as I heard the door closing behind me. His Grace then returned to his side of the desk and settled into his leather chair.

The meeting was brief, lasting only fifteen minutes. It began with all the usual formalities, there was an overly friendly welcome, an exaggerated smile, and offers of tea or coffee, which I declined. I just wanted the damn meeting to be over and done with. His Grace spoke about his long and cherished friendship with O'Connell, mentioning that they had known each other for over thirty years. He then expressed his understanding of the deep sadness I must be feeling during this very difficult time. If you only knew, I thought, as I sat opposite him in silence, his words entering one ear and going out the other.

After His Grace had finished reminiscing about his lifelong friendship with O'Connell, it became clear that the real reason for the meeting was to discuss the church's current struggles. He explained that the number of men entering the priesthood was at an all-time low and that the church was going through a very difficult period. After listening to him harping on about the struggles of the church, he finally revealed the purpose of the meeting. I was to become the new parish priest, replacing O'Connell. He also mentioned that another priest would eventually be sent to my parish to assist me, but for the time being, I would have to manage on my own. As soon as he finished speaking, he quickly stood up, shook my hand, and congratulated me on my new, yet unwanted, appointment. And just like that, the meeting was over. Not a single word was mentioned about O'Connell's suicide or the note.

My mind was a chaotic mix of anxiety, and uncertainty as I left the bishop's grandiose residence. The shock of becoming a parish priest was the last fucking thing that I needed or wanted. My life was already complicated, and taking on the responsibility of the entire parish only added to the burden. I can remember how busy O'Connell's days were; he never seemed to have a minute to himself. He was constantly occupied from early morning until late at night. Although, despite his hectic schedule, he still found time to seduce my mother and abuse me, and God only knows how many others. The only positive aspect of this chaotic situation was that I no longer had someone constantly watching over me. I was free from having to report and answer to O'Connell on a daily basis. Unless of course, I fucked up big time, which would result in me being summoned once again to His Grace's residence to be heavily reprimanded.

Once again, I sought solace in the stillness and silence of the sitting room. The curtains were drawn, the lights were off, and I was enveloped in darkness as I swigged from the whiskey bottle. The combination of solitude, silence, and a steady flow of alcohol had a calming effect on my chaotic mind. I found myself reflecting on the events of the past few weeks. I had committed the ultimate act of violence by murdering the two people I despised most in my own little chaotic world. Not only had I taken their lives, but I had done so without raising any suspicion. Both cases were closed, one deemed an accident and the other a suicide.

As I stood up from the sofa and approached the mirror that hung above the fireplace, I gazed intently at my reflection staring back at me. A sudden darkness swept across its surface, enveloping me in an eerie shroud. In complete silence, my lips trembled as I formed each word, my tongue carefully shaping them into sentences. When my lips stopped moving, I closed my eyes and bowed my head in reverence. The message reflected back at me was crystal clear, it was time to embrace my true identity and fulfil my destiny. Finally, my time had arrived.

Chapter 14

T he first few weeks of my new role as parish priest were incredibly challenging, to say the least. I was aware that my predecessor, O'Connell, had a busy schedule, but I never truly realised the extent of his workload until I stepped into his shoes. There were days when I felt completely overwhelmed by the workload that lay ahead of me and I just wanted to give up and disappear. I was sick to death of people telling me how much they missed Fr. O'Connell and how the parish wasn't the same without him. Listening to them was draining. I had to constantly bite my tongue and force a smile, struggling daily to hide my frustration and anger. It was a constant battle to keep my emotions in check. After enduring these exhausting and soul-destroying days, I often found myself in need of a couple of stiff drinks. On particularly difficult days, I would throw a Valium or two into the mix just to help me cope.

At the end of a long day, I would lie on the sofa, drifting in and out of consciousness thanks to the combination of alcohol and medication, which provided a temporary escape from reality. It was a beautiful feeling, a feeling that I regularly craved and needed, to maintain my sanity. In those moments, I was transported to my own happy place where no one could hurt or find me. However, as with any form of escapism, there was a downside – eventually, I would have to return to reality. Despite this, I found solace in the fact that most of the time spent in this altered state of consciousness was pure bliss. Although there were also moments when my mind would drift back to those long, dark nights that I had spent in the seminary. My time in the seminary had a profound impact on me, both physically and mentally. The intense and often oppressive environment had taken a serious toll on my well-being. Those crazy bastards attempted to brainwash us with their warped and outdated views. Sadly, they had succeeded with some of the weaker individuals, while the rest of us were left either confused or completely fucked-up.

One cannot endure such physical and mental abuse without it leaving a lasting impact. The severity of the abuse we endured was sure to have serious consequences. At the seminary, the priests instilled in us the belief that every thought and desire that ran through our minds was inherently sinful. This strict ideology was deeply ingrained in us, causing us to constantly question our own being and left us feeling conflicted and uncertain. The most damning and radical of their beliefs, which they tried to impose on us, revolved around women and sex. I found it surprising that those men, who had taken a vow of celibacy, would have such a strong interest in these topics.

In the seminary, women and sex were discussed with such venom and hatred, classifying them as deadly and poisonous. Even notable women from biblical times, such as Eve and Mary Magdalene, were not spared from this fury. One morning, during a sermon, a priest stated that 'Eve and Magdalene were nothing more than two common whores who had spent their lives tempting men and leading them to damnation.' Later that night, the same priest who had delivered those words with such fervour would visit our rooms and bugger us, with his Rosary beads still hanging around his neck. During another prayer service, one of the priests declared from the pulpit that,

'If two men had entered the Garden of Eden, instead of a man and a woman, the world would be a better place.' It was crystal clear what his preferences were.

The Bible is littered with sordid stories of women who are depicted as immoral and responsible for the downfall of mankind. In the seminary, Eve was often referred to as 'the mother of all whores' and was held accountable for committing the original sin that led to man's downfall. Additionally, we were thought, that Mary Magdalene, who had turned away from her immoral and sinful past and became a devoted disciple of Jesus, had attempted to seduce him in his final hours.

It was preached in the seminary, that women were the root cause of all evil since the beginning of time, while men were portrayed as weak and easily succumbed to their temptations. Those thoughts have been deeply ingrained in me, hidden away in some dark corner of my mind. However, there were times while I was drifting in and out of my relaxed altered state of consciousness, as the alcohol and medication mingled and rushed through my veins. I began to entertain the idea that maybe, just maybe, those crazy old bastards in the seminary who had tried to indoctrinate us with their warped beliefs, were probably speaking the truth.

After all, it was a woman who had caused all my pain and suffering throughout my childhood, albeit my own deluded mother. Not only was she a fucked-up sadist, she was also a priest's whore. And even worse, she had turned a blind eye whenever the priest preferred to indulge in her own son rather than her. Throughout my time in the seminary, those depraved priests who stood at the pulpit, preaching about hell, sin, and prostitutes, almost frothing at the mouth as they spat out the words, remained deep within me. I can vividly recall one priest in particular , Fr. Clark, was his name, once he got started on the subjects of sin and prostitutes, he seemed to completely lose the run of himself. One morning, as he preached from the pulpit, almost passing out as he poured his entire being into his sermon,

'A child born from the womb of a prostitute has a black heart and nothing but sin running through its veins.' It was ingrained in us that women were evil, but prostitutes were the worst kind of human beings.

I never doubted that women are the more cunning and powerful of the species. When a man succumbs to the temptations and charms of a woman, his life is no longer his own. Once he has tasted the forbidden fruit, he can no longer function without it. Of course, this is common knowledge among women, who are fully aware of men's weaknesses and know exactly how to exploit them. Innocent men are often blinded by the charms of vile, deceitful prostitutes, who roam the streets with their hearts and souls tainted by darkness, like hungry predators preying on their helpless victims.

History has repeatedly shown that those soulless women could easily tempt and seduce even the most powerful and disciplined of men. Some men have gone to extreme lengths, risking everything they have achieved, and some have even resorted to murder, just to satisfy their carnal desires and indulge in the pleasures of the flesh. Those vile whores possess a dangerous and formidable power to manipulate and control men. I had put an end to my own mother, a worthless priest's whore. Perhaps it was time for me to put an end to those vile creatures that stood on street corners every night, luring men into temptation.

As I lay on the sofa, drifting between this God-forsaken world and the beautiful haven created by my altered state of mind, I felt a terrible rage rising from deep within me. The come-down, that horrible feeling as the effects of the alcohol and medication began to wear off, and the harshness of reality awaits my return, was starting to set in. I reluctantly opened my eyes and found myself back in the cold, dark sitting room where my journey had begun.

As I sat in the darkness, I felt numb, devoid of any feeling or emotions. I had proven to myself that I was capable of ending someone's life with ruthless brutality, without feeling any sense of guilt or remorse. In my mind, I was fully convinced that I had done the world a great deed by removing those two twisted sadists from it. It was now time for someone to put an end to those vile whores roaming the streets, corrupting minds, destroying lives, and robbing the souls of innocent men. A chill ran through me as I returned to the chaotic reality that was my life, a reality I detested. With a pounding headache and a mouth as dry as the desert, I knew that I had to take matters into my own hands and cleanse the streets of these repulsive creatures.

Chapter 15

A s the sole priest in the parish, it was my responsibility to say the ten o'clock mass every morning and the three services on Sundays. Before O'Connell's untimely passing, we took turns presiding over the mass, which provided us with some respite away from the constant demands of the church. However, since he was no longer with us, the weight of this now fell solely on my shoulders. I was expected to officiate every mass, christening, wedding, and funeral, as well as make the hospital, school, and house calls. This left me with an overwhelming workload and very little time away from the church, and the often-overbearing presence of the blue rinse militia.

Each morning, as I stood at the alter and looked out among the congregation, the same familiar, aging grey faces with vacant eyes greeted me. The regular attendees, who were mostly members of the blue rinse militia, always sat in the first two rows, proudly displaying their devotion to the rest of the church, which was practically empty. They made quite a sight, with their eyes tightly closed and heads bowed, clutching their Rosary beads in their pale, wrinkled hands, and wearing their Sunday best regardless of the day.

Some of the women were accompanied by their husbands, who stood obediently by their sides like faithful pets. Some of the more fortunate husbands had already passed on, leaving their widows in a constant state of mourning for years on end. The few remaining husbands, who stood silently beside their busybody wives, appeared worn out. Their tired eyes told a sad tale, as if they had given up and were simply going through the motions to keep their wives happy until their own time came. Each of them wore the same blank expression on their old, grey faces. It was a sombre sight to be met with every morning as

I said mass, but I couldn't help feeling a sense of sadness as I looked down from the altar.

I was often tempted to say something irrelevant as I made my way through the service, just to see if any of those vacant eyes looking up at me would even notice. I knew they weren't listening; they were here only in body, their minds and thoughts elsewhere. I'm sure they were well aware that they had reached their sell by date and were now on precious borrowed time.

My duties as a priest were becoming overwhelming. I struggled to keep up with my workload and often had to take a moment to remind myself that being a priest was the perfect cover for my true vocation of eradicating those vile whores from the streets. Despite my personal struggles keeping on top of things, the black suit and the white dog collar that I donned every morning still commanded respect, and I knew that I needed to take full advantage of that. I suppose having been forced into the priesthood at such a young age, didn't help the situation that I found myself in. Struggling through each day and hating every minute of what I was doing, was really taking its toll on me. However, I knew that I needed to remain focused and avoid any slip-ups as my new vocation consumed my thoughts.

As I lay awake, sleep eluded me regardless of how much I begged for it to come and whisk me away to a far-off dreamland. Realising that it was going to be another sleepless night, I got out of bed and began pacing the hallway, hoping to induce sleep. After an hour or so of pacing the hall like a madman, I decided enough was enough, I grabbed my coat and car keys and left the house. I cannot recall if my destination was premeditated or if I had subconsciously known exactly where I was going. Either way, twenty-three minutes later, I found myself driving through a well-known red-light district in Dublin. I drove down Fitzwilliam Street and around by the famous Pepper Canister before making my way towards Baggot Street Bridge. There were a lot of women, young and not so young, roaming the streets, looking for business. What a fucking terrible way to end up, I thought to myself as I turned back over the bridge and parked on Upper Mount Street. I rolled down the window and lit a cigarette, and watched in amazement as cars pulled up and girls got in, no doubt going off to engage in immoral acts. Lost in my thoughts, I smoked and watched as the girls came and went, fascinated by the demand for their vile services.

A sudden, unexpected knock on the passenger door window startled me. I turned to see a young woman with long black hair and beautiful brown eyes peering in at me. I leaned across and rolled down the window.

'Do you have a light?' she asked in a strong Dublin accent, holding a cigarette between her nicotine-stained fingers. Reaching over, I handed her the lighter through the window.

'Not a bad night,' she said, before placing the cigarette between her bright red lips and flicking the lighter to ignite it.

'Yes, it's quite mild,' I replied, my voice quivering slightly.

'Are you lost?' she asked, taking a drag from her cigarette.

'No, I just pulled over for a smoke. I needed a break from driving, I was feeling a little tired,' I replied.

'It's just that I've noticed you driving up and down this road several times in the past half an hour,' she said, exhaling a cloud of smoke through her glossy red lips. Panic set in as I realised that if she had noticed me driving around, others probably had as well. I struggled to respond, sheepishly smiling while considering whether I should just turn the key in the ignition and drive off.

'Are you looking for some business?' she asked.

'Business? I'm not sure what you mean,' I nervously replied, as I shifted uncomfortably in the driver's seat.

'Don't waste my fucking time, you know exactly what I mean,' she snapped, her words were sharp and direct. I sat in stunned silence, never having been spoken to so bluntly by a stranger before. After a brief moment to process her words and tone, I managed to stammer out a few pathetic words in response.

'No, I'm fine,' I replied, trying to hide my nerves. I felt like a complete fucking idiot. I could sense she noticed how uneasy I was.

'If I stand here much longer, I'll turn into a fucking statue, can I get in?' she asked, taking one last drag from her cigarette before tossing the butt to the ground. Once again, I was lost for words, I just nodded, and without any hesitation she got in. I couldn't believe that such a beautiful young woman was sitting so close to me. I had to curtail my excitement; I was hard. You are going to be my first sacrifice, you filthy whore, I thought to myself, as I smiled at her, trying to hide my sinister thoughts.

'I think we should drive up the road a bit, the fucking filth are all over the place tonight for some reason,' she said. Smiling like a child on Christmas morning, I started the car, amused by the young whore's choice of words, referring to the police as 'the fucking filth.' It was clear that the poor creature was obviously unaware of her own social standing. I pulled out onto Fitzwilliam Street, drove through the cross-roads at the top of Lesson Street, and parked in a lay-by across from the hospital on Adelaide Road.

'So, what will it be?' she asked, breaking the silence. Once again, words evaded me. My mind was blank, and I had no idea how to respond. Although, the uncomfortable lump throbbing in my trousers was a clear indication of what I wanted. Despite this, the situation I found myself in was completely alien to me.

'You seem quite nervous. Is this your first time?' she asked. I was taken aback by her directness and felt uncomfortable being asked such a personal question. It almost felt like she was mocking me. A part of me wanted to tell her to get the fuck out of my car, but another part of me (the throbbing sensation in my trousers) was drawn to her.

'Yes,' I eventually admitted, feeling embarrassed. I kept my eyes fixed ahead, avoiding any eye contact with her.

'I'll give you a hand job for twenty euro,' she said with a mis-chievous smile. Feeling foolish, I simply nodded as she wrapped her cold, petite hand around my throbbing penis. I came quickly, much faster than when I did it myself. She took a pack of baby wipes from her handbag, wiped me down and then cleaned her hands, she smiled with her hand outstretched. Fumbling for my wallet, I eventually paid her, and for some unknown reason, I also thanked her. As she turned to open the car door,

'Wait, please don't go,' I said, my words sounded pathetic and needy.

'Why? Do you want more?' she asked, turning back to face me.

'I don't want you to leave. I'm enjoying your company,' I replied. She quickly shut me down, saying,

'Listen, I'm not a fucking charity worker. If you want my com-pany, you're going to have to pay for it.' Her tone and demeanour had changed; there was something nasty and disturbing about her. I gripped the steering wheel tightly as I struggled to control my rising temper. This vile little bitch will suffer dearly later, I thought as I steadied myself.

'Of course. I know how it works,' I replied, as I asked myself, what the hell am I doing? 'So, what are you looking for?' she asked, her piercing gaze unnerved me.

'How much to spend the rest of the night with me?' I asked, while somehow managing to keep my simmering rage at bay, at least for the moment.

'It depends on what you want to do,' she said.

'Not much, just go for a drive, grab a bag of chips, simple stuff. Look, I don't have a girlfriend, I'm just feeling a little lonely and I like your company,' I replied, aware of how pathetic I sounded.

'Okay, let's say four hundred for the rest of the night and I'm yours until six in the morning,' she said.

'That sounds fair enough,' I replied. Although I had no idea what the hell I was going to do with her. One thing was certain; she would be dead by six in the morning.

Chapter 16

We drove aimlessly around the city in silence for about an hour. I could sense her growing anxiousness, as she kept fidgeting with her handbag.

'By the way, it's cash up front,' she said, finally breaking uncomfortable silence. 'No problem, I just need to stop at a bank link,' I said as we left the city and headed towards Rathmines. I pulled into a spot just off the main street, directly across from McDonald's. There was a bank link machine just a short distance away on the other side of the road. She got out of the car, crossed the street, and went into McDonald's. Before leaving the car, I put on a baseball cap and pulled it down as low as possible, hoping that I wouldn't meet anyone I knew. I stepped out of the car and made my way to the cash machine. As I entered my pin number, I began to question my sanity. What the hell am I doing? Have I completely lost the fucking plot?

I withdrew the cash for the jumped-up little whore not giving it much thought, as I knew the money would be back in my wallet before dawn. As I made my way back to the car, the same unanswered question kept repeating itself over and over again in my mind, does she truly deserve to die? Am I certain that I want to go through with this? When I returned to the car, she was nowhere in sight. My heart raced and beads of cold sweat trickled down the length of my spine. This is fucking crazy, pure madness, I thought to myself as I got into the car and slammed the door shut. I turned the key in the ignition and was about to drive off when the passenger door suddenly opened, she lowered herself into the car, grinning like a child as she handed me a Big Mac Meal.

'Did you get the money?' she asked bluntly, as she settled into the seat and closed the car door. I handed her the wad of cash with a forced smile. The cheeky bitch counted it out in front of me before placing it in her handbag.

'Now, I'm all yours until six in the morning,' she said before sinking her teeth into her burger. I signalled and pulled out onto the main road in silence.

'Do you have a place we can go to?' she asked, wiping her mouth with the back of her hand.

'No, I'm afraid not,' I replied.

'Ah, I see. Little old wifey sitting at home all alone,' she said, her tone mocking. I didn't like the idea of this jumped-up whore mocking or making assumptions about my life, but I needed to remain calm.

'Fancy a drive out to Killiney Beach?' I suggest, not really knowing what to do or where to go.

'Whatever floats your boat, I'm all yours now,' she replied with a wink.

I couldn't help but smile back at her, thinking to myself, if you only fucking knew what was coming. We pulled into the car park across from Killiney train station and walked the short distance under the tunnel and onto the beach. The night air was warm, and the sky was clear, save for the bright moon. Its reflection created a magical pathway that seemed to stretch all the way to the distant horizon, as it rested on the calm sea. As I looked to my right, I could see the famous landmark, the cross standing tall and proud at the summit of Bray Head, and to my left the moon illuminated the Witch's Hat on Killiney Hill.

She removed her shoes as we walked along the water's edge, the cold dark water gently lapping over her petite feet and between her toes. I lit a cigarette and handed it to her; I then lit another one for myself. We made our way over to a grassed area. I took off my coat and placed it on the ground, she tossed her shoes to the ground as she sat down on my coat. She looked beautiful under the moon light as she stared out towards the sea.

I settled down next to her on the damp grass, the early morning dew was already making its presence known. She pulled me close, and we kissed, I was hard and excited. I wanted her. She was in complete control as she moved down along my trembling body, undoing my belt and trousers before taking me in her mouth. I lay back on the damp grass, my gaze fixed on the bright moon above as she pleasured me. As much as I enjoyed her touch, my mind drifted back to those dark nights I had spent in the seminary. I had been forced to perform this very same act night after night on priests, some of whom couldn't even keep it up. Their frustration often resulted in me receiving a beating. The memory made me sick to my stomach. As I looked down at the top of her head bobbing up and down as she pleasured me, my mind filled with disgust and regret. She was nothing but a vile whore, who spent her nights walking the streets and enticing vulnerable men into temptation. She had seduced me, like so many others, into indulging in disgusting and depraved acts that would ultimately lead to damnation. She needed to be stopped.

My train of thought was interrupted when she abruptly pulled away from me and stood up. She then proceeded to undress and lowered herself onto me, smiling as she guided me inside her. It was my first time entering a woman. I lay there with my eyes tightly closed, unsure of what to do. I was completely lost and unaware of my role in this immoral act. She was in complete control, moving at a pace that suited her. Her groans, which I'm sure, were as fake as her smile, only added to the experience. When I came, she lay on top of me, holding me tightly as she kissed my neck. My heart was racing and my entire body tingled with pleasure, I couldn't believe that I had a beautiful, naked woman lying on top of me.

'Well, did you enjoy?' she asked, lighting one of my cigarettes.

'Yes, very much,' I replied, still breathing heavily as I lay on my back. She began to laugh as she rolled off of me. I couldn't help but wonder what she found so amusing. Was it because she could tell that it was my first time? Or was the worthless whore laughing at the size of my manhood or how quickly I came with her bouncing up and down on me. My temper flared and I felt myself losing control.

'What's so fucking funny?' I snarled. But my question only seemed to make her laugh even harder, like a giddy child. The more she laughed, the more agitated I became until I completely lost it. I grabbed her by the hair and threw her face down onto the grass, landing several hard blows to the side of her head. The laughter stopped as I buried myself into her as deep and as hard as I could. Once I came, I tossed her aside like a piece of trash. That's all she was to me, a worthless piece of trash.

Breathing heavily, I lay down beside her. She was silent, curled up with her back to me. I lit a cigarette and gazed up at the luminous, full moon, and smiled. As I turned my head slightly to the right, I could see the silhouette of the cross at the summit of Bray Head. The sight of the cross reminded me of the story of Jesus being crucified. According to belief, Jesus had died on the cross so that all of humanity's sins would be forgiven and to save our darkened souls. And yet, I found myself, a priest who had taken a vow of celibacy, lying naked on a beach after buggering some vile whore. Nothing made sense anymore; our lives seemed to be a chaotic mess with no rhyme or reason. I turned my gaze back to the whore, her naked body curled up in the fetal position. It was all her fault; she had seduced me, led me into temptation, and enticed me to taste the forbidden fruit, just like Eve had with Adam in The Garden of Eden, how something's never change, I thought.

'Can I have a smoke?' she asked, as she stood up. I lay there in silence, admiring her naked body towering over me. I lit a cigarette and handed it to her; she smiled and then turned to face the calm water. I watched as she drew hard on the cigarette, I was unsure if her trembling was from the chilly morning air or from what had just happened between us. As she turned to face me, she flicked the butt away.

'Fancy a dip?' she asked, already making her way towards the calm, dark water. I got up and followed her, she stood waiting at the water's edge until I joined her.

As we entered the water together, she wrapped her hand tightly around mine. We both let out little shrieks as the cold water enveloped our naked bodies. When the water reached chest level, I stopped walking and turned to face her. I pulled her close and she rested her head on my chest. The only sound was the gentle lapping of the waves against the shore. I kissed her forehead and as she tilted her head back, our eyes met, she was beautiful. I pulled back slightly, before launching forward with all my strength, my forehead connected with the bridge of her nose, there was a sickening crack. I repeated the action several times.

I struggled to keep her upright, she was dazed, and her once beautiful face was now a bloodied mess. I grabbed her by the back of her head and submerged her beneath the water. Tears rolled down my face as I felt her struggling, trying desperately to save herself. When the struggling stopped, I knew she was free. Free from that vile life she had chosen. I pulled her lifeless body up and held her tight. With her body, now cleansed, and her soul free. I kissed her goodbye, as I slowly released her from my arms, and watched as her body disappeared beneath the gentle waves.

I dressed quickly. The sun was slowly creeping up on the distant horizon, casting a warm orange glow over the sky and water. I gathered up her clothes and neatly placed them just up from the water's edge. After retrieving my cash from her handbag, I placed it next to her clothes. No doubt, some early morning dog walker or runner would stumble across them and raise the alarm. I quickly made my way back to the car park, taking in one last look at the cross standing proudly at the top of Bray Head, as if it was admiring the vast ocean form its vantage point.

'Thy will be done,' I whispered softly, as I wiped away my tears.

Chapter 17

The journey from Killiney Beach back to my house was completed in record time. My heart was racing, thumping against my ribcage as I gripped the steering wheel tightly and pressed the accelerator to the floor. I drove recklessly, well above the speed limit as the roads were deserted at such an early hour. As soon as I entered the house, I ran upstairs and stripped before stepping into the hot, steaming shower. As the water ran over me, I tried to scrub away the lingering scent of revulsion from the sin of that vile whore.

As I stood under the showerhead, I closed my eyes and leaned my tired head against the tiled wall, letting the water run over my shoulders and down my back. Suddenly, the image of her struggling beneath the waves flashed before me, her eyes filled with fear as she fought for her life. I quickly opened my eyes and turned off the water, nervously taking in my surroundings. The faint scent of saltwater still clung to my skin, reminding me of the ocean's unforgiving power. Christ, what just happened? The memory of her thrashing beneath the waves, her hair plastered to her face and her arms flailing, was etched into my mind with startling clarity. What the fuck had I done to her? I asked myself, as I trudged into the bedroom.

Once inside the room, I opened the wardrobe and retrieved the leather whip from its resting place on the top shelf. The punishment was not optional; I had taken the life of a fellow human being, violating the most sacred of the Ten Commandments: 'Thou shalt not kill.' Despite my belief that I was making the world a better place by eliminating such filth, committing such an act has consequences. I removed the towel from around my waist and stood naked in front of the full-length mirror, just as I had done throughout the years in my mother's house. I raised the whip high above my head, my entire body tensed

THY WILL BE DONE

in preparation for the onslaught that was about to unfold. Closing my eyes, I took a deep breath before bringing the whip down fast and hard across my naked flesh, repeating the action until I had received ten brutal lashes. I dropped to my knees as my flesh tore open across my upper back. The pain was unbearable, as I rolled over onto my side, fighting back the tears, as I cursed the vile whore who disappeared beneath the dark waves.

I woke to the blinding glow of the alarm clock's crimson digits, it was four, twenty-three am. I was freezing, curled up naked and bloodied on the floor. It was a gruelling and torturous struggle to pull myself from the frigid, threadbare carpet. Finally, I made it onto the comforting warmth of the bed. I pulled the duvet over my shivering body, desperate for its warmth to seep into my bones. I must have drifted off; my battered and exhausted body succumbed to the pull of sleep. The alarm clock jolted me awake at eight-thirty am, dragging me back into the horrors of reality.

The short distance between my bedroom and the bathroom felt like a mammoth task, each step sent a jolt of pain through my entire body. As I braced myself and stood under the showerhead, the hot water penetrating my skin, reopening the fresh wounds, it felt like being whipped all over again. Closing my eyes, I fought hopelessly against the excruciating pain that ran through me. The girl, whose name I never got, appeared in my mind once again, her frightened face unnerved me. Every time I closed my eyes, even for just a split second, I saw her face drifting away beneath the cold, dark waves. It felt as though she was haunting me, and I suppose, I couldn't blame her. After all, I had taken her life. But the constant vision of her that lingered in my mind was beginning to freak me out.

After drying myself off, I made my way down to the kitchen. My body was craving caffeine, nicotine, and painkillers. Getting dressed was a difficult task, as my open wounds were still raw and any contact with my clothes caused them to bleed again. Despite the pain and discomfort, I decided to walk to the church to celebrate the morning mass, hoping the short journey would help loosen my stiff and sore body.

Just as I was about to leave the house, the news came on over the radio. The headlines reported that several items of women's clothing had been discovered on Killiney Beach by a woman out walking her dog. The authorities were notified, and the Coast Guard and the Lifeboat were conducting a search of the area in the hope of finding a body. As I was saying mass, the news headline echoed relentlessly in my mind, causing a sense of unease and distraction. Despite my best efforts, I found it difficult to focus on the service and stumbled over my words several times. Fortunately, it seems that not too many people pay much attention to priests harping on from the pulpit anymore, as my mistakes went unnoticed.

After saying mass, I slowly and painfully made my way back home. Once inside the house, I swallowed another handful of painkillers and downed a large glass of whiskey. As I lay on the sofa, suffering and cursing my mother and the girl with no name, an overwhelming urge came over me to return to Killiney Beach. I could not understand it; it was nothing short of pure madness. For some inexplicable reason, I felt the need to be there in case her body washed up onto the beach. The thought of her pale, limp body being tossed onto the beach like a discarded piece of driftwood haunted me.

There was no sense to all the madness that was playing out in my mind. Why on earth would I want to go anywhere next or near that beach after what had happened between us the previous night? As I struggled with my racing thoughts, my phone beeped, it was a reminder that I was due at the school for two o'clock for a meeting with the children who were going to be making their First Holy Communion later on in the year.

A classroom full of noisy children was the last fucking thing that I needed. School visits were a nightmare for me, simply because I didn't like children, period. No matter which classroom I entered, there was always one cheeky little fecker, who would try to show off in front of his classmates. I stood at the front of the classroom, feeling dazed and glassy-eyed, my body full to the brim with painkillers. A beautiful young blonde female teacher stood beside me, directing the children as they recited their hymns and prayers. Their young high-pitched, squeaky voices only added to the unbearable pain that was already crucifying me. My mind began to drift, as I thought about my latest perfect murder. I couldn't help but smile as I looked down at the classroom full of spoiled brats.

Chapter 18

I had officially crossed the threshold into the realm of a 'Serial Killer.' The esteemed title is given to a person who has killed three or more people. Although, I must confess, such a title did not sit well with me. I saw myself more as a saviour, a force of good in a world plagued by darkness. My actions were driven by a sense of justice, not by a desire to kill. I was convinced that I was doing what needed to be done to protect innocent souls from harm, and by eradicating such wickedness, I believed I was making the world a better place.

Ten days had passed since the beautiful girl, with no name, had disappeared beneath the cold, dark waves, and there was still no sign of her body. The same beautiful girl who had taken my virginity, and in return, I had taken her life. Every time I closed my eyes, her frightened face appeared before me. I could not shake the haunting image, her eyes wide open and her hair floating around her, as she drifted away beneath the waves. My nights were consumed by terror, and despite my exhaustion, I was unable to find sleep, for fear of closing my eyes.

I was hesitant to return to the red-light district in the city. It was a dangerous place, full of junkies, winos, and whores, certainly not suitable for a man of the cloth like myself. However, I could not afford to waste any more time; stopping these vile creatures from walking the streets had become my sole focus. One evening, while browsing the internet, I stumbled upon a site advertising escorts. I was shocked by what appeared on the screen in front of me. A list of all the escorts working in each county, complete with profile pictures, contact numbers, hourly rates, and a disturbingly detailed list of their perverted services. As I scrolled through the site, I could not believe how many of these vile whores existed and how boldly they advertised their services.

I couldn't believe my luck, stumbling across such a site. There was no need for me to risk driving in and around the dangerous red-light district as I searched for my next victim, or rather 'offering.' After browsing through the site for quite some time, I settled on a beautiful dark-haired girl from Brazil. I dialled her number, and she answered on the third ring. Her soft voice was barely audible, and she spoke in broken English, which made for a difficult conversation. During our brief chat, we struggled to understand each other, she eventually hung up and texted me her address. I replied to her message, and we arranged to meet later that night at her apartment in Inchicore.

As I sat in the living room, staring at my reflection on the blank television screen. I flicked the lighter and brought the naked flame up to meet the tip of my cigarette and took a long drag, it dawned on me that I had been smoking a lot more than usual lately. It was probably due to the fact that my stress levels were through the fucking roof, and the extra nicotine seemed to calm me and steady my nerves. At least, that's what I kept telling myself.

Shrouded in the darkness and silence of the room, I tried to figure what would be the best way to end the girl's life. It needed to be quick with as little mess as possible. The last thing I wanted was to leave a crime scene full of incriminating evidence and clues that could lead to my arrest and inevitable demise. Strangulation seemed like the most straightforward option, with the added bonus of no mess. However, just in case, things didn't go according to plan or worse, got out of hand, I decided to bring a hammer with me.

I pulled up outside her apartment block; the only parking available was directly across the road in a church car park, of all places. The car park was pitch black, the only light came from the faint glow of the streetlights, intensifying the eerie silence. Lowering my cap as I crossed the road, trying to remain inconspicuous. I took out my phone and read her text message, which instructed me to, 'Press number 78, then press the button with the picture of a bell on it.' I followed her instructions and immediately recognised her voice from the phone call earlier, as her words filtered through the intercom.

'Hi, come up to the third floor,' she said in a soft, almost whispering tone. Her broken English was incredibly alluring to me. I walked past the elevator and took the stairs, as a bad experience in a lift a number of years ago had left an indelible mark on me, and since then I have always used the stairs. I was a little out of breath when I finally reached the third floor. The hallway was dimly lit and a bad odour lingered in the background, as if something was rotten, or the trash bins needed to be emptied. I followed the numbers on the doors until I found myself standing in front of number seventy-eight. Just as I was about to press the doorbell, the door opened. A small, beautiful, tanned woman with long, dark hair stood before me. She greeted me with a warm smile, and although she was stunning, I couldn't help but notice that she was not the same girl as the one in the profile picture on the website.

'Hi, please come in,' she said, stepping aside to let me to enter before closing the door behind me. She then gestured with her hand for me to follow her. We walked down the narrow hallway until we reached the last door on the right. She gently knocked and exchanged a few words in her native tongue with whoever was on the other side of the door. After her brief conversation, she opened the door and ushered me inside. As I entered the room, there was another beautiful woman standing at the end of the bed, dressed in sexy black lace underwear. I instantly recognised her from the profile picture on the website. Confused by the situation, I turned back to the woman who had brought me to the room, but before I could say anything, she had already left and closed the door behind her.

Fuck, there was more than one person in the apartment. I never even considered that possibility, how fucking naïve of me.

'Hi, how are you?' she asked, as I turned back to face her. I was speechless, my mind racing to find a solution to this unexpected situation that I found myself in.

'Are you a little shy?' she asked, her sultry smile and broken English caught my attention.

'No, I'm fine,' I replied, just for the sake of saying something.

'Let me help you undress,' she suggested smiling. I stood in silence, gazing into her dark, brown eyes as she removed my clothes. We stood naked, facing each other, the flickering flame of the scented candle on her bedside table casting a warm glow on our bare skin and filling the room with the sweet scent of vanilla.

She playfully pushed me onto the bed. I lay there thinking, this vile whore does not know how lucky she is, there was no way I could remove her from this world with other people in the apartment. She expertly slid the condom down along my throbbing shaft using only her mouth, her tongue teasing me with every movement, quite a skill, I thought, the filthy bitch. But, I couldn't resist her, I closed my eyes and lay there defeated. I had succumbed to her temptation, fallen at her feet. I wondered was this how Adam felt when Eve seduced him in The Garden of Eden all those years ago. I felt completely helpless, bound to her womanly charms. Has anything really changed between men and women since the beginning of time, I thought to myself, as I entered her.

As I left her apartment, I was torn between the ecstasy of the experience and the frustrated of my own weakness. I felt like I had failed and was defeated by a cunning whore. She had exposed my weakness, and like so many others before me, I fell helplessly at her feet, completely at her mercy. When I arrived home, I was still feeling angry and disgusted with myself for having crumbled so easily. I immediately went straight up to my bedroom and retrieved my mother's whip from the top shelf of the wardrobe and began the cleansing ritual in front of the full-length mirror, mercilessly bringing the strips of leather down across my naked flesh.

Chapter 19

Almost three weeks had passed since the beautiful girl, with no name, had disappeared beneath the waves, and her body had yet to be found. After my previous experience, I was hesitant to use the escorts website, although driving around the red-light district posed its own set of risks and dangers. However, I was determined to continue on my quest. The dimly lit, sin-ridden streets of our capital's seedy underworld were not going to cleanse themselves.

Regardless of whether I was driving around the streets or browsing through the internet, I knew there would always be risks involved, I had accepted it as an occupational hazard. After much deliberation, I decided to take another chance on the escort's website. Although I was fully aware of the risks and consequences, I also understood that taking chances was necessary to accomplish my objective. After carefully browsing through dozens of profile pictures, I selected who was to become my next sacrificial lamb, and wasting no time, I dialled her number. Once again, and much to my delight, the phone was answered in broken English. After a short but pleasant conversation, she texted me the address of her apartment in Lucan. My only hope was that she lived alone.

After driving around in circles for what felt like an eternity. I finally found her apartment above a shop on the main street. I pressed the doorbell, but there was no answer. Frustrated, I muttered 'bitch' under my breath and pressed the bell again, this time I left my finger on it for a little longer as my impatience grew. A light came on, and I could see someone coming down the stairs through the glass panel on the door. The door opened to reveal a tall, slim woman in her thirties. She looked nothing like the woman in the profile picture; I began to notice a pattern emerging.

'Hi, welcome,' she said, extending her hand. She quickly glanced up and down the street before ushering me in. I followed her up the narrow staircase. The apartment was small and cramped, it seemed to have only one bedroom off the hallway. My senses were heightened, and I could almost smell the blood of my sacrificial offering as she led me through the apartment. She then took me to the bedroom, but just as she was about to close the door behind us, I asked if I could use the toilet.

'Of course,' she replied, directing me towards it. I quickly scanned the narrow hallway as I entered the bathroom. The only other room was a kitchen and dining area; I needed to check it, to see if there was anyone else in the apartment. I flushed the toilet, just for effect. On opening the bathroom door, I was taken aback to find her standing right outside, waiting for me. I didn't like her piercing gaze; it made me feel unease. I still needed to check the kitchen to make sure that we were alone.

I politely asked her if I may have a glass of water, she didn't respond. Instead, she simply nodded and gave me a forced smile before heading to the kitchen. I trailed behind her like a lap dog. She filled a glass with water and handed it to me, leaving me with no option but to drink it in front of her. She watched intently as I drained the glass, I thanked her, smiling to myself. The mission at hand was completed, and I now knew that there was no one else in the apartment. It was just the two of us, how romantic, I mused, as I followed her back to the bedroom.

Once we entered the bedroom, she quickly undressed. I could tell that she wanted to get this over and done with as quick as possible. Her demeanour suggested that she was clearly dreading the task ahead, a task she would rather poke her eyes out than go through with. Her forced smile, which seemed to be permanently fixed on her face, sickened me. As I unbuttoned my shirt, I told her to get on the bed and turn around on all fours. As she positioned herself, I reached for the hammer that was patiently waiting in the pocket of my overcoat which was draped over the chair. After four blows to the back of her head, she was dead. Her forced smile was gone forever.

As I picked up my shirt from the floor, I caught a glimpse of my blood-stained reflection in the mirror. Fuck, there was blood everywhere, on me, on the walls, on the bed. Even the ceiling had speckles of her dark red blood sprayed across it. In a panic, I rushed into the bathroom and frantically cleaned the hammer and washed her blood from my face, neck, and hands. I left her apartment, completely satisfied with my night's work.

She had received what she truly deserved: one less whore on the streets, no longer able to seduce and engage in depraved acts. As I drove home, I was overcome with euphoria, knowing that she was growing colder and stiffer as she lay lifeless on her bed, surrounded in a pool of her own poisonous blood. I had not succumbed to her womanly charms, I had resisted and remained steadfast, as she tried to entice me. The fact that I had refused to engage in any sexual acts with her, meant that I didn't have to subject myself to the cleansing ritual. Dear Old Mother's whip could remain safely hidden away on the top shelf of my wardrobe.

I was on such a high as I left her blood-splattered apartment. Everything had gone according to plan. It was almost midnight when I finally returned home, completely exhausted and drained from the events of the night. In an attempt to come down off my high, I poured myself a large whiskey and lit a cigarette as I sank down onto the sofa. The warm, golden liquid glimmered in the dim light, as I raised the glass towards my lips. As I slowly exhaled the smoke, I closed my eyes and a smile spread across my face as I replayed the memories of the last few hours, savouring every moment. After draining another couple of generously poured whiskeys, I stumbled up the stairs, and headed to bed, feeling content for the first time in weeks.

Chapter 20

I woke early the next morning, full of renewed vigour and a great sense of purpose. As I poured myself a second cup of coffee, I turned on the radio. At exactly eight o'clock, the news began, and the main headline read,

'A woman's body was discovered by her husband late last night when he returned home from work.' I was thrilled to hear that my work from the previous night had made the headlines.

'Filthy whore, she got what she deserved,' I muttered to myself. Carrying on like that behind her poor husband's back while he was out working hard. But then it dawned on me, I was lucky to have not been caught. What if her husband had arrived home while I was still there? He could have easily overpowered me and raised the alarm. The newsreader could have been reporting a completely different story over the radio. It was a disturbing thought. The risks attached to visiting those apartments were far too high.

I realised that I needed to reassess my plan of action. Continuing to put myself in harm's way or risking getting caught by the police was not a viable option. The thought of that whores husband arriving home while I was still there kept replaying in my mind. I would have had to kill him as well or he could have easily killed me or restrained me until the police arrived. The good mood I had woken up with quickly dissipated, leaving me with a heavy sense of unease. As the day wore on, my mind was consumed with a mix of anxiety, fear, and irrational thoughts of worst-case scenarios that kept creeping in.

As the evening slowly evolved into night, the streetlights came to life, casting a warm glow over the darkening sky. However, it wasn't just the sky that grew darker, my mood did as well. For some unknown reason, I just couldn't seem to relax. I paced back and forth in the hallway, chain-smoking one cigarette after another, feeling like I was wasting precious time. In a moment of pure frustration, I hopped into my car and drove into the city, scanning the familiar spots where the ladies of the night were known to gather.

As my senses heightened, I parked the car across from the Pepper Canister and rolled down the window to light a cigarette. As if on cue, a woman suddenly materialised out of thin air and approached my car. Her figure illuminated by the streetlights as she propped herself against the car, her body language exuding confidence as she asked for a light. I smiled and flicked the lighter, holding it for her. Now that I had overcome my initial fear of speaking to theses whores, I was becoming more confident when dealing with them. She appeared to be in her thirties or forties, with deep lines on her face that spoke of a difficult life. Despite the heavy makeup she wore, it was clear that she had endured a lot of hardship over the years.

As I watched her exhale a cloud of smoke, I thought to myself, let's get this over with quickly.

'How much?' I asked bluntly.

'Jesus, there's no beating around the bush with you. What are you looking for?' she asked.

'I need a shag,' I replied.

'Fifty,' she said, taking a deep drag from her half-finished cigarette.

'Hop in,' I said with a smirk, as she confidently strode around to the passenger door and settled into the seat. I drove up Lesson Street, turned onto Appian Way, and then on into Ranelagh.

'Where the hell are you taking me?' she asked, her voice quivering nervously.

'I live in Rathfarnham, we're almost there. Is that okay?' I asked, not really giving a flying fuck, if she was okay or not.

'you're taking me well away from my usual spot, so that will be extra,' she said.

'No problem, how does two hundred sound?' I asked. She simply nodded, smiling. I drove into the housing estate that borders Bushy Park, and said to her,

'I live just around the corner, but I have a fantasy of doing it in the park.'

'If that's what you want, could you drop me back into the city afterwards? she asked. 'Of course, no problem,' I replied. As I was about to exit the car, she reminded me, 'Aren't you forgetting something? Money first.' I reached into my coat pocket, retrieved my wallet, and handed her the cash. I knew all too well that I would be getting it back shortly.

She counted the money before placing it into her handbag.

We left the car and followed the various twists and turns along the dimly lit pathway that made its way around the perimeter of the park. At the far side of the park, there was a forested area.

'Jesus, it's really fucking creepy,' she said as we entered the dark woods. I slid my hand into the pocket of my overcoat and felt the smooth wooden handle of the hammer, the touch of the wood against my hand sent a thrill through me.

'I need to pee,' she said. She walked a few feet ahead of me and disappeared behind a tree. I waited for a minute or so before approaching her. When she heard me coming, she turned quickly and looked up from her squatting position.

'Jesus, you scared the fucking life out of me,' she said, visibly relieved when she realised it was me standing over her. As she started to stand up, I viciously swung the hammer and struck her on the side of her head. She fell to the ground; her jeans and panties were still down around her ankles. She lay motionless. I was certain that single blow had killed her, but I couldn't take any chances. I continued to strike her face and head with the hammer several more times.

Her lifeless body felt like a ton of bricks as I struggled to drag her over to a densely overgrown area. The very recently deceased whore was right; it was fucking creepy walking through the woods. The dark trees loomed over me, casting eerie shadows as I cautiously made my way out of woods. I was relieved to finally emerge from the dark woods and make my way back to where I had parked my car.

As I approached the entrance to the park, there was a police car parked a few spaces down from mine with two officers in it. Glancing at my watch; I saw it was two-thirty in the morning. I cursed them under my breath, I knew that if they noticed me leaving the park at such an ungodly hour, they would surely question me. Questions, that I would be unable to answer. I quickly hid behind a cluster of trees and watched as the two officers chatted and sipped their coffee. Fuck them, out of all the places in the city, they had to choose this one for their coffee break. All I could do was wait.

Forty-five minutes later, they sped away with sirens blaring, flashing blue lights, and coffee cups thrown to the ground. It felt like I was watching a poorly directed cop movie unfold before my eyes. Despite the bitter cold, I decided to remain hidden among the trees, just in case they circled back towards the park. After a few minutes had passed, I cautiously crept out from my hiding spot and made my way back to the car.

All the late-night excursions were taking their toll on me. I looked completely drained, my tired eyes were bloodshot and sunken, and my skin was pale and sallow from the lack of sleep. My appearance had drastically changed in just a matter of weeks. I was shocked by the reflection that stared back at me in the mirror. In what felt like such a short period of time, I had aged terribly.

One of the blue rinse militia had commented on how tired and run down I looked. I brushed it off with a smile, explaining that there simply weren't enough hours in the day. And, as the only priest in the parish, I was constantly chasing my tail. I had managed to garner sympathy from the entire parish, which was exactly what I wanted. They were all on my side, telling me that I was in their prayers. It was almost comical, the thought of the blue rinse militia praying for me, a serial killer. Although, I knew that eventually something would have to give, the chaotic double life that I was living would not end well.

Chapter 21

' Let us now go in peace to love and serve the Lord, Amen,' I said, as I raised my bowed head to face the congregation. I was sick to death of saying mass every morning, tired of repeating those same empty words day after day to the same vacant faces staring back up at me. It was all starting to weigh in on me. My days were a blur of early morning masses, confessions, and hospital visits, followed by late night committee meetings and paperwork, leaving me with very little time for myself. I was worn-out and becoming increasingly frustrated. I had to constantly remind myself that being a priest was the perfect disguise for my new vocation. No one in their right mind would ever suspect a member of the clergy of being involved in the disappearance and murder of women, especially sex workers. It was the perfect cover.

After saying mass, I returned home and made myself a cup of coffee and lit up a cigarette. A quick glance at the clock that hung above the door, it was almost eleven o'clock. I turned on the radio to catch the hourly news. The female newsreader delivered the headlines with a clear and concise voice. She reported that,

"A murder investigation had been launched after the discovery of a woman's body at Bushy Park in Rathfarnham earlier this morning." Closing my eyes, I tried to imagine what the newsreader looked like, the colour of her hair, her skin tone, and the shade of lipstick she wore to hide her pink tongue as she perfectly pronounced each word. Her voice reminded me of my old primary school teacher, someone who was well-educated and well-read. Or perhaps she resembled the elderly lady who worked at the library with her refined manner of speaking and was always sensibly dresses. However, I quickly dismissed both images, smiling to myself, as I took a long drag from my cigarette.

I eagerly took a seat at the kitchen table, listening attentively. The newsreaders voice filled the room, her words painting a vivid picture in my mind. It was a satisfying feeling to hear my accomplishments being read out over the airwaves. I felt that I deserved some sort of recognition or appreciation, perhaps even the freedom of the city. After all, my work was for the greater good of humanity. However, instead of being celebrated or thanked for disposing of those vile creatures, I often found myself having to slip back into the shadows of the city streets, hidden under the cover of darkness to avoid being discovered.

My obsession with cleansing the streets and disposing of prostitutes had become all-consuming. And just like any other obsession, it had a negative impact on my well-being. I couldn't escape the haunting images of my victims terrified faces, which kept me up, night after night and left me feeling drained and tormented. I tried to rationalise these haunting images as their lost souls seeking revenge. I left my thoughts and returned to the newsreader as she announced,

'The police have cordoned off the park and are searching for vital clues.'

'Enough,' I muttered to myself, as I turned off the radio. I would certainly like to think that I didn't leave any clues behind. No, I couldn't have, I was careful, clever, always one step ahead of the posse, as the saying goes. Surely there was no evidence that could link me to the crime scene or lead the ongoing investigation to my front door. Just before I abruptly turned off the radio, the newsreader mentioned that the body had been removed from the crime scene and taken to the city morgue for a post-mortem examination, to be carried out by the state pathologist.

Two days later, it was reported on the evening news that the body found in Bushy Park was identified as Sharon Daly, a forty-three-year-old mother of two. The cause of death was a fatal blow to the head with a blunt object. My trusted hammer had played a crucial role on that fateful night. After the news ended, I turned off the television and powered up my laptop and went straight to the escorts website where I was greeted by dozens of profile pictures. My initial plan was to eliminate every single one of them, although realistically, I soon realised that would be an impossible task. It was an oversight on my part, perhaps due to my naivety. In my defence, I had no idea that there were almost as many prostitutes as there were rats scurrying around the streets of the city. What I did know was that both were equally poisonous vermin, and a threat to society.

I never bought into the whole sad storyline that these women were someone's daughter, sister, or even a mother who had fallen on hard times and resorted to selling their bodies to make ends meet. Bullshit, I saw through their pitiful façade and knew that they were fully aware of what they were doing. I had no sympathy for them, and to hell with all the do-gooders, creating excuses trying to justify their actions. In my mind, they were beyond help or redemption and were nothing more than a scourge on the city, like rats scurrying around the streets.

I was hesitant about meeting girls from the website. My main concern was that I had no way of knowing if they lived alone until I entered their apartment, and by then it was too late. Picking up girls on the street also posed its own risks. No matter which route I took to find my next sacrificial offering, there were serious dangers involved. I wrote down the phone number of a stunning, dark–haired Spanish girl named Maria before shutting down my laptop. Just looking at her profile picture aroused me. After exchanging a few text messages, we arranged to meet later that evening.

When she opened the front door of her apartment, I immediately recognised her from her profile picture. This was a refreshing change from my past experiences, as most of the other girls I had met did not resemble their profile pictures at all. As she stood in the doorway, I was struck by her mesmerising beauty. She looked like a rare and exotic species, deserving of a place on a pedestal in a gallery, to be admired and desired but never touched. She greeted me with a friendly smile and invited me inside, closing the door behind me, before leading me down a hallway and into a large bedroom that reeked of sex and cheap perfume. The first thing that caught my eye was the en-suite bathroom in the corner of the room. After closing the bedroom door, she turned to face me.

'Eighty euro for one hour,' she said in broken English, while holding out her right hand waiting for the cash. No fucking about with this one, I thought to myself as I handed over the money. As she stood facing me, I suddenly realised that I had seriously fucked up. On entering the apartment, I was so captivated by her appearance that I forgot to check if there was anyone else in the apartment. And with an en-suite in the bedroom, I couldn't use my usual trick of asking to use the toilet. How was I going to find out if we were alone or not? I excused myself and went into the en-suite to relieve myself, buying some time as I gathered my thoughts. I needed to be absolutely sure that we were alone before I could carry out my plan to kill her.

When I emerged from the en-suite, she was lying naked on the bed. From that moment onwards, I didn't give a damn if there was anyone else in the apartment or not. Trying to resist what lay on the bed before me would have been a futile act. As I approached her, she sat up and moved to the edge of the bed, reaching out her arms to pull me closer to her. She was stunning in every way, her luscious long, black hair cascading down over her tanned shoulders and back. As she stared up at me, her dark, brown eyes sparkled with an alluring intensity, and her plump, perfectly shaped lips were irresistible. The colour of her lipstick matched the polish on her fingers and toes, and her beautiful formed rounded breasts and long, shapely legs made her a perfectly sculpted being. Her ethereal beauty was beyond compare.

I stood before her, my heart thumping against my chest with a mix of excitement and nervousness, as her hands gently caressed my body. I was defeated, completely lost in her touch. She lay back on the bed, pulling me down on top of her. Without hesitation, she guided me inside her. Her groans, whether genuine or not, were incredibly arousing. I didn't want the moment to end. Lost in a state of pure ecstasy, I held onto her tightly as I tried to prolong the experience. Once again, I had little control and came far too quickly. We lay side by side, holding each other. My heart was pounding as she smiled at me. Her arms and legs enveloped me in a warm embrace. The warm embrace that I had craved for so long did not disappoint, even though it was from a prostitute who was only holding me because I paid her, I still savoured the moment.

It didn't take much persuasion for my friend to stiffen again. She rolled onto her stomach and sensually raised herself onto all fours, like an erotic creature enticing her mate. Thankfully, I lasted a little longer the second time around, my performance seemed to be improving. Once again, we lay side by side, but this time she didn't embrace me. I released a contented sigh, feeling completely spent yet utterly satisfied. As I lay beside her, I could feel the warmth emanating from her body. My eyes followed the gentle rise and fall of her shapely, tanned breasts with each breath she took. Despite my lustful desires, I had nothing left in me. I would have been content to spend the rest of the night simply lying there, admiring her beauty, if she had allowed me to do so. As I gazed at her, a sudden wave of realisation washed over me, our time together was almost up, and I needed to snap the fuck out of my pathetic little love buzz. She would be expecting me to leave soon. But, to achieve my goal, I first needed to determine if there was anyone else in the apartment.

'It's very warm in here, would it be possible to get a glass of water? I asked politely.

'Of course, just help yourself in the kitchen. The glasses are in the press above the kettle.

And don't worry about covering up, my friend is at work,' she replied with a smile. My friend is at work; those five simple words were enough to give me another hard on. We were alone. I made my way into the kitchen and turned on the tap, letting the water run as I gathered my dark, twisted thoughts. Once the glass was filled, I returned to the bedroom and offered her some water, but she declined.

'You have fifteen minutes left,' she said, as she lay on her back staring vacantly at the ceiling.

'Bend over,' I said curtly, my mood had suddenly darkened. Although I'm sure she was use to people speaking down to her, considering her chosen profession. She smiled and turned around, positioning herself on the bed. As I stood at the end of the bed, admiring her from behind one last time, I felt a twinge of sadness knowing that she was so close to death. Despite her beauty and my longing for her, I knew there was no point in me even trying to get it up, I had nothing left in the tank. It would have only resulted in humiliation for me. After draining the glass of water, I placed it on top of the chest of drawers and then slowly reached down to remove the hammer from my coat.

I carefully eased myself back onto the bed and began to kiss and caress her exquisite ass. As my tongue gently entered her, I raised the hammer above my head. Suddenly, I felt the full force of her foot striking the side of my face, sending me flying off the bed. Although my head was spinning and my vision slightly blurred, I quickly regained my composure and jumped up, grabbing her tightly by the hair, and forcefully pulled her back onto the bed before she could reach the door or cry out for help. I held her face down, her voice was muffled by the pillow, barely audible as she struggled. The first blow of the hammer brought a sudden halt to her frantic movements; the second blow silenced her forever. I collapsed onto the bed next to her, and that's when I noticed the mirror on the wardrobe door, she must have seen my reflection as I raised the hammer.

I went into the en-suite and quickly washed her crimson blood from my face and hands. My entire being was consumed by adrenaline as I hastily threw on my clothes, my hands were trembling as I struggled to close the buttons on my shirt. Before leaving the room, I looked down at Maria one last time; even in her lifeless state, her features still held a serene beauty that sent shivers down my spine.

As I left the bedroom and walked down the hallway, I suddenly froze in shock and fear as I noticed the front door was slightly ajar. My heart pounded against my chest as I remained still and strained my ears listening for any signs of movement or voices. However, all I could hear was the frantic thumping of my own heartbeat echoing throughout my body. Panic quickly set in. Had someone entered the apartment? I was sure that Maria had closed the door behind me when I first entered. Yes, she had closed it. I distinctly remember it being closed when I went to the kitchen to get a glass of water.

I had a strong urge to shout out 'hello,' but the paralysing fear that consumed me quickly suppressed my voice. My curiosity was torn between investigating the apartment and my fear of the unknown dangers that may be lurking behind any one of the doors. One side of me wanted to check the place out, to see if anyone had entered and remained inside, while a small voice in my head screamed at me to get the fuck out as quickly as possible.

With a sense of trepidation, I cautiously approached the living room door, it was open when I first entered the apartment, but now it was partially closed. I peeked inside without entering, I found the room empty. Fuck this, I need to get the hell out of here, I thought to myself as I turned and made my way towards the front door. I hesitantly looked out into the main hallway through the gap in the front door, there was no sign of anyone. Just as I was about to leave, I suddenly remembered that I had left the hammer in the bedroom. Quietly, I crept back to the bedroom, my senses were on high alert in case I encountered any unexpected guests. Upon entering the deceased's bedroom, I saw the hammer lying on the blood-soaked pillow. I quickly grabbed it and left.

Sweat dripped down my face, stinging my eyes and blurring my vision as I ran down two flights of stairs and out to the car park, all the while, praying that I wouldn't meet anyone. My heart was pounding at a ridiculous rate as I pulled out onto the main road a lot faster than I should have. The car behind me sounded its horn aggressively as I sped away. My mind was in turmoil, making it difficult to think clearly. Who had opened the front door and the closed the living room door? And, if someone had entered the apartment, had they seen or heard anything?

When I finally arrived home, I went straight into the kitchen and grabbed a bottle of whiskey from the press. My hands trembled as I raised the bottle to my lips, the thought of her escaping sent a chill down my spine. If she had managed to escape, the consequences would have been disastrous. And as for the front door slightly ajar, I simply couldn't explain it. As I lay back on the sofa, taking swigs from the bottle, I felt like a cat who had just used up one of its nine lives.

Chapter 22

The following morning, I woke to a sharp, stinging pain that seemed to radiate throughout my entire body. I dragged my aching body out of bed and slowly made my way to the shower, each torturous step brought tears to my eyes. As I closed the bathroom door behind me, I winced at the sight of my reflection in the mirror. My wounds were caked in dried blood; the deep gashes and torn tender flesh made it difficult to move without feeling a sharp tug on my skin. Each movement caused a fresh trickle of warm blood to erupt, leaving a sticky crimson trail in its wake. The searing heat of the water felt like a thousand hot needles piercing my skin, my body writhing in agony, as my mother's cruel words reverberated in my mind, tormenting me,

'Watch the sin running off of you.'

After painfully drying myself off, I covered my open wounds with an antiseptic cream. I decided to remain naked, hoping that the thick layer of cream would penetrate the cuts and alleviate my suffering. I then sent a text to Michael, the church sacristan, to inform him that there would be no mass this morning because I had picked up a stomach bug and was feeling poorly, more lies.

As I descended the stairs, my body was crying out for painkillers and the soothing warmth of whiskey. I slowly navigated each crucifying step before shuffling wearily into the kitchen.

'Jesus, Ann, I never heard you come in,' I said in a complete state of shock, standing naked in front of my housekeeper.

'Oh my God, Father, what on earth happened to you? She gasped, her hands flew to her mouth, her eyes widening in shock as she took in my naked bruised and battered body, she couldn't help but stare in horror. Embarrassed, I quickly covered myself with my hands and replied,

'I had a little accident, it's nothing serious.' I turned away as quickly as I could, which was no easy feat given my condition. It was a humiliating journey as I slowly trudged, naked, from the kitchen and back up the stairs, with each step I took, I could feel Ann's scrutinising gaze following me. Fuck, I had completely forgotten that Ann was coming over to clean the house. How foolish of me, I thought as I struggled to pull a t-shirt over my head and then painfully slipped into a pair of tracksuit bottoms.

As much as I liked Ann, I was fully aware that she was the parish gossip. I knew there was no chance she would be able to keep what she had just witnessed to herself. After descending the dreaded stairs once again, each step crucifying me in its own sadistic way. I reluctantly re-entered the kitchen, not only was I in excruciating pain, but I also felt completely embarrassed.

'Ann, I'm so sorry for walking in on you like that,' I mumbled, unable to make eye contact.

'Father, there's no need to worry. I've been married for over twenty-five years, so I've seen it all before. Those cuts across your body do look quite painful,' she said. I thought I caught a glimpse of a flirtatious smile as she turned away from me.

'I went mountain biking with a friend yesterday and had a nasty fall. And I can safely say, it was my first and definitely my last time on a mountain bike, it was terrifying,' I replied, wondering where all these lies were coming from so effortlessly.

'Did you go to the hospital? she asked, her genuine concern was evident in her tone.

'No, I went to the doctor. He gave me the once-over and told me that nothing was broken. He also prescribed some strong painkillers and an antiseptic cream,' I replied, feeling a little guilty as the lies just poured out of me.

'Ann, my deepest apologies for walking in on you in that state. I feel very ashamed and embarrassed,' I said, still unable to make eye contact.

'Honestly Father, there's no need to apologise, and from what I saw, you have nothing to be embarrassed about,' she said with a mischievous smile. Did I hear her correctly? I wondered, returning her smile.

'I'll put the kettle on. You deserve a strong cup of coffee after that ordeal, or maybe even something a little stronger?' I asked.

'Coffee will be fine. I hope that you're going to be okay,' she replied, still smiling away to herself. Despite my craving for a stiff drink, I made two strong cups of coffee. I had to resist the temptation of whiskey, knowing that Ann would not approve of me indulging in it at such an early hour. As we sat across from each other, she still wore that foolish grin on her face. She reminded me of a teenage girl with a crush.

We chatted awkwardly, in between long periods of uncomfortable silence, as we sipped our coffee. As Ann stood up from the table and brought her empty cup over to the sink, she told me that she needed to go to the supermarket for some shopping. I offered to drive her there, I was still feeling a little guilty for putting her through that awkward situation earlier, and for all the lies that I had told her.

'If you insist, that would be great. It'll save me a walk,' she replied with a smile. I was still taken aback by her unexpected comment about me having nothing to be embarrassed of as I stood naked in front of her.

As she cleared the table, I could tell something was weighing heavily on her mind. She turned to face me,

'I apologise, Father. It was wrong of me to speak to a priest in such a manner. I am not sure what came over me. I am truly ashamed of myself,' she said, before her eyes dropped to the floor.

'It's fine, Ann. There's no need to apologies. Yes, I may be a priest, but I am also a man. And I'm taking your comment as a compliment,' I replied. She slowly raised her gaze from the floor until our eyes met. I stood before her, a man of the cloth, fully aroused. The outline of my throbbing penis was clearly visible, pushing hard against my tracksuit bottoms. I knew she had seen it; her eyes glanced back and forth to my crotch whenever she thought I wasn't looking at her.

'I really like you, Ann, a lot,' I said with a goofy smile, trying my best to flirt. She returned the smile and we both fell silent, looking into each other's eyes.

'I want to kiss you,' I blurted out, moving closer to her, but she quickly turned away, leaving me staring at the back of her head. I cursed myself, wondering if I had gone too far. What the fuck was I thinking? The silence remained for what felt like an eternity. Finally, she turned back to face me and said,

'Take off your clothes.' We stood facing each other in complete silence, as I painfully peeled off my clothes, wincing as they had stuck to my open wounds. I stood before her, naked and fully aroused.

She gently traced her fingers over my torn and scarred skin, the expression on her face was a mix of concern and curiosity. One thing was for sure, she knew damn well it was no mountain bike accident that had left me looking the way I did. She knelt before me, tenderly pressing her lips against my wounds as if trying to soothe the pain with each kiss. Then, with a hunger in her eyes, she took me gently into her mouth. Minutes later, I had her bent over the kitchen table, as I thrust myself into her, the wounds on my body reopened, causing a warm trickle of blood to run down my skin.

Chapter 23

Half an hour later, I pulled into the busy car park of the small, family-owned supermarket just off the main street. I sat in the car, tapping my fingers on the steering wheel, as I waited patiently for Ann to finish my weekly grocery shopping. My head was spinning, as I tried to figure out what the fuck had just happened between us. Ann, a priest's housekeeper, in her mid-fifties had seduced me and led me into sin. I had always looked on Ann as a motherly figure. Her actions had proven to me that all women were the same, nothing but filthy whores, the whole fucking lot of them.

As I sat in the car, waiting for her, my temper began to rise. I lit a cigarette, my mind racing as I inhaled the poisonous nicotine. What the fuck am I going to do? I repeatedly asked myself. Not only was she a vile whore, but she was also a gossip. There was no doubt in my mind that she would talk. She was bound to tell someone about what had happened between us, and it wouldn't be long before the entire parish was whispering about our dirty little secret. She had left me with no choice, I knew it was time for her to disappear without a trace.

In the rear-view mirror, I saw her struggling towards the car with several bags of shopping hanging out of her. I got out and opened the boot, taking the bags from her like a true gentleman before placing them in the boot. My mind was in complete chaos as I turned the key in the ignition and pulled out of the car park. Cold beads of sweat ran down the length of my spine as we drove away from the shopping centre.

I had landed myself in one hell of a serious predicament, and the worst part was, I had no idea how to handle it. As we drove along the motorway, I felt completely overwhelmed as I tried to gather my thoughts and come up with a plan to dispose of her.

'Are you free for the rest of the day, Ann?' I asked.

'Yes, I am, Father,' she replied. I couldn't stand her calling me 'Father,' it felt so wrong, especially after the wild passionate acts we had recently engaged in.

'Ann, please call me John,' I said, keeping my eyes on the road, pretending to focus on my driving, even though my mind was plagued with chaotic thoughts.

'Okay, John it is,' she replied with a sheepish grin.

'Do you fancy a spot of lunch?' I asked, trying to buy myself some time while I came up with a plan.

'That sounds lovely, John,' she said with a smile. 'It's just like a real date.' I couldn't help but wonder what was going on in her little, messed-up mind. Her own words had sealed her fate – she was a liability and had to go.

'I know a lovely little café in Enniskerry,' I said, trying to maintain a calm demeanour.

'Sounds nice,' she replied, smiling away to herself.

Although I had no choice but to dispose of her, I couldn't help feeling a twinge of guilt as I thought about the fact that in just a few short hours, she would be dead. Her face would appear on a missing person's list over the next couple of days. Then again, she had no one to blame but herself, seducing a priest, of all people, just to satisfy her own carnal desires. According to the Old Testament, she should have been dragged out into the middle of the street and stoned to death, in front of a blood-thirsty maddening crowd.

We barely spoke during lunch, as the café was filled with a cacophony of noise. The clattering of dishes, chattering of customers, and the hissing of the espresso machine, drowned out any conversation between us. The voices around us seemed to compete rather than engage with each other. And the background music was barely audible, completely overpowered by the loud voices and the hustle and bustle of the waiters. They hurried back and forth, balancing trays of freshly cooked food and wiping down tables as they went. I suppose the noise and activity in the café provided a welcome distraction from my chaotic thoughts.

As I sipped my coffee, a single thought consumed my mind: how was I going to murder and dispose of the woman sitting across from me? It seemed like an impossible task. Ann was not just my house-keeper; she was a kind and compassionate soul who had become a dear friend to me, the only true friend I had in my life. She was also well liked and respected within the parish committee, where she played a very important role and was always willing to lend a hand at the drop of a hat. The situation I found myself in was truly heartbreaking. As I watched Ann delicately dab at the corners of her mouth with a nap-kin, I couldn't help but notice how well-preserved she was for a mid-dle-aged woman. Her unblemished skin and clear, bright eyes made her look radiant. However, my attention was quickly diverted when I heard a plate shatter on the floor at the far side of the café, followed by a child's cries. In that moment, a wave of sadness washed over me, serving as a bittersweet reminder that nothing lasts forever.

After we had finished our meal, we left the café and stepped out into the blistering heat of the midday sun.

'Fancy going for a drive? I absolutely love this area,' I said, forc-ing a smile.

'That sounds lovely, you're really spoiling me, John, she replied. The look in her eyes had unsettled me. She seemed completely infatu-ated. As we drove up the steep hill, we left the charming village behind us. We drove a short distance and then pulled into a lay-by that led to a walkway through a beautiful forest. It was part of the Wicklow Way Trail, and a little yellow man was carved and painted onto a wooden post, pointing us in the right direction.

'How about a nice leisurely stroll through the forest?' I suggested, feeling my anxiety levels rapidly rising.

'Yes, that would be lovely,' she replied. 'The weather is abso-lutely beautiful today – clear blue skies and a gentle breeze. It's the perfect day for a walk.'

'I love being out here, the mountains, the forest, and the fresh air. It's so relaxing, a great way to escape from all the madness and pres-sure of the city,' I said, stepping out of the car.

As I lit a cigarette, I took a moment to appreciate the stunning scenery that surrounded us. I knew there was no point in offering Ann a cigarette; she had told me when we first met, that she didn't smoke. 'I'm far too sensible for that foolish carry on,' I'm certain those were her exact words. As I opened the passenger door, to my complete horror, I realised that I had left my coat at home. It was such a beautiful, warm, sunny day – there was no need for a coat. But for me, the problem was that the hammer was in my coat pocket.

'Fuck,' I muttered under my breath, slamming the car door closed in frustration.

'Is everything alright, John? she asked, her voice was beginning to irritate me. I needed to get this over with as quickly as possible. The slamming of the car door out of pure frustration made it clear that everything was not alright. Inhaling deeply, I steadied myself and filled my lungs with a mixture of the fresh country air and the deadly nicotine of my cigarette. It was a welcome change from the polluted shite we were forced to inhale in the city. I turned to face her and replied,

'Everything is fine. I thought I had my coat with me, but I must have left it at home.' 'You won't need a coat on a day like this. Sure, the sun is splitting the tree's; it's absolutely beautiful,' she said, looking at me as if I had ten heads. I forced a smile as she looked up at the clear blue sky.

We left the lay-by and ventured into the forest, following the directions of the little, yellow man. The pathway we followed was a narrow dirt track that meandered through the heart of the forest. The towering trees that lined the track seemed to stretch towards the heavens. I couldn't tell if they were fir or pine trees, and I felt too embarrassed to ask Ann. Geography was one of the many subjects that failed to capture my interest in school. As we leisurely strolled along the dusty path, rays of warm sunlight filtered through the branches and leaves, bathing us in its warmth, as we fully immersed ourselves in the beauty of nature.

The scenery was beautiful, and the tranquillity of the surroundings was truly awe-inspiring. As I turned to face Ann, I couldn't help but think that this was the perfect setting for her final moments upon this earth.

'Ann, are you okay with what happened between us back at the house?' I asked.

'Yes, I'm fine with everything. To be honest, I really enjoyed it. It made me feel so alive, something I haven't felt in a long time,' she replied. My heart was racing with anticipation as I stopped walking and pulled her close, our bodies pressed together as our lips locked in a passionate embrace.

'I want you right now,' I said, my heart pounding against my cheat and my penis throbbing with lust, as I held her tight. She didn't resist as I pressed my lips firmly against hers, unaware that her time to depart from this world was almost upon us.

I could tell from the way she reacted that she wanted it just as much as I did. As we left the dirt track and ventured deeper into the forest, the shadows deepened, casting an eerie cloak over the forest. The sunlight filtered through the leaves, creating a mesmerising dance of dappled patterns on the forest floor. We stumbled upon a clearing and began to kiss, the sounds of the forest surrounded us, adding to the primal nature of the encounter. Our clothes were discarded in a frenzy of passion, and as our limbs tangled together, we embraced like wild animals. In that moment, nothing else existed. I pulled her roughly to the ground and entered her as our entwined bodies rolled and tumbled on the forest bed.

I gently traced the warmth and softness of her flesh with my fingertips, savouring the sensation as I slowly ran my hand along the curves of her body. With a final thrust, I emptied myself into her, feeling a rush of pure pleasure and connection. She let out a soft sigh as her fingernails dug into my back. As I kissed her neck, I gently placed my hand around it, feeling her raised pulse beneath my touch. As I continued to kiss and caress her, my other hand slowly made its way up to her neck. She buried her head into my shoulder and tightly coiled her arms and legs around me. As my hands tightened around her neck, a dark impulse consumed me, urging me to squeezed harder and harder. I used every ounce of strength that was in me. Her eyes bulged with terror, as if they were about to burst from their sockets. She struggled for a lot longer than I had expected, her entire being fighting against my grip. When her body went limp, I released my grip and slowly removed myself from her lifeless corpse. As I rolled off her, I let out a deep sigh of relief, but my heart ached with sadness at the thought of never seeing her again.

After getting dressed, I sat down on a tree stump to catch my breath. The sun's rays illuminated her naked corpse through the trees, she looked so peaceful.

'Ann, what a beautiful setting for your final resting place,' I whispered, as I walked over to where she lay. As I looked down at her lifeless body, I realised that killing Ann was a mistake, a big fucking mistake. As the saying goes, 'never shit on your own doorstep,' and I had certainly done just that. I had really fucked up this time. Fuck her anyway, I thought as I repeatedly kicked her lifeless body. This whole fucking mess was her fault. She had seduced me and led me into temptation, just like that devious whore Eve did to Adam all those years ago.

I struggled to drag her lifeless body through the dense undergrowth, her pale skin scraped and battered by the rough terrain. It was hard to believe that this same lifeless body had given me so much pleasure only moments ago. I came across a small hallow in the ground, noticing that the earth surrounding it was soft and loose. Without hesitation, I dropped to my knees and using my hands and a thick branch, I dug out some of the soft soil and undergrowth. I rolled Ann's body face first into her final resting place and then threw her clothes in on top of her, before covering her with the soil and undergrowth that lay around. Exhausted, I knelt next to her grave and sobbed uncontrollably, like a little boy who had just buried his mother.

It took me some time to find my way back onto the dirt track. I began to panic, as it felt like I was going around in circles. Eventually, I managed to get back on the track and ran to where my car was parked. I decided to avoid driving back down into Enniskerry village, as I was worried that Ann's missing person appeal would be sent out in the coming days. I didn't want to take any unnecessary risks, as I was concerned that someone might remember having seen us in the café or driving through the village and then later seeing me driving back alone.

The last thing I wanted was to become a person of interest in Ann's disappearance. So, instead of taking the usual route home, I decided to take the scenic route over the mountains. Unfortunately, I was too distracted to fully appreciate the breathtaking views.

The road crossing over the mountains was narrow, with a steep drop on the left-hand side. I was driving at a dangerous speed, and one wrong move could have easily sent me over the edge, and Ann would have been the least of my worries. As I drove, I tried to convince myself that most people were far too preoccupied living their own lives, to pay any attention to a random couple walking into a café for a spot of lunch. We would have looked like any other mother and son just out for a bite to eat.

As I lit a cigarette and rolled down the window, my mind drifted back to Ann's final resting place. The longer she remained undiscovered, the better. I wanted her to be devoured by the merciless jaws of nature, leaving nothing but scattered bones behind. So, if she was ever found, the truth would remain a mystery. As I drove over the mountains, a smile spread across my face. I flicked the cigarette butt out the window and cranked up the volume on the radio. As Jonny Cash's voice filled the car, I sang along with the man in black as I gazed out at the lush landscape of 'forty shades of green.'

Chapter 24

T he situation that I found myself in was precarious to say the least. Having sex with Ann, was one thing, but killing and disposing of her body was another matter entirely. It should never have happened. If she hadn't seduced me, she would still be alive, and I wouldn't be caught up in this terrible mess. It was all her fault. All she had to do was come to my house, clean it, and then leave, like she had done so many times before. But, no, she had behaved like a common street whore, teasing me and testing the waters to see how far she could push me. With her seductive ways, she had me trapped and tormented, with no hope of turning back.

'Well, Ann, look where you ended up, with all your foolish game playing. Lifeless, and covered in leaves and undergrowth, in a dark forest, waiting to be devoured by wild animals,' I said as I turned to face the vacant passenger seat.

'Am I losing my mind?' I whispered under my breath as I lit another cigarette, desperately trying to calm the chaos in my mind. I knew there was no turning back from the irreversible consequences of my actions.

When I arrived home, I immediately headed to the shower to wash off the dirt from digging Ann's shallow grave on my hands and knees. Just as I had finished getting dressed, the doorbell rang. 'For fuck's sake,' I muttered as I made my way down the stairs. I opened the door to find Terry, Ann's husband, standing before me. My heart almost stopped. What was he doing here? My mind raced as I struggled to compose myself. I knew that I needed to remain calm and act normal, so I forced a friendly smile and offered a handshake. Terry was short, grey-haired man in his fifties, or at least that's how he appeared. He had a naturally friendly face that always seemed to be smiling. If Terry was getting the same treatment from Ann that she had so willingly bestowed upon me, it was no wonder he always seemed so happy, I thought to myself. However, there were no smiles on his face as he stood before me. Instead, her wore a look of worry and concern.

'Terry, how are you?' I asked, after finally mustering up the courage to speak, while trying to appear as normal and relaxed as possible. As we stood facing each other, a thought crossed my mind: how many other men have murdered a woman and then found themselves chatting with their victim's husbands shortly afterwards? I imagined it couldn't be too many.

'I'm sorry for disturbing you, Father, but I am concerned about Ann. She hasn't returned home yet and she's not answering her phone. Did she happen to mention that she might be going somewhere after leaving your house?' He inquired. Fuck, I suddenly remembered that her phone and handbag were still in my car. Ann had hidden them under the passenger seat before we went for a walk in the forest, a walk that will haunt me forever. I had completely forgotten to dispose of them. It seems Ann had achieved her goal of keeping them out of sight, out of mind. I made a mental note to get rid of her phone and handbag later. I quickly averted my attention back towards Terry.

'No, Terry, Ann never mentioned anything to me about going anywhere. I drove her over to the supermarket to get some shopping. (Christ, I just realised that the bags of shopping were still in the boot.) When we got back, I left her here to finish off a few things while I went to the hospital to visit some of our sick parishioners, some of them are in a terrible state, the poor souls. When I arrived back home, Ann was gone,' I said, glancing at my watch. It was almost eight o'clock and the clear blue sky from earlier in the day had now darkened as the night settled in. I slowly brought my eyes up to meet his; knowing that the eyes never lie. It was clear that he knew something terrible had happened to his beloved Ann.

'Terry, would you like to come in and have a cup of tea?' I asked, hoping that he would decline my offer.

'No, Father, I can't. I need to find her. I have a gut feeling that something isn't right. I can feel it. I have been in touch with her family and most of her close friends, but no one has heard a word from her,' he said. As we stood facing each other, I couldn't even manage to string a couple of words together. I simply nodded my head, as if completely bewildered by what I was hearing.

'I dropped her off earlier, so I knew she was here,' he said, 'I called by a couple of hours ago, but there was no answer. This is completely out of character for her. I'm really worried, Father,' he added, his voice quivered with anxiety, rising in pitch as he bravely fought back the tears. As I faced the suffering husband of my latest victim, a pang of guilt consumed me. The sadness in his watery eyes left me with no choice but to insist that he come inside for a while.

'Terry, please come in, I insist,' I said, gesturing for him to enter. 'I'll ring around the hospitals and see if Ann has been admitted, due to an accident.' He simply nodded his head and walked straight past me and went into the kitchen. For fuck's sake, this is all I need at the moment, I thought as I switched on the kettle. Terry sat down at the kitchen table; he placed his elbows on the table and then buried his head into his hands, without uttering a single word.

I decided to forgo the tea; something stronger was required to deal with such delicate circumstances. I poured two generous glasses of brandy, placing one in front of Terry before taking a seat across from him at the table. I took a large sip, struggling to find the appropriate words to console my unwanted guest.

'I'm sure everything will be fine, Terry. She probably just forgot to mention that she had somewhere to go,' I said gesturing towards the glass of brandy in front of him. Terry slowly brought the glass to his lips and took a small sip, grimacing before setting it back down on the table. It was then that I noticed the little pioneer badge on his jacket. Jesus, a pioneer, another religious nut, no wonder Ann was gagging for it. Just drink the damn thing for fuck's sake, I thought to myself, struggling to suppress my rising temper.

If only he knew that just a few hours ago, I had fucked his precious little wife across the very table he's leading on. As I watched him suffer in silence, I couldn't believe how badly I had fucked up this time. Terry sat across from me, his head buried in his hands and his eyes closed, as if he were deep in prayer. Feeling uneasy, I drained my glass. What the hell was I thinking, inviting him into my home? It's been over an hour since he first sat down at the kitchen table. It's high time he got up and fucked off home. I already had more than enough on my own plate to deal with. And the last thing I needed was the burden of someone's else's problems, even if his suffering was directly linked to my actions. Within the last few hours, I had fucked, murdered, and buried my housekeeper. If all of that wasn't enough of a burden, I also found myself consoling her distraught husband who seemed to have glued himself to my kitchen table.

Sitting across from him in complete silence was a nightmare. I couldn't take it anymore. I abruptly stood up from the table, forcefully pushing my chair back, causing it to screech against the floor. He didn't even flinch. I told him that I was going to call a few of the hospitals, even though I knew it was a complete waste of time, as I already knew the reply that I would receive. But I needed to put on a show and make him think that I was concerned and doing whatever I could to help him in his time of need. On entering the sitting room, I lowered two large swigs of brandy straight from the bottle before making the senseless calls. I took a few deep breaths and another couple of swigs from the bottle to prepare myself before returning to Terry at the kitchen table.

'Anything?' He asked, looking up from the table, as I entered the kitchen.

'No, she hasn't been admitted to any of the hospitals,' I replied, struggling to play the part of the concerned friend and, more importantly, the role of a caring parish priest. I remained standing, poured myself another drink and drained it in one mouthful, he didn't even notice. His eyes remained fixed on the table, his grey head bent over, resting on his arms. He looked frail.

I sat back down at the table and gently placed my hand on Terry's shoulder. He slowly raised his head until our eyes met.

'Terry, do you think we should call the police?' I asked, I couldn't believe what I had just suggested. He hesitated for a few moments, staring down at his brandy as he swirled the glass in his hands. I wanted to remind him that the brandy was for drinking, not for staring into, but I held my tongue.

'Yes, Father, I think it's time,' he said faintly, as he reached into his jacket pocket and pulled out his phone. I left the room, feeling that he needed a little privacy. The last thing I wanted to hear was the poor man explaining that his good, God-fearing wife had gone missing.

Chapter 25

Half an hour later, the doorbell rang. I opened the door to find the expected guests: two police officers.

'Hello Father. I am Detective Sergeant Conroy, and this is my colleague, Office Halligan,' Conroy said, the more senior of the two, I assumed. I invited them inside and led them to the kitchen, where Terry was still seated at the table. The officers took seats on the opposite side of the table, facing Terry. I refilled the kettle and turned it on before taking my place at the head of the table, after all, it was my house. I remained silent, only speaking when spoken to, my presence was solely for moral support for one of my devoted parishioners in his time of need. When the kettle boiled, I made four cups of strong coffee and placed one in front of each of my three unwanted guests. I then returned to my own seat, cradling the cup between my hands as if trying to warm them.

Detective Conroy asked the questions, while the junior officer kept himself busy scribbling down every word that left Terry's mouth. I remained silent and just listened; my eyes fixed on Terry as he described his missing wife. The pain was deeply etched onto his face; he truly was suffering. I never realised that one human being could be so much in love with another human being, until that night. Their voices became nothing more than a muffled noise in the background. I was bored and restless, my mind drifted back to the events that took place earlier that day. A vision of Ann wrapped tightly around me as we lay on the forest bed, the hot midday sun beating down on us through the trees, played out in my mind. It was hard to believe that they were talking about the same woman. If Terry only knew how his wife really liked it, the poor bastard, I thought to myself as I finished my coffee.

The two officers sat at my kitchen table for almost an hour before they stood up, simultaneously, like a pair of well-trained synchronised swimmers, to take their leave. They shook hands with both Terry and me, promising to be in touch soon. I walked them to the front door and thanked them once again for coming before closing the door behind them. As I returned to the kitchen, I saw Terry standing up and putting on his jacket. Thank fuck.

'I'm sorry Father, I didn't mean to stay for so long. I hope I haven't kept you from anything important,' he said. He appeared and sounded defeated, as if his entire world had just crumbled.

'No, Terry, you haven't kept me from anything. I am here to help you in any way that I can,' I replied.

'I'm very grateful, Father. I better get going just in case Ann arrives home and I'm not there, she'd be worried,' he said. I wanted to tell him that there was no fucking chance of that happening, but once again, I held my tongue.

'No need to thank me, Terry. That's what I'm here for. Now that you have my number, if Ann is at home when you get there, please let me know. And remember, you can call me anytime, day or night. My phone is always on,' I said.

As we shook hands, I could see the pain in his eyes. It was as if he knew that he would never see Ann alive again. I waved him off, closed the door, and returned to the kitchen, where I finished his practically untouched brandy and lit a cigarette, taking a long drag, as I asked myself, 'What the fuck had I done?' I knew that I needed to remain calm and collected from this point on. There was no room for mistakes or slip-ups. I picked up the bottle of brandy from the table and made my way towards the stairs, knowing that a long, sleepless night awaited me.

Chapter 26

The following morning, I woke suddenly, feeling a little shell-shocked. As I struggled to start a new day, Ann's handbag and her phone were the only two things on my mind. That was, until I tried to move, my head was throbbing, making it difficult to even sit up and my throat felt parched and scratchy, begging for water. I sat on the edge of the bed, trying to piece together the events of the previous night. I unscrewed the cap off the bottle of painkillers that permanently sat on my bedside table, and with the help of a glass of water, I swallowed a handful of pills.

It felt as though my body relied heavily on the combination of painkillers, alcohol, and nicotine just to keep functioning. I only ate the odd morsel of food when my stomach cried out for it. The weight of guilt and regret settled heavily on me, overshadowing the hangover from hell that was slowly crucifying me. How had I let myself reach this point? I had evolved into a serial killer, plain and simple. The realisation hit me hard, but I had gone well past the point of no return. I couldn't erase what I had done; there was no turning back the clock.

'Pull yourself together, for fuck's sake, and stick to the plan,' I told myself as I stood under the shower.

I had completely forgotten about Ann's handbag and phone, until Terry mentioned that she wasn't answering her phone. It was only then that I remembered Ann putting the phone into her handbag before sliding it under the passenger seat of the car. So that it would be out of sight from any potential opportunists passing by. Ann had always been cautious and had a keen sense for identifying potential risks and taking the necessary precautions to prevent them from happening. However, on that fateful morning in my kitchen, I don't know what came over her. Perhaps it was pure animal instinct, but she lost all control of her usually reserved self, and her recklessness ultimately led to her demise. It proved to be fatal.

After retrieving Ann's handbag from underneath the car seat, I made my way back inside the house, away from any prying eyes. Once safely inside, I opened the bag and found her phone. The screen displayed seventy-eight missed calls, most of which were from Terry. The ten most recent calls had been made within the last hour. I quickly dismantled the phone, throwing the battery in the bin. I then discovered a nice little bonus of ninety-five euro in her purse, which went straight into my back pocket. Well, in all fairness, she no longer had any use for it. I then carefully put everything back into her handbag and placed it in a black refuse sack, which I buried in the corner of the shed under a pile of old junk, while making a mental note to dispose of it properly later, when I wasn't under so much pressure. I then went into the sitting room, and knelt down by the fireplace, struck a match and held it to the firelighters until they caught fire. The fire was always left set and ready to be lit. A habit instilled in me by my mother at a young age, a chore that needed to be done before I left for school every morning. I watched, as the Sim card and the other plastic parts of Ann's phone melted in the heat of the orange flames.

A quick glance at my watch told me that I still had a little over an hour before I needed to be at the church to say the morning mass. As I looked at the time, my mind was consumed with the events from the previous day and night. The enormity of my reckless behaviour had only just begun to hit me. The taking of Ann's life was a huge mistake, and as for her henpecked husband, as far as he was concerned, I was the last known person to have seen his wife alive. He had even said it to the police, right in front of me, as if I wasn't there, as we sat around my kitchen table. I was concerned that the police might have me ear marked as the prime suspect in Ann's disappearance, all because of Terry's loose words.

There was no denying that I had fucked up big time. Although in my defence, Ann would never have been able to keep what happened between us a secret. My back was pretty much against the wall; she had left me with no choice in the matter, she had to go. I was convinced there was no incriminating evidence that could link me to Ann's disappearance.

As I walked out onto the altar to say the morning mass, the first face that I saw was Terry's. He looked terrible, completely devastated, as if he had aged ten years since he had left my house the previous night. His watery eyes never left the ground throughout the entire service. When the mass ended, I walked down to him and gently placed my hand on his shoulder and asked,

'Are you okay, Terry?' my voice barely above a whisper. With a heavy sigh, he slowly raised his head until our eyes met. His face appeared ashen, and his features were drawn, giving him a haggard appearance. He shook his head and replied,

'No, I'm not okay. Ann's gone, and I don't know what to do.' I struggled to find the right words to say. I couldn't speak; my mouth was dry as I looked into his tear-filled eyes. Did this broken, dishevelled man standing before me truly believe that I had something to do with his wife's disappearance? We stood in silence for a moment, neither of us able to utter another single word. Eventually, Terry lowered his gaze back towards the floor. I stood there, overwhelmed by a sense of helplessness. There was nothing more I could have done or said to ease his suffering. With a heavy heart, I watched him sink deeper into his sorrow, without a lifeline to cling onto. I quickly turned and made my way back to the sacristy.

Chapter 27

After saying the morning mass, I left the church and spent the rest of the afternoon at the hospital, where I celebrated another mass in the secluded chapel that was hidden away in a quiet corner of the building. However, I was only there in body, my mind was elsewhere consumed with thoughts of the worst possible outcomes. Following the brief mass, I aimlessly roamed from one ward to another, providing prayers and administering Holy Communion to the bedridden. I loathed the sight of old, sick people, their frail, wrinkled bodies and laboured breathing made me recoil in disgust.

I disliked everything about hospitals: the smells, the sickness, and the forced smiles on the faces of the overworked nurses. Exhaustion had slowly crept up on me, and I was still feeling slightly hungover as I wandered through the hospital. My stomach growled, crying out for food. I glanced at my watch; it had just gone four o'clock in the afternoon. 'Where did the day go?' I muttered to myself as I entered the hospital café and ordered a coffee and a toasted ham and cheese sandwich. Just as the waitress approached my table with a tray and a smile, my phone rang.

'Hello, Father. This is Detective Sergeant Conroy. My colleague and I were at your house last night to take a statement from a Mr. Terry O'Rielly, regarding his wife's disappearance,' he said. My heart skipped a beat, maybe even two, as I almost choked on my sandwich. What the fuck does he want? I thought, quickly pulling myself together.

'Hello, Officer Conroy, do you have any updates on Ann?' I asked, trying to remain calm. I'm sure there is a significant difference between the ranks of 'Officer' and 'Detective Sergeant.' I had hoped to piss him off by referring to him as a mere officer.

'No, I'm afraid we have no news to report as of yet. I was calling to see if I could drop by your house later this evening to go over a few things from last night?' he asked. What the fuck is going on? I thought to myself. He must know or suspect something; otherwise, there would be no reason for him to want to talk to me again, and so soon. It hasn't even been twenty four hours since he left my house. My mind was racing as I quickly realised that I had remained silent on the phone for much longer than I should have. I took a deep breath to steady myself before replying,

'I am free any time after seven-thirty this evening.'

'I thought I had lost you there for a moment, Father. Seven-thirty is perfect, I'll see you then,' he said before the line went dead. Why on earth did the police want to speak to me again? I thought, feeling agitated, as my temper rose.

How fucking dare, him, practically summoning me for questioning. Does he not realise that I am an esteemed parish priest and a well-respected pillar within the community? No one ever questions the clergy; we are untouchable. Who the hell does he think he is? Lost in a blind fury, I cursed Detective Conroy, as I pushed my unfinished sandwich away from me, he had turned me off my food. I quickly came to my senses when I realised that I was still sitting in the hospital café, surrounded by people. In a rush, I stood up and left the café, my eyes fixed on the ground until I was outside in the car park.

Chapter 28

Seven-thirty came and went, without any sign of the police arriving. I felt both annoyed and relieved. At seven-fifty-three, the doorbell rang. 'Here we go,' I muttered as I headed for the front door.

'Hello, Father. Sorry we are running a little late. Thank you for agreeing to see us. This is my colleague, Detective Maguire,' Conroy said, looking chuffed with himself as he introduced his attractive little blond sidekick.

'No problem at all, please come in,' I replied, trying to maintain a calm and composed demeanour. The three of us entered the kitchen, just as we had the night before. My heart raced as I turned on the kettle, and cold beads of sweat ran down the length of my spine.

'So how can I help you?' I asked, hoping my voice didn't betray my nerves.

'I just want to go over a few questions with you from last night,' Conroy said, his tone was serious, and the look on his weathered face was stern. I nodded and placed a cup of coffee in front of each of them before taking my seat at the opposite side of the table, avoiding eye contact. As soon as my ass hit the seat, the questioning began.

'Father, did you and Ann go anywhere else after leaving the shopping centre yesterday?' Conroy asked, his serious tone still evident. Detective Sergeant Conroy had returned to my house a very different man. Last night, he had played the role of a sympathetic listener, but within a few hours, his demeanour and tone had shifted dramatically. It was hard to believe that this was the same man I had sat across the table from just a short while ago. Now, he seemed to be indirectly accusing me, pointing the finger in a roundabout way, or was he just putting on a show, for his pretty little sidekick? I wondered.

'No, we came straight back here,' I replied, trying to remain calm despite the difficult circumstances.

'Did Ann mention anything about going somewhere or meeting someone after she left here?' Conroy asked, repeating the same questions he had asked me the previous night.

'No, she didn't mention anything. We came back here after getting some shopping, and then Ann finished off the remaining housework. When she was done, we had a coffee and chatted, as we usually do. She left around three-thirty, I explained. Conroy nodded to his sidekick when I mentioned the time of Ann's supposed departure from my house. She quickly jotted something down in her notebook.

'Okay, Father, let's recap. We are trying to trace Ann's last know steps. According to you, Ann left your house at approximately three-thirty yesterday afternoon and you didn't go anywhere else together after returning from the shopping centre. Is that correct? Conroy asked. I didn't like where this line of questioning was headed.

'Yes, that's correct,' I replied, while trying to quell my rising temper.

'And you haven't seen or heard from Ann since she left your house yesterday? He asked. I felt a surge of frustration rising up inside of me as I sat across from them. Was Conroy trying to trip me up, or put words in my mouth? I raised my head and stared into his piercing gaze and replied as calmly as I could,

'No, I haven't seen or heard from Ann since she left here yesterday.' My mouth was dry, and I was becoming anxious, struggling to keep my emotions in check. These police officers were trained to pick up on the slightest thing, I needed to keep it altogether.

Does this arrogant little fucker actually know something? Or maybe their line of questioning was meant to throw me off. I couldn't figure out their game plan; every word that left my mouth was written down by the blond sidekick. Conroy gave me a smug look as he stared across the table at me. All I could do was try to maintain my composure and not let Conroy's demeanour affect me.

'We're just making sure that we have all the facts we need to aid us in our investigation. I would hate to miss anything that might hinder us along the way,' he said. I did not like this Detective Conroy character at all. I simply nodded, hoping that my body language wasn't giving away any vital clues or arousing suspicion.

'Okay, Father, that's all for now. Thank you for your cooperation and time. We'll be in touch if there are any new developments,' he said, his serious tone softening slightly. I shook hands with both of them before we made our way to the front door. As they left, I wished them a safe night and closed the door behind them, although my true thoughts were far from that. With my back firmly pressed against the door, I slid down onto the floor and buried my head in my hands. After realising that I had given them a completely different story, than the one I had told Ann's husband, Terry.

Chapter 29

Two days had passed since my last visit from the police. I hadn't heard a single word from them. Well, as they say, no news is good news. I was on edge, or rather completely paranoid, if the truth be told. Was I a suspect? Were the police watching my every move, just waiting in the wings, ready to pounce when I slip up? The uncertainty was eating away at me, leaving me anxious and restless.

tried to carry out my daily run-of-the-mill priestly duties in my usual relaxed, lay-back manner. However, despite my outward appearance of calmness, internally I was struggling and falling apart at the seams. I was unsure of how much longer I could maintain this façade. The pressure was becoming unbearable, and I felt as though all eyes were on me. I was convinced that Detective Sergeant Conroy had a photo of me pinned to a board in an incident room, with prime suspect written in thick red marker, just like you see in the movies.

Saying the ten o'clock mass every morning became a tedious task. The same went for all the other duties that I had to perform. The hospital and house calls, the school visits, christenings, weddings, and funerals. I approached them all with such an intense loathing. My monotonous and unfulfilling life as a clergyman was draining me of my energy and passion. I felt the weight of these negative effects bearing down on me.

As I stood at the pulpit, head bowed, ready to deliver my well-rehearsed homily. After a brief moment of silence to gather my thoughts, I slowly raised my head and scanned the church. More than half the pews remained empty, it was a sign of the times, I thought to myself. However, what caught my attention and made me do a double-take, was the absence of Terry, Ann's husband. He wasn't in his usual spot. It fascinated me how the regular old-timers would always sit in the same places every morning, just like regulars at a pub, who have their designated stools at the bar and would be very upset if someone else occupied them upon their arrival. I proceeded to scan the church from my vantage point of the pulpit. Terry was nowhere in sight, not a good sign, I thought, as I began my homily. After the service concluded, I decided to swing by Terry's house and pay him a visit, a sort of courtesy call. After all, I needed to keep up the pretence of playing the dual role of concerned priest and caring friend.

When Terry opened the front door, I got a terrible shock as our eyes met. It seemed as though he had undergone a strange metamorphosis overnight. The once fit and sprightly man, who rose early every morning and walked his dog, regardless of the weather, now appeared hunched over and dishevelled. This sudden drastic change in his physical appearance was difficult to fathom in such a short period of time.

Christ, he must have really loved her, I thought as I followed him into the kitchen. He wore a few days of heavy growth on his face, and the rank odour emanating from him suggested that he hadn't showered in a while. He put the kettle on and then sank into an armchair next to the fireplace. When the kettle boiled, I made two cups of tea, the milk in the fridge had gone off, so we were left with no choice but to drink it black. I handed Terry a cup before settling into the armchair across from him, which I assumed was Ann's usual spot.

He stared blankly into the empty fire grate, never once lifting or turning his head in my direction. The heavy suffocating silence that hung between us was unbearable to sit through. I did my best to make small talk, but it was a complete waste of time, as he was miles away. As I watched Terry's blank expression and heard the clock ticking away in the background, I couldn't help but feel a heavy weight of guilt settle in my chest. I had not only taken his wife's life, but also his will to live. Fifteen slow and painful minutes dragged on, with not a single word escaping his lips. Enough, I said to myself as I got to my feet. I thanked Terry for the tea that I had made while quickly concocting some cock and bull story about having to attend a very important meeting and that I must be on my way. He simply nodded his head, still lost in a trance-like state, his gaze never left the fireplace. I let myself out.

Chapter 30

That night, I was restless. The image of Terry slumped in his armchair, haunted me. I was also fully convinced that bastard Detective Conroy was onto me. My mind drifted from one unpleasant scenario to another. The thought of a long prison sentence terrified me. Fuck that, I had already served hard time in the seminary, and I was determined to never be imprisoned behind large granite walls again. Once again, sleep eluded me as I lay in bed with my eyes wide open. My mind was consumed by the vivid and gruesome image of Ann's lifeless body, lying face down in a shallow grave. I also couldn't shake the intense feeling of Detective Conroy's piercing gaze, while his pretty little sidekick frantically scribbled down every word that left my mouth.

There was no point lying in bed tormenting myself. Realising that it was going to be another sleepless night, I quickly dressed and then made my way to the kitchen. As I lit a cigarette, I tried to distract myself, but my mind was flooded with a tsunami of stress and anxiety. It wasn't long before frustration took over and I found myself pacing the hallway. I was unable to relax or calm down; I felt the need to take action. Fuelled by a sudden surge of adrenaline, I grabbed my coat from the rack and left the house. Twenty-seven minutes later, I found myself parked in the seedy underbelly of the city's red-light district without considering the potential dangers, what if Detective Conroy was following me? Simple answer, I'd be fucked. There's only one reason a man would be snooping around this part of the city at night, and it wasn't to admire the splendour of the Georgian architecture. As I rolled down the window and lit a cigarette, my eyes were drawn to the deep, velvety night sky. The warm, humid air enveloped me as I exhaled the cigarette smoke, creating a hazy cloud that lingered in the

She lay curled up at my feet, completely at my mercy. I dragged her to the back of the car and threw her into the boot before pulling out of the laneway and onto the main road. Half an hour later, I pulled into the car park at the foot of the walkway that led up to the ruins of the notorious Hell Fire Club. The old, eerie building had always fascinated me, ever since I had visited it on a school tour many years ago. The stories of debauchery, human sacrifice, and the Devil himself appearing on a stormy night always captured my imagination.

Upon opening the boot, I realised she was still breathing. Which was perfect, as the night was still young. My twisted and malevolent mind revelled in the thought of her suffering, relishing the idea of her begging for mercy before meeting her inevitable end. However, removing her from the boot was no easy task, she fell to the ground with a thud, her limbs were heavy and sluggish, as if they were made of solid lead, making her almost impossible to lift. In a fit of pure frustration, I unleashed a series of brutal kicks to her well-maintained body, each one eliciting a faint cry from her. I reached down and firmly grasped her hair and pulled her up onto her feet. She was dazed and leaned into me as I placed my arm around her, struggling to hold her upright as we began to walk. She was completely disoriented and had no idea where she was or who she was with.

She had a deep, nasty cut above her left eye, causing blood to smear across the entire left side of her face. I became frustrated with her as she struggled to remain upright, and in a fit of anger I drove my clenched fist hard into the side of her bloodied face, before throwing her over my shoulders. The walk from the car park up to the old ruin wasn't that far, but carrying a woman slumped across my shoulders required a marathon effort to cover such a short distant. Once inside the eerie ruin, I dropped her to the ground, causing her to let out a groan as she landed hard. Exhausted, I collapsed to my knees. Gasping for air, I rolled onto my back, my muscles throbbed with an intense, searing pain that felt like they were being ripped apart from the inside.

'Where am I?' She asked weakly, her voice reduced to a faint whisper. She rambled on for a bit, her voice was faint, and her words barely audible. I ignored her, as I struggled to regain my breath. After a few minutes, my laboured breathing returned to somewhat normal. Slowly, I rose to my feet, my legs throbbing in agony. I dragged her limp body by the ankles to the far, shadowy corner of the ruin. I stood still, immersed in the darkness as I absorbed my surroundings. A dense, stifling silence filled the air, suffocating any noise that dared to break it. The crumbling walls, worn down by centuries of neglect, exuded a musty scent of decay and dampness that clung to my nostrils and filled my lungs with every breath. My heart raced as I heard the frantic scurrying of rats, unseen but definitely present.

Although the old ruin appeared empty, I sensed a lingering presence. Shadows flickered and swirled, as if they were alive and taunting me, creating an eerie and unsettling atmosphere. I believed that a malevolent deity lurked among the ominous darkness, watching my every move, eagerly anticipating the depraved acts I was about to inflict upon this vile whore. I refused to disappoint them. She began mumbling to herself, like a drunk in the corner of a pub at the end of the night. That was, until my boot connected with the side of her face, the sickening thud silenced her. She lay motionless on the ground, her once delicate features now marred by my brutality.

After taking a short breather, I left the ruin and made my way towards the wooded area. I gathered as many sticks and branches as my tired arms could carry, before returning to the crumbling remains of the abandoned building where she lay curled up on the cold, hard ground. Once back inside, I released my grip on the wood, the branches and sticks fell to the ground and scattered around my feet. As I knelt down beside her, I lightly pressed my fingertips against her neck, there was still a slight pulse. I then quickly removed her clothes and brought them over to the pile of wood.

I inhaled deeply, savouring the bitter taste of the cigarette as it filled my lungs. Her time had come, I flicked the lighter and held the solitary flame to her blouse, watching as it quickly engulfed in fire. I placed the burning blouse on the ground, adding the rest of her clothing on top. The sticks and branches I had gathered were dry, and they burned quickly as I continued to add to the growing fire. With a sinister smile on my face, I watched the vibrant orange flames dance before me as I warmed my hands. I made several more trips to the woods, the cold night air sent a chill through me as I gathered a large pile of wood to ensure I had enough to finish the task before me.

By the time the fire had reached a substantial size, her pulse had disappeared. It was unfortunate, as I had been looking forward to the sound of her screams as she burned and melted amongst the flames. With great effort, I heaved her lifeless body onto the bright, orange flames. Kneeling by her side, I retrieved a large kitchen knife from inside my overcoat and watched momentarily as her body slowly burned. With one final glance, I drove the knife deep into her chest. Her body shook violently as the flames rose up around her, causing me to fall backwards. For a brief moment, I feared that she had returned to life, her spirit seeking retribution for having been so cruelly taken from this world. I quickly regained my composure and, in one swift movement, I rolled her burning body back onto the blazing funeral pyre. The flames consumed her, and the smell of her burning flesh filled the air, making me realise the gravity of what I had just done. The haunting sight of her burning body would stay with me long after the fire had burnt out.

With a trembling hand, I reached down and grasped the wooden handle of the blood-soaked knife that lay on the ground and then proceeded with the sacrifice. I removed her perfectly sculpted breasts with relative easy, what a waste, I thought, before tossing them into the hungry flames. I struggled to cut deeper into her chest. It took several blows of the hammer to break through her ribs. The smell of charred flesh filled the air as I finally removed her blackened heart. Letting the knife fall to the ground with a clatter. I stood tall, brandishing her heart up to the shadows, offering it to the unseen spirits that lurked within. I could feel their malevolent presence as I held her heart aloft, my hands drenched in her tainted-blood as I waited for them to revel in my offering. As the ritual came to an end, I cried out to the forsaken spirits, entombed within these cursed walls. I then tossed the lifeless organ into the searing flames and watched as it shrivelled and blackened before my eyes.

As I stood in the eerie silence, with my blood-soaked hands outstretched, I was completely immersed in the atmosphere. The burning wood cracked and sent sparks flying across the ruin. The orange flames illuminated my dark silhouette against the back wall, making me look frightening as I moved my outstretched hands to and fro. I let the eerie stillness of the night, envelope me as I inhaled the scent of burning wood and flesh. With the ritual over, I began to place more wood on top of her burning body, I was secretly hoping to catch a glimpse of one of the spirits who may have witnessed my offering. Completely drained and breathless, I collapsed in front of the roaring flames. A sense of satisfaction washed over me as I watched the vile creature's lifeless body burn in the crackling, orange flames that danced before me.

The fire voraciously devoured each piece of wood that I threw into it, its flames reaching higher and higher. In a desperate attempt to reduce her to a charred, unrecognisable heap of ash, I kept adding more and more wood to the fire. The putrid stench of burning flesh filled the old ruin, causing my stomach to churn and bile to rise in my throat. I stumbled outside, my body convulsing as I retched violently, unable to contain the revulsion rising within me. I dropped to my knees onto the cool and dewy grass, feeling the cold droplets of the early morning dew seep through my clothes and onto my skin. I looked down at the silent city below, its streets and buildings cloaked in a deep, inky darkness that seemed to swallow everything in its path. The city seemed to hold its breath, as if waiting for something to break the eerie silence.

I woke suddenly, feeling cold and damp. I quickly got to my feet and ran back inside the old ruin. The fire had long since fizzled out. Christ, how long had I been asleep? All that remained was her badly burnt corpse. As I stood over her charred remains, a wave of nausea washed over me, I couldn't believe what that vile whore had made me do. What lay before me was disgusting and unrecognisable. The charred mess on the ground looked more alien than human. I turned away and placed my trembling hands against the cold, damp wall for support. I tried to vomit, but there was nothing left inside me. Standing in the cold, dark ruin bent over and dry retching under the watchful eyes of the dark spirits that never made it out alive, I longed for one of them to reach out to me. Their tormented souls were trapped within these cursed walls for all eternity.

I took one last look at what remained of the woman, who just a few hours ago was still beautiful. Now, she lay before me as nothing more than a foul-smelling carcass. Glancing down at my watch, I saw that it was four-twenty in the morning.

'Christ, it's late,' I muttered to myself, as I turned away from the grotesque sight of her smouldering body. There was no point in trying to hide the charred mess at this late hour, it would be daylight soon. A strange sense of calm washed over me as I pulled out of the car park, leaving her corpse and the eerie ruin behind. I quickly left the dark, narrow winding road and merged out onto the motorway. However, for some unexplained reason, I found myself turning the car around at the next exit and heading in the direction of Killiney beach.

The car park across from Killiney train station was completely empty, which was no surprise considering the ungodly hour of the morning. After parking, I walked towards the dark water. I stopped a few feet from the water's edge and undressed, never once taking my eyes off the imposing cross that stood on the top of Bray Head. The only sound was the gentle lapping of the water against the shore. I stood at the water's edge, gazing out at the vast ocean. The cold, dark water washed over my feet and then receded with the tide, repeating the same motion over and over.

With a deep, slow breath, I finally mustered the courage to wade into the water. I closed my eyes and surrendered to the icy embrace. As I continued walking, the water grew colder, causing me to take quick, shallow breaths in an attempt to fight against the chill. When the water reached my neck, I stopped and stood in silence, the dark water bobbing just beneath my chin. I was certain that I had arrived at the exact spot where the beautiful girl with no name had drew her final breath. I opened my eyes and gazed out across the serene yet formidable ocean, feeling a sense of awe and respect for its vastness and power. The distance line where the sky meets the sea, seemed to beckon me, but I was fully aware of its merciless nature towards those who dare to enter and explore its depths.

My teeth chattered violently, and my body trembled uncontrollably from the freezing water. I turned back to face the shore and decided to make my way out of the water. Just as I began to move, a strong breeze appeared out of nowhere and swept around me like a vortex, trapping me within its grasp. Then I heard it, the voice of the beautiful girl with no name.

'Murderer, murderer, murderer,' she whispered gently as the breeze encircled me. Fear rose within me as I closed my eyes and tried to convince myself that it was just my imagination. I opened my eyes and began to run, but the weight of the water held me back. I struggled until I finally reached the shoreline. Exhausted, I collapsed onto the sand.

My freezing naked body was coated in a layer of frigid, wet sand, causing me to shiver violently. As I looked back out over the ocean, the water stretched out before me, still and dark as a mirror, reflecting the moon's gentle glow, all was quiet. There was no strong breeze, no voice, nothing only complete silence and stillness. What the fuck just happened? Could I really have imagined the whole thing? No, it was real. I felt the breeze upon my skin, as it encircled me. I clearly heard her voice; it was unmistakable. It was her, calling out to me from the depths of the ocean. I struggled to stand up, my body trembling, I was cold, confused, and frightened. As I made my way over to where my clothes lay, I cursed my worthless whore of a mother. It was all her fault. She had created this monster that I had evolved into. My wet shivering body was covered in sand, making it difficult to dress. While dressing, my eyes remained fixed on the dark, unforgiving water. The same dark, water that had taken the beautiful girl away under its waves.

My hands shook as I struggled to light a cigarette, the flame dancing wildly in front of me. 'What the fuck just happened?' I asked myself as I inhaled deeply. Am I losing my mind? Going stir crazy? Was my mind just fucking with me, playing a little game, just to see how I would react? Or had that vile whore's evil spirit just paid me a visit. I drove home in a daze, my mind still reeling from what had just happened, my knuckles white from gripping the steering wheel so tightly.

Upon entering my house, I wearily made my way into the kitchen. My mind was still in a state of turmoil, and I was completely exhausted. Once in the kitchen, I noticed the half-empty bottle of whiskey still sitting on the table from the night before. Without hesitation, I unscrewed the top and threw it into the bin, I knew I wouldn't be needing it again. As I raised the bottle towards my mouth, I stared vacantly out from behind the kitchen window, into nothing but complete darkness. The thought of another sleepless night loomed over me.

Chapter 31

The following morning, I was abruptly awoken by someone repeatedly ringing the doorbell. I turned to face the alarm clock, wincing as the bright red numbers pierced through my closed eyelids, intensifying the throbbing in my head. The clock read Ten forty-three. Fuck, I jumped up out of bed, which was not a good idea, considering my fragile state. As my feet landed on the floor, I stumbled over the empty whiskey, its contents long gone, which explained my ferocious headache.

As I descended the stairs, the incessant ringing persisted. With my eyes barely open and a pounding headache, I reluctantly opened the front door to find five members of the blue rinse militia staring back at me. This was the last thing I needed.

'Are you alright, Father?' inquired Maura, the self-appointed leader of the blue rinse militia. Maura had taken over as chairperson of the parish committee after my mother's passing. She was just another busybody with nothing better to do, other than stick her nose into other people's business. She was a right pain in the arse. Maura always made a point of introducing herself as the chairperson of the parish committee, as if anyone actually gave a flying fuck.

'Good morning, ladies. Yes, I'm fine. I apologise for my absence at the morning mass. I am feeling a little under the weather. I spent most of the night up vomiting. I must have eaten something that didn't agree with me. And, at some ungodly hour, I must have fallen into a deep sleep. I never heard my alarm going off,' I replied. Maura let out a sigh of relief and said,

'Thank God you're alright Father. We were all so worried about you.' The other four women, all dressed in floral dresses with matching head scarf's, stood in silence, nodding their heads in agreement with their fearsome leader. They reminded me of those silly little bobblehead dogs that people put on their dashboards, constantly nodding away while you're driving.

'Thank you for your concern, but I assure you I'm feeling a little better. Once again, I apologise for sleeping through the morning mass,' I said politely, through gritted teeth, wishing they would just leave.

'Would you like us to come in and make you a nice pot of tea and some toast? That's always good for an upset tummy,' said Maura, looking and sounding ever so concerned. That would have been the last fucking thing I needed. Ideally, I would have loved for the five, nosey old bags, to just fuck off and die.

'No, thank you, ladies. I'll be fine. I really appreciated the offer, but I must excuse myself now, as I am way behind on the rest of today's busy schedule,' I replied. Maura chimed in, 'Are you sure Father? It would be no trouble at all. We could fix you up a little something to eat, it would do you the world of good.'

'No, honestly, I'm fine, thank you. I truly appreciate your kindness and concern. Thank you for checking in on me, I am very grateful to all of you,' I replied. As much as I wanted to tell them to fuck off and leave me alone, I resisted the urge and kept the thought to myself.

'Okay, Father. If you're sure we'll be on our way and leave you in peace,' said Maura. Thank fuck ran through my mind.

'Thanks again, ladies, for checking on me, it's very much appreciated,' I said, with a forced smile as I closed the door. I then slowly dragged myself to the kitchen, where I swallowed a handful of painkillers and then put the kettle on. My body was craving for a jolt of caffeine to shake off the morning grogginess and help me wake up. I scooped two heaped spoonful's of coffee into a mug and then poured in the boiling water. Upon opening the fridge, I realised there was no milk. I then checked the bread bin, no fucking bread either. My day seemed to be going from bad to worst. All I really wanted was to go back to bed, but I quickly dismissed the idea. Since I was already up and about, I thought it would be better to keep moving.

On entering the bathroom, I caught a glimpse of my reflection in the mirror. Christ, I looked rough. I splashed cold water on my face and attempted to tame my unruly hair, which was in bad need of a trim. Realising that there were hardly any groceries left in the house, I decided it was time to take a trip to the local corner shop. Ann usually handled all of my shopping, but with her gone, I needed to start taking care of myself.

Eight minutes later, I found myself standing at the shop's counter, handing over a loaf of bread, a carton of milk, and a copy of the local rag to Joseph, the owner. He had been sitting behind that very same counter for the past twenty-three years, or so he claimed. He seemed to take great pride in this fact and loved to share it with anyone who was willing to listen. I wasn't in the mood for his usual bullshit small talk. I just wanted to quickly grab the few things that I needed and be on my way.

'Good morning, Father. How are you keeping?' asked Joseph. Here we fucking go again. It was the same conversation every time I entered his godforsaken shop.

'I'm grand, Joseph, and how about yourself?' I asked.

'Oh, you know, can't complain. Sure no one listens anyway,' he said with an exaggerated sigh.

'I suppose you're right,' I forced a laugh.

'Did you hear about that young woman they found at the Hell Fire Club this morning?' He asked. I felt my knees go weak.

'No, I didn't hear the news this morning. I've had a bit of a hectic morning. What happened?' I asked, attempting to appear interested and curious.

'Apparently, a woman out walking her dog this morning discovered a badly burnt body up at the Hell Fire Club,' he informed me. Of course she did, it's always an early morning dog walker who stumbles upon these things, I thought to myself, as I struggled to maintain my composure.

'My god, that's terrible,' I replied, feeling myself growing weaker by the second.

'It's truly shocking. Sure, society as a whole seems to have gone completely mad. There's no sense of law and order, no respect whatsoever, nothing or no one is safe anymore,' Joseph said, with another sigh, shaking his head. I just nodded in agreement.

'Although whoever carried out the murder was not very clever. The murder weapon was discovered at the crime scene,' he stated. My heart raced as I struggled to remain standing on my trembling legs. I needed to get the hell out of his shop immediately before he noticed anything suspicious about my behaviour. Feeling weak, I leaned on the counter for support, fearing that I might collapse and hit the ground. The knife, how could I have been so fucking careless?

'Are you okay Father? You don't seem right all of a sudden,' Joseph asked with concern. I scolded myself, urging to regain composure.

'I'm fine, thank you. It's just difficult to comprehend that one human being could commit such a heinous crime against another. It's moments like these that truly challenge my faith in humanity and even in God. And I'm not ashamed to admit it. We live in a terrible dark world Joseph,' I replied, attempting to convey a sense of sadness and grief.

'Are you sure you're feeling alright? Would you like to come on through and have a seat in the back until you feel better? Mary will make you a nice cup of tea, or I can fix you something a little stronger if you think it might help,' Joseph offered.

'No, thank you. I'll be on my way,' I replied, managing to regain some strength.

'Would you like me to walk you home? It would be no trouble at all,' he kindly offered. I took a deep breath and steadied myself before responding.

'No, Joseph, I appreciate the offer, but I'll be fine, thank you,' I replied, before turning away from the counter and leaving the shop.

I left the shop and kept my head down, walking as fast as I could until I was safely behind my locked front door. How could I have been so fucking stupid? My fingerprints would be all over the knife. I walked into the kitchen and placed the bag of shopping on the table. My mind raced as I began to panic, and my pounding headache wasn't helping the situation at all. My punishment was well overdue. Slowly, I trudged up the stairs before entering the bedroom and removing the whip from the top shelf of the wardrobe.

As I stood in front of the tall, full-length mirror, revealing every inch of my nakedness, I examined the scars that marred by battered body. They had healed nicely since my last whipping. Despite the dark red and purple welts that still covered my skin, I refused to let them break me. They served as a constant reminder of the pain and suffering

I had endured. Each scar that ran along my skin was a testament to my inner strength and resilience. As the leather tore through my flesh, I bit down hard on my lower lip, drawing blood. Tears cascaded down my cheeks, as the intense sting seared through my body. The memory of her blood on my hands and her charred remains at my feet haunted me. The usual ten lashes paled in comparison to the heinous crime I had committed. As the whip tore into my skin for the sixteenth time, I collapsed to the floor, bloodied, battered, and in agonising pain. I curled up in a ball and wept bitterly.

Shivering in the cold, I lay there for what felt like an eternity. Eventually, I managed to get up off the floor. My cuts were jagged and deep, exposing layers of raw flesh. The slightest movement would send a fresh stream of blood trickling out of me. As I stood before the mirror, my tear-filled eyes opened to a gruesome sight, my skin was ripped apart, and pieces of raw flesh dangled from my open wounds. My blood had splattered throughout the bedroom, staining the wardrobe, mirror, and ceiling with a deep crimson colour.

My body was racked with pain, making each step a torturous ordeal. With great difficulty, I finally managed to make it into the bathroom, my movements slow and laboured. I opened the glass cabinet above the sink and reached for the bottle of painkillers. The temptation to swallow the entire contents and end everything was overwhelming. After a fierce internal battle, I settled on a handful of pills. As the painkillers coursed through my system, I lowered myself onto the bed. Even the slightest touch of the bed sheet brushing against my freshly opened skin sent a searing pain right through me.

As I lay on my back and closed my eyes, I hoped that the large quantity of pills I had taken would soon take effect. Despite the pain that I was fighting against, I couldn't help but envision her charred corpse in the old, dilapidated cursed ruin. The evil spirits that resided there were surely still feuding over her tainted dark soul. The smell of her burning flesh lingered in my senses, as if I were still kneeling beside her.

As the pain slowly began to subside and drowsiness set in, I struggled to keep my eyes open. A smile crept across my face as I willingly surrendered to the numbing effects of the painkillers, as I desperately needed to escape from the pain of reality, even if only for a short while. When the painkillers fully kicked in, I felt a deep, heavy sleep fast approaching, I smiled and welcomed it with open arms. Just before succumbing to the impending slumber, the same breeze from the previous night on the beach returned, as I drifted in and out of consciousness.

My eyes were too heavy to open, weighted down by fatigue as the cold breeze swirled around my pounding head. Then, I heard her voice, the voice of the beautiful girl with no name. At first, her voice was barely audible, but as the cold breeze intensified, her words grew louder and clearer.

'Murderer, murderer, murderer,' she whispered, her warm breath, like a gently caress, bushed against my face. Her words left me paralysed with fear, my body unable to move as I lay there, helpless and terrified. Suddenly, the cold breeze vanished into the night, I could feel the weight of fear lifting off my chest as a wave of relief washed over me. As the warmth of the painkillers spread through my body, the gently lullaby of the ocean waves lapping against the shore reached my ears, enveloping me in a feeling of calmness and relief.

As the darkness consumed me, a peaceful stillness settled in.

Chapter 32

The excessive amount of painkillers and alcohol I had consumed plunged me into a deep, unconscious stupor. Several hours later, I woke up to a stiff body that was screaming out in pain. I groaned in agony as I opened my eyes and tried to move. The room was bathed in a warm, orange glow from the streetlight, casting long shadows along the wall next to my bed. After surveying the chaotic mess of the room, I closed my eyes and let out a defeated sigh as I sank back onto the pillow.

After some effort, I was able to reach the edge of the bed. Despite the pain, I persevered and managed to stand up. Each step was accompanied by wincing and groaning as I made my way to the window to close the curtains. I turned on the light, as my eyes finally adjusted to the brightness, what lay before me resembled a crime scene. The shattered bedside lamp and overturned chair were accompanied by painkillers strewn across the floor and a whiskey bottle smashed against the back wall. I had no recollection of doing any of it. The sight of my blood splattered in a gruesome pattern across the mirror and bed sent shivers down my spine, intensifying the already disturbing atmosphere. I dreaded the daunting task of tackling the mess before me.

My next obstacle was the stairs. I tackled each agonising step, cursing the day I was born as the sharp pain jolted through my body. Thankfully, I had stocked up on the whiskey just a couple of days ago. In the kitchen press, two bottles of whiskey sat side by side, their amber hues tempting me to indulge. I quickly lowered a few mouthfuls straight from the bottle as I lit a cigarette and placed two slices of white bread in the toaster. It had been a couple of days since I had eaten anything substantial, and my stomach was growling painfully, reminding me that the consumption of food was well overdue. Sitting down was not an option, due to the open wounds across my lower back and legs. I stood in the kitchen, one hand resting on the counter for support as I ate my toast and washed it down with a glass of whiskey.

Out of the corner of my eye, I caught a glimpse of my phone flashing from where it lay on the kitchen table next to my car keys. It showed five missed calls and three new voicemails. Two of the missed calls were from Terry, Ann's recently widowed husband. He had left a message asking, if I could call around to see him whenever I got a chance. He also mumbled something about finding it very hard to cope without Ann. The final part of his voicemail was muffled and barely audible, his voice trembling with emotion as he tried to speak through the tears. I hung up.

I really had no choice but to visit him. I made a mental note to stop by his house as soon as I got a chance, after all, I was the cause of the poor bastards suffering. Although, I could argue that if his whore of a wife had not seduced me, she would still be alive, and they would still be sauntering through their mundane life together. The second voice-mail was from what sounded like a very annoyed school principal. I had arranged to visit the school and speak with the pupils about their upcoming First Holy Communion, an appointment that completely slipped my mind. I would need to come up with a damn good excuse to get myself out of this mess. The third and final voicemail was from Fr. Liam, the Bishop's personal assistant. Fuck, what now? I thought, as I listened with great difficult, struggling to understand Fr. Liam's rapid speech, I cursed under my breath. His thick Kerry accent made it difficult enough to have a conversation in person, let alone decipher a voicemail from him. After listening to his message several times, I was still none the wiser. With no other option, I reluctantly called him back, unsure of what to expect.

Fr. Liam answered the call almost immediately, as if he had been standing by the phone awaiting my return call. The call lasted less than three minutes, which was very unusual for him. There were times in the past, that you couldn't get him off the phone. Maybe he was under a bit of pressure, just like the rest of us, I thought as I hung up. The reason behind the call was that the bishop had requested to meet with me at his residence the following Friday at eleven-thirty.

Christ, it can't be good to be summoned to the big fella's residence again, especially so soon after the last visit. I knew that I had missed several masses, skipped numerous hospital and school visits, and arrived late on several occasions, sometimes a little worse for wear, to administer the Last Rites. Which often caused frustration for the bereaved family, as their loved one had passed away without receiving a final blessing. Perhaps someone had reported my shortcomings. Surely a few little slip-ups here and there wouldn't be enough to land me in any major trouble.

I had two full days to prepare and sort myself out before meeting with the bishop. After my brief conversation with Fr. Liam, I threw the remainder of my toast in the bin. The thought of another meeting with the bishop, had driven the hunger from me. Exhaustion had completely consumed me, as I struggled to make my way back up the stairs, crying out in pain as my cuts reopened with each step. Before collapsing onto the bed, I picked up a handful of painkillers from the floor and swallowed them. I couldn't remember how they had ended up scattered across the floor from the previous night. The combination of pills and alcohol quickly took effect, transporting me to a peaceful sanctuary of quiet stillness and darkness.

Chapter 33

The following morning, I woke naturally. The bright red numbers on the alarm clock informed me that it was five-fifteen am, a little too early to rise, I thought, as I painfully eased myself out of bed. Despite my suffering, I had managed to fall into a deep sleep, thanks to the combination of painkillers and alcohol. However, even the slightest movement caused excruciating pain. I cursed the vile whore whose charred remains had been found at the Hell Fire Club. As I stood under the shower, the water stung my skin like hot needles, causing fresh blood to flow from my wounds and intensifying the already unbearable pain. Drying myself off was like another form of torture. The once pristine white towel was now completely destroyed, littered with streaks of my crimson blood. I covered as many of the fresh wounds as possible with antiseptic cream, before attempting to tackle the dreaded stairs.

My body was yearning for the familiar jolt of caffeine and the calming effect of nicotine. After consuming two cups of coffee and smoking three cigarettes, I finally began to come around. I remained naked for as long as possible, allowing the cream to fully soak into my torn and battered skin. The mere thought of clothes touching against my ripped skin and sticking to it caused me immense distress. I waited until the last possible moment, before I donned my black suit and white dog collar. The room was a gruesome sight, with blood splattered on the walls and floor like a macabre painting. Physically, I was unable to tackle such a daunting task in my exhausted and weakened state.

As I left the house, I reminded myself to call by Terry's house straight after saying mass. I felt a little guilty for not returning his calls from the previous night. And the thought of him coming over to my house was the last thing I wanted. I knew that if he did call around, we would end up sitting in an awkward tense silence for hours.

With my head bowed in supposed reverence. I stood at the altar and solemnly recited the opening prayers of the mass. Each word that left my mouth felt empty and meaningless. Slowly, I raised my head and looked around the congregation, my gaze was met by a sea of elderly women, with their eyes tightly closed and hands clasped around their rosary beads. They looked almost childlike in their devotion. I couldn't help but wonder, what sins could they have possibly committed at this late stage in their lives? I smiled to myself, trying to push away my sinister thoughts. Most of the congregation appeared to be well past their sell by date, but some had managed to cling onto a little more borrowed time. Perhaps their longevity was due to the advancements in modern medicine, I thought, before continuing on with the service.

After the service, Martin, the Sacristan, informed me that the parish committee were having a meeting straight after mass in the parish hall.

'Oh, I wasn't aware of any meeting. What is it about? I asked, knowing that I couldn't avoid the damn thing. Martin replied with a mischievous grin,

'Your guess is as good as mine, Father. It's probably a meeting about a meeting. There seems to be a lot of those lately.' I smiled back and replied,

'Yes, I'd say you're probably right, Martin. A meeting about a meeting. God only knows what Maura and her band of merry women have in store for me.' We both shared a laugh as I left the sacristy and made my way across to the Parish Hall.

The table in the parish hall was well decked out, as it always was for such events. Pots of tea and coffee were placed alongside overflowing plates of biscuits and cakes. All the usual suspects were already seated and making pigs of themselves by the time I arrived. At the far end of the table, the blue rinse militia were huddled together, whispering amongst themselves as if they were planning a covert operation. These meetings, which I detested, seemed to hold great importance in the otherwise mundane lives of the committee members. Maura, the chairperson, stood up and gently tapped her teaspoon against her cup, while she wiped crumbs from the side of her mouth with her free hand. Once she had the full attention of the committee members, with all eyes fixed on her and complete silence in the room, she would begin the proceedings.

Maura began the meeting by reciting a list of items, using her finest telephone voice, that she had compiled in her notepad. Items that, in her opinion, needed to be discussed with great urgency. However, after an hour into the meeting, we had only managed to cover three out of the seven items that Maura so urgently needed to discuss. I was extremely frustrated sitting there. The more I looked at the large knife that was being used to slice the cake, the stronger the urge became to grab it and slit my wrists. Eventually, when item number three had been dealt with to Maura's satisfaction, we took a ten-minute break for refreshments and if one needed to use the bathroom.

As everyone busied themselves, either refilling their cups or waiting in line to use the toilet, I saw my opportunity and gently pulled Maura aside. I told her that I had to leave, giving her some bullshit excuse about having to attend a meeting at the school. It was only when I mentioned the word 'school,' I remembered that I had forgotten to return the principal's voicemail, regarding my absence from the First Holy Communion meeting. I thanked Maura for organising the meeting, even though, I had been unaware of it until the last minute. I told her that I would be in touch soon before quickly turning and leaving the hall without giving her a chance to say goodbye or ask me any further questions.

After leaving the parish hall, I drove to Terry's house with a heavy sense of guilt. It was an overdue visit that I had been dreading, I would have preferred to go to the dentist and have teeth pulled instead. As I parked outside his house, I lit a cigarette and tried to gather my thoughts on what I was going to say to him. The last few times we met, I had struggled to meet his gaze. After all, I had fucked and murdered his wife. I finished my second cigarette and was considering lighting a third when Terry appeared from behind his front door. He must have spotted me from the window and was probably wondering what the hell was I playing at sitting in my car. I got out of the car and walked towards him; I was completely taken aback by his appearance. He looked pale and gaunt, like a walking corpse.

'Jesus, what the hell have I done?' I asked myself as we shook hands.

'Hello Father, thank you for dropping by,' Terry said, his voice low and filled with sadness as he greeted me. His tear-drenched eyes remained fixed on the ground as he led me into the kitchen. He no longer walked; he shuffled, showing the weight of his emotions. The kitchen was dark, with the blinds pulled down, blocking any natural light from entering the room. The only source of light was a small portable television hanging on the far wall. The room exuded a repulsive blend of stale body odour and decaying food, assaulting my nostrils with its overpowering stench.

'Please, have a seat. I'm sorry about the mess, but with Ann gone, I just don't see the point anymore,' Terry said. My heart sank as I felt a wave of guilt wash over me. I sat down on Ann's armchair, facing Terry. He was truly a broken man; his shoulders were slumped forward and his watery eyes fixated on the floor. He sat across from me in complete silence, as if in a trance.

I felt extremely uncomfortable as we sat across from each other. To break the silence, I forced myself to cough. After all, he was the one who asked me to call in, so the least he could do was speak to me. He seemed to have taken my cough as a sign; he slowly rose from his chair and shuffled over to the sink. He then filled the kettle and rinsed two mugs under the tap before reaching up to remove a jar of instant coffee from the press. My heart went out to him; he was a harmless, decent old skin, who didn't deserve the fate that had befallen him.

On that fateful day in the forest, I had only buried one body, but in reality, I had taken the lives of two. The gaunt dishevelled figure of Terry standing before me was a haunting reminder of my actions. He looked like a mere shadow of his former self, his once vibrant energy now drained away. Fuck it, what's done is done, I can't change what had happened. No matter how much I wished I could turn back time and fix everything. There was no going back, no rewind button to press. Yet, every time I looked at him, I was consumed with overwhelming guilt and remorse. I needed to gather my thoughts and regain control of my mind. It was a struggle to focus; I had to constantly remind myself that I was not to blame for this tragic situation. It was all because of his deceitful wife, who had led me astray with her seductive feminine wiles. If he only knew the truth about her, it might ease his pain and suffering, but I could never bring myself to tell him.

He slowly shuffled back over towards me with two badly stained mugs of coffee. 'I'm sorry Father, there are no biscuits, I haven't been to the shops,' he said, his faint voice, reeked of sorrow, as he handed me a mug. I couldn't bring myself to make eye contact with him. He was an honest, hardworking, God-fearing man, and I had single-handily destroyed his happy little life. My anxiety levels were beginning to rise as I sat opposite him, staying in the same room as him was no longer an option, I needed to get the fuck out and quick.

'Tom, have you been to see a doctor?' I asked, trying to sound concerned.

'No, sure there's no point, he'll only fill me up with pills, sedate me, no, I don't want that,' he replied, shaking his head from side to side.

'Would you like me to drive you over to the supermarket to pick up a few things?' I asked, hoping he would decline my offer.

'No, I've enough to get by. I'll stay here just in case Ann comes home,' he replied. There was no fucking chance of that happening, I thought to myself, as I racked my brain trying to come up with an excuse to leave. As I sat there watching him, staring vacantly into the fireplace. I reluctantly took a sip of coffee from the filthy mug, its surface coated in a thick layer of dried coffee stains and greasy fingerprints. The cold liquid made me want to gag, but I forced myself to swallow it down. He mustn't have boiled the kettle. He sat across from me, rambling on about how he first met Ann, and how he knew straight away that he wanted to spend the rest of his life with her.

Christ, I 'd heard enough. Terry's reminiscing about the past had become unbearable. I rose from the comfort of Ann's chair, pretending that I had lost track of time. I told Terry that I was due at the hospital to say mass. As I walked over to the sink, I placed the filthy, stained mug of cold coffee on the draining board. Terry slowly got up from his chair and thanked me for dropping by. As we shook hands, I couldn't help but notice how frail his pale hand felt. He shuffled behind me as we made our way to the front door.

As I stepped out onto the porch, I turned to face him and told him that he could ring me at any time, day or night. He didn't reply, he simply nodded his weary head as a sad smile appeared on his face. As I drove home, the only thing on my mind was a large whiskey. I knew it would steady me, provide a temporary escape from the mounting pressure that threatened to consume me. Once inside the house, I collapsed onto the sofa and swallowed desperate gulps from the bottle of whiskey, the burning liquid numbing my mind for a brief moment.

Chapter 34

The raspy, deadpan voice of Lou Reed filled the room as the clock radio sprang to life at eight in the morning. He was singing about a 'perfect day.' I found it absurd that there could be such a thing and quickly hit the off button before getting out of bed. As I got dressed, I noticed that I was able to move a little easier and my cuts were no longer tender to touch. It was also the first morning in several days that I woke up feeling hungry, a positive sign that my body was healing. However, my rumbling stomach was surely disappointed as it was only fed my usual breakfast of two slices of toast, washed down with two strong cups of coffee, followed by three cigarettes.

I was feeling a little nervous as I prepared for the morning mass, knowing that I had an important appointment with the bishop at eleven-thirty. After the service, I quickly changed out of my vestments and left the sacristy. Within minutes, I was in my car and on the road to the bishop's residence. Fr. Liam, the bishop's personal assistant, buzzed me in through the imposing gates that guarded the bishop's hideout. The towering, black gates creaked open with a piercing squeak, pleading for a drop of oil as they revealed a magnificent mansion. As the tyres slowly rolled along the pebble driveway, the satisfying crunch of the gravel echoed through the quiet surroundings, adding to the grandeur of the scene.

As I reached the top step, Fr. Liam was waiting for me. He held the door open with his foot as we greeted each other with a firm handshake and exchanged pleasantries. It wasn't the first time we had met, so there was no uncomfortable awkwardness. Fr. Liam then led me to His Grace's office, which was located just off the main hallway of the house. Despite feeling nervous about the purpose of the meeting, I couldn't help but marvel at my surroundings as we walked through the building. It was like a palace, with its ornate details and grand style. Vow of poverty my arse, His Grace wanted for nothing.

'Please take a seat. His Grace will be with you shortly. Would you like a cup of tea or coffee?' Fr. Liam asked, although his mind clearly seemed to be elsewhere as he fidgeted with his hands.

'Coffee would be great, thank you. How is His Grace keeping?' I inquired, trying to keep the conversation flowing in an effort to soothe my nerves.

'He's in good spirits; despite the immense pressure he's under. The church is currently getting fired on from all sides at the moment. But he's handling it well, at least for now,' Fr. Liam replied with a smile.

'Fr. Liam, if you don't mind me asking, do you know why I have been summoned here today?' I asked hesitantly, my voice betraying a hint of concern.

'Summoned, sounds a bit harsh, but to be brutally honest, I haven't the foggiest. I am not privy to much information, as everything is on a need-to-know basis around here,' he replied, raising his eyes towards the heavens. We both shared a smile. His Grace's entrance into the room was quick and business-like. I took a deep breath and braced myself for whatever he was about to throw at me.

'Smiling and laughing, that's always a good sign,' His Grace said, extending his damp, chubby hand. His powerful voice echoed around the large, high-ceilinged room.

'How have you been, John?'

'I'm good, Your Grace. And how are things with you?' I asked, not really giving a flying fuck one way or another. His Grace let out a heavy sigh as he lowered his massive bulk down into his large leather chair, a sign of his struggles of late.

'Struggling like the poor farmer,' His Grace replied with a somber smile.

Fr. Liam returned to the room with a tray held between his two hands. He carefully placed it on a side table before pouring us both a cup of coffee. Then, with one swift movement, he left the room, closing the large wooden double doors behind him. It was evident that this was a task he had become accustomed to and had perfected its execution in a very professional manner.

'Well John, let's get straight down to business. I have one hell of a busy day ahead of me,' His Grace said as he lit a cigarette, without offering me one. What a miserable bastard, I thought, as I sat across from him in silence, sipping my coffee unsure of what to expect.

'I have some good news for you, John,' His Grace said with a wide smile. 'Next week, a new priest will be joining your parish. His name is Fr. Brian, he's fresh out of the seminary, so he will be full of enthusiasm from the get-go. He is currently visiting his family in Cork for a week before starting his priestly duties.

'That's great news. Having another priest will be a great addition to the parish. Sometimes, it can be overwhelming trying to balance everything,' I replied, discreetly letting out a sigh of relief, when I realised that the purpose of the meeting had nothing to do with my long list of shortcomings.

'John, have you heard any updates about your housekeeper?' His Grace asked with what seemed like genuine concern.

'No, unfortunately there hasn't been any news. The whole parish is in a state of shock and completely devastated. I spent some time with her husband Terry yesterday. He has been inconsolable since his wife's sudden disappearance, his life completely shattered without her by his side,' I replied, solemnly.

'Do you think it might be too soon or even a little insensitive to replace her with a new housekeeper?' His Grace asked. Jesus, did he really just say that? He's more heartless than I could ever be, I thought as I took the last sip of my coffee, trying to hide my shock and disbelief at his insensitive comments.

'Yes, I think it might be. The atmosphere in the parish is still quite raw. And to be honest, having to cook and clean up after myself is doing me no harm at all. I think it would be wise to wait a while before finding a replacement for Ann,' I replied, still taken aback by his suggestion.

'It seems like the man above is really testing you, John. First the tragic loss of your mother, then poor Fr. O'Connell, and now your housekeeper. It's almost as if you're cursed. If anything else is thrown at you, I might have to start calling you Job,' His Grace said with a sympathetic expression.

'I must admit, the last few months have been incredibly challenging. They have taken a toll on me both physically and emotionally. Some days are harder than others, but I start each morning by counting my blessings. I take a deep breath and put one foot in front of the other, doing my best to carry on. I have placed all my trust and faith in God's love, in the hope that he will guide me through this terrible dark period of my life,' I replied, trying to maintain a sombre demeanour. What a load of horse shite, I thought to myself, wondering where I had conjured up such words from? If His Grace only knew the true nature of the man sitting across from him. I'm sure he would either have a heart attack right there in his large comfortable leather chair or run out of the room screaming blue murder.

'John, you are absolutely right. The only thing you can do in this difficult time is trust in God's love. I believe that he will guide you through this difficult time. As long as you remain strong in your faith and continue to love and serve the Lord, I have no doubt that everything will work out in the end. Please know that you are in my daily prayers as well, John,' His Grace said with a smile. I returned the smiled, but deep down, I was filled with anger. I had heard enough of his bullshit, his empty words, it was sickening. As I watched him take a sip from his cup, I couldn't help but wonder if he, like his deceased friend Fr. O'Connell, also had a fondness for young boys. I couldn't shake the thought that he might have read the suicide note I had coerced O'Connell into writing just before I ended his miserable double like.

As I felt my temper rising, I quickly interrupted my dark thoughts. I knew that losing my temper in His Grace's office would be a regrettable mistake. We chatted away aimlessly for another ten minutes or so before he suddenly stood up out of his chair without warning. He was surprisingly agile for such a large man. His sudden movement reminded me of a Jack-in-the-box, as he sprang up from his chair.

'Well John, it was lovely to see you again. Unfortunately, I'm pressed for time as always. I have to make my way across the city for another meeting,' His Grace said, extending his hand. I stood up and shook his hand, thanking him for everything. He walked me out to the main entrance, and we said our goodbyes, shaking hands once again.

As I reached the bottom step, I turned to face him, but he was already gone, and the front door was closed.

'Ignorant bastard,' I muttered to myself as I got into my car.

I drove slowly down the winding pebbled driveway, lined with perfectly trimmed hedges and vibrant flowers. The imposing black gates slowly creaked open as I approached them, as if by magic. Once again, the unbearable squeaking assaulted my ears as I waited for the gates to fully open. Unable to resist, I turned my head for one last look at the grand Victorian mansion that stood proudly amidst its lush garden and towering trees. In that moment, I caught a glimpse of Fr. Liam peering out from one of the windows on the top floor. Our eyes met briefly before he stepped back into the shadows.

'What a strange creepy place,' I muttered to myself as I pulled out onto the main road.

Chapter 35

His Grace did not disappoint; as promised, a new priest arrived within a week. Fr. Brian was a handsome young man with a full head of wavy jet-black hair and an athletic build. I'm sure the senior priests at the seminary visited his dorm regularly after dark, as he lay petrified and helpless in his bed, completely at their mercy. I knew that his dark smouldering eyes and chiselled jawline were sure to cause a stir in the parish. He was very polite and friendly, with an outgoing personality, he had a strong manly handshake and an even stronger Cork accent.

Fr. Brian shadowed my every move during his first few days, never straying too far from my side, like a young pup clinging to its mother. I didn't mind too much, after all, everything was new to him and I'm sure a little overwhelming at times. I introduced him to the parish committee, and he was warmly received by all the members of the blue rinse militia. They welcomed him as if he was a long-lost grandson. And naturally, the young lad was loving all the attention.

During his first few weeks in the parish, I continued to say all the masses. I wanted to ensure that he did not feel overwhelmed or pressured. Of course, I had my own agenda and intended to mould him into the kind of priest that I wanted to work with. So, I eased him in gently, and when he felt comfortable in his new surroundings, we began to say mass on alternating days. This arrangement worked out well for both of us, as it allowed us to have every other morning to ourselves.

As the new kid in town, everyone wanted a piece of Fr. Brian, which took a lot of pressure off me. As the weeks turned into months, I gradually immersed Fr. Brian into every aspect of parish life. From the dreaded parish committee meetings to the hospital and house calls, and my least favourite, the school visits, an area in which he seemed to excel. I must admit, he did come across a lot more child friendly than I did, he had a natural way with children that I lacked. As I seamlessly integrated him into the running of the parish, everything seemed to be running smoothly. I began to fade into the background, unnoticed, as he took on more responsibilities.

Within a relatively short period of time, Fr. Brian had settled into his role and, more importantly, he was warmly embraced by the parishioners. I had full confidence in his abilities to carry out his duties and no longer felt the need to constantly supervise him. However, I soon realised that his youth and eagerness to please made him gullible and easily fooled. The poor lad took every word that left my mouth as gospel, making him the perfect understudy. It was the perfect working relationship. With my newfound freedom, I could once again focus my full attention on the task at hand: ridding the streets of those vile whores.

The story of the charred remains found at the Hell Fire Club had faded from the headlines, for which I was grateful. However, I still struggled daily with the regret of leaving the knife at the murder scene. And if that wasn't enough to deal with, the image of Ann's lifeless body lying on the forest bed, her brown eyes wide open staring into nothingness, tormented my thoughts. Maybe it was because she was so close to home, and every second person I met throughout the day mentioned her name. Though I was certain that wild animals had already devoured her carcass.

Every day, thoughts of Ann and that other vile whore who met her tragic end at the Hell Fire Club consumed me. Their haunting images seared into my mind, tormenting me with their presence. And just when I thought, the situation couldn't possibly have gotten any more chaotic. The breaking news that a young woman's body had been discovered washed up on Killiney Beach, almost sent me over the edge. As soon as I heard the headlines, being read out over the airwaves, I knew it had to be the body of the beautiful girl with no name. The girl whose tormented spirit whispered to me each night as I closed my eyes. She was the one who had taken my virginity before she drifted away under the cold, dark waves. And, as per fucking usual, her naked, lifeless body was discovered by an early morning dog walker. As the newsreader continued on with the headlines, I jumped up from the kitchen table, left the house and drove straight out to Killiney Beach. I have no idea why I felt drawn to return to the scene; it was as if some strange magnetic force was pulling me towards it.

Her body lay on the beach, hidden from view by a large blue tent that was taken a battering from the sea breeze. The police had cordoned off the area. I lit up a cigarette and slowly walked over to where a young police officer was standing, with a clipboard wedged between his chest and folded arms.

'Good morning, Father,' he said, in a toned-down Dublin accent, quite similar to my own. 'Good morning. What a terrible tragedy,' I replied, making the sign of the cross for dramatic effect.

'That it is, Father. The number of young people taking their own lives these days is shocking,' he said with a shiver as the sea breeze wrapped itself around us.

'Is it definitely suicide?' I asked, taking a long drag on my cigarette.

'It certainly appears that way. Most cases like this are,' he replied, as he tried to wrap his arms tighter around himself, in what seemed like a feeble attempt to either warm or shield himself from the sea breeze.

'It's a tragic situation,' I said, trying to sound like the voice of reason.

'If only people would open up and talk, so many unnecessary deaths could be prevented.' 'I agree with you, Father,' the young officer replied. 'But as you know, people tend to keep their problems bottled up, allowing them to fester and grow in their troubled minds. Which usually leads to tragic outcomes, such as people being washed up on beaches or found hanging from a tree. It's a terrible waste of life and the devastation they leave behind is unimaginable.' As he spoke, his eyes welled up with emotion. Christ, I wasn't expecting a counselling session, time to quickly move on, I thought as I tossed the cigarette butt onto the sand.

'I am going over to sit on one of those benches and say a few prayers for the poor troubled soul, hoping that she has finally found peace,' I said.

'That's very thoughtful of you, Father,' the young windswept officer replied, as he dried his eyes with the back of his hand. After saying our goodbyes, I walked the short distance to one of the green benches. I sat down and took out my rosary beads, pretending to pray as I often did. I cannot recall ever consciously praying with true intent. No one could ever discern if I was truly praying or not, and that's part of the beauty of it. I was aware that the young officer might occasionally glance in my direction. So, I tried to appear as authentic as possible, as I held my rosary beads tightly and bowed my head in a solemn manner.

I couldn't help but wonder what the hell was going on inside the tent. Could they uncover any evidence that would elevate the case from suicide to murder? It seemed unlikely, considering the body had been in the water for a significant amount of time. Over to my right, I noticed a television camera crew setting up and a female newsreader, whom I recognised from the television preparing to go live with the latest's update on the grim discovery.

My attention was quickly drawn back to the blue tent when I noticed a woman in white overalls and a hooded face mask emerging from it. She made her way to a white van, which was parked close by, followed by a man dressed in the same attire. I watched them, as they engaged in a brief conversation, removing their masks while they spoke and enjoyed a cigarette, taking shelter from the harsh sea breeze inside the van. After a short while, they put their masks back on and returned to the tent. I assumed they were part of the forensics team, searching for clues that I hoped they would never find.

As I sat on the unforgiving cold metal bench, I felt the chill seeping through my clothes and into my bones. As my eyes shifted from the blue tent to the news crew and back again. I began to feel uncomfortable, wondering if I looked out of place and if my presence might raise any suspicion.

'Jesus Christ, just listen to yourself, you're fucking paranoid,' I whispered under my breath. I struggled against the sea breeze as I tried to light another cigarette, but it was futile. I gave up and abandoned the craving. Despite my paranoia, I decided it would be best to leave the scene. I didn't want any unwanted attention, and I still couldn't figure why the hell I had come back here in the first place?

I stood up from the cold metal bench and made the sign of the cross, adding to the dramatic effect in case anyone was watching. I waved to the young police officer, his feet planted firmly on the sand with his slim body leaning slightly against the wind, still clutching his clipboard as if his life depended on it. He looked as though he could be swept away at any moment. He returned my wave with a friendly smile. Just as I turned to make my way back to the car park, a high-pitched scream pierced through the sound of the wind and waves. The tormented cry of a cursed banshee flashed through my mind as I turned towards the direction of the scream.

A dark-haired woman was running towards the blue tent, pursued by an overweight middle-aged man who was calling out her name. I couldn't make out her name over her wailing and the strong sea breeze. As she approached the tent, her high-pitched screams intensified. Nearby, two police officers sitting in a patrol car quickly jumped out and ran towards the woman, intercepting her just as she reached the cordoned off area. The young police officer with the clipboard seemed frozen in time, watching in amazement as his two colleagues struggled to contain the frantic woman. Despite being in her forties and of a slight build, she put up a strong fight against the two burly officers. She desperately tried to break free from their hold, clearly distressed as she called out, 'Lisa, please, no, not my Lisa.'

The man chasing her had finally caught up, visibly struggling to catch his breath as he pulled her free from the two officers. They seemed both thankful and relieved to be free of her, yet they both remained vigilant, no doubt expecting her to try and push past them at any given moment. The wailing woman turned to face the man who had freed her from her captors, and they both fell to their knees. The young officer, still holding his clipboard, cautiously made his way over to the distraught woman. Her face was contorted with grief, and undoubtedly, he wished he was anywhere else but where he found himself. Reluctantly, and very foolishly, I joined him. After witnessing such a traumatic event, I should have just walked away while I had the chance. The scene that faced me was way beyond fixing. It was nothing short of total carnage.

I approached the man who had his arms tightly wrapped around the frantic, grief-stricken woman, who was wailing uncontrollably. He looked up at me through tear-drenched eyes and said,

'Father, we need to see if that's our daughter, Lisa.' As fresh tears rolled down his hardened face, the woman's wailing had subsided and was replaced by uncontrollable sobs as she buried her face into the man's chest. They both knelt on the wet sand, clinging to each other for support. My hand trembled as I reached out and placed it on her shuddering shoulder.

'I am deeply sorry for your loss,' I said, feeling completely out of my comfort zone. 'That's my baby, my beautiful Lisa. My only child. Why? Why?' she cried, before burying
her face back into the man's chest.

I wanted to tell her, that the girl lying dead inside the tent was truly beautiful, and how she had spent her last remaining hours upon this godforsaken earth. But I didn't. How could I have brought myself to tell a grieving mother that her daughter, her only child, was nothing more than a common whore? That would have been unethical. Instead, I tried to calm and comfort her, for all the good it did me, she wasn't having any of it. The poor woman was completely distraught; her heart had been ripped right out of her. Her only child lay naked, dead on a beach, inside a blue tent, while men and women dressed in white overalls were prodding and poking at her decaying corpse.

The distraught woman needed a doctor urgently; she was in desperate need of sedation, even if only temporarily, to alleviate her pain as she struggled to come to terms with her new reality. My words, or anyone else's for that matter, would be of no use. In such devastating circumstances, words were futile. She raised her head; her swollen and teary eyes briefly met my gaze. I couldn't help but notice the striking resemblance between the mother and daughter. They both had the same mesmerizing hazel eyes and shoulder-length dark brown hair, with their high cheekbones and perfectly shaped full lips, they could have easily been mistaken for twins. As I looked down at the grieving woman's distraught face, my mind briefly wandered, and I began to fantasise about having both the mother and daughter. Fucking sluts, the pair of them, I thought to myself, as I quickly snapped out of my inappropriate fantasy and brought my depraved mind back to the harsh reality, I found myself in.

Feeling the heavy weight of the situation, I attempted to ease the tension. 'Would you like to join me in prayer?' Sure, what else could a priest say in such devastating circumstances.

'Prayers? Fuck you and your prayers. Fuck you and your God. Go on, fuck off. Go find yourself an altar boy to play with. You lot are all the fucking same, a bunch of fucking perverts,' she screamed at the top of her voice as she struggled to get back on her feet. In her anger and grief, she threw a closed fist in my direction but thankfully missed.

'Please, Father, just go. You're only making her worse,' he pleaded, his voice trembling with emotion as he struggled to restrain her.

I was filled with anger and wanted to retaliate. How fucking dare, she label me as a pervert and suggest that I go play with an altar boy. Without saying another word, I quickly made my way back to the car park. My hands trembled with rage as I lit a cigarette and sped out of the car park, not giving a flying fuck who saw me. That grieving whore had pushed me over the edge. As I drove along the motorway, I struggled desperately to calm myself, chain-smoking one cigarette after another.

Lisa, no longer the beautiful girl with no name, now lies lifeless beneath a blue tent on the very same beach where she drew her last breath. On their knees, her distraught parents clung to each other on the damp sand. The unforgiving sea breeze showed no mercy towards the grieving parents, its relentless force adding to their pain as they wept uncontrollably, their hearts shattered forever by the loss of their only child. As tears streamed down my face, I cried out, 'Please forgive me, Lisa,' through broken sobs.

Chapter 36

T he evening news showed the harrowing scene of a black body bag being removed from the tent and loaded into the back of a hearse. While in the background, the poor distraught woman was being restrained by her husband and two police officers. It made for difficult viewing, as the woman wailed like a fucking deranged banshee, she had turned me right off my dinner.

I hit the remote and turned off the television, 'damn woman,' I muttered, as I stood up from the table. The remaining food on my plate was scraped into the bin, as the image of the hysterical woman had ruined my appetite. I gazed out the kitchen window into the still and dark night; while washing the few dishes I had used throughout the day. Leaning closer to the window, my nose almost touching the glass, my reflection stared back at me. It was pitch black outside, so the window acted as a mirror.

'Mirror, mirror, on the wall,' I whispered, laughing to myself.

'Mirror, mirror, on the wall, who is the cleverest of them all,' I whispered, smiling at my reflection in the window. However, to my surprise and horror, my reflection did not smile back, but instead stared back at me with a blank, emotionless expression. Startled, I dropped the plate I was drying, causing it to shatter into pieces on the tiled floor. I frantically rubbed my eyes, bringing my face up close to the windowpane for a second time. Every line, spot, and blemish on my face was clearly visible. I forced a nervous smiled, but my reflection remained stoic and unresponsive, causing me to jump back from the window in fear and confusion.

'What the fuck is happening to me?' I whispered to myself, as I stared at my reflection in disbelief.

I quickly pulled down the blind, concealing the ominous darkness that lurked beyond the window. My heart raced as I sprinted up the stairs, taking two steps at a time. On entering the bathroom, I turned on the light and looked deeply into the mirror that hung above the sink. I wore a serious, determined look upon my face, with my fore-head furrowed and my lips pressed into a thin line. I held that gaze for a minute or so before I nervously shed a weak smile, my reflection mimicked the smile. Slowly, I lowered myself onto the toilet seat, my elbows resting on my knees, as I buried my face into my trembling hands. A wave of relief washed over me, followed by a surge of fear. I grappled with the reality of what had just happened, my mind reeling as I tried to make sense of it all. I returned to the kitchen and left the blind down, panicked, I tried to convince myself that the experienced was just a trick of the light.

Despite my attempts to push the incident out of my mind, I couldn't shake off the uneasiness that lingered within me. I lit a cig-arette and took a long drag, while pouring myself a little something to steady my nerves. A half an hour or so had passed before I began to feel more relaxed. I had just settled onto the sofa and turned on the television when the doorbell rang. Glancing at my watch, it read eight thirty-four.

'For fuck's sake,' I muttered as I made my way to the front door. To my surprise, Fr. Brian was standing facing me as I opened the door. Although, I hadn't a clue what he wanted, I was relieved that it wasn't the police or Terry, Ann's husband.

'Hello John,' he said, with a big friendly goofy smile across his young fresh face.

'Ah Brian, come on in,' I replied, wondering what the hell he wanted, as I stepped aside so he could enter the hallway.

'I hope I'm not disturbing you?' he asked. And even if you were, would you just turn around and fuck off, I thought to myself.

'No, not at all. Is everything okay?' I asked, half expecting there to be a problem. 'Everything is fine and dandy. I just fancied a few glasses of the good stuff, and a bit of a chat,' he replied, smiling as he pulled a bottle of Bushmills whiskey out of a brown paper bag.

'Well Bushmills and a chat it is. You go on into the sitting room and make yourself at home, while I fetch a couple of glasses,' I replied.

'That sounds like a good plan to me,' he said, smiling as he made his way to the sitting room. I headed to the kitchen, feeling frustrated, 'a bit of a chat,' that's the last fucking thing that I needed. Christ, if I didn't have enough going on in my own head at the moment, and now the thought of having to engage in small talk for the rest of the night, galled me, as I grabbed two glasses and returned to the sitting room.

'Now, Brian, pour away,' I said, trying to hide my contempt as I placed the glasses on the coffee table in front of him. He smiled as we clinked our glasses, which were filled with a generous measure of what he called 'the good stuff.' I forced a smile in return.

'You must feel quite settled and accepted in the parish by now? I asked, trying to start a conversation.

'Yes, the people around here have been incredibly friendly and welcoming towards me. I couldn't have wished for a better start,' he replied.

'They're not a bad bunch around here, although the old parish committee can be a bit heavy going at times. But they mean well. Other than that, everything else seems to run smoothly enough on its own,' I said.

'Yes, good old Maura and her band of merry women will certainly keep us all in line,' he replied with a laugh.

'You're dead right, Brian. She's a rare one all right, is our Maura,' I said before draining my glass.

As the night progressed, we chatted and drank freely, and I found myself becoming more relaxed. The incident involving my reflection in the window had faded into the depths of my mind, like a distant dream that I could barely recall. And the generous pours of whiskey undoubtedly played a significant role in my mellowing out on the sofa. Surprisingly, I was genuinely enjoying Brian's company. In the background, a political program blared on the television, with two politicians engaged in a heated argument, both were red-faced and practically foaming at the mouth. Brian and I couldn't help but laugh as we watched the intense exchange. Suddenly, Brian turned to me and asked,

'John, do you mind if I ask you a personal question?' The laughter died down. He seemed hesitant, his gaze fixed on the floor. I had no idea what the fuck was going to come out of his mouth next, but what else could I say,

'Ask away, Brian.'

'Are you happy being a priest? Do you believe you made the right decision?' he asked. I paused, considering his question, as if deep in thought. I had no idea where this conversation was headed.

'I would say that I am content,' I replied, choosing my words carefully. 'But let's also be honest, do any of us truly make all the right decisions in life? Sometimes, the biggest decisions are made for us by those close to us, who may have their own hidden agendas.'

'I'm not sure I understand you, John,' he said, his brow furrowed in confusion. 'I may have had a bit too much of the good stuff,' he added with a sheepish grin. Christ, this could turn into a very long night, I thought as I cleared my throat.

'Well, let me share my own story with you. My mother always wanted me to become a priest, but I never even considered it,' I explained. Fr. Brian sat up straight, suddenly alert.

'So do you regret becoming a priest?' he asked. I hesitated, searching for the right words, which wasn't easy due to the large amount of alcohol I had consumed.

'I wouldn't say I regret it. It's just all I've ever known. I became an altar boy at the age of eight, and the parish priest at the time was a close family friend. My father had passed away when I was three, cancer, I was told. Fr. O'Connell took me under his wing, so to speak, and I simply followed him into the priesthood without giving it much thought. I knew it would make my mother proud and happy,' I replied. If only he knew the whole story.

'The group you refer to as the 'blue rinse militia' filled me in about the terrible house fire. An awful tragic way to lose your mother, and then the death of Fr. O'Connell. How in the name of God did you manage to keep going?' he asked, his eyes growing hazy as the alcohol took effect.

'To be honest, it is only by the grace of God that I am still here today. He gave me the strength to carry on and keep moving forward,' I replied. I was impressed with myself for being able to come up with such convincing bullshit.

'Brian, may I ask you the same question? Are you truly satisfied with your vocation? I inquired, this should be good, I thought smiling to myself.

'To be completely honest, John, I am extremely passionate about my work. It brings me a great sense of fulfilment. However, I must admit, (here we go) there are times when I feel quite lonely. Like when I arrive home late in the evening to a silent, and empty house, I can't help but feel a sense of loneliness and isolation. It can be difficult and even depressing at times. I often find myself daydreaming about arriving home in the evening after a long day to be greeted by a loving wife and children, surrounded by the joyful chaos of family life,' Brian mused, gently cradling his glass as he gazed down at the floor. 'Do you know what I mean, John?' he asked, his voice tinged with a hint of wistfulness. It's clear that whiskey isn't for everyone, I thought as I prepared to answer.

'Of course I do Brian,' I replied, 'It's only human to have those types of thoughts from time to time.'

'John, do you often entertain thoughts like that?' Brian asked. As I carefully considered my response, to his question, I kept him waiting while I finished my drink.

'Not as much now, but there have been times over the years when I've questioned my faith and vocation. I've had my fair share of sleepless nights because of it,' I admitted. As the conversation continued, I grew increasingly frustrated with Brian's silly questions. I just wanted him to fuck off home so that I could catch up on some badly needed sleep. I wasn't sure if it was due to the several drinks I had consumed or if it was simply because I was exhausted from all the stress that I was under. But I could feel my temper flaring up, and I struggled to conceal my growing irritation.

Behind it all, Brian was a nice, innocent lad who was just feeling a little lonely and needed to get a few things off his chest. Despite my growing anger, I somehow managed to suppress it and conjured up the strength to continue on with his pointless conversation.

'John, I'm really sorry for showing up unannounced like this. I must have wrecked your head over the last couple of hours. I'm ever so sorry, I just needed someone to talk to,' he said, his words slurred. I forced a smile, trying to hide my impatience.

'It's okay, don't worry about it. That's what friends are for my door is always open for you, Brian. Don't ever keep things bottled up, always come and talk to me, no matter what's on your mind,' I replied, silently hoping he would leave soon.

'Thank you, John. I really appreciate you listening tonight,' he replied gratefully, as he poured the last of the whiskey into our glasses. I didn't have much choice; I wanted to tell him. He raised his glass, swaying slightly, and said,

'To our calling.' Once again, we clinked our glasses and downed the remaining whiskey.

The bottle of Bushmills sat empty on the coffee table. As I stood up, he looked up at me with bleary eyes. His expression said it all, he was finished. I helped him up off the sofa and guided him towards the front door. I watched with great amusement as the young, lonely, and confused Fr. Brian stumbled down the garden path and struggled with the latch on the front gate before finally managing to open it. He turned and waved before drunkenly making his way down the street. My eyes followed him until he turned the corner at the end of the street and disappeared from sight. I locked the front door and set the alarm. My watch read, twenty past three in the morning. As I staggered up the stairs and collapsed onto the bed, I couldn't help but smile as I kicked off my shoes, relieved that it was Brain's turn to say the ten o'clock mass later that morning and not mine.

Chapter 37

The following morning, the bright sunlight streaming through the gap in the curtains jolted me awake. I was still feeling the effects of my unexpected night of drinking with Fr. Brian. The only consolation was that I didn't have to wake up early to say mass. As I thought about Fr. Brian, a smile crept onto my face. I couldn't help but imagine him standing at the altar, his face drenched in sweat as he fought the urge to either vomit or pass out. My head throbbed with a dull, pulsating ache and my throat felt painfully dry. I struggled to force my heavy eyelids open as I turned to check the time. The glowing red digits on my alarm clock blazed like fire, searing my tired eyes. It was eleven-thirty in the morning. I threw back the duvet and swung my legs over the side of the bed, surprised to see that I was still wearing the same clothes from the night before. After quenching my thirst with a cold glass of water, I indulged in a steaming, hot shower.

My wounds had healed nicely from the last whipping I had endured. It no longer hurt to stand under the shower as the hot water did its best to penetrate my badly scarred body. As I dried myself off in front of the full-length mirror, I couldn't help but notice the resemblance of my body to the body of the actor who played Jesus, in the movie The Last Temptation of Christ. My skin was marred with deep, jagged purple scars, resembling the brutal wounds on his battered and lacerated body in the movie. In fact, I could have easily been his body double, with the added bonus that all my scars were real. No need for heavy makeup or sneaky camera tricks, I was the genuine article.

It was no wonder that poor Ann got such a fright when she saw me naked on that fateful morning, which ended up being her last day on this earth. Ironic, how things pan out for some people. Maybe if Ann hadn't seen me naked, she just might still be alive today. My scarred and battered torso was undeniable evidence of the abuse that I had endured over the years. Ann's witnessing of my dark secret ultimately sealed her fate, making her another unfortunate victim of being in the wrong place at the wrong time.

After getting dressed, I headed down to the kitchen. I couldn't stomach food, but I desperately needed caffeine and nicotine. As I opened the backdoor and lit a cigarette, I closed my eyes and let the warmth of the sun wash over my face. Inhaling deeply, I savoured the heat and my first nicotine fix of the day.

The radiant rays of the sun and the crisp, invigorating breeze seemed to be beckoning me to join them outside, and I simply couldn't resist their alluring charm. Leaving my dirty mug in the sink, I stepped out of the house and embarked on a leisurely stroll, hoping the fresh air would alleviate my hangover. I wandered aimlessly for about an hour, but even the beautiful day couldn't shift my bastarding headache. On my way back home, I stopped by the local corner shop. Joseph, the ever friendly, yet extremely nosy shopkeeper, was sitting in his usual spot behind the counter. It appeared to be a struggle for him to get up from the stool that seemed to be permanently attached to his large frame.

'Good morning, Father,' he greeted, wiping beads of sweat from his forehead with a handkerchief before returning it to his trouser pocket. 'What a beautiful day,' he added.

'Indeed it is, Joseph. God is surely smiling down on us today,' I replied. As we continued our brain numbing conversation, he brought up the tragic news of the young girl who had washed up on Killiney Beach.

'Such a terrible tragedy,' he said with a heavy heart.

'Very sad. Her name was Lisa,' I responded, a little too quickly, as a wave of guilt washed over me.

The memories of that fateful night are etched deep in my mind. Every night, as the witching hour approached, her face suddenly appeared before me, her ghostly visage haunted my every thought. I could almost feel the icy chill of the ocean water against my skin, and the ebb and flow of the waves, lapping onto the shore, drowning out all other sounds as she disappeared beneath them. These secrets will accompany me to the grave. While my mind drifted into a momentary lapse, Joseph's monotone voice derailed my train of thought, and I quickly regained my focus.

'Lisa, you say. The news report stated that her name would not be released until after a post mortem had been carried out,' he replied with a confused look on his fat, red face, as his hand reached into his trouser pocket and retrieved his sweat stained handkerchief, and began to wipe his brow. I cursed myself for being so foolish as to mention the girl's name, especially to Joseph of all people.

'After hearing the news headlines yesterday morning about a body being washed up on Killiney Beach, I drove out there. When I arrived, I met the distraught parents of the victim. It was a heart-wrenching scene. I spent some time with them, offering prayers and trying to provide some comfort. However, I knew that no words or prayers could ease the pain of losing their only child in such a tragic manner. The girls' father told me her name,' I explained, hoping to dispel any doubts or suspicions that may have been floating around in Joseph's head. Christ, I'm so fucking paranoid, I thought to myself, as I looked across the counter wondering what was going through Joseph's mind.

'Another suicide, I suppose,' Joseph said, nodding his head somberly.

'Yes, it certainly looks that way. It's shocking. I have witnessed a great deal of it in hospital morgues. It's frightening, and the numbers seem to be increasing every year,' I replied. After several more minutes of idle chatter, I paid Joseph for the groceries, thanked him and then left the shop, breathing a sigh of relief as I stepped outside into the warm air.

Fifteen minutes later, I arrived home. As I put away the few groceries, I made myself a strong coffee before sitting at the kitchen table to read the morning paper. The main headline nearly sent me into cardiac arrest:

'Police following definite line of enquiries as vital evidence found on the murder weapon used at the Hell Fire Club.' I couldn't believe what I was reading. What kind of evidence could they have found? I felt the police were using the headline as a tactic to unsettle the killer and provoke a mistake. As I delved further into the article, I found myself increasingly spooked and panicked. According to the newspaper, the police were making significant progress in the case and were following concrete leads, which I found quite unsettling to read.

I knew my fingerprints would be all over the knife. After all, I had used it many times over the years at home, but purely for culinary reasons. However, I had never had my fingerprints taken before. So, what were they going to match the prints on the knife to? I was convinced that it was all nonsense. It was just the police trying to convince the public that they were onto something. When in reality, they had sweet fuck all evidence. As I stood up from the table, I crumpled the newspaper into a ball and tossed it towards the bin, I missed, and the paper ball landed on the floor. I told myself that the newspaper article was nothing but lies and propaganda.

As the evening slowly transitioned into night, the natural light faded, and I found myself enveloped by the darkness and silence of the sitting room. Suddenly, the old streetlight outside my house flickered to life, casting a warm glow through a gap in the curtains, illuminating a flurry of swirling dust particles, dancing wildly in mid-air, breaking the stillness of the room. Lost in a deep reverie, I sat motionless, my eyes fixed on the beam of light that illuminated the room.

The newspaper headline had darkened my mood and plunged my mind into a chaotic whirlwind of unpleasant scenarios, all of which had unfavourable outcomes. The twenty well-chosen and carefully crafted words that made up the headline had unsettled me. I knew I had seriously fucked up by leaving the knife at the murder scene. However, I did not need some smug journalist constantly writing about my stupid mistake.

Chapter 38

The microwave pinged, dragging me back into reality as I removed the hot plate and made my way into the sitting room. After the second mouthful of what was supposed to be a microwavable dinner of lasagne, the hunger left me it tasted absolutely horrendous. I was on the verge of retching as I scraped what remained on the plate into the bin. The after taste in my mouth was disgusting, how the hell were these companies getting away with producing such shite ready meals and charging a fortune for them.

As I settled in to watch the evening news, I lit a cigarette in the hope of getting rid of the unpleasant taste that lingered in my mouth. However, my attention was quickly diverted by the newsreader as she announced that a man had been arrested in connection with the murder at the Hell Fire Club. I eagerly perched on the edge of the sofa and turned up the volume to catch every word that left her perfectly formed lips. But my excitement was short lived as she delivered the crushing news that the man had been subsequently released without charge. I was gutted, for a brief moment I believed that someone else would be tried and convicted for the murder I had committed, no such fucking luck. Sadly, I sank back down on the sofa, feeling completely deflated by the time the newsreader had finished her report.

As the news ended, I felt disappointed and frustrated. I drained my glass of whiskey before turning on my laptop. As I scrolled through page after page, I was bombarded with images of one vile whore after another, shamelessly flaunting their immoral services. Based on my past experiences, I knew that the first few phone call I made might not be answered. Therefore, I made sure to write down several numbers and worked my way through them until someone picked up. The third number I dialled was answered by a Polish woman who offered a 'very sexy massage' as it was worded on her profile.

Two hours later, I found myself lying naked, face down on a massage table in an apartment on Thomas Street, for what was to be my first real massage, as opposed to the inappropriate touching and stroking I had experienced in the seminary. I felt completely relaxed as she slowly moved her warm hands over my scarred body. She began with my shoulders and back, then gradually worked her way down along the length of my body and onto my legs. The room was shrouded in a peaceful silence as she skilfully plied her trade, she didn't need to speak, her hands did all the talking. As I lay there, basking in the tingling warmth of her touch and the gentle pulsing of new sensations flooding my body, I began to drift off. As she massaged my legs, she gentle parted them, allowing her hands to glide freely along the inside of my thighs. Each time her hands reached the top of my thighs, she slid one hand underneath me and caressed my penis. With each sensual stroke, she gradually wrapped her warm hand around my penis and started moving it up and down along my shaft. Once I was fully aroused, she asked me to turn over onto my back.

I followed her command, and she wasted no time in cupping my balls in one hand and started to massage them.

'Would you like a blowjob or full sex?' she asked, her broken English adding to the excitement.

'Just a hand job,' I replied. As soon as the last word left my mouth, she began to work her magic. She had truly mastered the art of giving a sensual hand job. I assumed she had plenty of practice, the filthy whore. With one hand, she removed her t-shirt and threw it to the floor, exposing her beautifully formed tanned breasts. She leaned over me and placed my throbbing penis between her perfectly shaped mounds of flesh, pushing them together and keeping the momentum going until I exploded all over them. As soon as I came, she stood up and grabbed a pack of baby wipes. I watched as she wiped my cum from her breasts before cleaning me off. She was probably getting herself ready for her next client, I thought, the filthy whore. As I got up from the massage table, I could feel my anger rising within me, despite the lingering pleasure in my body.

'May I use your toilet?' I asked politely.

'Yes, of course, it's the first door on the left,' she replied. Without bothering to get dressed, I walked out into the hallway completely naked. I didn't actually need to use the toilet, it was just a test. I was certain that if there was someone else in the apartment, she would not have let me leave the room naked. After flushing the toilet for effect, I returned to the room.

She was standing in the corner with her back towards me, facing the wall, like a bold child. Maybe she was trying to be polite by not watching as I dressed, I thought as I began to put on my clothes. Although, deep down, I knew that my repulsive, scarred body was the real reason for her looking the other way. Once I was dressed, she turned to face me.

'Eighty euro please, sixty for the massage, and twenty for the hand job,' she said with a smile, revealing perfectly straight, white teeth, of which I was envious when I thought of my own badly stained and crooked teeth. I removed my wallet from my coat pocket and handed her a hundred euro note.

'One moment please, I'll get your change,' she said, smiling once again as she left the room. I couldn't help but think how polite she was. I put on my overcoat and slid my hand into the pocket, tightly gripping the wooden handle of the hammer. As the door opened, she entered the room with her hand outstretched, holding a twenty euro note.

'Your change,' she said, with a beautiful smile that would be her last on this earth. 'You can keep it as a tip for a job well done,' I said, as I quickly swung the hammer and landed the first blow on the side of her head. She dropped to the floor with a heavy thud, the twenty euro note floated slowly towards the ground, before finally landing beside her tanned bare feet. I struck her head several more times, just to ensure that she had indeed departed from this world. Turning to face the mirror that hung on the back of the door, I noticed a few specks of her blood on my cheek and forehead. I quickly cleaned my face with the baby wipes that she had used to wipe my cum from her filthy body. I then cleaned the hammer and slid it back into my coat pocket.

I looked down at her lifeless body, her face grotesquely disfigured, courtesy of my hammer. She looked so peaceful in a strange kind of way, although the growing pool of blood surrounding her head suggested differently. I knelt down beside her and dipped my middle finger into the pool of her crimson blood. Sniffing, as I raised my blood-soaked finger to my nose, I couldn't quite discern the scent of her blood. It simply smelt like blood, I supposed. I stood up and walked over to the mirror, and used her fresh blood to write the letter T. I then repeated this process, going back and forth between the pool of blood and the mirror, my right hand trembled with each stroke, until the words,

'THY WILL BE DONE' were etched in crimson across the mirror.

Chapter 39

T he darkness of night no longer brought the peaceful embrace of slumber; sleep had become elusive. The thick and suffocating darkness seemed to taunt me, rendering sleep an unattainable dream. I often wondered, as I lay awake, if sleep had ever existed, or if a good night's sleep was nothing more than a figment of my imagination. I would lie awake night after night, staring at the cracked ceiling, and as soon as I closed my eyes and began to drift off, those dead girls faces would appear before me, one after another. As if their ghostly figures formed a line, each one patiently waiting for their turn to haunt me.

It had reached the stage where I was running on autopilot. I would stand at the pulpit, looking down over the congregation and mindlessly recite one prayer after another, without any conviction, I felt nothing, the prayers were just empty words. And when it came to the sermon after reading the Gospel, I would simply wing it. I often repeated the same sermon many times and the fact that nobody seemed to notice, only confirmed my belief that no one listens or really gives a flying fuck to what the priest is harping on about from the pulpit.

As the weeks passed, it felt as though my responsibilities and obligations were not only catching up on me, but they were also over-taking me. I was constantly on the back foot, struggling to keep up with the demands. I knew that my double life would eventually crumble, and I feared the consequences that would follow. Burning the candle at both ends had taken a toll on my appearance, leaving me looking haggard, exhausted, and much older than my actual years. My reflection in the mirror showed the signs of my deteriorating appearance, dark circles under my tired eyes, unkempt hair, and my slumped posture.

Fr. Brian was the first to comment of my dishevelled appearance. I would simply dismiss his concerns, telling him that I hadn't been sleeping well since my mother's death and that it was just lack of sleep finally catching up on me. One morning over coffee, as I constantly yawned and chain-smoked, it seemed Fr. Brian had seen enough.

'John, maybe you should go and see a Dr. Frank. He'll surely give you something that will send you off to dreamland,' he said. But will he give me something to block out the terrified looks on those girl's faces that keep appearing every time I close my eyes? I thought to myself as I lit a cigarette and offered one to Fr. Brian. I wanted to tell him about the haunting images that seemed so real to me. It was as if the girls had come back from the dead, their eyes wide open, filled with terror as they looked up at me, suddenly realising their time was up. These haunting images will undoubtedly accompany me to the grave.

'Yes, I think I will. I really do need to get back into some sort of sleep pattern,' I replied, stubbing out the butt in the ashtray.

'Good old Dr. Frank, just down from the spar shop, sure he'd give you anything, whether you're sick or not,' he said, laughing. In all fairness, Fr. Brian had a valid point, good old Dr. Frank had earned himself a bit of a reputation for being a soft touch when it came to giving out prescriptions and sick notes.

'I'll try to stop by and see him later today, if I get a chance,' I replied. As much as Fr. Brian had a tendency, unbeknownst to himself, for getting under my skin, his suggestion to see a doctor made perfectly good sense. And surprisingly, I took his advice and made an appointment to see Dr. Frank later on that afternoon.

When the time of my appointment rolled around, I nervously entered the waiting room. I wasn't even five minutes in the surgery and left with a prescription for sleeping tablets. Sure, it's no wonder people are addicted to the damn pills. They're so easily available, I thought to myself as I handed the prescription over to the young woman standing behind the counter in the chemist. A few minutes later, she handed me a small brown plastic bottle full of pills. She then explained to me that the tablets were very strong and that I was only to take one right before bedtime, and under no circumstances was I to drink alcohol or drive after I had consumed a tablet. I thanked her and paid for the prescription, leaving the chemist with a smile at the thought of finally getting a full night's sleep.

The young woman behind the counter at the chemist, had not exaggerated about the strength of the little white pills. I took one about half an hour before going to bed. I had been watching a documentary, which claimed new evidence had been discovered, suggesting that Jesus, and Mary Magdalene, were married in secret and had a family together.

'Magdalene, that fucking slut,' I snarled at the television before draining my glass. I stumbled from the sitting room and what a fucking job I had conquering the stairs. If felt like I was standing at the base of Mount Everest, staring up at the summit.

The following morning, I woke up feeling extremely drowsy, still in my clothes from the previous day and lying face down on the bed. I couldn't believe the effect that one little pill had on me. How could something so small have such a powerful impact? Struggling to drag myself out of bed, I cursed my stupidity for not heeding the young woman's advice at the chemist about not mixing alcohol with the sleeping pills. I slowly undressed and stood under a cold shower for at least twenty minutes, hoping to shock my body into coming alive. I sauntered down the hallway towards the kitchen. My limbs were heavy like lead and my mind was foggy. Even after I had consumed ridiculous amounts of caffeine, I still felt completely drained.

It was well into the afternoon before I came around and was able to function somewhat normally. I swore to myself that I would never take another one of those sleeping pills again, they were far too strong for me. I felt like a zombie, aimlessly wandering around the house. As the effects of the medication began to wear off, I realised how hungry I was. It dawned on me that I hadn't eaten anything since the previous day, all because a little white pill had left me comatose on the sofa for most of the day. My body craved food and fresh air, so I decided to take a stroll down to the local chipper. A smoked cod and chips would see me right.

I had just placed my order when I heard a familiar voice behind me say,

'Evening, Father.' I turned around to see that arrogant prick of a detective, Conroy, with one of his sidekicks looming over me. My initial reaction was to run, but I quickly regained my composure and responded.

'Good evening, gentlemen. How is your night going?' I forced a smile and tried to appear calm and collected.

'All is quiet at the moment,' Conroy said. 'But one call over the radio could change that quickly enough.' I stepped aside to let them pass so that they could make their way to the counter and order their food. While we chatted and waited for our food to be cooked, I was surprised that Conroy, never mentioned Ann's name. I was feeling very uneasy standing in front of the two dicks and was only delighted when my phone rang. I retrieved the annoying piece of plastic from my coat pocket and noticed 'caller unknown' displayed across the screen. I excused myself from Conroy and his colleague and went outside to take the call.

'Hello,' I said, unsure of who was on the other end of the line.

'Hello, Father,' a soft, feminine voice replied.

'May I ask who I am speaking to?' I asked, not recognising the voice.

'I know what you've been up to, Father,' she said. The line suddenly went dead, and a surge of terror engulfed me. Panic set in as I frantically scanned the area around me, trying to make sense of the call. I noticed the young man behind the counter waving at me, holding up a brown paper bag, my food was ready. I nodded to acknowledge him and made my way back inside the chipper. The phone call had left me shell-shocked and completely disoriented.

'Are you alright, Father?' asked Conroy, as I approached the counted to get my food. 'You look as though you've seen a ghost.' I tried to steady myself as I replied, 'I just received some bad news. It came as a bit of a shock, that's all.'

'Can I offer you a lift?' Conroy asked. He was the last fucking person I wanted to be around.

'No, thank you,' I replied, trying to quell the nervous quiver in my voice.

'I best be off now. I hope you both have a safe and quiet night,' I said as I turned and left the bustling chip shop.

'Goodnight, Father,' they said in unison as I walked away. I wondered if their synchronized words were a result of their police training.

As I walked home, my mind was filled with unease and chaos, I felt shocked, paranoid, and constantly looked over my shoulder. Who the hell had called me? I had no idea. The voice on the other end of the line was definitely female, and her words were spoken in broken English, indicating that she was a foreign woman. What exactly did she know? How could she possibly know anything? I wondered as I quickened my pace. And as for obtaining my phone number. Well, I suppose that wouldn't be too difficult. It was boldly displayed on the notice board in the Parish Hall, so anyone could have easily taken it down. But the part that completely freaked me out was what she said. Could someone possibly know what I was up to? No, surely not. I was clever, meticulous, except for my monumental fuck-up of leaving the knife up at the Hell Fire Club. I had learned a valuable lesson from that mistake, one that will never be repeated again. The thought of someone potentially watching or knowing my every move sent shivers down my spine, but I was determined to stay one step ahead.

'No, there's nothing to worry about,' I reassured myself. It was just a crank call, nothing more. I imagined that a couple of youths had taken down my number from the notice board in the parish hall and were simply having a laugh at my expense.

Upon arriving home, I went straight to the kitchen and emptied the contents of the vinegar-stained brown paper bag onto a plate. Despite my intense hunger and the alluring aroma of the food, I couldn't bring myself to eat even a single chip. Frustrated beyond belief, I angrily tossed the plate, along with the smoked cod and chips that I had been longing for, into the bin. In an attempt to calm my nerves, I poured myself a generous glass of whiskey and made my way upstairs.

I sat on the edge of the bed and opened the drawer on the bedside table, revealing the small brown plastic bottle of sleeping pills that I swore I would never touch again. As I opened the bottle and gazed in at all the beautiful little white pills lying on top of each other. They were small, yet deadly. Each little white pill possessed the power to block out everything and transport me to another world. A new world shrouded in stillness and darkness, where I no longer saw or felt any-thing. I placed two of the pills on my tongue and washed them down with a mouthful of whiskey. Just as I was about to twist the lid back onto the bottle, 'Fuck it,' I muttered under my breath and swallowed one more pill, draining my glass.

Chapter 40

The only problem with escaping from reality is that eventually, you must return to it. Unfortunately, as I have found out, this is never a pleasant experience. Despite my dislike for the terrible drowsy feeling that followed the next morning after taking one of those sleeping pills, I was always grateful for the hours of uninterrupted sleep that they granted me. There was no way I would have been able to sleep after receiving such an unexpected phone call. However, even in my groggy and disoriented state, I could still vividly recall the exact words of my mysterious caller:

'Hello, Father, I know what you've been up to.'

I was still none the wiser as to who the caller might be. I desperately tried to convince myself that it was nothing more than a hoax call from some of the youths that hung around the parish hall. However, a nagging voice in the back of my mind suggested something completely different. Since receiving the call, I became even more paranoid than I already was. I had the eerie sensation of being constantly watched and found myself glancing over my shoulder whenever I was out and about. Even inside the safety of the four walls of my house, I found it impossible to relax. I spent most of my time peering out of my bedroom window, scanning the street below for any signs of unusual activity or suspicious strangers lurking about. I couldn't deny the overwhelming fear that consumed me as I tried to process the sudden unexpected situation, I found myself in.

A quick glance at my watch informed me that I had enough time for another cup of coffee, before facing the intimidating blue rinse militia and celebrating the morning mass. Saying mass had become a tedious chore for me. Over time, I had managed to reduce the length of the service from forty minutes down to twenty-five minutes, and no matter what I tried I couldn't get it any lower. Although, I was pretty sure that I must have set some sort of a precedent with that time. During the service, my mind often wondered, and I would imagine myself stepping down from the altar and walking among the congregation. However, my daydreams would take a dark turn as I envisioned violently dragging one of the blue rinse militia, preferable Maura, their leader, up to the altar by her hair. I would then lay her down on top of the altar and sacrifice her soul to the lurking spirits that dwelt within the church. Similar to what I had done with that vile whore at the Hell Fire Club. That would certainly liven things up, I thought, as I looked down towards the sorrowful lot staring back at me. Their eyes and faces were devoid of emotion. They appeared to be merely going through the motions, as they waited for their inevitable judgment day.

During every mass, the congregation would stare up at me as if they were waiting for me to perform some sort of miracle that would change their mundane lives for the better. The image of sacrificing Maura on the altar regularly entered my mind as I became bored during the service. I would smile to myself, picturing the chaos that would ensue – the screaming, the panic, the blue rinse militia crying out to a God that doesn't exist, begging for salvation. However, I quickly removed the image from my mind before it could fully consume me and I acted on it. Sadly, the thought of sacrificing Maura on the altar was nothing more than a fantasy, a pleasant dream, just my vivid imagination running wild. Exactly twenty-five minutes after I had said the opening prayer of the mass, I raised my bowed head from the altar and looked down at the first three rows of pews, the rest of the church was empty.

'Mass had ended, let us go in peace to love and serve the lord, Amen.' Thank fuck, ran through my mind as I blessed myself and made my way back to the sacristy, my footsteps echoing throughout the empty church.

Once again, I had fallen way behind on my other priestly duties, such as the hospital and house calls, and the dreaded school visits. In fairness to Fr. Brian, he had been extremely helpful and went above and beyond the call of duty on many occasions to assist me in catching up on tasks that I had either genuinely forgotten or simply neglected. As the parish priest, I knew that I needed to smarten up and take responsibility for my duties. The last thing I wanted was to be summoned to His Grace's abode again. I needed to remain well under the radar and out of sight in order to avoid any unwanted attention.

There were several people who were very unhappy with me. The school principal for one, he had left a number of voicemails on my phone, sounding quite agitated. I put it down to him being under a lot of pressure, as I'm sure it must be very stressful trying to manage a school full of cheeky, entitled brats. The hospitals were also displeased with me. They had called multiple times, requesting that I come and administer the Last Rites. However, I did not answer their calls or respond to their voicemails. This caused a lot of distress for the hospitals, as the families of the deceased were devastated that their loved ones had passed away without receiving a final blessing to guide them on their journey to the afterlife.

I decided to treat Fr. Brian to a spot of lunch. I felt that I needed to explain my recent shortcomings and slip-ups. He was definitely the one person who I needed on my side. We met at a local establishment that doubled as a café by day, and a restaurant by night, which surprisingly had an extensive menu and more importantly a very impressive wine list. However, food no longer played a significant role in my daily routine. I rarely cooked, and even when a dinner was placed in front of me, I usually just picked at it. This lunch was no different; I ordered a Caesar salad, even though I disliked salads and anything that was green and healthy. I only ate the small pieces of chicken that lay scattered around the plate.

'Is your appetite not with you today?' Fr. Brian inquired, as he looked down at my barely touched plate.

'Man does not live on bread and water alone,' I quipped, as we shared a laugh. 'Ah, but wine, now that's a different story. One of life's necessities some might say,' I added, as I poured us both a glass of a fine red wine from the south of France.

'You look tired, John,' Fr. Brian said, from across the table as he shovelled a fork full of food into his mouth.

'I am tired, in fact, I'm completely exhausted,' I replied, punctuating my statement with a yawn.

'I take it you didn't get a chance to go and see the doctor,' he said, while wagging his finger at me in a chastising manner.

'Actually, I did. He prescribed me some sleeping pills and let me tell you, they worked like a charm. The only downside is that I'm completely wiped out for most of the following day,' I replied.

'Jesus, he must have given you some really strong stuff. Maybe you should go back to him and explain the side effects. I'm sure he'll give you something else,' he said, before emptying another fork load of food into his mouth.

'I might have to, I'll see how I feel over the next couple of days. I don't take them every night, and in fairness to the old quack he did mention that they might take a bit of getting used to,' I replied.

'Well, you'll know what's best for yourself,' he said, as he wiped tomato ketchup from the side of his mouth with the back of his hand. It was like watching a child eat.

'Brian, I wanted to thank you for all your extra help and support over the past few weeks. You have truly gone above and beyond. I must admit, I have been struggling to keep on top of things, and I have let a few things slip through the cracks. I just wanted you to know how grateful I am for all your help. I couldn't have managed without you during this time,' I said, trying to sound sincere. I laid it on thick and heavy. Surely, that would be enough to inflate his young ego. If that didn't work, my next step would be a blowjob, but I really didn't want to go down that route. I haven't had to resort to such drastic measures since my days in the seminary.

'No bother at all. Sure, isn't that what I'm here for, to be your lackey,' he replied breaking out into a fit of uncontrollable laughter. I raised my glass to meet his and smiled as they clinked.

The hours drifted by as we sat there drinking and talking pure shite. The more wine I consumed, the more I enjoyed his company. I didn't notice the time passing. It was only when I realised that the second bottle of wine was empty and the attractive waitress, who spoke in broken English, was asking if we would like another bottle. It was then that I knew it was time for us to be on our way. I paid the bill and left a generous tip for the beautiful waitress. She had stirred something inside of me that I knew I had to ignore. As we rose from the table, we were a little unsteady as we made our way outside into the bright, warm afternoon. I hadn't noticed how dimly lit the café was until we stepped out onto the street. The sudden brightness momentarily blinded me, until my eyes adjusted to the warm rays of the sun shining down on us. As we made our way along the street, both of us a little unsteady on our feet, but neither of us willing to mentioned it. We just struggled on.

As we stumbled along the street, I silently prayed that we wouldn't run into any members of the blue rinse militia. I was sure that some nosy old biddy would notice the two priests walking up the road, half-cut and giggling like two good-for-nothing corner boys. The scandal of the two drunken priests roaming through the town would surely spread throughout the parish before I even made it home. Fuck them, I thought smiling drunkenly, as we both stumbled merrily on up the road. However, our drunken giddiness was short – lived.

I eventually left Fr. Brian at his house, bidding him farewell and declining his offer to join him for a strong coffee, which was probably just what us drunken pair of fools needed. I just wanted to go home, lie on the sofa, and sleep it off. Upon opening the front door, I unset the alarm before bending down and picking up the pile of mail from the floor. There were five envelopes: four white and one brown with a black harp printed on it. Straight away, I could tell that two of the white envelopes were bills. I carefully placed the two bills and the brown envelope on the cluttered telephone stand in the hall before making my way into the sitting room. I kicked off my shoes and collapsed onto the sofa, my head was spinning from the combination of alcohol and exhaustion. It felt good to lie down. It was far too early in the day to be drinking that much wine. I opened one of the two remaining envelopes; it was a thank you card from someone that I had helped out a little while ago. I couldn't for the life of me remember what I had done to help that person, and I couldn't make out the signature on the bottom of the card. So, I hadn't a clue who sent it, not that I cared anyway, as I tossed the card onto the coffee table.

After briefly dozing off, I dragged myself up off the sofa and made my way to the kitchen. I filled and turned on the kettle, maybe Fr. Brian's suggestion of a strong coffee was the way to go. While waiting for the kettle to boil, I sat down at the kitchen table and opened the last envelope. I was shocked to see seven words spelt out in black letters cut from a newspaper and pasted onto a sheet of white paper, like something out of a movie. The words read,

'I SEE YOU LIKE CALL GIRLS, FATHER.' A sharp, bone-chilling shiver shot down my spine, causing my entire body to tremble. My hands shook violently as I tightly gripped the letter, my mind unable to process the words on the page.

'This can't be happening,' I whispered as I read the letter over and over, in complete disbelief.

Chapter 41

The letter and phone call consumed my entire being, their words echoed through my mind, haunting my every waking hour. I couldn't escape their grip, no matter how hard I tried. Even in my drunken, sleeping pill induced slumber, the call and letter crept into my dreams, transforming them into terrifying nightmares. Each time I reread the letter and replayed the phone call in my mind, a surge of fear and anxiety washed over me. I felt like I was suffocating, unable to escape from the constant reminder that someone was watching my every move.

Although the days were dull in comparison to the terror that awaited me once darkness had descended. Each night, the ethereal apparitions of those I had sacrificed would materialise before me one after another, as if letting me know that their spirits were never too far away. Their hollow eyes and pallid skin chilled me to the core. I would jolt awake, my heart racing and my trembling body drenched in a cold sweat. I sought solace in the depths of a whiskey bottle, drowning my fears and numbing my senses with each mouthful.

Three days had passed since I received the letter and read the seven words that were boldly staring back at me. For the past three days and nights, those seven words consumed my mind, leaving no room for any other thoughts to enter. Yet, I still couldn't answer the only question that kept repeating itself in my mind: who could have sent the letter? Not a single name came to mind of someone who might have a vendetta against me. I had dismissed the thought that it was a hoax; I knew the letter was serious. Everything about it had sent a chill right through me. I was scared, someone was watching me closely, and I was completely clueless as to who it could be.

I was consumed by intense paranoia and constantly on edge. I spent endless hours looking out of my bedroom window, scanning the street below. Despite my vigilant watch, nothing ever seemed out of the ordinary or suspicious. The street was always quiet, with no signs of anyone lurking or watching my house. I wasted countless hours just staring out of my window, watching the same old familiar faces pass by as they went about their daily routines. And despite the normalcy of the street, I couldn't shake off the feeling of being watched. It was a constant battle between my rational mind and my irrational fears.

There was never anyone hanging around, acting suspiciously, or any cars parked with someone sitting in them watching my house. Nothing ever stood out or caught my eye or gave me cause for concern. For hours on end, I stood hidden behind a curtain, looking down at the street below, tormented, frustrated, and above all, scared shitless of the unknown that awaited me.

After hours of careful consideration and weighing up all the evidence, I finally arrived at the conclusion, that it had to be one of my neighbours. Although, I struggled with the thought of one of them stooping to such a depraved low, it was the most logical explanation, it made perfect sense. The culprit had to be right under my nose, someone, who had taken a very unhealthy interest in me and has been closely monitoring my every move. As unsettling as the realisation was, my neighbours were the only ones who could monitor my daily routine and movements, without causing any suspicion.

I was completely baffled; none of it made any sense to me. And the last thing I needed was all this added burden and stress entering my already chaotic and fucked-up life. The phone call and the letter only added to the constant madness that was swirling around inside my messed-up head day and night, without any reprieve. I knew that I needed to get to the bottom of this before it escalated any further, but I had no idea where to begin.

My thought process was that anyone living near me could be a potential suspect. I couldn't relax and found myself constantly pacing the hallway, chain-smoking and feeling on edge. I craved some kind of confrontation to release my pent-up frustration. So, I decided to go out for a walk, hoping that whoever was watching me would follow on foot. As I strolled along, I reminded myself to stay calm and act normally, while also remaining vigilant and cautious. I carefully observed my surroundings with each step, checking to see if I was being followed. Even though the situation that I found myself in was anything but normal, I needed to give off the impression of being care-free, without a worry in the world, just your average priest out for a leisurely midday stroll.

I stopped by the local shop and bought a pack of cigarettes. I had a quick chat with Joseph, the life-draining shopkeeper, before con-tinuing on my way. The more I walked, the more paranoid I became, knowing that someone was closely watching me. The voice on the phone that evening belonged to a woman, and I assumed that the let-ter was from her as well. So, my stalker was a foreign woman, as she spoke with broken English. I cursed her under my breath as I entered the local park and followed the narrow, winding pathway that com-pleted a full loop around the perimeter of the park. Once again, noth-ing or no one stood out or caught my attention.

As I strolled along the winding path, everything felt surreal. It was as if my life was no longer my own. I came across a heavily graffitied bench and sat down, lighting a cigarette as I scanned the park. Despite my paranoia, nothing seemed out of place. No one had followed me into the park, and those already in the park seemed obliviously to my presence. I flicked the smouldering cigarette butt to the ground, watch-ing as it sizzled and died out on the pavement. Slowly, I rose from the cold metal bench, my eyes scanned the bustling crowd, which mainly consisted of mothers and their young children. Disheartened, I made my way to the main entrance of the park and headed for home. Once safely back inside my own four walls, I poured myself a large whis-key and sat down at the kitchen table. As I stared vacantly at the back wall, I couldn't help but wonder why I had never hung a picture on it to break up its blandness. But my thoughts quickly returned to the real problem at hand: my stalker, my tormentor, the invisible woman who was slowly driving me insane. I needed to set a trap and lure the devious bitch out into the open. One careless slip-up and she would be at my mercy.

As the evening slowly drifted into the night, the sky darkened and the streetlights flickered to life, casting eerie shadows along the pave-ment. I had spent the last couple of hours looking out of my bedroom window, observing the quiet street below, and as per usual, every-thing appeared as normal. Suddenly, a wave of anger and frustration washed over me, I quickly descended the stairs and slammed the front door behind me. I had no idea where I was going, but I needed to flee from the claustrophobic walls of my house, which seemed to be slowly suffocating me. As I reversed out of the driveway, the clock on the dashboard read eight-thirty, although it felt much later. The sky was shrouded in a thick, impenetrable darkness, like a heavy blan-ket draped over the world. Even the bright moon struggled to pierce through the thick veil that cloaked the sky above.

I cautiously drove down the quiet street, constantly checking my surroundings for any signs of being followed. With no specific destination in mind, I merged onto the main road. The tension in my body was evident as cold beads of sweat trickled down my spine and my knuckles turned white from gripping the steering wheel so tightly. Eventually, I ended up in Dun Laoghaire and pulled into the car park across from Teddy's famous ice cream parlour. No cars followed me into the car park, but if someone was tailing me, they may have driven a bit further on down the road before parking where they could still keep an eye on me though their rear-view mirror, I thought as I lit up a cigarette.

I sat for a while, gazing out at the vast expanse of the dark sea. As I exhaled a cloud of cigarette smoke out the car window, my eyes constantly shifted between the rear-view mirror and the side mirror, searching for any signs of a lurking presence or someone watching me from a nearby parked car. Even though I couldn't see her, I knew my nemesis was out there, hiding in the shadows and patiently watching my every move, invisible to the naked eye. With a sense of unease, I stepped out of the car, acutely aware that someone was probably watching me.

As I made my way towards the pier, I couldn't help but admire the peacefulness of the night. The moon cast a soft glow over the still water, and the warm air enveloped me as I stepped onto the pier, although my mind was anything but calm. My hands trembled as I reached for another cigarette, my mind racing with anxious thoughts. I couldn't seem to calm my nerves, no matter how many times I lit up. Halfway down along the pier, I approached the old, weathered bandstand. I stopped and leaned against its railings, which were in bad need of a fresh coat of paint. Memories flooded back from many years ago, when I was forced to endure the deafening noise of a brass band playing on this very bandstand. I can still vividly recall the vice-like grip of my mother's hand, as I stood by her side with an ice cream from Teddy's in my other hand. As I reminisced on the past, a shiver ran through me as the sea breeze wrapped itself around me. Or perhaps it was the ghost of my sadistic mother that caused me to shudder as I looked out over the sea.

I left the bandstand and continued down along the pier. Couples walked past holding hands, while others were cuddled up tightly, arms wrapped around one another, all loved up. Secretly, I envied them as they walked by. My life could have been so different if my mother had not been so fucked up. A wave of sadness and bitterness washed over me as I watched the couples completely lost in each other, a feeling I have never experienced and never would.

The bustling pier was a popular spot for dog walkers and joggers. As someone who wasn't an animal lover, and had no interest in sports, I found the incessant barking of dogs and the heavy thud of footsteps pounding the ground grated on my nerves. A small group of joggers sprinted past, their faces red and sweat dripping down their foreheads, as if attempting to break a world record. However, their heavy breathing made me wonder if they should even be jogging at all. As I strolled and smoked my way back up along the pier, I felt invisible and insignificant among the horde of people, who seemed too consumed by their own self-importance to even spare me a passing glance.

'For fuck's sake, show yourself, you worthless whore,' I muttered under my breath as I discreetly scanned every face passing by. Frustrated, I flicked my half-smoked cigarette to the ground and continued walking back up the pier. My mission had failed, and I left the pier feeling defeated and disheartened, annoyed that I was unable to spot my stalker. As I made my way towards the car park, I stopped and rested my arms on the railings, taking in one last look at the majestic beauty of the ocean before me. The water was so calm that it appeared one could walk across it. A smile crossed my face as I thought about the crazy story of Jesus walking on water.

'Where the hell are you?' I muttered to myself, rage boiling inside me as I scanned my surroundings one last time.

Upon returning to my car, I was seething with rage over the failure of my plan and the continued mystery surrounding my stalker's identity. Despite my efforts, I remained clueless about who was tormenting me. Although, part of me wanted a confrontation, another part felt relieved that no one had approached me. I don't know how I would have reacted if a stranger had accosted me. Fuck it, I thought, as I turned the key in the ignition. Just as I was about to leave the car park, out of the corner of my eye, I spotted a white envelope tucked under one of the windscreen wipers. I slammed on the brakes, jumped out of the car, and removed the envelope, my eyes darting around frantically, but there was on one in sight.

I quickly drove away from the car park; my mind was consumed by a tumultuous storm of violent and vengeful thoughts. My rage surged through every inch of my being as I sped down the road at breakneck speed. After about a mile, I pulled into a lay-by, my hands shook uncontrollably as I opened the envelope. The words were scrawled in thick black capital letters:

'ENJOY YOUR WALK, FATHER?' I couldn't fucking believe what I had just read. What kind of twisted game was she playing? I slammed my fist down on the dashboard in frustration.

'You messed-up bitched,' I snarled, hitting the dashboard again. I got out of the car and scanned the quiet road, but there was no one in sight. The worthless whore had completely outsmarted me, making me look like a fool.

I was completely at her mercy; the bitch had me right where she wanted me. I was nothing more than a puppet on a string, pulled for her amusement and pleasure whenever she pleased. My mind was spinning, stuck in overdrive. She must have been so close; I probably walked right past her as I made my way down along the pier. The cheeky bitch had watched my every move before placing the envelope on my windscreen. Not a single person I passed on the pier raised any suspicion. Who the hell am I dealing with? The invisible woman? A ghost of one of my victims?

By the time I arrived home, I was exhausted and completely freaked out. I stepped out of my car and lit a cigarette, leaning against the front door, scanning the eerily quiet and dimly lit street. Once again, everything seemed normal, which only made things worse. Because things were far from being normal, everything was fucking abnormal. I could not shake the feeling that at any moment, someone or something would emerge from the shadows and end my life. I could sense it; the feeling was real. Even though, I couldn't see anything, I knew it was there, just waiting for the right moment to pounce. I inhaled deeply, as I took one last look up and down the street. Still nothing.

'Fuck the lot of you,' I whispered, as I threw the butt to the ground and went inside.

Chapter 42

Having a stalker completely disrupted my life. Overnight, I had gone from predator to prey, a role I had previously sworn never to take on again. As I said mass, I carefully observed the congregation while placing a piece of Holy Communion on an ugly pink tongue that was extended towards me. It could be anyone, even this old fogey kneeling in front of me on her arthritic knees.

'Body of Christ,' I said, followed by a darker thought, go to fucking hell, as I moved on to the next parishioner, whose tongue protruded eagerly, like a well-trained dog waiting for a treat.

After celebrating mass, I enjoyed a pleasant chat and a coffee with Fr. Brian. We discussed what needed to be done in and around the parish and then divided the list between ourselves. After finishing our second cup of coffee, we said our goodbyes and went our separate ways to begin tackling our respective to-do lists. However, my day took an unexpected turn when I received a phone call, informing me that I had to rush over to a neighbouring parish to perform a funeral mass. The priest of that parish was unwell and confined to bed, therefore he was unable to perform his duties, so I had to step in. The sudden change in plans was a major inconvenience and put me on the back foot for the rest of the day.

The day flew by and before I knew it, it was late in the evening. Exhausted, I arrived home and collapsed onto the sofa, with the remote in one hand and a glass of whiskey in the other. As tired as I was, I couldn't shake the thoughts of the phone call and the letter from my mind. I reminded myself that I needed to stay focused and alert, as the stakes were now higher than ever. One mistake on my part could be detrimental. How close was she? The conniving bitch had me cornered and I was growing impatient. Her presence, though unseen, was not just affecting my work, but also my well-being. It had become increasingly difficult to rid the streets of those vile whores while under surveillance.

As I peered out from behind a curtain in my bedroom down onto the street below, it felt as though I was under house arrest. As if my stalker had penned me in, I felt trapped and confined within the walls of my own home, afraid to leave the safety of my cocoon. My frustration grew as I thought about those vile whores freely roaming the streets, luring innocent and unsuspecting victims with their tainted bodies, leaving a trail of destruction in their wake, while I cowered within the safety of my room as I waited for my nemesis to strike. I couldn't just sit and wait while they carried out their disgusting acts in secluded street corners under the cover of darkness.

As I lay on the sofa, completely drained and unable to relax, my mind was in overdrive as my thoughts spiralled out of control.

'Fuck this,' I whispered as I got up and went into the hallway. I grabbed my coat from the rack and felt a surge of excitement as I reached into the pocket and touched the hammer.

'Let's see how clever my invisible stalker is,' I muttered as I left the house through the back door. I walked down to the end of the garden, unlocked the back gate, and made my way down the dark, narrow, and foul-smelling laneway. Five minutes later, I was sitting in the back of a taxi. When we reached the city centre, I got out at the taxi at the top of Fitzwilliam's Road and paid the driver.

As I lit up a cigarette, I leaned against the railings of an old Georgian house, now converted into solicitors' offices, according to the two brass plaques that were fixed to the wall, beside the front door. I casually scanned the street, taking note of a group of five women standing at the corner of a side street just a short distance away. However, I quickly dismissed the idea of approaching them. It was far too risky to target a group; I needed a lone worker. If there were two of them, there was a chance that one could identify me if something went horribly wrong. Although I highly doubted that possibility, as most of the girls working the streets were addicts, and completely off their heads on gear as they wandered from one punter to the next. It was an unnecessary risk that I was not willing to take.

I made my way over to the corner of Fitzwilliam's Square, where I noticed a woman smoking alone under a streetlight. As I crossed the road, I kept a watchful eye all around me, paranoid, and with good reason, that I might be followed. As I approached the woman from behind, the sickly-sweet scent of her cheap perfume and the pungent smell of cigarette smoke assaulted my senses. She must have heard me approaching and quickly turned to face me.

'Are you looking for a bit of business?' she asked, blowing smoke from her bright red lips. 'Yes,' I replied a little too eagerly, with a sheepish smile, feeling like a complete fucking idiot.

'Well, what are you looking for?' she asked, bringing the cigarette back up to her mouth.

'A shag,' I replied, my eyes fixed on the pavement, unable to meet her gaze.

'Sixty euro,' she said. I raised my eyes to meet hers. Her penetrating stare bore into me, as if searching the depths of my soul. The intensity of her stare was unsettling, her eyes sharp and unwavering.

'Do you have a place we can go to?' I asked, avoiding eye contact once again.

'Sure, follow me. We just need to hop over the railings and into the park. They're not very high, it's easy,' she replied with a smile, making me feel a little less uneasy. I could tell from her response that she had hopped over these railings many times before. Well, tonight will be the last time she hops over any railings, or does anything else for that matter, I thought to myself as I followed her across the road. The sound of her heels clicking against the pavement with each step echoed off the nearby buildings, there was nothing discreet about this vile whore. The railings surrounding the park were low and easy to climb over. Once inside, she led me to a secluded spot that she clearly frequented. She lowered herself onto the soft, green grass and turned to me with a smile.

'We'll be grand here,' she said, extending her hand towards me.

'And it's money up front.' I mirrored her smile as I handed her the cash, before removing my coat and settling down on the soft grass beside her.

'Nice one,' she said, as she carefully counted out the crumpled notes and placed them in her worn leather handbag.

I lay back on the grass and without wasting any time, she unbuckled my belt and pulled down the zip on my trousers. Her cold hands began to move around my penis. As soon as I was hard, she turned and lay down on her back. I entered her roughly, wanting to get the disgusting deed over and done with. She lay beneath me, her eyes closed and her body tense, as if lost in her own thoughts. Probably thinking how the fuck had her life gone so terribly wrong, I imagined, as I worked away on her. She seemed miles away, not even bothering to fake a groan. Fucking bitch, what the hell was I paying her for, I thought, as I tried to suppress my growing anger.

Once spent, I rolled off of her, breathing heavily, fucking cigarettes, I thought as I struggled to regain my breath. She quickly sat up and began fixing herself up.

'Are you in a hurry?' I asked, still a little out of breath.

'Why, you got your money's worth,' she replied, taking a cigarette from the pack in my outstretched hand.

'It's just, I'm really horny tonight, I'd like to go again,' I said, suddenly feeling embarrassed as the words left my mouth. I felt like a greedy child asking for more sweets after already indulging in a whole bag.

'Okay, another sixty euro,' she replied, her tone business-like. I smiled as I handed her the money, knowing that her life was almost over. At that very moment, she may as well have been staring into the eyes of the grim reaper.

'I'll just have this smoke first,' I said. She simply nodded; her expression was easy to read. It was clear that the poor girl would rather be anywhere else, but her unfortunate circumstances had landed her here, getting fucked in a park by a stranger just to make ends meet. As I lay back on the grass, smoking, savouring the moment, the calm before the storm, I thought as I stared up at the heavens. The sky was a deep, velvety black, with the moon struggling to break through the dark clouds. Its soft glow illuminated the peaceful park, which was otherwise shrouded in a starless sky.

I turned to face her. She was looking right at me, or maybe even right through me. She remained silent, as she brought her knees up towards her chest and wrapped her arms around them. With a slight turn of her head, her eyes shifted towards the far side of the park, as if something had caught her eye. I finished my cigarette and stood up, before walking over to the trees to relieve myself. Glancing over my shoulder, I saw that she hadn't moved, she was still lost in her own little world, staring into space. Fucking nut job, I thought to myself as I made my way back to where she was sitting. Standing over her, she turned and raised her head, her vacant eyes met mine.

'Suck it,' I demanded, my tone leaving no room for negotiation. Slowly, she got onto her knees and took me into her mouth. As she worked away on me, my hands tightly grabbed a fistful of her silky, jet-black hair, I quickly pulled away from her, much to her surprise, before roughly turning her around on all fours. I slid down and entered her, taking it easier the second time around. My entire body trembled with pleasure as I reached climax. When I came, she lowered herself onto her stomach with a slow, deliberate movement. A deep sigh of relief escaped her lips, relieved that the ordeal was finally over. I gently eased myself down on top of her, savouring the feeling of her body beneath mine. A tingling sensation coursed through me as I caressed my lips along her warm, smooth skin. I bypassed the overpowering scent of cheap perfume, and the faint hint of stale sweat that lingered on her skin, not wanting to let her go.

As I held her, a strange feeling washed over me, a feeling that I had never experienced before. I wanted that brief moment of tenderness to last. Reluctantly, I released my hold on her and stood up. I was confused; it felt like good and evil were rising up against each other from deep within me as I fixed my clothes. The silence and stillness, which shrouded the park created a beautiful setting. I reached out my hand to help her up off the ground, trying to be the perfect gentleman. She thanked me, as she got to her feet. I watched as she took a small mirror out of her handbag and checked her hair and makeup. She applied some red lipstick, to her perfectly shaped lips before putting the items back into her bag. Then, without a single word, she began making her way towards the railings.

Ignorant, ungrateful bitch, I though as I reached into my coat pocket and retrieved the hammer. Just as I raised the hammer above my head, she turned to face me. In a moment of panic, I brought the hammer down onto her forehead, but not before, she had released a loud piercing scream. In a complete frenzy, I quickly landed several more blows. What if someone heard her scream? I though, as I dragged her lifeless body over to a densely overgrown area of bushes. I hid among the bushes and trees, fearing that someone may have heard her scream and might decide to investigate. I remained silent and motionless, hidden among the foliage next to her lifeless corpse for several minutes. Nobody entered the park, it was time to move. After carefully surveying the surrounding area from inside the railings, I climbed back over onto the pavement. I lit a cigarette and walked calmly towards Baggot Street Bridge.

The temptation to run was strong, almost egging me on, but I resisted and remained steadfast, trying to appear carefree as I exhaled smoke into the warm night air. As I crossed the bridge, I hailed down a taxi and twenty-seven minutes later, I was sitting at my kitchen table, savouring a well-deserved glass of whiskey and feeling completely satisfied with my night's work. Closing my eyes as I drained the glass, the only thought still consuming my mind was: who the fuck is stalking me?

Chapter 43

A s I lay on the bedroom floor, curled up in a tight ball of pain, my warm blood trickled down my battered body like a crimson river. The rough texture of the threadbare carpet, combined with the musty smell of old stains, pressed against my cheek as I lay there, unable to move a muscle. The metallic smell of my blood and the taste of salt in my tears overwhelmed my senses, as the burning pain radiated from the deep gashes on my skin. Tears cascaded down my contorted face as I stared at my pitiful reflection in the mirror. The leather whip lay discarded on the floor beside my blood-soaked feet, a painful reminder of the torture I had endured.

'You're a pathetic excuse for a man,' my dead mother's voice echoed in my head as I remained on the floor, cowering like a beaten animal and whimpering in pain.

I struggled to lift myself onto my knee's multiple times, but each attempt ended in failure. Eventually, I surrendered and collapsed onto the blood-soaked carpet, crying as I drifted in and out of consciousness. I must have dozed off for a brief period, only to awaken in excruciating pain, my body trembling uncontrollably, chilled to the bone. After much struggle and effort, I finally managed to stand up. I was in a terrible state, my already scarred body now covered in fresh wounds, all because that vile whore had lured me over the railings and into the park.

My tears flowed freely as I cried out in agony, the hot water from the shower felt like a barrage of lashes raining down on my skin, sending unbearable jolts of pain through my body. The intensity of the pain made it impossible for me to dry myself off, so I resorted to swallowing a handful of painkillers and smothering my open wounds with antiseptic cream. On returning to the bedroom, I collapsed face down on the bed, thankfully, I didn't have to leave the house, it was Fr. Brian's turn to say the morning mass. I also, didn't have to worry about my nosy housekeeper walking in on me.

As I lay there in agony, waiting for the painkillers to kick in, I couldn't stop thinking about Ann. She didn't deserve the fate she met. Ann was never part of my agenda; she was just another innocent person caught in the wrong place at the wrong time. It's a tragic cycle that seems to repeat itself endlessly. I can only imagine that by now, the animals of the forest have feasted well on her decaying body. And as for her henpecked husband, Terry he was completely devastated by her disappearance. I found it so hard to believe that someone could be so deeply in love and attached to another person. I just couldn't comprehend it. What a cruel twist of fate for that poor, innocent soul.

I tried to lift myself off the bed, but the pain was too much. The painkillers I had taken seemed useless, just like that vile whore I had engaged with in the park last night. As the pain persisted, fresh tears rolled down my cheeks. I buried my face in the pillow, muffling my sobs as I released all the pent-up pain and frustration.

Chapter 44

A week had passed since I received the letter, and with each passing day, my paranoia only intensified. Whenever I was in the house, I found myself constantly pacing the hallway or anxiously peering out of my bedroom window, desperately searching for any signs of suspicious activity on the street below. Each one of my neighbours had now become a potential suspect, and I firmly believed that the perpetrator must be living on my street, closely monitoring my every move.

The evening news featured a reporter interviewing the park warden who had discovered the woman's body earlier that morning while opening the park. As I watched, I couldn't help but mutter,

'Fuck him,' at the television screen. Finding the body the next morning was far too soon for my liking. The immense pressure of my double life was taking a heavy toll on me. I had gone from smoking one pack of cigarettes a day to two, and on particularly stressful days, I even managed to make it halfway through a third pack. This stalker of mine had completely turned my life upside down. What kind of a twisted game was she playing? And what was her ultimate goal? These were the questions, I could not answer.

I couldn't figure out her motive. It was evident that she had not gone to the police, as they would have already been in contact or possibly even arrested me by now. The only motive I could think of was money. Although she hadn't mentioned it in her letter, I couldn't think of any other explanation for her foolish games. If money was her objective, I did have a significant amount stashed away, thanks to my mother's untimely departure from this cruel world. The sale of her house, her savings, and insurance policy all added up to a substantial sum and was safely hidden away in a second back account. Due to the nature of my profession, which required me to take a vow of poverty,

I had to be discreet about my acquired assets. However, if necessary, I would reluctantly dip into my secret stash to get rid of this crazy bitch.

The idea of someone constantly watching my every move made my skin crawl and filled me with a sense of unease. In passing, I glanced at the faces of my nosy neighbours, searching for any signs of suspicious behaviour. But none of them seemed to fit the profile of a potential stalker. Then again, I suppose anyone of us could have the potential to become a stalker, or even worse, if our circumstances drove us to it. Although I was fairly certain that not many people would have suspected their local Parish Priest of being a serial killer. A title that still didn't sit well with me.

That night out in Dun Laoghaire, as I strolled along the pier, continued to haunt me. I realised that I must have been so close to her, perhaps even walked right by her on the pier or in the car park. Her perfume may have even aroused my senses as we passed each other.

Despite my personal opinion of her, a certain part of me couldn't help but admired her tactics, whether they were underhanded or not. She had me on the ropes, cornered, toying with me, just waiting for the right moment to finish me off. First the phone call, then the letter, and the incident that left the deepest mark on me – the note left on my windscreen. I can only assume that she had followed me from my house that night, all the way out to Dun Laoghaire. She must have watched from the shadows as I walked along the pier and then had the audacity to leave the envelope under the windscreen wiper. She had managed to deceive me and carry out her plan right under my nose, without me noticing or suspecting a thing. One could not help but admire her cunningness.

The following morning after another hellish night filled with tossing and turning, plagued by haunting images and fears. I met Fr. Brian for a coffee after he had finished saying the morning mass. After the rough night I had, I would have preferred to meet for a few glasses of whiskey, but it was only eleven o'clock in the morning. Not that the early morning hour would have deterred me from drinking, but I'm sure many would have disapproved, including Fr. Brian.

After buttering him up a little, I subtly mentioned to Fr. Brian that I was considering taking a short trip, curious to see his reaction. I fabricated a heart-wrenching story, explaining that an old friend of mine was in poor health and I felt compelled to visit him in case he didn't recover.

'Sure, that would be no problem at all, John. I am more than capable of managing things here for a few days on my own. You go and visit your sick friend,' he replied with a smile, as he raised a chocolate éclair up to his mouth. I had to look away.

'Thank you, Brian. But only if you feel comfortable being alone for a few days,' I responded. I knew Fr. Brian was more than capable, he could run the entire parish on his own, much better than I could, any day of the week.

He attempted to speak, but a large piece of gooey, chocolate-covered éclair that he was chewing on temporarily prevented any words from leaving his mouth. After washing it down with a mouthful of coffee and wiping his mouth with a paper napkin, he finally managed to speak.

'It won't be a problem at all. Sure, I have the blue rinse militia wrapped around my little finger. They'll give me all the help I need. You go ahead and do whatever you need to do,' he said as he stuffed the last piece of éclair into his mouth.

'I know it's short notice, but I just received the call from my friend's distressed mother as I was leaving the house, less than an hour ago. I was thinking of leaving early tomorrow morning,' I explained.

'That's no problem. You leave whenever you like. Everything will be fine here,' he replied, wiping his chocolate-stained mouth with the back of his hand.

I politely waved over to the young foreign waitress, who had brought our coffee and cakes to our table with an exaggerated smile. It appeared that she remembered the generous tip I had given her the last time, as she quickly made her way over to us. I requested the bill and she promptly returned, holding it in one hand and a credit card machine in the other, her beautiful face still wearing the exaggerated smile. Fr. Brian always seemed to avoid looking at the bill. I paid, and left a generous tip once again, courtesy of the weekly collection at the Sunday mass. As we got up to leave, I thanked the waitress, and we said our goodbyes. Outside the café, I lit a cigarette and offered one to Fr. Brian, which he gratefully accepted.

'Thanks again, Brian. And remember, you can call me anytime, day or night. If you need anything or any issues arise, my phone is always on,' I said, before inhaling deeply on the cancer stick.

'Thanks, John. I appreciate it. Hopefully I won't have to bother you while you're away,' he replied. We shook hands, exchanged our farewells, and then went our separate ways.

On my way home, I decided to stop by Terry's house, Ann's husband. Why? I haven't a fucking clue. Perhaps it was because I had single-handedly ruined his once happy little life. Deep down, I felt guilty for all the pain and suffering I had caused him. He was the innocent party in all of this. His only mistake in this nasty situation was marrying a woman who turned out to be a worthless whore, which he could not have predicated all those years ago as he watched her walking down the aisle towards him, both of them caught up in a tangled web of love and lust. I had completely shattered his perfect little life. He was a broken man, hurting to his very core. I knew Terry would never fully recover or be able to move on from the loss of his beloved Ann.

I pulled up outside Terry's house and took a moment to compose myself, before approaching his front door. I pressed the doorbell; a smile appeared on my face as I reminisced about how much I enjoyed fucking his wife before she tragically departed from this cruel world. No answer. I rang the bell again, still no response.

'Fuck this,' I muttered to myself, as I felt my anger rising. I decided to try one last time, third time lucky, I thought. But as I reached for the doorbell, I stopped myself.

'Fuck him,' I snarled under my breath, as I turned and made my way back to the car. What the fuck was I even doing here? There was nothing that I could do or say to ease Terry's pain and suffering. I closed the gate behind me.

Chapter 45

It felt as though everything was closing in on me. I found myself spending more and more time hiding in my house, pacing back and forth like a caged animal or peering out from my bedroom window, constantly scanning the street below as if I were on sentry-duty. I knew that I needed to escape from it all before I completely lost my mind. I had already successfully planted the seed with Fr. Brian, by filling him with a load of bullshit, about my imaginary sick friend, (little did he know, that all my friends were imaginary) and he had given me his blessing to take a few days off to go and visit my sick friend that doesn't exist. Oh, the lies we weave, it always amazed me how easily we can deceive others, I smiled to myself, as I picked up the phone and made a reservation at a small family-run hotel just outside the town of Kenmare in County Kerry.

It was the same hotel where I had sought refuge after my mother's funeral. I retrieved my suitcase from its perch on top of the wardrobe and hastily packed enough clothes to last me a couple of days. For me, taking a short trip out of town for a couple of days was not a straightforward task. It was not a matter of simply tossing a few items of clothing into a suitcase and hitting the road. No, I was being watched, not just casually, but with an intense scrutiny that made me feel uneasy. The last thing I needed was for my stalker to follow me down to Kerry. My mind raced as I desperately tried to come up with a plan to mislead her.

I had spent the last few hours racking my brain, trying to come up with a plan before leaving my house and driving to the church car park. As expected, the car park was empty at such a late hour. I rolled down the window with a creak and lit a cigarette, taking in the quietness of the main road. No one seemed to have followed me or if they did, they certainly didn't pull into the car park. Although that was not to say that someone wasn't watching from the other side of the main road. Silence enveloped me as I nervously smoked, my mind in turmoil.

As I sat there, smoking and scanning my surroundings, I noticed several people walking past the entrance to the church car park. Some had children hanging out of them, while others were walking their dogs. I couldn't help but think, what's the difference? They both required cleaning up after. I exhaled smoke into the cool night air and let another fifteen minutes pass as I sat in the car, chain-smoking. Feeling satisfied that no one had followed me, I left the car and walked the short distance to the corner shop. I needed to stock up on a few supplies for my couple of days away. Whiskey and cigarettes were my top priorities, as they played an important role in helping me maintain my sanity. However, I was well aware that my heavy consumption of both would eventually come back to haunt me.

Upon entering the shop, I was relieved to see that Joseph, the owner, was nowhere to be seen. Instead, his great oaf of a son, whose name I could never remember, was sitting on the long-suffering stool behind the counter. I was glad to avoid a pointless conversation with Joseph, as my mind was far too preoccupied to be dealing with his nonsense. Although his son, unlike his father had no people skills at all, he just sat and stared. I always found him a bit odd, as if he wasn't quite all there. I didn't bother thanking him as he handed me my change, knowing it would have fallen on deaf ears. As I Stepped out of the shop, I discreetly looked all around before beginning my short journey home. I constantly glanced over my shoulder, checking to see if I was being followed.

'I know you're watching me. Come out and show yourself, you cowardly bitch,' I whispered to myself as I continued on my way, trying to appear nonchalant. However, it was much easier said than done given the circumstances.

Once back inside my house, I put away the few groceries that I had bought, before pouring a large whiskey and resuming my sentry-duty from behind the curtain. As I stood in the shadows, the darkness of the room seemed to swallow me whole. Whiskey in one hand, cigarette in the other, as I gazed down at the quiet street below. Looking for what? Anything. My thoughts drifted aimlessly, like a ship lost at sea without a rudder, desperately seeking a safe refuge.

I clawed through my chaotic and fragmented thoughts, only to be plunged back into the harsh reality of the nightmare I was living in. Now was not the time to be drifting off to some imaginary happy place. I needed to remain focused. My plan was to leave my car parked overnight in the church car park, hoping to confuse my stalker and throw her off my trail. I set my alarm clock to sound at four o'clock in the morning. Fucking crazy, I know, but my plan was to be on the road while the rest of the town slept, which hopefully included my stalker.

It felt as though my head had barely touched the pillow, before the alarm clock sprang to life. Annoyed, I forcefully slammed my fist down on the piece of plastic that was creating the awful racket at such an ungodly hour. What the fuck was I doing getting up at such a ridiculous hour? I began to question my sanity, as I dragged myself out of bed. I dressed quickly under the cover of darkness, not wanting to switch on any lights just in case someone was watching my house from outside. Once dressed, I descended the stairs, my eyes barely open and my body heavy with exhaustion. I placed my suitcase by the backdoor. In an attempt to wake up, I downed a very strong coffee, hoping that it would help to kick start my day, despite my body clock telling me that it was still the middle of the night. It was far too early for me to contemplate eating anything, so I settled for a cigarette.

I drained my cup and left it unwashed in the sink. Glancing up at the clock on the wall, it read four thirty-three in the morning. I must be stone fucking mad, I thought to myself as I quietly slipped out the back door with my suitcase in hand and made my way down the narrow, filthy laneway that reeked of piss. I didn't meet another soul as I walked towards the church car park. The only other living being I encountered was a black dog with a lost, vacant look in its eyes. When I reached the car park, I quickly placed my suitcase in the boot. As I lit a cigarette, I paused for a moment to take in the soft golden light of dawn streaming through, announcing the start of a new day filled with endless possibilities. With a smile on my face, I pulled out onto the main road, feeling confident that I had outsmarted my stalker.

Chapter 46

I drove for a solid two hours along the motorway, smoking and singing along to every song that played on the radio, regardless of whether I knew the lyrics or not. Eventually, I took an exit and followed a sign that promised,

'BREAKFAST SERVED ALL DAY ONLY 2KM AWAY.' The sign led me to a quaint little village, whose name I didn't catch on my way in. The café was located halfway down the main street and seemed to have just opened. There was nothing enticing about the exterior of the café, but upon entering, I was pleasantly surprised by the bustling atmosphere, especially considering the early hour of the morning. As I looked around, there were a few early risers scattered throughout the café. Some were glancing through the morning papers, while others were already digging into their breakfast. I chose a cosy window seat and ordered a hearty full Irish breakfast. After all, I was on a bit of a holiday and decided to treat myself.

These few days away were badly needed. I was feeling completely overwhelmed and in desperate need of a break from everything. My house, the church, and the haunting images of the dead girls' faces, were all weighing heavily on my mind. I found myself spending countless hours staring out of my bedroom window, trying to figure out who was watching me. I was feeling extremely stressed and in dire need of some time away to clear my mind, disconnect, and simply unwind. As I signalled for the waitress to bring me the bill, I hoped that these few days away from all the chaos would grant me the temporary reprieve that I so desperately craved.

I left the café feeling satisfied and refreshed, having been fed and watered. I decided to take a seat outside and finish my coffee while indulging in a cigarette. As I sat there; watching the world go by, the quaint little village slowly came to life. People gathered at the bus stop directly across the road from the café. It was clear that the café was a popular spot among the locals, as I noticed that many of the customers and staff were on first-name basis. After finishing my coffee and extinguishing my cigarette in the overflowing ashtray, I leisurely strolled back to the car. The early morning sun was doing its best to make its presence felt, casting a warm glow down upon the street, as it began to stir from its slumber. I checked the time and saw that it was approaching eight o'clock in the morning, a smile spread across my face. I was in no hurry. I had all the time in the world, as Louis Armstrong reminded me in his beautiful song, 'What a wonderful world' which had lodged itself in my head since hearing it earlier in the café.

After enduring another couple of monotonous hours behind the steering wheel, I finally arrived at the hotel. A stunning old country house that had been beautifully restored, with many of its original features still intact, as the friendly manager had eagerly pointed out during my last stay. The exterior was adorned with ivy and various coloured rose bushes, giving it a picturesque charm reminiscent of what one might see in a grand period drama. I checked in without any delays or issues and made my way up the old, creaky staircase, avoiding the lifts due to my deeply ingrained fear of them. Upon entering the room, I kicked off my shoes and sank into the soft mattress. Exhausted from my early morning start, I placed my hands behind my head, letting out a content sigh as I closed my eyes.

A chilling dream jolted me awake, my body drenched in a cold sweat. The lifeless faces of those girls, with their wide, unblinking eyes and twisted, open-mouthed screams continued to haunt my dreams. Glancing at my watch, I realised I had slept for almost three hours. My clothes clung to my skin with sweat; I removed them and took a refreshing shower. It was a nice change to be able to shower without the water stinging my wounds. As I stood naked in front of the bathroom mirror, a sense of dread washed over me a I took in the gruesome sight of my skin, marred by deep, jagged scars that seemed to pulsate with anger.

After getting dressed, I made my way down to the small but taste-fully designed lounge area. I ordered a pint of Guinness and perused the menu. A local girl with a strong Kerry accent took my order, flashing a well-rehearsed smile. I returned her smile out of politeness, remind-ing myself to let go and enjoy my short break as I looked around the busy lounge. Throughout the meal, I kept my head down, avoiding eye contact unless absolutely necessary. I didn't want to be pulled into idle chit-chat with a stranger who just wanted to pass the time.

I thoroughly enjoyed my meal, which I washed down with a few pints of the world renowned 'black stuff,' After finishing my meal, I decided to take a walk outside to inhale some much-needed fresh air and enjoy some peace and quiet. The lounge had become very crowded and stuffy, due to the busy lunchtime trade. It was a pic-turesque afternoon as I strolled through the meticulously maintained grounds of the hotel. The warm air was occasionally interrupted by a gentle breeze, serving as a gently reminder that summer had not yet fully arrived. The outdoor seating area was bustling with people, all enjoying their drinks and the pleasant atmosphere. Couples occupied most of the outdoor tables, with some appearing a lot more loved up than others. As I scanned the beer garden for a seat, my mind began to wander, envisioning the debauchery that would unfold as the night descended and darkness shrouded their naked bodies, fuelled by alco-hol and primal desire.

I felt safe, confident that no one had followed me down from Dublin. My cunning plan had successfully outsmarted my stalker. Back in my room, I reached into my suitcase and pulled out a bottle of Bushmills, my go-to whiskey. The smooth liquid poured effortlessly into the glass, the sound of it hitting the bottom echoing in the quiet room. The room boasted a grand bay window that offered a pictur-esque view of the courtyard below, as I stepped back from the window with a smile, I reminded myself that there was no need for sentry-duty tonight. I drained my glass and poured another.

Feeling both tired yet restless, I lay down on the bed and turned on the television. After flicking through the channels a number of times, I settled on a documentary about the Vietnam War, not exactly ideal viewing for someone who just wanted to chill the fuck out. Just as I started to dose off, I was abruptly jolted awake by loud noises coming from the room next to mine. The sound of the headboard banging against the wall made me think they might crash through and join me at any moment. The woman on the other side of the wall seemed to be either having the best sex of her life, or she was one hell of an actress.

Chapter 47

I slept late the following morning; it was after eleven by the time I rose. I had missed the breakfast serving, as the sign clearly stated, 'Breakfast served between seven and ten only.' I didn't bother asking if I could order something. Looking out the window of my room, I could see that it was another beautiful day. After showering and getting dressed, I decided to take a walk into the village and grab a bite to eat. I stumbled upon a charming little café and chose a table in the far corner next to a window. Although I felt relaxed just sitting and watching the world go by, my stalker was never too far from my thoughts.

A waitress arrived shortly after I had settled into my seat. She took my order and then quickly disappeared behind the counter. Before long, she arrived back at my table and set down a plate full of food in front of me. As I sat there, gazing out the window and savouring my succulent steak, which had been sourced from the upper field just across the road, the waitress had informed. My entire being was filled with a newfound sense of freedom, as if I had been liberated from a hellish concentration camp and was finally able to indulge in a proper meal after what felt like an eternity. Time meant nothing to me; I didn't have to be anywhere at any particular time. If only my life could be like this every day, I thought. How nice it would be if I didn't have to return to Dublin. If I could just disappear, I smiled at the happy thought, but realistically, that's all it was, a happy thought.

I could only imagine the chaos that would ensue if I didn't return home. Maura and the rest of the blue rinse militia would surely be on the case, forming a search party and scouring the length and breadth of the country looking for me. And if that wasn't enough, what if my stalker spoke up and revealed what she knew, hinting that I had done a runner? That would certainly cause all sort of problems. Although it was just a fleeting thought, the idea of disappearing brought a smile to my face. I reminded myself to relax and enjoy my few days away from all the chaos. I needed to embrace the peace and quiet while I could, knowing that it wouldn't be long before I was back in Dublin, surrounded by the madness and mayhem that I had somehow found myself in.

The problem with random thoughts entering my mind was that they lingered. They would burrow into a dark corner of my mind, incessantly replaying like a scratched record, causing me great anxiety and agitation. In an attempt to calm my mind, I took a deep breath and poured another glass of wine, quickly draining it as I tried to steady my thoughts. The crowded and noisy café, combined with the unbearable heat, made me feel claustrophobic, I craved fresh air. Overwhelmed and extremely anxious, I knew that I needed to leave. I quickly paid the bill and stepped outside onto the street, my heart was racing, and my shirt was clinging to me, drenched in cold sweat. Once outside, I lit a cigarette and inhaled deeply, the nicotine seemed to soothe my panicked state.

I followed the narrow and crowded footpath that ran alongside the busy street. It was barely wide enough to accommodate the constant stream of people walking on it. Every second person I passed by collided into my shoulder. Despite the beauty of the village, it seemed far too small to handle the footfall that passed through it. I struggled through the throngs of people as I made my way out of the village. A fresh, gentle breeze brought a brief moment of relief from the warm sun. After walking for about twenty minutes and smoking three more cigarettes, so much for wanting fresh air. I came across a lake surrounded by a thick, dark green forest and overlooked by a large, grey mountain. The sight before me was truly breathtaking. Finally, some peace and quiet, I thought to myself as I kicked off my shoes and sat down on the warm grass, taking in the majestic view. After finishing another cigarette, I lay down on the grass, basking in the heat of the mid-day sun. As the sun's rays lulled me into a state of tranquillity, my mind began to ease, and my eyelids grew heavy.

Chapter 48

Half an hour or so had passed when I was abruptly awoken from a nap. I must have dosed off under the hot sun.

'Excuse me,' I heard someone say. I opened my eyes, but the bright sunlight made me squint, and I quickly closed them again. I sat up and shielded my eyes with my hands, before attempting to open them for a second time. A tall man was standing over me, looking down.

'Sorry, did I wake you?' he asked. He appeared to be middle-aged and had a strong local accent. I remained on the ground, craning my neck to look up at him. I felt small and insignificant as I gazed up at his towering figure.

'No, I just had my eyes closed, enjoying the sun,' I replied.

'I'm sorry for disturbing you, would you have a light? he asked, dangling a cigarette in his right hand.

'Yes,' I replied, reaching behind me for my jacket, which I had been using as a pillow. I began to shift up onto my knees.

'Stay where you are, my friend. I'll come down to you,' he said as he lowered himself onto his hunkers. He was invading my personal space, which made me extremely uncomfortable. He was far too close for my liking. I lit his cigarette as he held it to the lighter. He dragged on it hard, twice, until the top of the cigarette glowed brightly.

'Thank you, I'm very grateful,' he said as he sat down beside me. I felt very uneasy. Just as I was about to stand up, he offered me his outstretched hand and introduced himself,

'I'm Michael, although everyone calls me Mick.' He wore a friendly smile on his large, round, red face. I couldn't tell if the colour on his face was natural or if he had spent too much time in the sun.

'Nice to meet you, Michael. I'm John,' I replied, shaking his hand. He had a strong, firm grip, a real man's handshake.

'It's such a beautiful place,' I said, feeling a little uncomfortable as I attempted to make small talk. What I really wanted was for him to just fuck off and leave me alone.

'Yes, it truly is,' he replied, flicking his cigarette butt to the ground.

'I come here every day, all year around. It's equally as beautiful in the winter, but in a different way.'

'So, you're a local man, I assume?' I asked.

'Yes, I was born and bred just outside the village. My house is only a mile out the road from here,' he said with a smile, before asking,

'Where are you from yourself?'

'I'm from Dublin. I'm just here for a couple of days to relax and recharge the old batteries,' I replied.

'Are you staying nearby? he asked. What's with all the fucking questions, I was beginning to get seriously pissed off.

'I'm staying at a small hotel just out the road, not too far from here,' I replied, trying to remain calm.

'Ah sure, I know it well, that's' my local watering hole. It's a grand little spot; to be honest, it's the best around,' he said.

'Yes, I really like it there, the staff are lovely, so warm and friendly,' I replied.

'Are you down with the wife and kids?' he asked. Now, he was really getting on my fucking nerves. I came down here to relax and unwind, not to be interrogated by some fucking overgrown local.

'No, I never married,' I replied, my tone was sharp and short, hoping he would pick up on the underlying annoyance in my voice.

'Oh, how come, a good-looking man like you?' he said with a big, stupid grin across his fat, red face.

'I'm sure there were plenty of women sniffing around back in the day.' Obviously, my short, sharp answer didn't have the desired effect that I had hoped for on the great big oaf.

'I suppose I just never found the right one. Are you married yourself?' I asked, immediately regretting having asked the question. What the fuck was I thinking?

'God no, married life is not for me. I enjoy my freedom too much,' he replied. Thankfully, his line of questioning stopped. We sat shrouded in an uncomfortable silence, staring out over the lake. His presence completely unnerved me.

'Well, Michael, I must be on my way. It was nice to meet you,' I said as I stood up. He quickly raised himself up, once again invading my personal space.

'Ah, we're just a pair of like-minded souls,' he said. I remained silent as I lit a cigarette and offered him one.

'Thank you, that's very kind of you,' he said. We both stood in silence, smoking and staring out over the lake.

'It's truly breathtaking,' I said, trying to break the uncomfortable silence. I felt trapped, as if his mere presence had a powerful hold over me, chaining me to the very spot where I stood.

'Yes, it's a wonderful sight. Do you swim?' he asked.

'No, I was never too fond of the water,' I replied.

'That's a pity. There's a lovely little private spot just around to the left of the lake. I swim there all the time. I call it my own private little cove,' he said, that stupid grin appearing on his face once again.

'It sounds lovely, your own private little cove,' I replied.

'Sure, come on around and I'll show you. It's a little piece of heaven in this crazy old world,' he said. Without giving it a second thought, I found myself walking alongside the great oaf as we made our way down by the edge of the lake. We followed a narrow, winding dirt track, barely wide enough for one person, which veered off to the left of the tranquil, still water. As we rounded the corner, a beautiful, secluded oasis appeared before us like a mirage.

'Well, what did I tell you? A little piece of heaven,' he said, smiling.

'Yes, it's absolutely beautiful and so secluded,' I replied, as we walked closer to the edge of the lake. I sat down on the soft warm grass, my mind racing. What the fuck was I playing at? Does this guy think that I'm fucking stupid? I knew exactly what he wanted, but he had no idea what was about to unfold for him. As I gazed out over the serene lake, the sun's rays glistened off the calm, mirror-like surface of the water.

After taking a long hard drag, he threw his cigarette butt to the ground and began to undress.

'Time for my daily dip,' he said, as he pulled his t-shirt up over his head and dropped it to the ground. Christ, he was big, well-built, he must lift weights, I thought to myself. He definitely won't be a pushover. I gave his heavily tattooed body a quick once-over as he sat down next to me on the grass and began to untie his boot laces. He then removed his socks and stood back up, with a mischievous grin, he slowly unbuttoned his jeans and let them fall to his ankles before kicking them off his feet.

'Care to join me for a swim?' I hesitated before replying, unsure of how I was going to handle the impending showdown.

'Unfortunately, I can't swim, and I also have a skin condition that is aggravated by the sun,' I replied, exaggerating a dramatic, sad frown across my face.

'That's a shame, the water is lovely and warm around this time of day,' he said, while removing his boxer shorts. I couldn't help but stare at his manhood. The sight of his penis dangling before me transported me back to those horrendous nights I had suffered in the seminary. Feeling a wave of embarrassment wash over me, I quickly averted my gaze, realising that I had been staring far too long.

'You seem to like what you see,' he said with a smirk, clearly noticing my lingering gaze. 'Yes, it's quite nice,' I replied, feeling a little flustered. What the fuck was I playing at? I scolded myself. This situation was on the verge of spiralling out of control at any moment. 'Would you like to touch it? he suggested, his words laced with a hint of perversion,

making my skin crawl. Dirty bastard, I though to myself, determined to teach him a lesson he would never forget.

'Yes, I would, but not here. Let's go into the forest,' I suggested. He quickly slipped his big, hairy, ugly bare feet back into his boots and gathered up his clothes. We made our way into the forest, which was just a short distance from the lake. Before venturing into the densely formed forest, I carefully scanned my surroundings, the place was deserted, not a single soul in sight. So, this is what the dirty bastard gets up to down at his own private little cove. Seducing men, he's no better than those filthy whores that prowled the street at night. As we walked deeper into the thick, forest my anger and disgust grew.

We stumbled upon a small, grassy clearing surrounded by tall, dense trees. He dropped his pile of clothes to the ground.

'So, are you going to strip or do I have to rip your clothes off?' he asked, his tone and demeanour had suddenly changed.

'What's the big rush? I'm enjoying the view,' I replied, smiling sheepishly, playing along as best I could, just waiting for the right moment to strike. He approached me with that twisted smirk on his face once again, saying,

'I knew you were gay the minute I saw you.' His words struck a nerve. I was not gay; I hated that word. Yes, I had been used as a plaything for all those fucked-up perverts who had used and abused me night after night in the seminary, just to satisfy their twisted fantasies and dark desires. I had no choice back then. But gay? I was not. I took great offense at his judgment of me. I wanted to kill the bastard and make him disappear forever, and this dark, isolated forest was just the place.

He stood less than six inches away from me, I cupped his hairy balls in one hand and ran my other hand up and down along his hard shaft. This guy was big all over. He closed his eyes and tilted his face towards the sun, basking in its warm rays, as I stroked him. My eyes scanned the forest floor in search of the perfect weapon. There were plenty of rocks and large branches scattered around; any one of them would suffice to finish off this vile pervert.

Suddenly, he grabbed me by the hair, catching me totally by surprise. He then dragged me down onto my knees, with incredible force. I quickly realised that I had seriously fucked up and completely underestimated my opponent. His muscular frame loomed over me, his powerful grip clenched tightly on my hair as he dragged me closer.

'Suck me dry, bitch,' he commanded, as he slapped me across the face with an open hand. Fuck, I was in serious trouble, the bastard had me right where he wanted me. I should have hit him over the head with one of those rocks as soon as we entered the forest. I was paying dearly for my mistake. Once again, his open hand made contact with my face. One whole side of my face stung like hell, and tears welled up in my eyes, he was so fucking powerful.

I was in a state of panic, realising the gravity of my mistake. He forcefully entered my mouth, repeatedly hitting me across the face and head. I was gagging as he rammed himself down my throat. He grabbed the back of my neck tightly, leaving me unable to move or break free. After several more forceful and rapid thrusts, he emptied himself into my mouth. When he was fully drained, he tossed me to the ground like a ragdoll. I gagged on my hands and knees, desperately trying to spit out his disgusting taste. It had been a long time since I was forced to swallow a mouthful of that shite. I could hear him laughing in the background.

'You're meant to swallow, not spit it out,' his laughter echoed through the thick, towering trees of the forest. I tightly gripped a jagged rock in my fist, ready to strike with all my might. Failure was not an option; the first blow needed to do damage. I was well aware of the vast difference in size and strength between us. Physically, I was no match for him. If the first blow didn't make contact, he would easily overpower me, and I would be the one left on the forest bed for the animals to feast on. I remained on all fours, biding my time for the perfect moment to strike. From the corner of my eye, I saw him approaching.

'You're in the perfect position, bitch. Just drop your bags,' he said as he knelt down behind me, and tried to pull off my trousers. Thankfully, my belt was too tight.

'Wait, wait. I'll take them off,' I said, reminding myself that I had only one chance of survival, so don't fuck this up.

'You just can't get enough, can you?' he laughed to himself.

'Just give me a minute. I need to take a piss,' I said as I stood up and quickly turned, striking him across the face with the rock. With a loud thud, he stumbled backwards and crashed to the ground, completely caught off guard by my sudden attack. I quickly pounced on top of him and viciously pounded his face and head with the rock clenched tightly in my right hand.

Exhausted, I rolled off him; he was dazed and bleeding heavily. As I struggled to regain my breath, I lay down beside him. His massive chest and shoulders rose and fell slowly as he lay still. Fortunately, he was still breathing. I didn't want him dead just yet. No, this fucked-up pervert was going to endure immense suffering. I wanted him to pay for his actions. With great difficulty, I flipped him over onto his stomach and secured his hands tightly behind his back using my belt, making sure that the leather was cutting into his wrists.

Completely drained, I sat on the ground, lit up a cigarette and inhaled deeply, savouring the nicotine rush, as I gazed in awe at his huge naked frame. I was furious with myself for having made such a foolish mistake. He could have easily killed me. What the fuck was I thinking? As I looked at him, memories of Ann flooded my mind. The difference between my two victims was stark, he deserved to die, but Ann did not. As I exhaled a cloud of smoke into the warm air, a disturbing image of Ann's naked corpse being devoured by wild animals flashed through my mind. There couldn't be much left of her by now, I thought as I shook the brutal image from my mind.

My head throbbed, and one whole side of my face was numb from his powerful blows. I cautiously approached the edge of the dense forest to ensure that no one was lurking around before completing the task at hand. His private little cove was still deserted, providing the perfect opportunity for some fun. As I returned to where my friend lay eagerly waiting. I stuffed his socks into his bloodied mouth and blew hard on the tip of my cigarette, until it glowed brightly. Smiling at him, I grabbed his flaccid penis and sank the burning cigarette into the top of it. His entire body jerked violently in pain; I laughed as I repeatedly slapped him across the face.

'Not laughing now, bitch, are you?' I taunted, as I watched him roll around in agony. After taking a long drag, I once again blew on the tip of my cigarette until it glowed bright orange and continued to torture the vile oaf. His head thrashed violently from side to side, his eyes wide open and brimming with tears, as his entire body convulsed in agonising pain and overwhelming fear. As much as I relished in his suffering, I knew I had to be cautious. If this beast managed to break free, he would surely tear me apart limb by limb. I watched and smoked until he eventually stopped writhing like a fish out of water and curled up in a ball. I knelt down behind him, dropped my trousers and entered him. He lay there, defeated and powerless, forced to endure everything I gave him. When I finished, I rolled him over onto his back. As he gazed up at me, the menacing look had vanished from his eyes, replaced with one of helplessness, as if pleading for mercy.

The expression in his eyes revealed his fate, he knew he would never leave the forest alive. Exhausted and desperate to end this horrific ordeal, I scanned the area for a large rock, my eyes landed on an old beer bottle. Fuck it, I thought, let's have a little more fun before he draws his final breath on this godforsaken planet. I grabbed the bottle, his eyes widened with terror as I approached him, brandishing it menacingly. With a firm grip on the neck of the bottle, I smashed it against the side of his head. The force of the impact left his already bloodied face, disfigured and unrecognisable. The broken bottle now had a threatening, jagged edge-just what I needed.

I tightly gripped his severely burnt member as he frantically struggled to move, but his efforts were in vain; he was beaten, only a few precious breaths of life lingered in him. With the jagged piece of broken glass, I mercilessly dragged it across his member, causing a gush of blood to spring up into the warm midday air. A great deal of force was required, sawing the piece of glass back and forth until his manhood was completely severed and fell into my blood-soaked hand. He seemed to pass out from the pain. I tossed what remained of his member into the nearby undergrowth, knowing that it would be devoured by wild animals.

I dragged his large and extremely heavy frame deeper into the dense forest, and finished off his miserable existence, courtesy of a large rock, and a series of brutal blows to his head. I removed my belt, which had been used to bind his hands and threw his clothes down on top of him. Then, I covered his body with branches and undergrowth that lay scattered around.

Christ, what an afternoon, I thought as I washed my face and hands in the cold, fresh water of the lake, and watched as the water around me turned red. Completely drained, my legs trembled and my breath came in ragged gasps as I staggered away from his private little cove. The leisurely stroll that I had enjoyed earlier in the day now felt like an insurmountable task. My entire body ached and cried out in pain, and one whole side of my face was still numb from that bastard's open hand.

When I eventually arrived back at the hotel, I moved quickly through the lobby and reception area. My eyes remained fixed on the floor, determined to avoid any eye contact or unwanted interactions.

I was concerned that I might still have traces of his blood on me, despite my frantic efforts to wash it off in the lake. Unfortunately, I had no way of checking my appearance before leaving the crime scene. Despite my weakened state, I avoided taking the lift because of my inherent fear of them. Instead, I opted for the daunting task of climbing the stairs, my legs felt like lumps of lead as I slowly dragged my body from one step to the next. Exhausted and out of breath, I finally reached my room and collapsed onto the soft, plush bed. The cool sheets provided a welcome relief to my overheated skin.

Chapter 49

T he following morning, I woke up to the sun's rays filtering through a gap in the curtains, casting a bright beam across the bed that demanded my attention. As I lay there, sleepily gazing at the particles of dust dancing wildly in the bright, warm stream of light, my mind suddenly filled with dread at the thought of the long drive back to Dublin. After reluctantly pushing my breakfast around on the plate, unable to muster much of an appetite, I checked out of the hotel and began my journey home. So much for my nice relaxing break, I thought as I pulled out of the hotel car park. I felt completely drained from my little escapade down by the lake. My muscles ached and burned with every movement and my eyelids drooped with exhaustion. I had been on the road for almost four gruelling hours before I finally turned the key in my front door. Fatigue consumed my entire being, so much so that I couldn't even find the energy to bend down and pick up the pile of mail that lay scattered on the floor just inside the door.

I left my suitcase at the bottom of the stairs. Exhausted, I walked into the sitting room and kicked off my shoes before collapsing onto the sofa. It was a relief to finally be able to lie down on the sofa in the comfort of my own home. The thought of climbing the stairs to my bedroom felt daunting and almost impossible. My few days away had started off exactly as I had hoped, relaxed and stress-free. However, everything changed when I met that depraved pervert. He turned my break into a complete fucking nightmare. I was still in shock at how brazen he was and how casually he had tried to seduce me. In the end, he got what he deserved, reduced to nothing more than animal fodder for the creatures of the forest to feast on.

As I lay on the sofa, reliving the events of the past couple of days, it dawned on me how lucky I was to be alive. I was convinced that he would have murdered me once he was finished with me. While I lay there counting my blessings, I sent Fr. Brian a text, letting him know that I was back home and that I would say mass the following morning. He responded quickly,

'That's great, John. We'll catch up over a coffee after mass.' Great, that's all I fucking need, I thought sarcastically as I lit a cigarette.

Two hours had passed since I arrived home and collapsed onto the sofa. As I lay there, my mind drifted absently, Suddenly, my stomach growled, as it clenched and ached with hunger, interrupting my fragmented and disjointed thoughts, reminding me that I had not eaten since the previous night. Eventually, I managed to prise myself up from the comfort of the sofa and stumbled into the hallway. I noticed a pile of mail on the floor that I had stepped over when I first entered the house. I was too exhausted at the time to bend down and pick it up. As I made my way into the kitchen, I threw the mail onto the table and then filled the kettle. With my stomach now demanding food, I quickly threw together a ham and cheese sandwich and brewed a strong cup of coffee to satisfy my cravings.

Having devoured the sandwich in just a few bites, I pushed the crumb-laden plate aside and began sorting through the mail. The usual crap, bills and quite a bit of junk mail. However, my eye were immediately drawn to one envelope that stopped me in my tracks. My name and address were written in block capital letters with a black marker. It sent a shiver right through me; I knew straight away that it was from her. With a sense of trepidation, I slowly opened the envelope, as if half-expecting something to jump out at me. Inside, just like her first letter, were neatly cut out letters from a newspaper, and arranged in a specific order to form the following message,

'ENJOY YOUR BREAK, FATHER. I MUST ADMIT, YOU REALLY DID FOOL ME. WHO'S A CLEVER BOY? GAME ON.'

'Fuck,' I shouted, jumping up from the table and causing my chair to crash to the floor. I crumpled the letter into a ball and hurled it against the wall. That fucking bitch, how the hell did she find out? Did she follow me? Who the fuck am I dealing with? My mind raced with thoughts as I grabbed a bottle of whiskey from the kitchen press. In the last twenty-four hours alone, I had been beaten, forced to perform oral sex on a vile, overgrown beast, who almost killed me. I was lucky to be alive. And, as if that wasn't enough, upon arriving home, I was met with her threatening letter. The weight of her words suffocated me, a heavy burden that I could not escape. In that moment, I felt a deep sense of hopelessness and despair, knowing that I had no one to turn to for help. I was alone, with no one to throw me a lifeline.

'Game on.' What the fuck does she mean by that? Is she implying that this is all just a fucking game to her? I thought to myself, as I drained my glass and reached for the bottle. This clown has no idea who she's dealing with or what I'm capable of. If only she had witnessed what happened down by the lake in Kenmare, I'm sure that would have put an end to all her childish games.

'Game on, fuck you and your game on,' I snarled, taking a long swig from the whiskey bottle. I picked up the crumpled piece of paper from the floor and flattened it on the table with the palm of my hand. I read it again, several times, hoping for a clue to jump out at me, but found nothing. The letter could have come from anyone, even the man in the moon. I couldn't think straight, my thoughts were scattered. How could I entice her out of the shadows where she lurked and watched my every move?

I grabbed the whiskey bottle from the table and slowly made my way upstairs to my bedroom. My bed was crying out to me, but my body ached with exhaustion and my mind churned in turmoil. Despite my fatigue, I was certain that sleep would elude me once again without the aid of a sleeping pill. However, I resisted the temptation, knowing that I needed a clear head for the morning. Tomorrow, I would begin my day by saying the ten o'clock mass, reciting the same empty words to the same vacant faces, who remained motionless and unresponsive as I trudged through the service.

'Yes, tomorrow everything will be back to normal, just as it should be,' I reassured myself. But as I closed my eyes, I couldn't help but wonder what 'normal' even meant anymore.

Chapter 50

Once again, sleep avoided me. I found myself tossing and turning, unable to drift off, the temptation to slip a little white sleeping pill onto my tongue was almost unbearable. The pill would have induced a deep, comatose sleep, plunging me into a state of unconsciousness. There was no denying that. However, it was the side effects that I couldn't handle. The following morning, I would be imprisoned in a foggy, lethargic state. I needed to remain alert and on top of my game. I couldn't afford to spend half the next day completely whacked out of it.

As I lay in bed, my eyes fixated on the intricate web of cracks in the ceiling, my mind was consumed by a chaotic parade of disorganised and nonsensical scenarios. Each one more absurd than the last, they only served to intensify my already overwhelming anxiety. At seven bells. My alarm clock radio went off as expected. The great Leonard Cohen sang, 'Everybody knows,' by my bedside. I reached over and hit the off button, abruptly silencing Mr. Cohen's golden voice and enchanting lyrics. I wondered if the song was a sign.

'Everybody knows. I hope you're wrong, Leonard,' I whispered. But someone certainly does know, and I needed to find out who. I reluctantly got out of bed and drew back the curtains, feeling a slight hint of a hangover creeping around in my head.

Upon entering the sacristy after saying the morning mass, I was greeted by Fr. Brian, who was sitting in the corner, eagerly waiting for me.

'Welcome back, John,' he said with an exaggerated, childlike smile on his face. He jumped up from the chair and extended his hand towards me. You would swear that I had been gone for months and had just returned from a tour of duty in some war-torn country.

'Thanks, Brian,' I replied as we shook hands.

'Well, did you enjoy your break?' he asked, still wearing that goofy smile across his face.

'Yes, thank you. It was just what I needed,' I replied, if only he knew, I thought.

'And how is your friend holding up?' he inquired. I had completely forgotten about the fabricated story I had told him before I left.

'To be honest, he's not doing well at all. I don't think he has much left in him,' I replied, trying to sound as despondent as possible.

'I'm sorry to hear that. Breakfast, my treat,' he said, as he grabbed his coat from the back of the chair he had been sitting on.

'That sounds lovely, just what the doctor ordered,' I replied, unsure if he had picked up on my sarcasm. His expression gave nothing away.

To be honest, having breakfast with Fr. Brian was the last fucking thing I needed or wanted. The thought of sitting across from him while he devoured a full Irish breakfast was not very appealing. He had a disgusting habit of talking with his mouth full, chewing away on his food while trying to speak, which I found difficult and even sickening to watch. Although I couldn't refuse his kind offer, and I was unable to come up with an excuse quick enough to take my leave.

In fairness, it should have been me treating Fr. Brian to breakfast. After all, he was the one who looked after everything while I was away. We took a window seat in the café, which was always a good source of distraction if the conversation was boring or worse, had dried up completely. There was always so much happening as you looked out onto the busy street. I often felt guilty after having breakfast or lunch with Fr. Brian, it was never as bad as I had anticipated, and sometimes I actually enjoyed his company. Although, I found that Fr. Brian was best dealt with in small doses. After breakfast, we parted ways outside the café. Fr. Brian set off on his merry way, probably going off to save the world or something equally noble. Meanwhile, I decided to take a stroll around the local park. I was feeling a little bloated after indulging in the full Irish breakfast and thought a walk might help the digestion.

The park was quiet, with not too many people hanging around, which was just the way I liked it. It was mainly mothers with their young children, and a couple of grandparents who had been roped into child-minding duty. They were all gathered in the playground area, trying to keep the children amused. I noticed the grandparents seemed to be struggling, and the expressions on their faces suggested that they would rather be anywhere else, so long as it was away from their whining and clingy grandchildren. As I continued walking, I came across a wooden bench, it was covered in obscene graffiti and chewing gum. Despite this, I sat down and lit up a cigarette, I had a clear view of the entire park from where I was sitting.

As I sat on the grimy wooden bench, I scanned the park while the smoke from my cigarette swirled around me, providing a sense of comfort. However, a sense of unease lingered in the back of my mind, as I couldn't shake the feeling that she was watching me. The words from her letter,

'Game on,' kept replaying in my mind. What the fuck does she want from me? She clearly had the upper hand. I could sense her presence, too close for comfort, yet completely invisible. As my anger and frustration intensified, I felt the urge to stand on top of the park bench and scream,

'Come out, you worthless whore! Show yourself!' Although I knew the consequences would be severe if I had resorted to such drastic action. I would have been carted off to the looney bin, declared insane, certified, and then heavily sedated before being locked away in a padded cell with no chance of escape.

The game she was playing was unfair and completely one-sided. I felt powerless and unable to retaliate against her. And to make matters worse, I didn't even know who she was or what she looked like. I was like a sitting duck, vulnerable to her attacks whenever she pleased. I needed to find a way to lure her out of hiding and into the open. She was undoubtedly close, yet she kept her distance. She was clever and had not made any mistakes or revealed anything about herself. I was backed into a corner, with her having complete control over me. These thoughts raced through my mind constantly.

My chaotic line of thought was derailed by the sound of my phone beeping. I reached into my pocket to retrieve it and quickly opened the message.

'Good to have you back, Father. I missed not having you around.' I looked all around me, trying to locate the sender. It had to be someone in the park, I thought, watching me and enjoying my reaction to their message. Although the park was still quiet, just as it had been when I first entered. The same few mothers and grandparents were minding and playing with their children and grandchildren, and no one else had entered the park. None of them were looking in my direction or holding phones in their hands. They were too engrossed in watching their children to even notice me. I stood up from the bench and made my way towards the park entrance, seething with anger and tired of playing this woman's foolish games.

'Come out of the shadows, you pathetic piece of shit,' I muttered under my breath, throwing my half-finished to the ground in temper. As I walked towards the entrance, I scanned the entire park. What the fuck am I supposed to do? I thought to myself. I can't compete against the invisible woman. If only she would come out and tell me what she wants instead of playing these stupid games. I needed to remain calm and remember that she was watching. I couldn't let her see me panicking. I tried to act like I didn't have a care in the world as I left the park, but who was I trying to kid? Myself? Definitely not her. That bitch has already made a fool out of me multiple times. I swore to myself, when I finally discover her identity, I will crucify her to a tree and stare deep into her eyes as she draws her final breath.

Chapter 51

By the time my alarm clock sounded the following morning, I had received another eight text messages from her. I was fuming and completely freaked out. I wanted her blood, her fucking head on a platter. But I knew that I needed to calm the fuck down and regain my composure before making any rash decisions. After a quick shower, breakfast consisted of a large glass of whiskey and four cigarettes smoked in quick succession while I tried to gather my thoughts. I knew that this was exactly what she wanted, for me to be in a state of panic and chaos. All I needed was for her to make one mistake and I'd be down on her like a ton of bricks.

While I was being held captive in my own house by an invisible woman, the mere thought of those vile whores working the streets tormented me. I was stuck between a rock and a hard place, but I couldn't simply sit back and allow them to freely roam the streets. As I scrolled through the escort's website, their alluring faces and bodies lured me in, but as I looked closer, I saw a haunting emptiness in their eyes. Their hearts were consumed by darkness, beyond all hope of redemption. I needed to act, but I also needed to be extremely cautious. My goal was to stay one-step ahead of my psycho stalker at all times, which was almost impossible since she was invisible.

After browsing through the website and jotting down several phone numbers, I turned off the laptop. Feeling uneasy about returning to the city centre, I opted to venture further afield, Bray, a destination well off the beaten track. I pulled the same stunt as the last time and left the house by the backdoor in an attempt to fool the psycho bitch again. Emerging from the dim and foul-smelling laneway that ran behind the houses, I scanned my surroundings before crossing the street and hailing down a taxi.

Thirty-eight minutes later, and my ears burning from an overzealous taxi-driver, who just didn't stop talking throughout the entire journey. I was standing in front of an apartment block, pressing the bell for apartment number six. The door buzzed open, yet no one spoke over the intercom, which I found a little unsettling. Upon entering the building, my senses were immediately overwhelmed by a combination of cooking smells and a pungent odour that resembled raw sewage. I walked along the corridor until I found myself standing in front of apartment number six. As my hand reached for the door, it swung open to reveal a breathtakingly beautiful woman standing before me.

'Welcome, please come in,' she said in a low voice, her words spoken in broken English. She stepped aside to allow me enter the apartment. I followed her down a narrow, dimly lit hallway and she opened the first door on our left, leading into a bedroom. Before entering the room, I noticed two other doors one on either side of the hallway. I assumed one was a bathroom and the other a second bedroom. At the far end of the hall, there was a kitchen and dining area. As she closed the bedroom door behind me, I couldn't tell if we were alone or not.

She wasted no time in removing her clothes, smiling as each item of clothing fell to the floor. She strode around to the far side of the bed, sat on the edge, pulled open the drawer on the bedside table, and removed a tube of lubricant and some condoms. She then lifted her beautiful, toned, tanned legs up onto the bed, and lay on her back.

'How long do you want, one or two hours?' she asked, her broken English only adding to the excitement that was already building in my boxer shorts. I quickly undressed, and to my surprise, she didn't even flinch at the sight of my badly scarred body, unlike many in the past who adverted their eyes as soon as I exposed my naked flesh.

'One hour,' I replied, almost forgetting to answer her question. Although, I would be easily forgiven for being so distracted. Her long, straight black hair cascaded down her back framing her dark alluring eye makeup, giving her an ethereal resemblance to an Egyptian goddess.

'One hundred euros, please,' she said with a smile, extending her hand. She placed the money in the drawer of the bedside table and then wasted no time in getting down to business. I closed my eyes and lay back on the bed. Suddenly, I heard a door open and muffled voices coming from the hallway. I opened my eyes and sat up quickly, brushing her aside. There were two voices, one male and one female, I couldn't make out what they were saying. Then, I heard the front door of the apartment being closed. My sudden movements had startled the girl.

'Relax, it's just my roommate. Please lie back down and enjoy,' she said. Fuck, we weren't alone. I was so preoccupied with the voices in the hallway that I lost all interest in what was happening between us in the bedroom.

'You don't like, you're not hard anymore?' she asked, with a stupid looking frown on her beautiful face. I looked down and felt embarrassed. There he was lying flaccidly to one side, wearing his protective raincoat.

'I'm very tired,' I blurted out, it was the first thing that came to mind.

'It's okay,' she replied, smiling. No, it's fucking not okay, I'm paying you good money, I thought to myself, as I roughly grabbed her and flipped her onto her hands and knees. My member quickly rose and conquered the vile whore who presented herself to him.

Despite being sexually satisfied, I was filled with anger and frustration as I left her apartment. I had travelled all the way out to Bray, only to have my mission abruptly aborted when I realised, we were not alone in the apartment. The despicable, soulless life of the whore had been spared by her roommate. If only she had known how close she came to death, perhaps she would have sought forgiveness and redemption, desperately pleading for her life and vowing to amend her wicked ways, I thought to myself as I flagged down a taxi. Upon entering my house through the backdoor, I grabbed a bottle of whiskey and made my way into the sitting room. I chose to keep the lights off and embraced the stillness and darkness, as I settled onto the sofa. With a heavy heart, I took another swig from the bottle, my mind raced with thoughts of my stalker's identity. Frustration built within me as I remained clueless.

Chapter 52

I woke suddenly. The bright red digits on the alarm clock glowed, it was three-fifteen in the morning. Even though I had just woken, my mind was already racing. I was still annoyed about the previous night, my wasted trip out to Bray. Although, in retrospect, I should have been thankful that I had heard their voices in the hallway. Only God knows what the outcome would have been, if they had remained silent.

I felt trapped and claustrophobic, as if everything seemed to be closing in on me. My mind was completely consumed by that bitch taunting me. The phone calls, letters, and text messages were becoming too much for me to handle. In a desperate attempt to clear my head, I got out of bed and drew back the curtains. The faint glow from the streetlight that stood directly outside my house illuminated one side of the bedroom, leaving the other side shrouded in darkness. I stood naked, hidden by the darkness, as I scanned the empty street below. It was no surprise that at such an ungodly hour, there was no one around. Despite the early morning hour, I knew there was no point in trying to go back to asleep. Once again, sleep had abandoned me, and I knew it wouldn't return anytime soon.

I got dressed and made my way down to the kitchen, my unease growing with each step. I couldn't rid myself of the nagging sensation that something bad was about to happen. But what? I couldn't tell. It felt as though a dark, ominous presence loomed over me, it felt tangible, making my skin crawl. Although, I couldn't quite describe it, even though if felt so real. As I topped up my coffee with a generous drop of whiskey, I began to question my sanity. Was I losing my mind? Was all of this just a bad dream? Perhaps the evil spirits of my mother and O'Connell were haunting me for having ended their miserable fucked-up lives, so violently. Was I in the midst of a mental break-down? Or had madness already taken hold of me with its merciless claws? I drained my coffee and stood up from the table, unable to relax or clear my mind. I lit another cigarette and began to pace the hallway, as I walked from one end of the hall to the other and then back again, it felt as though the walls of the house were closing in on me.

'Fuck this,' I muttered, my anxiety and temper rising. I grabbed my coat and locked the front door behind me. My watch read, four twenty-three in the morning.

The cold morning air blew away the cobwebs and any lingering drowsiness, leaving me feeling refreshed, alert, and fully awake. A nice early morning brisk walk should help to clear my cluttered and overactive mind, I thought to myself as I lit a cigarette. I had walked for over an hour without encountering a single soul. I could have strolled through the streets naked, and no one would have known. It felt as though the entire village belonged to me; I was like the sheriff in an old western cowboy movie as I strutted through the village. Despite the cold, there was a peacefulness that felt almost surreal. I had never ventured out for a walk at such an early hour before, and the experience was both eerie and exhilarating. Even in the quiet darkness, I constantly looked over my shoulder, half-expecting to see someone following me. However, I saw nothing, only darkness.

It was approaching six in the morning; I still had a few hours to kill before I needed to be at the church to say the morning mass. As I strolled through the dimly lit streets, I was enjoying the peacefulness and solitude. The last place I wanted to go was back home. Strangely, I felt drawn towards the church, as if some unseen force was guiding me there. I couldn't quite understand it, as I had no particular reverence for the place of worship. Although, my feet were killing me from all the walking. My leather shoes, although stylish, they were not suitable for long walks and were cutting into my heels and pinching my toes, I needed to sit down.

As I emerged from a side street, I found myself facing the church. What the fuck was happening to me? Confused and overwhelmed, I entered the sacristy and turned off the alarm. The room was cold; I made my way over to the makeshift kitchen in the corner and turned on the boiler and the kettle. As the boiler came to life, I sat on one of the hard stools, sipping my coffee and listening to the old pipes over-head as they rattled and groaned, as the water made its way through them.

After draining the last dredges of my coffee, I rinsed the cup under the tap and placed it upside down on the draining board. I then left the sacristy and entered the cold and desolate church. I couldn't for the life of me understand what I was doing there. Was I searching for a clue or maybe seeking divine intervention? As I gazed up at the crucified Jesus that hung above the altar, I knelt and bowed my head, feeling a sense of shame wash over me.

The sight of the thick, rusted nails that were brutally driven into his hands and feet, and the wound from the spear that pierced his side, as the soldiers laughed and played dice as they callously watched the crucifixion. His mother Mary and his lover Magdalene, knelt at the foot of the cross, their faces twisted in anguish and their bodies trem-bled with fear, unsure of their fate without their saviour's guidance and love. As I struggled to process everything that was playing out in my mind, years of unshed tears filled my eyes. I was completely over-whelmed by the image of the crucifixion.

'Stop,' I scolded myself, as I slammed my fist down onto the wooden pew in frustration. What the hell was happening to me? I didn't believe a single word that was written in the Bible. It was all lies, propaganda, nothing but an elaborate, well-crafted piece of fic-tion designed to instil fear and control the masses. What had come over me? How did I end up on my knees, gazing up at the crucifixion, with tears streaming down my cheeks? As if I was searching for a sign from a higher power.

'Stop it, for fuck's sake, stop it,' I whispered between the sobs. I'll drive myself insane with all this madness playing out in my head. I got up from my knees and looked around, as if waiting for someone to appear before me.

As I approached the Stations of the Cross, I dried my eyes and gazed up at the first of the fourteen Stations. Despite my disbelief in this supposed religious event, I still found myself making the sign of the cross as I examined the first Station. However, as I continued to move from one Station to the next, I couldn't help but wonder: what if, by some unknown phenomenon, the story of the Crucifixion was actually true? It was difficult for me to fathom, and even more difficult to believe that I was entertaining such ludicrous thoughts. What was happening to me? I questioned myself, doubting my sanity, and my very existence as I stared at the gruesome images displayed before me.

If the Crucifixion really did happen, which I wholeheartedly doubted, the man they called Jesus must have been terrified and felt so isolated as he walked through the maddening crowd, the weight of the cross pressing down on his freshly opened wounds. He knew that he was walking towards his own death. I closed my eyes and tried to imagine the fear and pain that he must have felt, abandoned in his hour of great suffering and need. And yet, in some strange way, I could relate to this man they called Jesus, whether he was a fictional character or not. I have always felt abandoned, unwanted, and unloved, as if this cruel world had turned its back on me, without even giving me a chance. Like Jesus, I stood alone and embarked on my own crusade. And just as he was, I too was met with disapproving glances and whispers behind my back. As Jesus sought to cleanse the world of sin, I sought to cleanse the world of sinful women. Maybe this Jesus character and I were not so different after all, I thought to myself as I continued to walk from Station to Station.

As I studied the haunting images, a sense of foreboding washed over me. I approached each new Station with great trepidation. As I looked into the eyes of Jesus, the pain etched into face was palpable, and I could almost feel the weight of his suffering. His skin was torn and bleeding, the crimson liquid trickled into his eyes as the soldiers pressed the crown of thorns onto his head with great force. The echoing voices of the soldiers tauntingly rang in my ears,

'Save yourself. King of the Jews,' they sneered. I wept uncontrollably at the thirteenth Station, when the solider pierced his side.

'Enough, enough,' I cried out, falling to my knees. My voice echoed in the vast, empty church. As I raised my head, with tear-drenched eyes, I spoke the final words that Jesus himself had supposedly uttered to God, his heavenly Father, as he hung abandoned and dying on the cross.

'My God, my God, why have you forsaken me,' I recited, bowing my head in silence as my tears continued to flow.

Exhausted, I struggled to rise up from my knees, before shuffling over to sit down on one of the pews. I wept bitterly as I stared up at Jesus hanging above the altar. I closed my eyes. What was happening to me? I clutched my head in my hands, trying to make sense of the chaotic thoughts racing through my mind.

'I must be losing my mind,' I whispered to myself. I was scared. I slumped my head in shame as my tears flowed freely, there was no point in trying to hold them back.

Suddenly, I felt a hand on my shoulder; my body jolted upright, my eyes snapping open as I sprang up from the pew like a jack-in-the-box.

'Jesus, Brian, you frightened the fucking life out of me,' I yelled at him, once again, my voice echoed in the background.

'I'm sorry, John, I'm so sorry. I called you a couple of times, you didn't answer, and the way you were slouched down over the pew, well, I thought, something terrible had happened to you. I'm truly sorry,' he said, his face and voice were laced with fear and concern. I struggled to pull myself together, my heart was pounding, I slowly lowered myself back onto the pew.

'It's alright, Brian,' I replied, my voice low, as I tried to calm myself after the shock caused by the idiot standing in front of me.

'I was lost in prayer, completely immersed in the Holy Spirit and the presence of our loving Father,' I said. However, a nervous quiver ran through my voice as I spoke, still feeling the effects of the recent encounter.

The Stations of the Cross had left me physically and emotionally drained. And on top of that, the sudden and unexpected shock brought on by Fr. Brian had put the heart crossways in me, how I didn't have a cardiac arrest, I'll never know. Once again, I surprised and impressed myself with the answer that I had given Fr. Brian. Where all the bullshit came from and so quickly when I needed it most, I couldn't say. There seems to be an endless supply of it buried deep in my subconscious, and it instinctively appears at just the right moment. And as for that gobshite, who believed every word I said, well, that certainly made my life a little easier.

'Jesus, John, I got such a fright when I saw you slouched over the pew,' he exclaimed, his face wore a mix of shock and relief.

'Brain, you really scared the fucking life out of me. But as you can see, I'm alive and well,' I replied with a forced smile, as I reflected on the intense experience we had just gone through.

'Let's go into the sacristy. I have a bottle of brandy hidden in the back press, just in case of emergencies like this. And I think we definitely need a drink after that ordeal,' I suggested, putting my arm around his shoulder with a grin.

'Yes, I could certainly do with a stiff drink after that. I think I'm still in a state of shock,' he said with a smirk. We both laughed as we walked towards the sacristy.

I retrieved a bottle of brandy from the press and poured a generous measure into our cups, since there were no glasses in the sacristy. After the fright I had just experienced, it wouldn't have bothered me if we had to drink it straight from the bottle. Despite the generous amount, I drained my cup in one gulp. I watched as Fr. Brian, still pale, and visibly shaken, struggled to lift the cup to his lips. I refilled my cup and took a seat across from him. I felt the need to explain to him why I was in the church at such an early hour, but then I wondered why he was here so early as well. Fr. Brian was well aware that I usually arrived at the very last minute before saying mass. I offered up a half-hearted excuse.

'I couldn't sleep, so I came here to do the Stations of the Cross. After I had finished, I knelt down in the pew and completely immersed myself in prayer. And, well, you know the rest,' I said with a forced smile, my heart was still trying to return to its normal pace.

'Well, I suppose there are worse things you could be doing than praying at the Stations of the Cross at this hour of the morning,' he said with a faint smile. I didn't like the last line that came out of his mouth.

'I suppose there are worse things you could be doing.' What the hell was he implying? Did he know something? I thought to myself. No, no, he couldn't possibly know anything. What he said was just a figure of speech. Everyone uses that phrase, 'there are worse things you could be doing.' I needed to relax, for fuck's sake, and stop my mind from running wild with loose thoughts. It was just Fr. Brian's way of trying to shed a little humour to the situation that almost gave the two of us a fucking heart attack. I watched in silence as he struggled; his hands were still shaking as he drank from his cup.

Although, I began to wonder if sweet innocent, Fr. Brian, whom everyone loved and adored, could be somehow involved with my stalker, passing on information to her of my whereabouts? My comings and goings? He would have a fair idea of my schedule. Christ, surely not, Fr. Brian. I forcefully pushed that thought to the back of my mind as I drained my cup and smiled over at him.

Chapter 53

I had just left the church after saying the morning mass and was about to get into my car when I heard someone calling me.

'Father, hello Father,' I turned in the direction from where the voice was coming from and standing before was a strikingly beautiful, dark-haired young woman. She appeared to be of Eastern European descent, although, I couldn't be certain from the distance. We walked towards each other and met halfway.

'Hello, can I help you?' I asked, trying to portray a sense of genuine concern.

'I need you to hear my confession,' she said.

'Confessions are heard every Thursday between two and four in the afternoon. If you come back then, I will gladly hear your confession,' I replied.

'Please, Father, I can't wait until then. It is urgent,' she said, her voice filled with distress. I looked into the beautiful brown eyes of the pretty little creature that stood before me, wondering what the hell could be so important. What terrible sin could she have committed, I thought to myself. This was the last thing I needed; my body was yearning for a drink and my sofa.

'I'm quite busy this morning, but I suppose I could spare a few minutes to hear your confession,' I replied, trying to convey that I was going out of my way to accommodate her.

'Thank you, Father. I am very grateful,' she said. It was then that I noticed her broken English. We entered the church, and I led her to where the confession boxes were located. Upon entering the box, I sat on the small wooden stool, muttering all sorts of obscenities under my breath. I was not in the mood to listen to a meaningless confession, just so some foolish whore could ease her conscience, any more than I was in the mood to have my teeth pulled out.

Closing my eyes, I sat in silence for a few minutes, taking the time to compose myself and allowing her to prepare for her recital. Once she seemed settled and there was no more movement on her side of the screen, I drew back the curtain on the lattice. Instead of turning to face her, I remained still and looked straight ahead, trying to maintain a serious and contemplative expression. What I really wanted to say was,

'Come on, hurry the fuck up, and get this bullshit over and done with.' Instead, I opted for the more traditional route. I took a deep breath, blessed myself, and said,

'In the name of the Father, and of the Son, and of the Holy Spirit. Now, my dear child, in the presence of our loving and forgiving Almighty Father, please tell me, what is troubling you so deeply?

'Father, my friend was murdered,' she said, her tone, matter-of-fact and almost blunt. Despite the gravity of the situation, her broken English and perfectly shaped lips were a real turn-on. I sat in silence, trying to process what I had just heard.

'My God, that's terrible. I am so sorry for your loss. How are you coping? I asked, at a loss for words. I had heard many crazy stories in the confession box over the years, but this was on a whole other level.

'I'm not coping well. I can't sleep, (welcome to the club) I'm not eating, (here's your brother.) You see, Father, I know who killed my friend,' she said. I turned to face her.

'Have you gone to the police?' I asked, my patience were beginning to wear thin. I couldn't care less about you or your murdered friend, I thought to myself, as my body cried out for a drink.

'No, I can't. I am an illegal immigrant. If I go to the police, I will be deported,' she said. Jesus Christ, I couldn't fucking believe what I was hearing. The allure of her broken English had disappeared.

'But if you know who murdered your friend, you must tell the police. That person needs to be sent to jail, and you need to get justice and closure for your friend,' I replied. She remained silent, her head bowed.

'Let me help you,' I offered. 'Are you absolutely certain that you know who killed your friend?' I asked. She raised her eyes from the ground and said,

'Yes, I have proof.'

'May I ask what kind of proof?' I inquired, feeling bored, yet a little curious.

'We have CCTV cameras in our apartment. I have all the footage on a disc,' she said. Who the fuck has CCTV cameras in their apartment? I thought to myself, as I studied her closely.

'That's perfect. I will take you to the police station and arrange for a solicitor. I'm sure that if you have vital evidence to solve a murder case and put a killer behind bars, some sort of a deal could be reached for you in relation to your immigration status. I will do everything in my power to prevent you from being deported,' I said, wondering what the hell was I getting myself into.

'There's only one problem, Father,' she said, looking straight into my eyes.

'And what might that be, my dear?' I asked, feeling a mix of anger and boredom as I listened to what I assumed would be complete nonsense.

'The killer is you. You killed my friend with a hammer. I have it all on a disc,' she stated. I turned to face her, trying to convince myself that I had misheard her.

'Who the hell are you? What the bloody hell do you think you are playing at? Money, is that what you're after, is that your motive? Well, let me make one thing crystal clear. If you don't get out of my sight immediately, I will have you deported in the morning. Now, fuck off out of here and never come back,' I snarled through the lattice, trying my best to remain composed with my voice lowered in case there were other people in the church.

'No, fuck you. Now you listen and listen very carefully you murderous pig. I have you on a disc, first fucking my friend and then brutally killing her with a hammer. I was there that day. When I entered the apartment, I heard the grunts and groans coming from her bedroom, so I knew she had a client with her. I went into the living room and laid down on the sofa. A short while later you opened the living room door, had a quick look around, and then closed the door. I clearly saw your reflection in the mirror above the fireplace. It was obvious that you didn't see me lying on the sofa, as the back of the sofa faced the doorway. Your behaviour seemed suspicious to me, your footsteps were fast and loud as you ran down the hallway and slammed the front door behind you. I jumped up off the sofa and ran to the front door. Looking through the spy hole, I caught a glimpse of you before you turned the corner of the corridor and made your way down the stairs. I knew something was wrong, I called out my friend's name and then raced into her bedroom, I threw up, trying to stifle my screams. I knew straight away that she was dead; there was nothing I could have done to save her, you fucking animal. I quickly ran out of the apartment and down to the car park. I saw you pulling out of the apartment block, I jumped into my car and followed you. You are not a holy man; you are nothing but an evil murdering bastard,' she spat out. I sat in stunned silence, unable to believe what I had just heard.

Every word that came from her mouth was undeniably true. As she recounted the events of that day, I found myself reliving each moment as if it were happening in real time. When I first entered the apartment on that fateful day, I vividly remembered the living room door being open. I quickly glanced into the room, but there was no sign of anyone. However, when I emerged from the bedroom later, I noticed that the living room door was partially closed. I popped my head in for a quick look, how had I missed her lying on the sofa? I remember the back of the sofa faced the doorway, I never thought of entering the room and having a proper look. Although, in fairness, I had just murdered some-one and was in a panic to flee the apartment. Christ, I had slipped up badly. I was completely overwhelmed at what I had just heard. I sat there dumbfounded, rendered speechless, my thoughts were scattered unable to process what was happening. My gaze remained fixed on the floor, as my entire being shook with disbelief.

No, this can't be happening, I must be fucking dreaming, I kept telling myself. Slowly I raised my head from the floor and met her gaze. Once again, I tried to speak, but words failed me.

'Like I said, it's all on a disc. I have a copy here for you to look at, you sick fuck,' she said. I just sat and stared at her; I was completely lost.

'Now, just in case you try anything stupid, there is a woman sitting at the far side of the church. She recorded us entering the church together and also entering the confession box. She's recording as we speak. If anything were to happen to me, I have entrusted copies to people who are very close to me. They have been instructed to give a copy to the police and the press If I were to go missing, or have an accident, of heaven forbid, end up dead. Do you understand me? Am I making myself clear?' she asked, her tone now menacing. I looked straight into her cold, hard stare. She didn't flinch, her unwavering gaze made it clear that she had complete control over the situation. I was fucked. I meekly nodded, feeling defeated and unable to respond.

'I will give you a few days to let everything sink in, then I'll be in touch. Goodbye Father,' she said as she stood up and left the confession box. I wanted to go after her, but there was no point. I remained seated, in shock and silence, trying to comprehend what the fuck had just happened.

A few minutes passed before I left the confession box. The church was empty, thank Christ. The last thing I needed was for some old holy Joe to approach me and start up a conversation just for the sake of killing time. As I opened the door to the confession box, that she had just left minutes earlier, I saw the disc sitting on the bench. As I placed the disc into my coat pocket, it was a tangible reminder of the event that had just unfolded.

I stumbled out of the church in a daze, consumed by shock and panic. My heart raced and my hands trembled as I fumbled with my keys, feeling their weight slip from my grasp and hearing them clatter to the floor. As I bent down to retrieve them, I winced as my head made a loud thud against the unforgiving steering wheel. On my third attempt, I finally managed to pick up the keys and start the car. The short drive home and parking the car in the driveway were a blur. Entering the house and unsetting the alarm felt as though I was operating on autopilot, my mind unable to process the life-changing event that had just occurred.

As my eyes met my reflection on the dark television screen, a tumultuous sea of emotions crashed against the shores of my mind. How could this be happening? I gazed into the dark screen, as if desperately searching for a solution to my problem as tears streamed down my face. I carefully removed the disc from my coat pocket and gently placed it on the coffee table. I couldn't bear to relive the events captured on the disc. In a fit of rage, I sprang to my feet and drained my glass before hurling it against the fireplace, sending shards of glass flying around the room.

'I am finished, defeated, it is all over," I whispered to myself, my voice quivering with fear and sadness. My heart sank as I realised there was no way out of this mess. With tears streaming down my face, I tightly gripped the bottle by the neck and took a long swig, desperately trying to drown out the overwhelming feeling of despair that consumed me.

Chapter 54

I must have drifted off on the sofa. I squinted and blinked several times before my heavy eyelids finally lifted. My head throbbed with a dull, persistent ache and my mouth was dry and scratchy, as if I had been eating sand. A sudden chill crept through the room, causing me to shiver. I wrapped my arms around myself in the hope of generating some heat. The empty whiskey bottle on the coffee table, and the faint smell of alcohol that lingered in the room, explained my current physical state.

I struggled up off the sofa and trudged over to the window, the curtains were still open, allowing the streetlight to filter into the room. My watch read two-thirty in the morning. I wondered if the bitch was outside watching as I closed the curtains. As early as it was, there was no point in going up to bed. Regardless of how much my body craved sleep, I knew it would not come. I slowly made my way to the kitchen, my body yearning for a strong coffee and a handful of painkillers.

Back in the sitting room, I lit a cigarette and picked up the disc from the coffee table. I inhaled deeply, feeling the smoke fill my lungs and the nicotine rush through my body, as I examined it in my hand. It was hard to imagine that this small piece of plastic, or whatever the hell it was made of, could possibly seal my fate. After tossing the cigarette butt into the fireplace, I inserted the disc into the DVD player. The bitch wasn't lying; there I was on the big screen in my own sitting room. In one scene, I'm fucking her like a porn star, our bodies tangled in a frenzy of desire, and in the next scene, I had morphed into a deranged, bloodthirsty murderer. The recording was crystal clear there was no denying that it was me on the disc. The date and time of the recording ran along the bottom of the screen. I was under illusions. I was fucked, big time.

After watching the recording, I pressed the rewind button and played it again. As I watched myself on the screen, I felt a surge of arousal. Based on my performance, I couldn't help but wonder if I had missed my true calling as an actor. After relieving myself from my heightened state of arousal, I let it sink in that what I had just watched was not a work of fiction, but a real event. The woman on the screen was being fucked and then brutally beaten with a hammer, while the man playing the lead role was not an actor, it was me, and the woman in the supporting role was now dead.

It was all too much for me to take in. Now, I was the one being fucked, good and proper. I couldn't see a way out of the fucking mess that I had landed myself in. Once the police receive a copy of the disc, I will spend the rest of my days behind bars. Her last words to me before she left the confession box were, 'I'll be in touch soon.' What the hell does she want? If she was planning to turn me in to the police, she would have done so by now. No, she definitely has a game plan. I'm certain all she wants is money, so that she can return to her own country and set herself up to live happily ever after. Money won't be an issue; the death of my mother had set me up nicely. I could just bite the bullet and make her an offer, I'm sure that's what she wants. Isn't that what they all want? money, and plenty of it. Worthless whores, the fucking lot of them.

All I could do was sit tight as I anxiously waited for her to contact me. Three long, endless days and sleepless nights crawled by without hearing a single word from her. Finally, on the fourth day, I received a letter in the same style as the previous ones. The black letters had been cut out from a newspaper to form the words. The letter read,

'MEET ME AT THE MAIN ENTRANCE TO STEPHEN'S GREEN PARK AT TWO O'CLOCK ON FRIDAY. IF YOU DON'T SHOW UP, THE POLICE AND THE PRESS WILL RECEIVE A COPY OF THE DISC.'

'Fucking bitch. What the hell is she playing at?' I snarled as I began to pace the hall. She was clever, choosing to meet in a public place, a busy park on a Friday afternoon. There would be plenty of people around, shoppers, office workers on their lunch breaks, clever little bitch, I thought as I lowered a mouthful of whiskey straight from the bottle.

Even if I knew where to find her, I couldn't risk trying to dispose of her. I'm sure she's long gone from the apartment where the incident took place, and I can only imagine what happened to the dead girl's body. She claimed that others had copies of the disc and were instructed to send them to the police and the press if anything untoward should happen to her. Whether she was bluffing or not, I couldn't take any chances. Although I had no reason to doubt her, she had thought of everything and was always one-step ahead of me. I had no choice but to play by her rules, at least for the time being. I needed to figure out her game plan and where she was headed with all this. Thursday crawled by, I was exhausted and extremely anxious. I hadn't slept since our meeting in the confession box.

Thursday night seemed never-ending as I paced the hallway, chain smoking and consuming excessive amounts of caffeine. By the time Friday morning rolled around, I was running on autopilot. I don't remember saying the morning mass or anything else that happened that morning before I made my way into the city for my two o'clock rendezvous with my stalker. As I stood at the entrance of Stephen's Green Park, I was a bundle of nerves, feeling anxious and completely drained. The park was bustling with people on their lunch breaks from the nearby office blocks. Some were holding paper cups of coffee, while others were munching on sandwiches or bread rolls. I couldn't seem to settle, I was constantly shifting from having my hands in my pockets to crossing my arms in front of my chest.

She arrived promptly at two o'clock, just as her note had instructed.

'Let's walk,' she said, brushing past me without stopping or slowing down. It was a command not a request. Her demeanour was businesslike; she was in total control of the situation and seemed to be enjoying her little power trip. I walked beside her in silence, feeling like a chastised child running alongside his annoyed mother. She sipped from her tightly held paper cup without breaking her steady stride. With each step, my frustration grew until I finally stepped in front of her, blocking her path.

'Tell me, what the hell do you want?' I asked, trying to remain calm despite the tense situation. I was fully aware of my surroundings and the potential consequences of causing a scene in public.

'Ideally, I would like to cut your balls off and then slit your throat. But fortunately for you, you're of no use to me dead,' she replied, her words dripped with hatred and malice. Hearing her say that I was of no use to her, dead, brought me some relief. It was clear that she wanted to make some sort of deal. A deal, I could handle that, I thought to myself as she moved around me and continued walking. I couldn't help but smile as I walked behind her. Eventually, we came across an empty bench and sat down.

'So, I assume it's money you're after? I asked, eager to resolve the situation as quickly as possible.

'I'll let you in on a little secret, holy man. The people who smuggled me into this shit hole of a country are also the same people who set me and my friend up in that apartment. They have numerous apartments scattered throughout the city, each housing girls like me. These individuals also install hidden CCTV cameras in their apartments. And now, because of you, they are experiencing significant financial losses. Not only did you kill one of their top earners, but you also caused them additional trouble by forcing them to dispose of her body,' she said, her stare cold and menacing as she locked eyes with me. I had heard enough; it was clear that I was way in over my head.

'So, what exactly do these people you work for want from me?' I asked, fearing the worst. 'They want half a million euro, or else they will contact the police and the press,' she replied.

'Half a million? There's no way on this earth I can come up with that sort of money,' I replied.

'You don't seem to understand how dangerous the people I work for are. Taking a human life means nothing to them. Then again, after watching the footage, it seems like you have no regard for human life either. Remember, I have been watching you since the day you fled from my apartment. I have seen you entering other apartments and climbing over railings to access parks late at night with women who are now dead. I have it all recorded - dates, times, everything. You are one sick, twisted bastard. I hope you burn in hell,' she spat out her words with such venom, and her cold stare sent a chill right through me.

'Who the hell hides CCTV cameras in apartments where girls are working as prostitutes? That's seriously fucked up,' I said.

'You are quite naïve for such an educated man. We use the footage to blackmail our clients. After they've had their bit of fun, someone follows them home. Most of our clients are wealthy businessmen, lawyers, and even some well-known people from the television and sports. We also get quite a few of your sort as well. It's a simple process. We stalk them for a couple of days, observing everything about them, gathering information. Their workplace, social hangouts, their wives' workplaces, and their children's schools. We take a few photos of our client's wives and children just to show that we have done our homework on them. Then, we pounce, like a hungry tiger, and hand them the disc, just like I did with you. We tell them to watch it and that we'll be in touch soon. The client's watch their homemade porn movie and can't believe what they see. We then inform them that if they don't hand over a specified amount of money by a given time, their beautiful wives' and innocent children will be forced to sit and watch them in action. It's a very lucrative scam, and it works every time,' she said, her tone as cold as fucking ice.

'Bastards, fucking scumbags,' I snarled.

'Now, now, those very words could easily be used to describe you. Then again, you don't just fuck them, no, you also murder them. My people only kill, when necessary,' she said, as she drained the last mouthful from her paper cup.

'I can't get half a million euro's, that's way out of my reach,' I said. I'm sure she could smell the fear and desperation emanating from me.

'You belong to the Catholic Church, one of the wealthiest and most influential organisations in the world. It ranks high on the rich list. The people I work for are not fucking stupid. This is not up for negotiation – it's either half a million, or the disc will be delivered,' she stated firmly.

'I don't have access to church funds, and even if I did, it would not come close to that amount. I am just a priest in a small parish in Dublin. It is the Pope in the Vatican City that you are after, seeking that sum of money,' I replied, my voice raised a few octaves as fear and panic consumed me.

'Spare me the bullshit. Like I said, this is not negotiable. I will be in touch over the next couple of days to see how things are coming along, and don't try anything stupid. You are being watched day and night. If you attempt any heroics, you will be exposed for the evil bastard that you truly are. Even now, two members of the gang are watching us as we speak,' she said, her cold, unflinching gaze fixed on me.

This crazy bitch sitting next to me is like ice, she's fucking fearless. She may only be the messenger, but her words sent a shiver right through me. Her captivating dark brown eyes held an unwavering, penetrating gaze that seemed to draw me in, as if I was being held captive. I couldn't help but wonder what secrets they held. Under different circumstances, those very same eyes would be considered beautiful. As she rose from the bench, she flashed me an exaggerated smile while adjusting her expensive looking coat. I wondered how many blowjobs she had performed to afford it.

'Sleep well, holy man,' she said, before turning and walking away, as if we were just two friends parting ways after a casual coffee and a chat.

Chapter 55

O nce again, I found myself pacing back and forth in a restless
state, swigging from a whiskey bottle and chain-smoking. I was
drained from lack of sleep, my body felt heavy and sluggish, and I
could hardly keep my eyelids open. Thoughts of defeat and hopelessness consumed my mind as I gave up pacing the hallway and made my
way back into the bedroom.

'I'm finished, it's all over,' I muttered, as I crawled under the
sheets, 'There's no way out of this mess.' Even if I could pay them
off, who's to say that they wouldn't keep coming back for more? Plus,
they could still send the disc to the police after I had handed over the
money.

I was trapped in a never-ending cycle of terror, my mind a prisoner to its own torment with no escape in sight. As I lay there, shivering in the cold and shrouded in darkness and the musty smell of fear,
my mind was a battlefield, constantly bombarded by endless scenarios
that played out in excruciating detail. Each one more terrifying than
the last, leaving me gasping for air and desperate for a way out.

I drifted in and out of a restless slumber, my mind plagued by
terrifying dreams. Eventually, I woke in a cold sweat, my heart racing
and my breaths coming in short, panicked gasps as my eyes adjusted
to the dark. I struggled to drag my drunken self out of bed and into
the bathroom. As I stood over the white porcelain bowl, emptying my
bladder, a thought born out of pure desperation entered my mind –
what if I could just disappear, vanish into thin air, and never return
to this forsaken and miserable place? Although I knew it wasn't that
simple – the bastards were watching me, following my every move.
Simply getting up, filling a suitcase, and doing a runner was not an
option. However, I had managed to fool them several times before

by sneaking out through the backdoor of my house. I needed to come up with a plan, I really had fuck all options, but I also had no intention of handing over any money to some Eastern European criminal gang, whom I viewed as nothing more than a bunch of lowlife pimps. Shivering with the cold, I wrapped the thin blanket tighter around me, determined to come up with a plan.

Their figure of half a million euro was preposterous and defiantly out of reach. Even if I pooled all my resources together, the money inherited from the sale of my mother's house, her savings, her insurance policy, and my own savings would still fall short of what they demanded. My combined resources would amount to a substantial sum of money. The main issue was that I had no intention of parting with any of my money, despite my vow of poverty. That little nest egg stashed away in a second bank account was my retirement fund. And I firmly believed that I deserved every single cent of that money, considering all the hardship that I had endured over the years.

My mother, O'Connell, and those perverts at the seminary all played a significant role in ruining my life. I viewed that money as a form of compensation for all the suffering I had experienced throughout my life, and the thought of simply handing it over to a gang of thugs, no, that was never going to happen. Although I was well aware that I was in way over my head, I still couldn't justify giving those bastards anything. They had no idea of my capabilities when I was backed into a corner. I needed to find a way to outsmart them, but I also had to proceed with extreme caution. One wrong move in the heat of the moment could lead to my downfall. I felt trapped, like a cornered animal. However, I also knew that this was when an animal becomes most dangerous. My opponents were clever, they had gathered enough evidence to potentially have me locked up for the rest of my life. I knew it wouldn't be as simple as just handing over the money and then returning to my normal life, as if my life had ever been normal. There was no way a ruthless gang would let me live after I handed them such a substantial sum of money.

The thought of packing a bag and running away had crossed my mind, but I quickly dismissed the idea as foolish and reckless, an act of desperation. I knew that if I were to go missing, the police and the press would receive a copy of the disc and my profile would be all over the news, making me a wanted man. It would have been impossible for me to pass through any airports or ferry ports undetected. Even if I had been guaranteed that the situation would be resolved when I handed over the money, I probably might have considered it. Although deep down I knew that there was no way in hell I could ever trust those ruthless bastards.

Suicide had crossed my mind. Realistically, it seemed like my best option when considering everything. A part of me longed for the peace that death would bring, but another part fought fiercely to hold on to life. I didn't want to die; I just needed a way out. I wanted to live; there was still so much unfinished work to be done. The streets weren't going to rid themselves of all those vile whores parading around on darkened corners. After much deliberation, I finally dragged myself out of bed for the second time that morning. I was relieved that it was Fr. Brian's turn to say the morning mass. As I impatiently waited for the kettle to boil,

'Fuck the coffee,' I muttered, and poured a generous amount of whiskey into an unwashed cup that was lying in the sink. I refused to let it all end like this, being controlled by a gang of pumped-up pimps. I refilled my dirty cup, determined not to go down without a fight.

Chapter 56

U pon entering the sitting room, I caught my reflection in the oval-shaped mirror that hung above the fireplace. The sight of my reflection was a stark reminder of how much I had aged since hearing that whore's confession. My once youthful appearance now appeared haggard and beaten, with pale skin, sunken eyes, and dark circles. As I stared at myself in the mirror, I couldn't help but think that I resembled one of the addicts from the day centre. In an attempt to clear my mind, I decided to go for a walk. Some fresh air and a nice stroll would sort me out, I thought, as I put on my coat and left the house.

The cold, fresh breeze certainly blew away the cobwebs. I pulled my collar up and glanced at my watch: it was eleven-seventeen in the morning. After another sleepless night and what felt like an eternity staring at the blank television screen, my mind numb from the whiskey I had been drinking from a dirty cup, I was relieved to be outside in the fresh air. I walked aimlessly with no particular destination in mind. However, about half an hour into my walk, the heavens opened. Realising that I was closer to the church than my house, I ran towards it for shelter.

As I stepped inside the church, my clothes were drenched and clung to my body, and I could feel the water squishing between my toes with each step. The church was empty except for two elderly women kneeling in front of the altar, reciting the Rosary. Their low voices reverberated throughout the vast empty space, filling it with deep, rumbling tones. I quietly made my way down the aisle and took a seat on one of the old wooden pews, observing the two old dears with their heads bowed and fingers slowly moving the rosary beads around their pale, wrinkled hands. Despite my scepticism towards their devotion, I couldn't help but think that they were completely delusional for fervently praying to a God that doesn't exist. But as I watched them, I felt a sense of admiration for their unwavering faith and dedication. Although it was also possible that the two women were just stone fucking mad.

As I sat on the hard wooden pew, the sound of the rain pounding against the churches stained-glass windows filled my ears. It suddenly dawned on me that I was in God's house, a place of worship, and as a priest, I should act accordingly. The church was the last place I wanted to be. Christ, I had already wasted far too much of my life in the damn place. However, in my desperate attempt to escape the relentless downpour, the church was my closest refuge. I knelt down and made the sign of the cross, feeling a little self-conscious as I noticed the two old dears were watching my every move. It was ironic, a priest who didn't believe in God, a murderer of at least ten people, and being blackmailed by a criminal gang. And yet, I found myself in a church, down on bended knee, pretending to pray, all because of the watchful eyes of two deluded old women. I got up from my knees and sat back down on the hard wooden pew. I closed my eyes, trying to give off the impression that I was deeply engaged in prayer.

I quickly grew tired of pretending. As I opened my eyes, I noticed that the two women were gone. I wondered if God had answered their prayers or simply ignored them, just as he had ignored my prayers and desperate pleas for help during my darkest trials. As I looked around, my eyes were immediately drawn to a dark-haired man kneeling a few pews away on my right. His gaze was firmly fixed on the crucifix that hung above the altar. He hadn't been there when I first entered the church. He must have come in while I was on my knees, pretending to pray with my eyes closed. I could tell he wasn't a local by his skin tone. He appeared to be in his mid-forties, well-dressed, with jet-black hair slicked back. Not too many men from around this area, especially in that age bracket, would set foot inside the church unless it was absolutely necessary. They only attend for funerals, or special occasions, such as Christenings, or their children's First Holy Communion, or Confirmation. He defiantly stood out, his confident demeanour demanding respect.

He must have sensed my gaze fixed on him, as he turned abruptly without warning. His dark brown eyes, although beautiful, seemed to penetrate right through me, leaving me feeling exposed and vulnerable. He rose up from the pew, powerfully, like a great silverback ready to defend his territory. I turned quickly to face the altar, as if that was going to save me. The sound of his heavy footsteps reverberated through the vast, empty church, filling the silence with a haunting echo. With my heart racing and nowhere to hide, all I could hope for was divine intervention, or even better, for the ground to open up and swallow me. As he descended onto the pew beside me, his massive bulk casting a dark shadow over mine.

'Hello, Padre,' he said. I turned to face him, my whole body was shaking, as the reality of the situation hit me. Everything had become far too real. I already knew who he was before he even spoke.

'Hello,' I replied, my voice quivered slightly as I fidgeted with my hands. He slid his right hand into the inside of his overcoat; I noticed the Armani tag on the sleeve as he pulled out an envelope.

'Time is running out for you, Padre,' he said, as he handed me the envelope. Reluctantly, I brought my trembling hand up as he placed the envelope in it. Without another single word, he stood up and walked towards the large wooden doors at the front of the church, before disappearing outside. My eyes remained on his massive shoulders and back until he was out of sight.

As soon as he had left the church, I turned back and looked down at the envelope clutched tightly in my trembling hands. Inside was a note, again written with the letters cut out from a newspaper. It read,

'YOU HAVE THREE DAYS.' Those four simple words sent a wave of terror through my entire body, causing my heart rate to skyrocket. After reading the note, I noticed that there were some photos in the envelope. As I looked through them, I dropped the envelope to the floor. The images were of the woman that I had murdered in her apartment. They were close-up shots of her severely caved-in face and head.

The images were gruesome. I bent down and tried to pick up the photos that had fallen out of the envelope when I dropped it. My trembling hands struggled to get a proper grip on them. Eventually, after several failed attempts, I managed to retrieve them and placed them back in the envelope. Sick, deranged bastards, I thought to myself as I looked around the empty church, the envelope still shaking in my right hand. I was consumed by an overwhelming sense of fear and terror that coursed through my veins as I struggled to stand up before leaving the church.

Outside, the rain continued to pour down. I walked around to the back of the church, where I usually parked my car. As I turned the corner, I was surprised to see that my usual parking spot was empty. It was then that I remembered I had been out for a walk and had only entered the church to escape the heavy downpour.

'For fuck's sake,' I muttered. I must be losing my mind, I though as I hunched my shoulders and pulled up my collar, for all the good it would do against such heavy rain. With my head down, I left the church car park and walked as quickly as I could, hoping to avoid meeting anyone. The bastards were definitely following me; otherwise, they wouldn't have known I was in the church. They must have been tailing me as I aimlessly walked around the village, and I was completely oblivious to their presence.

By the time I arrive home, I was once again soaked to the skin. My hands were still shaking uncontrollably as I tried several times in vain to light up a cigarette. Not until I had drained the second glass of whiskey did the shaking begin to subside. I sat down at the kitchen table, and placed the photos one by one before me, there were eight gruesome and disturbing photos in total. I lit up a cigarette as I studied each photo individually. Who in their right mind would record and print such sick images? I thought to myself, as I inhaled the deadly nicotine.

The close-ups of the dead woman's badly beaten face and head were absolutely horrendous to look at. Just as I was about to exhale the smoke from my cigarette, a wave of nausea rose up in my throat. And before I could stop it, I threw up all over the vile images. I felt completely overwhelmed with a sense of helplessness and entrapment as I looked down at the images now covered in vomit. I placed my arms on the table and rested my spinning head on top of them. Tears streamed down my face as I let out a gut-wrenching cry, my body shaking with sobs. The vile images were now drenched in a repulsive blend of the murderer's own tears and vomit. It was a sickening reminder of the brutal murder I had committed.

Chapter 57

I woke to the revolting smell of stale vomit, which almost made me gag again. My head was pounding, too much fucking whiskey, I assumed, as I looked across the table at the empty bottle facing me. The sight of those repulsive images covered in vomit greeted me as I slowly raised my head from the kitchen table. The daunting task of cleaning up the mess loomed over me as I struggled to pull myself together.

After spending a few minutes with my head held under the cold tap, I grabbed a couple of towels from the hot press and began the arduous task of cleaning up. When I was finished, I threw the soiled towels in the bin, as there was no point in trying to clean them. I left the back door open in the hope of airing out the kitchen, as the smell that lingered was horrendous. After wiping away the vomit from the soiled photos, I brought them into the sitting room and threw them into the fire grate. As I flicked the lighter, I watched the flames consume each vile image one by one, reducing them to nothing more than a pile of black ash.

Only two days remained before the police and the press would receive a copy of the disc. As my impending demise rapidly approached, my entire being was engulfed by fear and panic. My opponents were powerful, ruthless, and seemed to have abundant resources at their disposal. The overwhelming chaos and uncertainty of my current situation consumed my every waking hour. It felt like a never-ending battle of wits, with my opponents always one step ahead. Although, in reality, if felt more like a deadly game of Russian Roulette, and now it was my turn to place the gun at the side of my head and see if the barrel was loaded or not.

I could clearly see it all playing out in front of me. My bank account being emptied, and then I would go missing. A day or two later, the police and the press would receive a copy of the disc. It would look as though I had fled and was as guilty as hell. Without a trace, I would disappear, my fate unknown, my body never to be found. I would become another forgotten statistic on the ever-growing list of missing persons. My mind was racing. What if the gang decided not to kill me, but instead turned me in to the police after I had handed over the money? I could already envision the sensational news headline:

'Irish Priest Brutally Raped and Murdered Young Asylum Seeker.' And, then just to top off everything. My stalker came forward with the evidence, she claimed to have, which I didn't doubt, linking me to the other women that had been murdered. I would undoubtedly spend the rest of my life behind bars and would probably end up becoming a plaything for the real hardened criminals.

My options were far from ideal. I could ignore them and call their bluff, but that would likely result in either my death or imprisonment – neither of which appealed to me. Another option that I considered was to do the decent thing and end my own life. At least if I took my own life, the pain would be fleeting, and the end would come swiftly. However, I imagined it would be a completely different scenario if the gang decided to pay me a visit and bundled me into the back of a van. The mere thought of them keeping me alive and torturing me for days on end, just to satisfy their own sadistic pleasure sent a shiver right through me. In their hands, I would undoubtedly meet my end writhing in agony, my unheard screams echoing through the air as they tortured me mercilessly. They would never allow me to pass from this life to the next without suffering. After all, I had eliminated one of their valuable assets and cancelled out one of their sources of income. So, in other words, I fucking owed them big time.

The idea of faking my own death had occurred to me. I had read stories about people who had successfully pulled this off, often defrauding insurance companies or mortgage lenders in the process. However, there were also numerous accounts of individuals who were apprehended and served a considerable amount of time in prison for their actions, probably wondering how the hell it had all gone so horribly wrong, as they stared at the walls in their prison cell. I was convinced that those who were caught must have made some serious mistakes along the way, which ultimately led to their downfall. The more I contemplated the idea, the more plausible it seemed. If I could convincingly stage my own death and flee from here, I might just have a chance of outsmarting those merciless bastards who were relentlessly pursing me.

The harsh reality of my situation suddenly hit me: the clock was ticking. With only two days remaining until my deadline, time was running out. I needed to buy myself a little more time to figure out a plan. Perhaps I could persuade these low-life pimps who were blackmailing me to give me another couple of days to come up with the money. I could try to feed them some bullshit story about needing to apply for a bank loan, which would take a few days to be approved due to the large amount of money I needed. The gang had no idea of what I had stored away in the bank, and if they believed my story, it would alleviate some of the pressure while I set my plan in place.

In my chaotic mind, a plan was beginning to form – an elaborate, even far-fetched, yet a plan, nonetheless. In my state of pure desperation, any idea or plan was greatly welcomed. The first necessary step to initiate my plan would be to have a serious conversation with the bank manager first thing in the morning. During which I would inform him that I need to close my account with immediate effect and withdraw my entire balance of three hundred and fifty thousand euro in cash. I knew that attempting to withdraw such a large sum of money would be problematic and could potentially raise suspicion. However, with my back against the wall, I saw this as my only chance at freedom.

I knew that I needed to come up with a very convincing story for the bank manager if I was going to have any chance of pulling this off. The first step was to empty my bank account. I would explain to the bank manager that the money in my account had come from the sale of my late mother's house and her other assets. However, the most challenging part of my plan – the outrageous lie. I would proceed to tell him that it was my mother's dying wish for me to donate all of her assets among her favourite charities. And in order for me to fulfil her dying wish, I would need to withdraw all of the funds and close my account.

Surely, when he hears that it was my mother's final wish, it won't be a problem to close the account and withdraw everything at such short notice. My main concern was whether the bank manager would be allowed to hand over such a large sum of cash, or would he insist on using bank transfers due to the substantial amount. If I couldn't persuade him to give me the cash, my plan would be doomed, and I'd be fucked.

As my mind raced with possible outcomes, a surge of adrenaline coursed through my body, triggering my fight or flight response. Could I actually pull this off? Could I convincingly fake my own death and fool everyone around me? Time was of the essence, and every second from here on in was precious. I needed to empty my bank account, fake my own death, and leave the country. And all of this needed to be accomplished within the next thirty-six hours.

The only idea that came to mind in regard to faking my death was staging a house fire, similar to the one that tragically took the life of my poor dear old mother, the sadistic bitch. May she rest in peace, my arse; I hoped the evil bitch burns in hell for all eternity. After all, I had some experience in this area. If my house were to accidently burn down, the fire department would conduct an investigation to determine the cause of the fire. However, the biggest obstacle was that they would need to find a body in order for me to be pronounced dead at the scene. Without a body, my plan was useless.

In theory, the solution to my problem seemed simple enough: find a man of similar height and build to myself and murder him. Then I would plant the unfortunate victim in my house, making it appear as though I was the victim since I lived alone. Fucking genius, I thought to myself as I stood under the shower, embracing the soothing warmth of the water as it rained down on me. It felt as though I had received a new lease of life. For the first time since hearing that whore's confession, I could finally see a light at the end of the tunnel.

Chapter 58

As the words 'Game On' from her letter echoed in my mind, I knew I was ready to declare war on my opponent. My mind was racing with intricate details and strategies. All that was left was for me to execute each stage with precision. After getting dressed, I spent some time on sentry duty, looking out from my bedroom window. And as always, nothing or no one seemed out of place on the dimly lit street below. Fuck them, I was determined to succeed, no matter what obstacles stood in my way. If I am going to pull off this brazen stunt, it's now or never. I slipped out the backdoor and hurried through the putrid laneway, the stench filling my nostrils, grew stronger with each step. My eyes darted back and forth, constantly scanning my surroundings, on high alert for any signs of being followed as I made my way towards the village.

'Conyngham Road, please,' I said to the taxi driver as I settled into the back seat. Twenty minutes later, I found myself walking through the Phoenix Park. My heart was racing – I had never tried to pick up a man before, I was completely out of my comfort zone. It was well-known that the rent boys frequented the area around the Wellington monument. As I continued walking further into the park, I followed the pathway that led towards the monument. On the far side of the road, I noticed a young man standing alone, smoking with his back to me. From the distance, he appeared smaller in both height and build compared to me. Beggars can't be choosers; I reminded myself as I checked him out from a safe distance.

All I needed was a dead body. As I was sizing him up, much like a hunter taking aim at his prey, my attention was drawn to another man across the road. He, too, was alone and appeared to be closer to my height and build. I crossed the road and stopped on the footpath, pretending to tie my shoelace as I bent down. I just needed a moment to calm my nerves and gather my thoughts. What the hell was I going to say to him? I stood up, took a deep breath and cautiously made my way towards him. He must have heard my footsteps as I approached him. He spun around, his curious blue eyes meeting mine. We were almost the same height which was perfect. He had a thick, lustrous mane of jet-black hair, neatly combed to the right side. The soft, amber glow of the streetlight cast a warm halo around the man's features, making his clean-shaven face seem to glisten in the dark.

'Hi,' he said with a friendly smile.

'Hello,' I replied, my voice quivering with nerves.

'Would you happen to have a spare cigarette?' he asked.

'Sure,' I replied, removing the pack from my coat pocket and handing him one. I flicked the lighter and held the bright orange flame up towards him. He bent slightly with the cigarette between his lips to meet the flame. He thanked me with a genuine smile. He seemed like a nice, charming sort of fellow, I wondered how he ended up selling his ass to make a living. I couldn't help but to feel sorry for him, knowing that his life as he knows it will soon come to an abrupt end.

'Not a bad night,' I said, trying to keep the conversation flowing as I lit a cigarette. 'Yes, it's nice and mild. Not too bad at all,' he agreed. Then, the moment I had been anxiously anticipating finally arrived. An uncomfortable silence fell between us as we stood smoking, our eyes remained locked in a tense, unspoken exchange. Thankfully, my new friend broke the dreaded silence, by asking,

'Are you looking for some business?' He quickly turned his head in the opposite direction as the words left his mouth, as if he was checking to see who had just spoken.

'Yes,' I replied, blowing smoke up into the warm night air.

'What are you looking for, anal or oral? he asked, his eyes never leaving the ground as he drew hard on his cigarette.

'Both,' I replied, my mind raced, and I felt increasingly uneasy as I looked around me.

'A hundred euro,' he said, avoiding eye contact. He seemed embarrassed as we negotiated the deal.

'Fine, but not here,' I replied.

'Where then?' he asked, looking a little confused.

'My house is only twenty minutes away in a taxi,' I suggested.

'No way, fuck that. This could be a set-up for all I know,' he said, quickly rejecting my suggestion. I could see he was getting agitated.

'Look, I'll give you two hundred euro when we get in the taxi and another two hundred when we're finished,' I offered, realising the clock was ticking and I couldn't risk losing my body double.

'You're fucking with me. I don't have time for this bullshit,' he said, flicking the cigarette butt to the ground before starting to walk away.

I stepped in front of him and quickly scanned the area before pulling out my wallet. I then counted out four hundred euro in front of him, suddenly realising how fucking foolish I was to do such a thing. He could have easily attacked me and taken the money, knowing that I couldn't report it to the police. In all honesty, who in their right mind would willingly walk into a police station and admit,

'I have just been mugged and robbed by a rent boy?' As I counted the money, his eyes widened and the expression on his face sent a chill right through me. Had I just made a grave mistake? I had no way of knowing what dark thoughts were running through his mind. I had thrown all caution to the wind; I desperately needed him to leave the park with me.

'It's all yours, if you want it,' I said, trying to sound casual. He appeared uneasy, as he shifted his weight from foot to foot and kept glancing around anxiously before finally meeting my gaze.

'Alright, but just so you know, if this turns out to be a set-up, I swear, I'll hunt you down and slit your fucking throat,' he threatened, his tone aggressive. I didn't appreciate his aggressive words or tone. I had no choice but to brush it off, as time was of the essence.

We walked back through the park and out onto the main road, smoking as we waited for a taxi. Half an hour later, we entered my house through the backdoor, he never questioned anything. Once inside, I poured us each a large whiskey.

'I take it the bedroom is upstairs?' he said with a cheeky grin.

'Yes, follow me,' I replied, returning his smile as I led the way. Dead man walking, I thought to myself as we climbed the stairs in silence.

'Make yourself comfortable, I just need to use the loo,' I said, smiling as I left the bedroom, humming away to myself, as I locked the bathroom door behind me.

My nerves were shattered. I needed to regain control and pull myself together before I could follow through with my plan. As I threw cold water on my face, the young man in my bedroom brought back memories of Ann, another innocent victim of a senseless crime. History is filled with such tragic stories. As I looked into the mirror, I reminded myself that this was my only chance for survival. If I fucked this up, it would be game over. The harsh reality was the brutal choice of kill or be killed. I took a deep breath, trying to calm my nerves before returning to the bedroom.

Upon entering the bedroom, he was sprawled out on the bed, naked and caressing himself. Dirty bastard, I thought to myself, as I smiled down at him. He sat up and extended his toned arms, pulling me closer to him by my belt. Without hesitation, he undid my belt and unbuttoned my trousers, slowly sliding them down my trembling legs. I kicked off my shoes and stepped out of my trousers, which were now heaped around my ankles. His warm hands slowly caressed the inside of my thighs, and within minutes, he had me aroused and was taking me in his mouth. With his skilled tongue, he brought me to new heights of pleasure. After I came, I lay down beside him. We were roughly the same height, which was ideal, although we looked completely different. He was handsome, with a strikingly chiselled jawline, piercing blue eyes, and a well-toned body. As I lay next to him, I felt very self-conscious about my own appearance. I was far from handsome or toned. Though I was confident that by the time the fire crew stumbled across his severely charred corpse, he would be beyond recognition, and everyone would just assume that the body was mine.

'Did you enjoy?' he asked, as he lit up another one of my cigarettes without asking. 'Yes, it was beautiful,' I replied, smiling as I savoured the moment. The soft rustle of the sheets and the faint scent of his cologne filled the air as I lay next to him, my body still tingling from his touch. The beautiful moment was suddenly derailed. For the life of me, I couldn't remember where I had left the hammer, and panic began to set in.

'Would you like another drink?' I asked, needing an excuse to leave the room and find the hammer.

'Yes, that would be nice, thank you,' he replied. He was so polite, I thought as I picked up the two empty glasses from the bedside table and then made my way down to the kitchen. Where the fuck did I put the hammer? I repeatedly asked myself as I refilled the two glasses. A sense of unease washed over me as I heard him moving around upstairs, I then heard the bathroom door being locked. I remembered cleaning the hammer in the sink after its last outing. As I mentally replayed each step, from the last time I had used the hammer, my memory was restored. After I had cleaned the hammer, I placed it in the press under the sink.

Upon opening the press door, there it was lying on the shelf, cleaned and ready to go.

As I grabbed the two glasses and the hammer, I could hear the sound of running water echoing throughout the house. He was still in the bathroom. My heart raced as I hurried up the stairs, my knuckles turned white as I clenched the hammer tightly, praying that he wouldn't come out of the bathroom. Just as I reached the top of the stairs, I heard the toilet flush. I rushed into the bedroom and placed the hammer down at the side of the bed where I was lying. As he entered the room, I handed him a glass of whiskey, he accepted with a smile.

'Cheers,' he said as we clinked glasses. It was a great pity, although I had no choice but to take his life in order to save my own. He was a nice guy and, strangely enough, I was enjoying his company. However, I had to suppress my emotions and focus on what needed to be done. He finished his drink and placed the empty glass on the bedside table before lying face down on the bed.

'I suppose you want to fuck me?' he asked. I thought his manner of asking was a little crude, but then again, how does one ask such a question? He slowly raised himself up on all fours and I positioned myself behind him before entering him gently, almost lovingly. In that moment, I was completely consumed by him. All my thoughts and fears simply faded away as I indulged in the intoxicating and sensual pleasure. As soon as I came, he lay back down on his stomach, his handsome face buried in the pillow. Slowly, I eased myself off the bed and reached down to retrieve the hammer. He remained still as I raised the hammer above my head.

'How thoughtful of you,' I whispered as I repeatedly struck him on the back of the head. His dark red blood sprayed out in every direction, it dripped down the walls, pooled on the bed, even the ceiling was not spared from the spray of crimson. After the eight blow, I dropped the hammer to the floor.

I walked over to the chair in the corner of the room and slumped down, as I lit a cigarette. What a fucking mess, I thought as I surveyed the room. But then a smile slowly crept onto my face, as I realised that there would be no clean up required. In just a few hours, this place would be reduced to ashes. A sense of satisfaction washed over me as I drained my glass, knowing that a crucial part of my plan had fallen into place. I had obtained a body similar to my own height and build, which would be discovered by the fire crew as they battled the blaze.

'You truly are a clever fellow,' I whispered to myself as I stood up and walked over to the bed and gazed down at my recently deceased friend. He had unknowingly given his life for my chance of freedom, the ultimate sacrifice.

'Thank you,' I whispered, as I stubbed out my cigarette on his left buttock.

Chapter 59

As I slowly opened my eyes, I was greeted by the soft glow of the moon, still illuminating the room and casting a tranquil aura over everything. Glancing at my watch, it read three forty-seven. Depending on one's perspective, this could be considered either the middle of the night or very early in the morning. Knowing that the bank wouldn't open until nine, I had a few hours to kill. So, I decided to use the time to mentally prepare myself for the daunting task that lay ahead. After showering and getting dressed, I made my way down to the kitchen to brew a strong cup of coffee. My mind and body were consumed by a mix of fear, anxiety, and complete exhaustion. As I sat at the table, sipping my coffee and blowing smoke towards the nicotine-stained ceiling, the serene silence of the early morning enveloped me, the calm before the storm.

The kitchen was shrouded in a thick impenetrable darkness, with only a faint sliver of moonlight seeping through the gap in the blinds. I sat there savouring the moment, knowing that soon the rest of the world would awaken and fuck-up everything. I drained my cup and made another, this time making it even stronger to help combat the fatigue that was creeping up on me.

My mind wandered as I gazed out the kitchen window, lost in thought. The soft morning light was gradually filtering in, and I knew that I needed to brace myself for the day ahead – a day that would undoubtedly determine the course of my life. Despite my fears about the outcome, I was determined to see my plan through. After all, as I reminded myself 'it's a matter of life and death.' The bitter taste of the extra strong coffee snapped me out of my daydream, causing me to grimace as I forced it down.

With only one chance to accomplish so much in such a short period of time, it was up to me to decide my own fate. As I sat at the kitchen table, my mind was racing with thoughts of the challenges that lay ahead. I was engulfed by a tumultuous wave of conflicting emotions, each one threatening to pull me under, the serene aura I had awoken to had dissipated.

My feet pounded against the hardwood floor as I restlessly traversed the length of the house, traipsing from the backdoor to the front door and then back again. As I paced back and forth, I wondered if my behaviour mirrored that of a condemned man, counting down the final moments of his life on death row before being led away to the death chamber. I smoked one cigarette after another until the box was empty. In a fit of rage, I crushed the box in my hand and threw it to the floor, as I climbed the stairs.

Upon entering the blood-splattered room, I was struck by the beauty of my naked, lifeless friend against the gruesome scene. Despite the horror, he appeared almost serene, like a beautiful marble sculpture. It was as if he belonged in an art museum, among the great masterpieces, to be admired but never touched. However, I quickly scolded myself, 'Snap the fuck out of it and focus on the task at hand.' Reaching up, I carefully removed the two suitcases from the top of the wardrobe and placed them on the floor, making sure to avoid any contact with his blood. I quickly filled the suitcases with as many items of clothing as possible; I found myself having to kneel on top of each case to close them. Once they were packed, I then carried them downstairs and left them by the backdoor.

My next task involved more lies, I sent Fr. Brian a text, informing him that I was suffering from a severe case of food poisoning. I went on to say that I was doubled over in pain and couldn't keep anything down and asked if he wouldn't mine covering for me. To say the morning mass and to handle any issues that might arise throughout the day. Time was running out; my deadline was only one day away. The consequences of my failure to meet the deadline, were something I didn't even want to think about. The though of the police and the press receiving a copy of the disc was terrifying.

My primary focus was on the bank manager; I saw him as the main obstacle standing between me and my freedom. After my mother's untimely death, I had inherited around three hundred and fifty thousand euro, which was a nice little bonus, considering all I ever wanted was for her to be dead. My plan was to withdraw all of the money and close my account. However, the more I thought about it, the more ludicrous it seemed. What I was trying to pull off resembled a far-fetched movie plot. It was sheer madness, a wild and unstable idea born out of pure desperation. I glanced at my watch, it read, eight forty-five, game on. I left the house by the backdoor.

Chapter 60

The short walk to the village was spent rehearsing the story I had created about emptying my bank account and donating the money to my late mother's favourite charities, as per her dying wish. As I strolled up the main street towards the bank, my eyes darted back and forth and my senses were on high alert, scanning for anyone out of the ordinary. A subtle grin crept onto my face as I thought to myself, if the bank manager believes my story, he'll believe anything. Despite my nerves, I tried to exude a sense of calm and composure as I prepared to enter the bank. Taking one final, deep drag of nicotine, I steeled myself for what was to come.

Thankfully, the bank was quiet and there were only two people ahead of me in the queue. After a few of minutes had passed, I found myself standing before the counter. The young woman behind the glass screen looked up at me and smiled.

'Good morning, Father. How may I help you today?' she asked, forcing a smile on her plain face.

'I would like to speak with Frank about a small matter. Is he available?' I inquired, hoping that by using the bank manager's first name, the young clerk would think we were friends, and just send me on into his office. No such fucking luck.

'Do you have an appointment, Father?' she asked. Her false smile disappeared, as I replied, 'No. I'm afraid I don't. I just wanted to seek his advice on a financial matter. I promise not to take up too much of his time.'

'Okay, Father. If you would like to take a seat, I'll give Frank a call and see if he can fit you in,' she said, her smile returned.

'Thank you,' I replied, as I turned away and made my way over to the three bright red plastic chairs that were lined up against the wall.

I sat down on the middle chair, but without any apparent reason, I swiftly shifted to the one on my left. I sat nervously and waited, feeling like a bold child outside the school principal's office, about to be reprimanded.

After what felt like an eternity, Frank's obese frame emerged from behind a brown door marked 'private.' Frank always gave off the impression that he was extremely busy, scurrying around like a headless chicken. I was always drawn to his round, red cheeks, a sign of high blood pressure, I assumed. I knew that my request would not help his condition. Christ, he still has that ridiculous comb over, get a decent haircut for fuck's sake, I thought to myself as I stood up from the uncomfortable plastic chair as he approached me.

'Fr. Doyle, I apologise for keeping you waiting. It's hectic in here at the moment,' Frank said, extending his pudgy, sweaty hand towards me. Looking around, I was little flummoxed as the bank was empty except for me.

'No problem at all, Frank. I really appreciate you fitting me into your busy schedule,' I responded, with a hint of sarcasm, firmly shaking his sweaty hand. He motioned for me to follow him, as he confidently strode back towards the door he had just emerged from, I followed closely behind, discreetly wiping his sweat from my hand onto the leg of my trousers. He held the door open for me and then gently closed it behind me as I entered his office. He gestured for me to take a seat before he sank into a plush leather chair on his side of the desk.

'Now Father, how can I be of service to you?' he asked, panting and breathing heavily, as if he had just completed a hundred-meter sprint.

'I need to withdraw a large sum of money,' I replied, my voice quivering slightly as I lowered my trembling hands beneath the desk out of sight.

'That shouldn't be a problem. How much are you looking for?' he asked, his mind was clearly elsewhere as he impatiently tapped his fat fingers on the desk. He gave off the impression that I was wasting his precious time.

'The entire amount. Three hundred and fifty thousand euro. I want to close my account,' I replied. His fat fingers came to a sudden halt. I now had his full attention.

'My word, that's a significant amount. May I ask why you want to close your account with us?' Frank inquired, leaning forward and resting his large forearms on the desk, clasping his hands together.

'The reason for opening this account was due to the passing of my mother. I needed an account to deposit the proceeds from the sale of her house, as well as her other assets. As you may know, Frank, as a priest, I have taken a vow of poverty since my ordination. My salary is deposited into a separate account each month. The account in question was only meant to be temporary, until I sorted out my mothers' affairs. It was her dying wish to donate the proceeds from her assets among her favourite charities. That is why I am here today, to withdraw the funds and fulfil her final wishes. I am also concerned that if anyone were to discover that I, a priest, have a second account with such a significant sum of money, it would definitely be frowned upon,' I explained.

'I understand your concern, Father. Another scandal the church could do without,' he said, grinning to himself, pleased with his sly remark. I didn't like the smug grin on his face as he stared across the desk. I let his snide comment slide as I composed myself. I had hoped that when he heard it was an old woman's dying wish, that would have been enough to convince him to close the account, no questions asked. However, as I met his gaze, I couldn't decipher his thoughts, his stoic expression revealed nothing. The phrase, 'your move creep,' entered my head, but I quickly dismissed it. He straightened up and sat back in his plush chair, causing it to groan under his massive bulk. His smile had transformed into an evil smirk, reminiscent of a Disney villain.

'That is a significant sum of money for a priest to have stashed away. I can only imagine the sensational headline the newspaper would run with. And not to mention the potential payout for such a story,' he said, with a smug expression on his fat, red face. I couldn't believe what I was hearing, had he just attempted to blackmail me? Who the fuck does he think he is? As if, I didn't have enough on my plate at the moment. I struggled to maintain my composure, resisting the urge to lunge across the desk and choke the fucking life out of him.

'Yes, you're right Frank. I suppose a story like that getting out wouldn't do me any favours at all,' I replied, my voice seething with rage. 'I can only imagine the scandal that would ensue.' Frank's smirk grew by the second as he responded,

'Indeed, Father. It would be quite scandalous for a priest to have such a large sum of money hidden away. The public outcry would be immense.' I stared deep into his eyes, thinking to myself, you patronising little prick. I needed to control my rising anger, as time was running out.

'That is precisely why I wish to close my account and fulfil my late mother's final wishes,' I stated firmly. Frank's response was dripping with sarcasm,

'How very noble of you, Father. You have just restored my faith in the Catholic Church.' I clenched my fists and took a deep breath, trying to contain the surge of rage that threatened to consume me. I couldn't give him the satisfaction of seeing me provoked.

'Frank, is there a problem with me closing the account?' I asked, my tone and demeanour dramatically changed. I could tell from his expression, that he had noticed. I was really struggling to keep my rising temper under control. I couldn't understand why he was making such a big deal out of it. After all, it was my money. I wasn't asking for a loan. To me, it was a straightforward transaction – close my account and give me my money. It's that simple. But for whatever reason, this overgrown, worthless prick, sitting across from me seemed to be enjoying playing God. However, all good things must come to an end, and I was only seconds away from knocking Frank off his high horse.

'Well, you see Father. This situation is not as simple as you may think. I feel somewhat morally obliged to inform your superiors, and maybe even the authorities. After all, I have no idea how you came to be in possession of such a substantial amount of money, regardless of the story you just spun me. And more importantly, you are not fulfilling the vows you took when you were ordained,' he said, his words igniting a surge of rage deep within me and an insatiable desire to retaliate. Who the fuck does this prick think he is? Fuck him, if he wants to play dirty, then let's play, I thought to myself as I reached for the photo frame on his desk. I quickly turned it towards me to see the picture.

'What a lovely photo, Frank,' I said, admiring the picture.

'Does your wife know that you're fucking that young girl sitting out there behind the counter?' He nearly choked on his words.

'I beg your pardon,' he sputtered out, clearly offended.

'How dare you come in here and make such a false accusation.' He reached out to grab the photo frame, but I snatched it away before he could get a hold of it.

'How dare you accuse me of such a thing,' he continued, struggling to keep his voice down. I calmly placed the photo frame back on his desk and then stood up and walked towards him. I looked him directly in the eye as I sat down on the edge of his desk.

'Listen carefully, Frank. I will only say this once. I do not have much time, and the people that I'm dealing with are not only impatient, but they are also very dangerous. If they do not receive what they are owed, I'm fucked. I lied about my mother's final wish. The real reason I need to empty my account is that I have accumulated a significant amount of debt through gambling. I foolishly got involved with a money lender to pay off some of the debt. At the time, I didn't realise that I was dealing with a criminal who, as I have recently found out, is a prominent figure in the underworld. Now, he is putting a lot of pressure on me to pay up. So, Frank, I am asking you to stop fucking around, close my account and give me my money so that I can sort out this mess that I got myself into. It's that simple. So, stop trying to complicate the matter,' I said. Frank's body went rigid, and his eyes widened in shock, his mind was reeling in complete disbelief as he stared up at me with his mouth agape.

'I can't believe what I am hearing,' he said, desperately trying to comprehend my words. 'I'll call the police,' he said, wiping beads of sweat from his forehead with the back of his hand. 'We have procedures in place for incidents like this.'

'Don't be so fucking stupid. Have you not listened to a single word I just said? These people are extremely dangerous. They have been watching you and your family for the past week, monitoring your ever move. If I don't leave here with my money, we're both fucked,' I replied, trying to sound convincing. Once again, the lies came so easily. I spoke confidently, my words flowing effortlessly as I spun my web of deceit. And judging by the look of fear on Frank's face, my lies seemed to have the desired effect I was looking for.

'Jesus Christ, I can't just hand over three hundred and fifty thousand euro in cash, even though it is your money. That amount of money is usually electronically transferred from one account to another, without anyone even seen, let alone touching the money. I doubt we even have that amount of cash in the safe,' he said, leaping up out of his seat and reaching for his mobile phone that was sitting on the desk. I quickly snatched it from him.

'What the fuck are you doing?' I snarled, turning off his phone.

'I need to call head office. I am not authorised to release such a large sum of money, I need to get clearance. The bank has strict procedures that must be followed. I could lose my job if I were to hand over that amount of money,' he said, as he sank back into his chair, looking completely defeated.

'Frank, calm down and listen carefully. You can't get head office, or the police involved in this situation. All I am asking is for you to close my account and give me my money. It is a simple request and once it is done, the matter will be resolved, and head office will never need to know. However, if the police become involved, it could have serious consequences for both of us,' I said, trying to remain calm.

'Jesus, this is unreal, I can't believe it's happening,' he said.

'Frank, it is real, and it is happening. We need to act quickly,' I explained. Frank's breathing became more laboured with each new breath that he took, his round face flushed a deeper shade of red. I feared that he might have a heart attack before he could close my account, which would have completely fucked up everything.

'Frank, you need to calm down. You only have yourself to blame. If you hadn't been such a prick when I first came in, none of this would have happened. All you had to do was close my account, no questions asked, but no, you just couldn't resist the opportunity to try and blackmail me. You thought you had me over a barrel, and now look at the mess you're in,' I said, struggling to suppress my anger. I had already wasted far too much time in the bank and Frank had really thrown a spanner in the works by delaying everything with his unnecessary bullshit. If I left the bank without the money, my entire plan would crumble, and my life would be over.

'I don't know if we have that amount of cash in the safe,' Frank said, visibly shaking as he leaned on his desk. His massive arms trembled as they strained to support his weight.

'Let's hope and pray that you do, for both our sakes. If not, we're both fucked,' I replied as I began to pace the small office.

'How the hell did you end up in such a dangerous predicament? he asked, slumping back down into his chair.

'I was consumed by the curse of gambling and didn't realise it until it was too late,' I replied.

'Surely, we could set them up,' Frank suggested. 'If I call the police and explain everything, they could be lying in wait, ready to arrest them as soon as you hand over the money.'

Christ, I couldn't take much more. How fucking stupid is this man? I thought to myself. 'Jesus, Frank, do you have a death wish? This isn't a fucking movie, it's real life. We're dealing with real gangsters, that hurt and kill people,' I said, my voice raised as I slammed my clenched fist down onto the desk. I couldn't control my frustration any longer. We were wasting valuable time that I didn't have.

'Frank, we need to act quickly. We've already wasted too much time. Please just sort out the paperwork so I can close the account and get out of here before it's too late,' I urged, my heart raced, as I sat down and stared deep into his eyes.

Frank's fat fingers flew over the keyboard with surprising agility, as if they were performing a graceful dance as he entered my details into the computer. Beads of sweat dripped down Frank's beet-red face as he puffed and panted, frantically loosening his tie with one hand, while his other hand continued to pound the keyboard. He was a prime candidate for a heart attack; I prayed that it wouldn't today as I watched him sweating profusely and almost gasping for air.

Several minutes had passed before he finally raised his sweat-drenched head from the screen and said,

'All done.' As he stood up from the desk, he wiped the sweat from his forehead onto the sleeve of his suit jacket. I had never witnessed anyone sweat and breathe so heavily in my life.

'I need to check the safe to see if we have that amount of cash in it,' he said. I turned to follow him as he made his way towards the door.

'John, you can't come with me. That would be a breach of our security policy. If any member of staff sees you entering the safe room with me, they'll know that something is wrong, and the protocol is to press the panic button. The Armed Response Unit will have the bank surrounded within minutes,' he explained. We stood facing each other in silence, our eyes locked in a challenge. The only sound in the room was the heavy breathing of Frank and the faint hum of the computer. I couldn't tell if he was lying or if he was trying to call my bluff. As he reached for the door handle, I quickly grabbed him by the arm and warned,

'Remember, Frank,' tightening my grip on his arm. 'Don't do anything stupid or try to be a hero. The consequences will far out-weigh your brief moment of heroism.' I released my grip, the air in the room was thick with tension, making it almost suffocating. Frank simply nodded and then swiftly left the room, his footsteps fading away down the hallway.

As the door closed behind him, I closed my eyes and sank back into the chair, feeling vulnerable and helpless, knowing that my fate was now in Frank's hands. He was gone for what felt like an eternity but was probably only about ten minutes. I had visions of him return-ing with a team of heavily armed police officers. When he eventually reappeared, he was alone. The door to his office swung open with a forceful sweep, causing me to jump out of my seat. He had removed his suit jacket, revealing a pale blue shirt that was heavily stained with sweat and clinging to his body. He placed a sports bag on the desk.

'It's all there,' he said, gasping for breath as he collapsed onto the chair. I could see the stress etched on his plump face, and I was still terrified that he might have a fucking heart attack at any moment. That would surely be the icing on the cake.

'That's good,' I said, trying to reassure him. 'It will all be over soon and we can go back to living our own mundane lives.'

'I'll never be the same after this,' he replied, as he counted out the money in front of me. He then handed me several papers to sign; his hand was shaking as I took them from him. I had never seen so much cash in my life, and it was all mine. He zipped the sports bag closed and pushed it towards me.

'That's it, we're all done. Your account is officially closed and completely empty,' he said, his voice trembling with exhaustion and relief, as he constantly mopped sweat from his forehead with a handkerchief.

'Thank you, Frank,' I said, 'I'm sorry that you got dragged into this whole fucking mess. But, if it's any consolation, I didn't choose to be in this predicament either.' I opened the bag and removed ten thousand euro and handed it to him.

'No, no, I can't take it,' he said, shaking his sweat-drenched head from side to side. 'Please take it and bring your lovely family on a nice holiday. Remember, your time with them is precious,' I said. After a brief moment of hesitation, he finally reached across the desk and took the bundle of money as I knew he would. We shook hands firmly, and for the second time, I felt his sweaty palm against mine.

'Goodbye, Frank. It's all over now. And remember, this little incident never happened,' I said, tapping the side of my noise with my finger.

'Are you going to be, okay?' he asked.

'Yes, as soon as I hand over this money and clear my debts, everything will be fine, and we can all live happily ever after,' I replied. Before we left his office, I asked him if there was a back entrance that I could leave by. Frank led me down a narrow corridor that was cluttered with rows of dusty filing cabinets and stacks of cardboard boxes, which led to a large steel door. Frank entered a code on the keypad and then turned the key in the deadbolt lock. Just as I was about to step out into the lane that ran behind the bank, Frank put his hand on my arm and asked,

'John, how did you know about me and Amy, the young girl who works behind the counter?' I replied with a smile,

'Take a good look at her Frank. Who the fuck else would give her one?' He slammed the door behind me as I left.

As I walked up the street, the sports bag gripped tightly in my right hand. I half-expected to be pounced on by the police, but thankfully they never showed. Poor Frank, he had believed every word that I told him, the gullible fool. A smirk spread across my face as I realised that the second part of my plan had fallen into place, leaving only one more step to be completed.

Chapter 61

D espite feeling somewhat relieved, as I lay on the sofa, a cigarette dangling from between my fingers, and a glass of whiskey in my other hand, my eyes were fixated on the bulging bag of cash resting on the coffee table. I was still a little anxious that Frank, the Bank Manager, might let his conscience get the better of him and contact the police. This was the main reason I gave him the ten grand, as soon as he accepted it, whether he was aware of it or not, he became an accomplice.

Two crucial pieces of my plan had fallen into place. I had acquired a dead body and a substantial amount of cash. However, the most daunting and risky part of the plan still remained, leaving the country without anyone knowing. Undoubtedly, the journey that lay ahead of me would bring its own trials and tribulations along the way. The thought of what awaited me filled me with a sense of dread and a paralysing fear of the unknown gripped me like a vice. I had no way of predicting how the next few hours would unfold. I could do nothing but bide my time and wait for nightfall before making my move.

The only flight leaving Dublin airport that night, was for a place called Carcassonne. It was described as a charming medieval town in southern France and was scheduled to depart at ten o'clock. I had never heard of the place and had no interest in going to France. The thought of visiting a country where snails and frogs were considered delicacies did not appeal to me. Furthermore, I was also concerned about the language barrier as I did not speak French. However, it was the last available flight out of Dublin. For any other destination, I would have to wait until the following morning, a luxury that I did not have. So, with no other options available, I booked a seat.

One major obstacle that I had not considered was how to conceal the cash. If the cash was discovered going through customs, all of my efforts would have been for nothing. The thought of carrying such a large amount of cash from one country to another had never crossed my mind. I was so preoccupied with everything else that was going on around me that I never even considered it. Realistically, at this late stage, my only option was to take my chances and to hide the money among my clothes in the two suitcases. At one point, I briefly entertained the idea of strapping the cash onto my body. I had seed it done in a movie where the fugitive strapped the cash onto his body and successfully went through customs. Nevertheless, I quickly discarded the ludicrous idea as unrealistic, nothing more than a Hollywood fantasy.

I had left myself no other option but to accept the risk, regardless of what might happen at the airport. My only hope was that a priest walking through customs would be waved on without any issues. I spent the rest of the day and well into the evening either pacing the hallway or looking out of my bedroom window. Every time I entered the bedroom, I couldn't help but look down at my dead friend, lying naked on the bed. It was such a waste, another tragic case of being in the wrong place at the wrong time. As I lit up a cigarette, I glanced at my watch, it was a little after six in the evening. I still had a couple of hours to kill before I needed to leave for the airport. I needed to remain calm and composed, now more than ever.

My freedom, though tantalisingly close, still felt uncertain. Just as I entered the kitchen to prepare something to eat, my phone rang. I knew straight away who it was without looking at the flashing screen, I had been expecting her call all day.

'Hello,' I answered, knowing only too well that the cunning little bitch was on the other end of the line.

'Hello, Padre. I hope for your sake you have everything in order?' she asked. Her broken English was no longer a turn-on.

'Almost,' I replied. 'I have an appointment with the bank manager at eleven o'clock in the morning. I needed to get clearance on a loan due to the large amount of money I was looking for, which took a couple of days. Tomorrow, I have to sign the terms and conditions of the loan, and then the bank will release the funds.' I hoped she hadn't seen through the web of lies I had just spun, but I couldn't be sure if she believed me or not.

'Okay, that sounds good. I knew you wouldn't let us down. We will be watching you very closely. As soon as you leave the bank, call me on this number, and I will arrange for someone to meet you,' she instructed. A wide smile spread across my face and my tense shoulders relaxed as I let out a deep sigh of relief. She seemed convinced by my story.

'Okay, I'll call you as soon as I have withdrawn the money and left the bank,' I replied, attempting to convey a sense of desperation, as if I were completely defeated.

'And, Padre, don't try anything stupid. Just do as you're told and everything will end well,' she said before abruptly ending the call.

I had been anticipating her call all day, unsure of how it would play out. I felt relieved that it was finally over. As I returned to the kitchen, I remembered that I had been in the process of making something to eat before she had rudely interrupted me. I picked up where I left off and finished making a sandwich. I ate greedily, not realising how hungry I was. Once I was fed and watered, I left the kitchen and made my way upstairs. I shaved, showered, and then entered my bedroom, where my naked, deceased friend lay on the bed. He was such a fine specimen of a man, I thought as I looked down at him. How unfortunate.

I carefully removed my black suit from the wardrobe and dressed, taking care to fix my white dog collar in the blood-splattered mirror. As I gazed at my reflection, I whispered, 'It's time to start my new life.' As I looked around the room, a mix of emotions washed over me as I prepared to leave for the very last time. This house had been my sanctuary, a place where I escaped from the harsh realities of the outside world. But now, it was time to let go of the past and move on.

'Enough of the reminiscing,' I scolded myself as I lit up a cigarette. I wished I could have thanked my deceased friend while he was alive, for the selfless sacrifice he had made. Even though he was completely unaware, he had sacrificed his life for mine. Despite all the blood and his caved-in head, he looked so peaceful. He died so that I could live, similar to Jesus, I thought to myself with a smile.

When the fire crew discovers his body, they would most likely assume it was mine since I lived alone. It was a very clever plan, if I do say so myself. I took one last, deep drag from my cigarette, savouring the nicotine before tossing the butt onto the bed. With a flick of my lighter, I set the blood-soaked sheets alight. Once the flame caught hold of the sheets, I quickly left the room and made my way down the stairs. My heart pounded against my chest as I frantically grabbed the two suitcases and slipped out the backdoor. Leaving behind the burning room, as the raging orange flames devoured my saviour and the haunting memories of my past life.

I didn't realise how heavy the suitcases were, despite having packed them myself. Their weight significantly slowed me down as I made my way through the dark, foul-smelling laneway. If anyone saw me leaving and dragging two suitcases behind me, my carefully crafted plan would crumble, and I'd be fucked. With my collar up and head down, I quickened my pace. The sound of my footsteps echoed in the empty street as I pushed forward. I knew that the fire would spread quickly, and it was only a matter of time before someone raised the alarm.

Upon arriving at the main street, I quickly flagged down a taxi. The driver promptly got out and loaded my suitcases into the boot. I thanked him as he held the door open for me. The black suit and white dog collar were still revered by the older generation as a symbol of authority and respect.

'Airport, please,' I said with a friendly smile, trying to appear calm and collected as I settled into the back seat. However, my mind was anything but calm.

'Heading anywhere nice, Father?' the driver inquired, as many taxi drivers tend to do. For some reason, the majority of taxi drivers seem incapable of driving in silence. I resisted the urge to tell him to mind his own fucking business and instead kept my response polite.

'I am heading over to Rome for an audience with His Holiness and I have some conferences to attend and speak at. All rather boring, I must admit,' I replied reluctantly.

'That sounds interesting. I actually saw the Pope when he came here back in 1979, I think it was, at the Phoenix Park,' here we fucking go, I thought to myself as he continued to ramble on.

'I can still vividly remember it, as if it were just last week,' he said, glancing at me through his rearview mirror with a set of Rosary beads hanging from it. I couldn't believe my luck – not only was I stuck in the back of a taxi listening to an opinionated taxi driver, but a fucking religious one at that. I could only hope that he wouldn't remember me from his back seat, when the shocking headlines announced that a priest had tragically died in a house fire. I subtly ignored him by turning my attention to the passing scenery outside the window, lost in thought. Thankfully, this put an end to the small talk for the rest of the journey and the only sound in the taxi was the gently hum of the engine as we made our way through the dimly lit, empty streets. I felt nothing as we drove through my hometown, the place where I had spent my entire life surrounded by the same people every day. I was glad to see the back of it as the taxi pulled out onto the motorway.

Twenty-eight minutes later, the driver removed my suitcases from the boot. I paid and tipped him, to which he responded,

'Thank you, Father. That's very generous of you. I hope you have a pleasant trip in Rome. With a smile on my face, I adjusted the handles on my suitcases and dragged them behind me as I strode towards the entrance.

Chapter 62

The airport was a bustling hive of activity, as people scurried from one side of the building, with bags slung over their shoulders and dragging cases behind them as they rushed to catch their flights. The constant hum of inaudible announcements echoed throughout the terminal, creating a background noise that seemed to never cease. Children were running wild, releasing piercing screams that filled the air as they chased each other. And the wails of crying babies only added to the mayhem, causing people to shoot annoyed glances in the direction of the noise. There were suitcases and bags strewn across the ground, which created a chaotic obstacle course as I weaved through the madness and made my way towards the check-in area.

After joining the queue, I soon found myself standing at the counter and looking down at a young woman as she sat on her designated perch. Her uniform was immaculate and neatly pressed. She wore stylish glasses with designer frames, and her lustrous, jet-black hair was tied back in a bun, spare a single strand that cascaded down the left side of her heavily made-up face. She greeted me with a warm smile as I handed her my passport and plane ticket. As she keyed in my details, she asked me to place my suitcases on the conveyor belt. Once she had confirmed that everything was in order, she returned my documents and attached a sticker with my details to each suitcase. She then wished me a pleasant flight, to which I thanked her before moving on.

The airport was far too crowded for my liking. The sheer volume of people confined in one area was completely overwhelming to me. People were frantically running, dragging their suitcases behind them in a desperate attempt to catch their flights. It was a scene of pure mayhem. I never imagined that the airport would be so busy at such a late hour. In an attempt to escape the madness, I made my way to the departure lounge, in the hope of finding a more peaceful setting. With less than an hour until my flight was scheduled to take off, I struggled to keep my nerves in check as my thoughts raced and swirled, making it impossible to maintain my composure. As I spiralled into an endless loop of 'what ifs,' each one more terrifying than the last, my mind became consumed with fear.

In an attempt to quell my increasing stress and anxiety, I sought solace at the bar and ordered a brandy, hoping it would calm my racing thoughts and soothe my frayed nerves. To the naked eye, I may have appeared calm and carefree, but internally I was reduced to a bundle of nerves, my entire being trembled from head to toe. The thought of the cash hidden in my suitcases weighed heavily on my mind as I savoured a sip of the warm, golden liquid. If customs were to discover it, I would be fucked. No excuse, no matter how elaborate, could justify the significant amount of money I had in my possession. Even my status as a Parish Priest would not be enough to save me.

I knew that I wouldn't fully relax until I had made it through the airport in Carcassonne. The idea of starting a new chapter in my life, where I could completely reinvent myself, brought a smile to my face as I raised my glass. My mind drifted, consumed by thoughts of my house being engulfed in raging flames and reduced to a pile of smouldering ash, and my charred remains being discovered. The parish would surely weep and mourn, and no doubt give me a proper send off. As I tried to imagine the chaotic scene at my house, with the fire crew battling the blaze and Maura and the rest of the blue rinse militia, wailing and saying decades of the Rosary, praying for my soul, as the rest of the ghouls lurked in the shadows and whispered among themselves. My phone beeped, interrupting my train of thought. It was a text from Fr. Brian. I dismissed it, cursing myself for not leaving my phone on the bedside table, as I had originally planned. How could I have been so fucking careless? I thought as I drained my glass.

As I left the bar and headed towards the toilets, a wave of panic washed over me. I quickly entered the first available cubicle and turned off my phone before removing the SIM card. In my panicked state, I briefly considered flushing the SIM card down the toilet. However, I quickly realised that it was made of lightweight plastic and would probably not flush away but instead remain floating on top of the water in the bowl, taunting me. I dismissed the idea and instead opted to dismantle the phone into four pieces, carefully placing them into my coat pocket. As I left the toilet, I discreetly disposed of the back of the phone case and the SIM card in the waste bin just outside the toilet door. My mind was plagued by a constant sense of dread and paranoia, causing me to nervously scan my surroundings, fearing that I was being watched.

Directly across from the toilet was a shop. I went in and bought a newspaper. On my way out, I tossed the phone's battery in the waste bin that sat next to the coffee machine. Only fifteen minutes remained before boarding, and it couldn't come quick enough for me. As I entered the bar for the second time, I ordered another brandy, my hands trembled slightly as I tried to calm my nerves. I couldn't help but think that this would be my final drink in this godforsaken country. I took a slow sip from the glass, hoping it would calm me and drown out the bitter memories. This was it, my last taste of this dreary place before I left for good.

I was constantly plagued by the fear of bumping into someone I knew and getting dragged into some polite small talk. My main concern was that when the news of the tragic house fire and my supposed death broke, and I happened to run into someone, they would surely remember speaking to me at the airport. Furthermore, if they were to contact the authorities, and inform them that the charred remains recovered from my house could not possibly belong to me, as they had spoken to me on the very night of the fire, just before I boarded a plane. My mind was flooded with a multitude of scenarios. Finally, I heard my flight number being called; I let out a sigh of relief as I drained my glass. On my way to the boarding gate, I tossed the front cover of the phone into a waste bin beside a food stand. Twenty-three minutes later, I was comfortably seated on the plane, patiently waiting for take-off.

Chapter 63

'Ladies and gentlemen, please return to your seats and fasten your seatbelts as we will be preparing for landing shortly,' a male voice announced over the intercom in broken English. This was the final hurdle, the last piece of the puzzle that needed to be gently slotted into place before I could finally taste freedom. All that remained was for me to get through customs without any issues. If the cash was discovered, it would be game over and I would be fucked good and proper. I would be looking at a lengthy prison sentence in France for smuggling money into their country. Then, once the criminal gang back in Dublin realised that I had deceived them and fled the country, they would send a copy of the disc to the police and the press. The Irish authorities would seek my extradition to question me about the disc and the identity of the charred remains recovered by the fire crew while they battled the blaze at my house. There would be countless questions that I could never answer.

The plane seemed to glide gracefully onto the runway, its wings slicing through the air like a bird in flight, as the wheels touched down with a gentle thud. I trailed behind the exhausted crowd of travellers, their weary steps resembled the slow and steady pace of a herd of wildebeest in search of water during the dry season, as we trudged towards the conveyor belt to retrieve our luggage. It felt like an eternity before a single suitcase appeared from behind the black curtain. My nerves were frayed, my mouth parched, and my hands trembled. Every fibre of my being yearned for the soothing effect of nicotine. My mind was consumed with worst-case scenarios. While everyone around me appeared to be collecting their luggage and moving on, there was no sign of mine.

'Christ,' I muttered under my breath, my heart racing with fear. What if customs had searched my cases and had found the cash? What if they were on their way to arrest me?

As I watched the conveyor belt continuously loop, a suffocating wave of anxiety engulfed me. My suitcases were still nowhere in sight. In a brief moment of madness, I considered cutting my losses and leaving the airport without my cases, while I still could as a free man. I needed to quell the racing thoughts and overwhelming anxiety that were consuming me. What I really needed was a stiff drink and a cigarette. As I looked around, I counted five other people that remained scattered around the conveyor belt still waiting on their luggage. I took some comfort knowing that I wasn't the only one.

Several more agonising minutes dragged passed before my two suitcases finally emerged from behind the black curtain and slowly crept along the belt towards me. I scanned my surroundings; there was no sign of any police or customs officers lurking close by. My heart raced and my hands trembled as I retrieved my cases from the conveyor belt. I quickly pulled up the adjustable handles before making my way towards the exit sign, dragging my cases behind me.

'I'm almost there,' I nervously whispered to myself, as cold beads of sweat slithered down the length of my spine. With each step that I took, I was anticipating a hand to roughly clamp down on my shoulder. I could picture myself turning around to find a group of intimidating, heavily armed police officers facing me, wearing bulletproof vests and their guns pointed at me. And one of the officers speaking in a thick French accent, saying, 'Excuse me, Padre. You need to come with us.'

As I approached the exit, I noticed a group of four armed officers stationed around the doorway. Their tense postures and vigilant expressions indicted that they were on high alert. This was my final obstacle, after overcoming countless challenges; my freedom was finally within reach, just beyond the door. I took a deep breath to steady my nerves and strode confidently towards the officers who were guarding the exit.

I reminded myself to avoid making eye contact with any of the officers. As I neared the group of officers, my heart began to race. I couldn't help but worry that my behaviour and body language might raise suspicion if I kept my head down while passing them. In a split-second decision, I lifted my head and smiled as I passed the first two officers at the main exit.

'Bonjour, Padre,' greeted the towering, handsome officer on my left.

'Bonjour, messieurs,' I replied with an exaggerated smile. To my relief, all four officers smiled back at me. Bless them, I thought as I let out a sigh of relief and left the airport.

As I stepped out of the airport and onto French soil, my first instinct was to let out a triumphant scream. However, I resisted and instead reached for a cigarette. The nicotine provided a temporary distraction from the overwhelming rush of emotions coursing through me. My body tingled with a sense of liberation as I exhaled the first drag of my cigarette on French soil.

Over the last few hours, I had nonchalantly passed by police and customs officers in two different countries, concealing three hundred and fifty thousand euro in cash, without anyone even batting an eyelid. I now understood why so many people risked smuggling drugs and money in and out of countries all around the world. As I lit my third cigarette, I struggled to contain my overwhelming emotions. I was no longer held captive by the chains of fear that had crippled me for so long. As I sauntered towards the taxi rank, the weight of my dark past simply dissipated. With a renewed sense of being, I was ready to leave my past behind and start a new chapter in my life as a free man.

Chapter 64

My destination was the old medieval town of Carcassonne, located just a thirty-minute drive from the airport, according to the research I had conducted online. After waiting in the taxi queue for fifteen minutes, I finally reached the front. When the next available taxi pulled up, the driver, a short and well-presented elderly man, slowly eased himself out of the taxi, flicking a cigarette butt to the ground as he closed the car door behind him. His head was topped with a full mane of snow- white hair, and his moustache curled at each end in a way that would make any young modern-day hipster envious.

'Bonjour, Padre,' he greeted me with a warm, friendly smile.

'Bonjour, monsieur,' I replied as he loaded my suitcases into the boot of his car. I settled into the passenger seat and said,

'The town of Carcassonne, please.' The taxi driver replied with a smile,

'Oui.' He then pressed a few buttons on the meter before pulling away from the bustling taxi rank, clearly amused by my unsuccessful attempt to correctly pronounce the name of the town.

The first ten minutes of the journey were a nightmare. The driver spoke no English, and the few words of French that I knew seemed to go right over his head. When he finally realised that having a conversation with me was impossible, he shook his head and raised his hands in the air while laughing out loud. An awkward, heavy silence hung between us for the remainder of the journey, with neither of us even daring to make eye contact. After thirty minutes of sitting next to a total stranger in complete silence, we were both relieved when we arrived in the old medieval town of Carcassonne.

I thanked the driver and generously tipped him. As we shook hands, he rattled off something in his native tongue. I had no idea what he said. I quickly removed my white dog collar as he drove away, my days of being a priest were well and truly over. I reached for my cigarettes and lit one, the smoke curling around me as I surveyed the narrow, cobblestone streets and the towering medieval walls.

Although it was well into the wee hours of the morning, the town was still very much alive, as the sound of music and laughter filled the air. I noticed a bar across the street, just a stone's throw away, it was dimly lit yet seemed lively from the distance. I took a seat at one of the empty tables outside and within minutes, a handsome young waiter approached me with a notepad and a friendly smile. His sleek black hair was neatly tied back in a ponytail, and his deep, dark brown eyes looked directly into mine.

'Bonjour, monsieur,' he greeted me, pulling a pen from behind his ear. I couldn't remember any other words that fell from his perfectly formed lips. Assuming he was asking for my order, I tried to explain that I didn't speak French. However, he just stood towering over me, holding his notepad and pen, patiently waiting for me to place my order. Frustrated, I gave up and simply said,

'Brandy,' hoping that the drink was universal. He nodded, then turned swiftly, and disappeared into the dimly lit interior of the bar.

It was a beautiful night, almost enchanting, with a warm, gentle breeze caressing my skin and a sky full of bright twinkly stars. The bar was lively both inside and outside, with revellers embracing the warm night and each other despite the late hour. The last forty-eight hours had left me completely depleted, both physically and mentally. As the adrenaline slowly left my body, a heavy fatigue weighed down on my limbs. My heavy-lidded eyes struggled to keep up with the dancing shadows cast on the cobblestone street, by the soft glow of the moonlight. I closed my eyes and was enveloped by the mingling and echoing of footsteps and voices, blending together in a symphony of urban life.

As the waiter placed the drink down in front of me, I returned his smile. I was relieved that he didn't try to make conversation, as I didn't have the energy to search through my mind for the right words. I was grateful for the silence. In one swift motion, I drained my glass, hoping to drown any lingering nerves. I then signalled to the waiter for another brandy. He was leaning against the doorway, observing the patrons who were sitting outside, enjoying the warm night, ready and willing to meet their demands. Thankfully, he understood what I meant without me having to say anything.

I couldn't help but envy the loved-up couples that were sitting around me. As they held each other closely and gazed seductively into each other's eyes. The waiter promptly returned, snapping me out of my envious gaze, as he replaced my empty glass with a full one. The brandy had worked wonders; I felt completely relaxed. I approached my second glass with a more reserved pace, savouring my newfound sense of freedom. After the long journey, which had been littered with so many potential dangers, I was utterly drained. Nevertheless, I had made it, and I couldn't help but smile at the thought. My entire being, mind, body, and soul were crying out for sleep. I was desperate to find a hotel. Just as I placed my empty glass on the table, the waiter swiftly swooped in like a bird of prey, removing it from the table and placing it on his tray. I slowly lifted my heavy eyelids to mee his gaze, and our eyes locked in a brief moment of confusion as he spoke in his native tongue. I couldn't understand a single word, that left his mouth, but I assumed that he was asking me if I wanted another drink. I shook my head and said,

'No, no more.' Hoping, that would answer his question. I thanked him in English, and a look of complete bewilderment crossed his chiselled features, indicating that he had no idea what I had just said. After a brief pause, the penny dropped when I reached into my wallet and handed him the cash.

When the waiter returned with my change, I tipped him and said, 'Hotel.' He turned towards the entrance of the bar and called out a name that I didn't catch. Suddenly, a stunning, dark-haired woman with piercing brown eyes emerged from the doorway and walked over to my table. The waiter spoke to her in their native tongue, and she nodded at him before turning to face me.

'Bonjour, monsieur,' she said with a charming smile. I simply smiled up at her from my seat, having given up on attempting to speak the few French words that I knew. Besides, the brandy had gone straight to my head, and I was feeling a little worse for wear.

'Are you from England?' she asked with a curious tone, her broken English flowed effortlessly from her alluring lips. I gazed up into her beautiful brown eyes, the brandy was beginning to play tricks on me. I quickly composed myself, not wanting to say anything foolish.

'No, I am from Ireland,' I replied, fighting against fatigue and the impure thoughts that were creeping up on me.

'What a beautiful country. I visited with my family a few years ago,' she responded. I could have listened to her all night, her words rolled off her tongue with a soft and seductive accent. Snap out of it, for Christ's sake, I thought to myself as I quickly pulled myself together.

'Did you enjoy your time in Ireland?' I asked, trying to keep the conversation flowing. Despite my exhaustion, I was completely captivated by her. My head was starting to ache, too much fucking brandy, I assumed.

'Yes, we had a lovely time in Dublin. We spent three days in Ireland and then travelled to London for a couple of days,' she replied with a smile. Meanwhile, I was fighting against the numbing effects of the brandy and the overwhelming exhaustion that threatened to consume me.

'That's nice. I'm glad you and your family enjoyed your stay in Ireland,' I replied.

'So, you are looking for a hotel?' she asked.

'Yes,' I replied. Before leaving Dublin, I made the decision not to book a hotel. I didn't want to tempt fate, as there were several potential obstacles that could have easily prevented me from reaching my final destination: the criminal gang, the police, and the customs. I had decided to wait and see how my journey unfolded, and if I managed to outsmart all of my opponents, then I would find a place to stay. And thankfully, I found myself in that fortunate position.

'There are two hotels in the town, Hotel La Grande and Hotel De Chateau. They are both very nice,' she said. The beautiful waitress then proceeded to give me directions to each of the hotels, which went in one ear and out the other. I was far too distracted by her looks, to pay any attention of what was being said. I thanked and complimented her on her excellent English. As we shook hands, I reluctantly released my grip on her soft, petite hand. As I looked deep into her eyes, I couldn't help but think what a beautiful treat she would be. I promised myself that I would return for her someday. She returned my smile, completely oblivious of the dark thoughts that were swirling around in my mind. She quickly turned and went back into the bar to call a taxi for me.

The Hotel La Grande was the closest, only a ten-minute taxi ride from the bar. It looked very impressive as I stepped out of the taxi. I was completely exhausted and dishevelled as I approached the reception desk. Thankfully, the young woman sitting behind the desk spoke perfect English, albeit broken. I wouldn't have been able to handle another language barrier like the one I had experienced earlier with the taxi driver who drove me from the airport. Despite the ungodly hour, the friendly and very efficient receptionist quickly checked me in, for which I was grateful as I struggled to keep my eyes open and carry my own weight. Without delay, a friendly elderly porter took my suitcases and led me to my room.

The porter kindly opened the door to the room and stepped aside, holding the door as I entered the room. I thanked him and handed him a ten euro note. He smiled, then turned and left the room without saying a word. Ungrateful bastard, I thought as I closed the door behind him. Exhausted, I collapsed onto the bed and lay there with my hands behind my head, staring up at the ceiling. A smirk spread across my face as I thought about how I had outsmarted them all. The whole fucking lot of them, the gang, the police, and the customs. I had accomplished the unimaginable. It was hard to believe that I was lying on a bed in a hotel room in France, instead of lying in a prison cell or a shallow grave.

Despite my heavy eyelids, I couldn't help but smile. This was the beginning of my new life. I was a new man, unburdened by the shackles of my past. As I closed my eyes, the image of the beautiful waitress lingered in my mind. Her dark brown eyes, and perfectly formed, plump, rosy lips, that begged to be kissed, were etched in my memory. The way she playfully twirled a strand of loose hair between her fingers as we spoke, and her seductive lilt with its broken English and alluring accent, had awakened a primal desire within me for her touch. As her words rolled off her tongue, I was enraptured and consumed by an insatiable desire, aching for her skin against mine. I knew that one day, that desire would have to be satisfied.

The end, or is it just the beginning?